Gregorius

BENGT OHLSSON was born in 1963, and since his critically acclaimed debut in 1984 he has risen steadily to become one of Sweden's most celebrated younger novelists, recently winning the country's top literary award, the August Prize, for *Gregorius*. He lives in Stockholm.

SILVESTER MAZZARELLA has been translating Swedish and Italian prose, poetry and drama professionally since 1997. He learned English from his mother, Italian from his father and Swedish in Finland, where he used to teach English at Helsinki University.

'Bengt Ohlsson's novel is based on Hjalmar Söderberg's great Swedish classic, *Doctor Glas*, but it reinvents the century-old story by softening Gregorius into a tense, embarrassed presence. The power of the book comes from the difficulty of giving tenderness and humanity to his perspective... I imagine that Hjalmar Söderberg would read *Gregorius* with admiration and perhaps envy. Bengt Ohlsson is not content to be categorized as a successor. He has his own ambition and formal mastery. Silvester Mazzarella's translation succeeds in capturing the power of this unusual book, one that will be widely discussed.' *TLS*

Gregorius

Bengt Ohlsson

Translated from the Swedish by Silvester Mazzarella

with a preface by Margaret Atwood

Portobello
BOOKS

First published by Portobello Books Ltd 2007
This paperback edition published 2008

Portobello Books Ltd
Twelve Addison Avenue
London
W11 4QR, UK

The publication of this work was supported by a grant from the Swedish
Institute (Svenska instutet).

First published in the original Swedish by Albert Bonniers Förlag in 2004.

A CIP catalogue record is available from the British Library

9 8 7 6 5 4 3 2 1

ISBN 978 1 84627 017 8

www.portobellobooks.com

Designed by Nicky Barnaby
Typeset in Monotype Van Dijck by Avon DataSet Ltd,
Bidford on Avon, Warwickshire

Printed in Great Britain

To Helena

Thanks to Ingemar Glemme, Åke Abrahamsson,
Hans Isaksson, Håkan Johansson, the Schrenckh family,
Erik Satie and Ministry.

Preface

By Margaret Atwood

Note: Readers are warned that the plot is revealed here.

Gregorius, which won Sweden's August Prize for Bengt Ohlsson in 2004, is a tribute by a living author to 'the novel I return to when I periodically lose faith in literature.' (p.419) It's also both a riveting novel on its own merits and an astonishing gloss on an earlier masterpiece.

This is a hard trick to pull off. Novels that snitch characters from other novels or stories and re-tell events from their point of view can give a reader the uneasy feeling that a previous author's work has been violated. Nonetheless, such books now constitute almost a separate genre. The earliest attempts – such as *Shamela*, in which Fielding took the stuffing out of Richardson's pious *Pamela* – were often satiric, but the twentieth and twenty-first centuries, with their interest in the scorned, the marginalized, and the voiceless, have approached this task with more seriousness. Jean Rhys looked at *Jane Eyre* through the eyes of Mr Rochester's mad wife in the brilliant *Wide Sargasso Sea*; John Gardner has Grendel the Monster give a capering, blood-swilling, tragic rendition of *Beowulf* in the equally brilliant *Grendel*. Classics such as *Rebecca*, *Gone with the Wind*, and – endlessly – *Dracula*, have had their shadow versions, as have many other books. The mere doing of such a thing is no longer a novelty, and thus the doing of it well has become a considerable challenge.

Pastor Gregorius, the eponymous narrator of Bengt Ohlsson's novel, would seem at first glance to be a most unpromising subject for such an attempt. He appears in *Dr Glas*, Hjalmar Söderberg's extraordinary 1905 shocker, where he has no redeeming features and makes not one single good impression. Every time he heaves into view we experience a shudder of revulsion, just as Dr Glas himself does. Gregorius is not only a mealy-mouthed self-righteous minister, but he's physically repulsive. In addition to that, he sweats a lot and smells bad, and he's stupid; and – worst crime of all, in the eyes of Dr Glas – he's married a much younger wife who is very beautiful.

It is this youthful wife who seeks out Dr Glas, and – in the manner of a maiden imprisoned by a degenerate ogre – begs him to rescue her. Her story is that she married Pastor Gregorius – a family friend during her childhood – out of early piety, well before she had any idea of what marriage really meant. Now she finds herself forced to have sex with this loathsome man, whose touch she cannot bear. Can't Dr Glas tell her husband that she has some sort of 'condition', and that he has to forgo his 'rights', at least for a while?

Dr Glas, a romantic who's never had a lover and who tends to idealize women as long as they stay at a certain distance, rises to the appeal. Why should the hateful Pastor impose his disgusting lusts on this flower of – well, not exactly purity, for Mrs Gregorius immediately confesses to Glas that she has a lover – but of charm and desirability?

Dr Glas's first ploy is to tell Gregorius – in accordance with his wife's request – that marital relations at this moment would be damaging to his wife's health. That doesn't work – essentially, Gregorius rapes his wife – so Dr Glas then convinces Gregorius that he has a bad heart, and that such violent exertions might kill him. But trolls are creatures of unbridled carnality, and even this threat can't frighten Gregorius into keeping his nasty paws off his cringing, increasingly desperate wife.

Glas packs Gregorius off to Porla for a spa 'rest cure', which gives Mrs Gregorius a little breathing space and a happy time with her lover; but then back comes Gregorius, as disgusting and as sexually energetic as ever. Finally, when Mrs Gregorius threatens suicide – a thing Dr Glas has considered for himself, from time to time – the doctor decides to remove Gregorius from the scene. Then, with the aid of a little cyanide pill he tells Gregorius is heart medicine, he neatly does it.

Dr Glas isn't found out and punished for his crime, but neither does he benefit from it. Mrs Gregorius doesn't benefit either – the lover who was keen to pursue her during their clandestine affair throws her over for a rich bride, now that she's really available, and Dr Glas can do nothing, this time, to relieve her suffering. He has failed as a shining knight and has become a murderer in the process. Yet he feels no obvious guilt for having killed Gregorius. It's as if he's squashed a louse.

It's this louse upon whom Bengt Ohlsson sets his sights. His object is to de-lousify Gregorius; to portray him – in Ohlsson's own words – not necessarily as "sympathetic", but at least as "human". Rendering monsters as more worthy of consideration than their societies have been prepared to admit – or, at the very least, allowing them the courtesy of their own narrative voice, or providing them with an explanatory back story – has been an ongoing project of the past two hundred years. The line of partially-redeemed monsters stretches all the way from the Creature in Mary Shelley's *Frankenstein*, to Erik, the Phantom of the Opera, to Mr Hyde in Robert Louis Stevenson's classic, to the many furry werewolves and misunderstood trolls that now populate the Fantasy shelves in bookstores and the many sympathetic Hulks, vampires, and X-men that rampage, bite, and sizzle their way into the film-viewer's heart.

But is Gregorius really such an extreme monster? Ohlsson suspects he may have been more human all along than Dr Glas would ever have allowed.

Dr Glas is written in the form of a diary, so we must necessarily view everything and everyone in it through the rather cold and reflective eyes of Dr Glas himself. What man in love with a woman has ever considered the sexual partner of that woman – especially when the sex is being forced upon the woman in question – to be a fine and admirable fellow? As Gregorius himself says in Ohlsson's novel, 'If it's someone you feel hostile to you'll furnish them with a set of unattractive qualities, so that in the end your antipathy will appear entirely comprehensible, even logical.' (p.276) Thus Glas is not prepared to give Gregorius the benefit of the doubt in any way. When the childless Pastor Gregorius uses his longing for a child as his reason for enforcing his marital 'rights', Glas immediately labels him an old fraud. But what if Gregorius is simply telling the truth?

Similarly, what if Helga Gregorius is lying? She's been lying to her husband for some time – she must have been, to have been cheating on a regular basis behind his back. She's willing to pretend to have a non-existent medical condition, and she joins Glas in the bad-heart charade, so she's something of an actress, too. Yet Glas never suspects she might also be lying to him.

What might she have lied about? Very possibly, the nature of her marriage to Gregorius when it first took place. She tells Glas that she never found Gregorius attractive – quite the reverse. Because of her extreme religiosity at the time, she was ashamed of her sinful sexual longings and felt she should marry someone repulsive in order to chastise such longings. She blames him for taking advantage of her ignorance and youth, and there's something to this, since Gregorius has longed for Helga even when he was still married to his first wife and Helga was technically still a child.

She also describes how he pesters her for sex and badgers her with notions of her 'duty' when she is reluctant to come across, and then forces himself upon her. But what if the marriage was more like a real one at the outset, with mutual desire and mutual satisfaction, and tenderness? Then the story would take quite another turn; and, in the hands of Ohlsson, it does. He doesn't excise the rape – Gregorius feels he's at the mercy of his 'stump', which like many such stumps has a life of its own and leads its owner into dark places against his will – but, with Helga as a fully-sexualized wife, the event becomes ambiguous.

Ohlsson plays out another possibility not suggested, but also not absolutely forbidden, by the parent text: Gregorius, far from living in self-satisfied ignorance of his wife's affair, learns about it. Moreover, he learns about it from a man who says he has the power to stop the affair – he has some hold over the lover – and will do so out of friendship, if Gregorius requests it. Surprise number one: Gregorius has a friend! Surprise number two: he says thank you very much, but he'll handle it himself. (He doesn't.)

Thus the ignorance and stupidity Glas accuses him of are in fact an act, too. Gregorius is playing a part – the part of a man who doesn't know. From within this part, he watches his wife playing her own part. She doesn't deceive him for a minute, but he deceives her. However, he takes no pleasure in this: he experiences it as a form of subtle but excruciating torture. Thus tormented, he walks the sordid back-alleys of his city, dishing out what meagre comfort he can to its equally tormented citizens.

★

Ohlsson also gives us a couple of characters not present in the parent novel, but not excluded by it either. When Gregorius is out of sight of Dr Glas, he can of course do some things Glas knows nothing about. Away from Glas, the troublesome stump of Gregorius gets into some adventures of its own, thus complicating the pattern of love and rejection laid out for us in *Dr Glas*.

Any fictional love story must have more than two elements in it to hold our attention for long. John loves Mary and Mary loves John is a satisfactory ending for a romantic novel and also a desirable state of affairs in real life, but it's not very useful for fiction unless the two are separated for a time – a war, a sea voyage, or a hurricane will do – or unless, even better, a third person intervenes. Otherwise there's nothing much to say about the heavenly happiness of Mary and John except 'That's nice'.

But the lover-beloved structure of *Dr Glas* involves more than the usual threesome. Glas loves Helga, and so does Gregorius – at any rate, he lusts after her – but Helga loves neither of them. Instead she loves young Klas Recke, who – ultimately – doesn't love her. It's a Commedia del'Arte situation, with pretty Columbine fixated on a dashing Harlequin, while a pompous old Pantalone and a sad and pathetic Pierrot yearn for her – two fools chasing a butterfly who's chasing the moon.

Ohlsson gives this twisted cable one more twist. When Gregorius is sent off to Porla for his health, he gets involved with an unfortunate woman called Anna, who's married to a husband much meaner and more hateful than Gregorius ever could be. The woebegone Anna sees Gregorius as her only hope. Unfortunately he can't reciprocate, and thus he plays both a rejected husband and a rejecting lover. But it's refreshing to find that Gregorius – old and ugly, smelly and sweaty, and we're spared none of this – can be the object of such adoring love.

There's another character in *Gregorius* who is only suggested in

Dr Glas, and that character is God. Glas himself is a man of his sceptical turn-of-the-century age. He acknowledges the reign of science, though he finds it arid. His morality stems from his fear of public opinion, not from inner conviction. He considers the Pastor a hypocrite, though Helga says the truth is not that the Pastor doesn't believe what he preaches, but that he feels his strictures should apply to everyone. It's the fact that he's a believer that makes her despair of his ever granting her a divorce. No, she's trapped – even if he found out about her affair, he'd just nauseatingly *forgive* her. What a dreadful fate.

Ohlsson explores this facet of the Gregorius character much more fully. What if, for Gregorius, God is real? In that case, in what way has Gregorius offended Him? Why is Gregorius being tormented so much by his fate, and why is his life such a nightmare?

It isn't always a nightmare, of course. As Gregorius himself says, 'The joy of being alive. The joy of being a human being, with all that involves. The joy of being exactly who one is.

… Yes, that's rare indeed. Sometimes you find it, then it slips out of your hands, and you think you've lost it for ever. But then you find it again when you least expect it.' (p.276)

This is what Dr Glas accomplishes with his little cyanide pill: he stops Gregorius short in the middle of his life's journey, and cuts him off forever from the possibility of rediscovered joy.

Gregorius is a full, touching, and artful re-imagining of its ungainly hero. It's also an unsettling but thoroughly engaging exploration of the seedier sides of human nature, and of the power men and women wield over each other in their most intimate relationships. No wonder it won a prize.

After the evening meal Helga says she's thinking of going for a walk. Meanwhile Märit's busy clearing the table. I think I see something change in Märit's tired, yellowish face, like when a blind goes up.

And I wonder whether Helga's planned the whole thing. Perhaps she knows I'll think twice before asking her compromising questions with Märit in the room. Or perhaps she just suspects it.

I say I suppose that's fine, since I'll be busy planning the Confirmation class.

She nods and gets up. I'm desperate to stop her. I don't know why.

'My dear,' I say.

'Yes?'

But then, when she looks at me, I do understand why.

I want to see if she has that expression on her face this evening. That little smile with lips tensed till they're almost white.

'Mind where you go.'

She lifts her eyebrows.

'It's hot outside,' I say. 'Have you any idea how hot it is? On an evening like this everyone goes out, and they go out for the wrong reasons. I mean, not because they think it'll be pleasant, but because it's unbearable to stay indoors. On an evening like this, you know, the only people who stay in are those who for one reason or another can't go out. Do you understand what I mean?'

She nods. I detect a thrill of fear in her eyes, as if she's worried this will take a long time. Perhaps that's the very reason I can't bring myself to stop.

'The sick and the old,' I continue. 'Sitting in their hovels, coughing themselves to death. Perhaps with festering wounds, and flies buzzing around their dirty bandages. There they sit, listening to the cheerful voices from the street, children laughing, hawkers going about with their carts and calling their wares. They hear life passing them by out there and curse their fate, that on an evening such as this they're forced to sit there with a knee useless since birth or a foot that was crushed under a packing case... Or very small children, perhaps also sick. With stomach cramps perhaps, shrieking, whimpering, moaning, sweaty, filthy, with matted hair...'

She lowers her eyes, nods vigorously.

'Do you understand?' I say.

'Yes,' she whispers.

'The streets are full of people who've fled from this inferno. All I ask is that you bear this in mind, and exercise a certain caution. That's all.'

'I shall. It was good of you to remind me.'

A few seconds' silence. Märit's hurried off with her rattling tray. My wife clings tightly to the arm of her chair, restlessly chafing its smooth surface with her thumbs. There's that smile again. She gives a little nod and leaves the room. There's a lively rustle from the fabric of her dress.

That little smile. Those tense lips. Why does that memory come back to me?

I sit still in front of the empty dining table, rubbing my knuckles against my temples with short slow movements as if to knead away the image that has surfaced from my memory, as if to press it back into the hidden places of the brain. But it is pointless. Just as with everything else I try to knead away. I can clearly see the monkey in front of me.

The square, Stortorget, many years ago: I saw a crowd and went over to them. There was some sort of travelling mob, gypsies presumably, I don't remember. The little monkey had been dressed up in a sailor suit, complete with cap and everything. The gypsies had constructed a roundabout for it from an old cartwheel, with a little chair where it was sitting lashed fast while a gypsy made the wheel turn, round and round. The crowd shouted with delight every time the gypsy jerked the wheel. The monkey was terrified, looking about itself and pulling its lips apart so it looked as if it was laughing. From time to time, perhaps when the fear became more than it could bear, it would push its mouth forward, giving the crowd the impression that it was pouting seductively at them, and then their shouts of joy grew louder than ever, supplemented by coarse comments from a drunken shoemaker.

It was particularly heartrending to see how the monkey kept one hand pressed to its head to hold its sailor cap in place (hardly an action that would come naturally to a monkey, so the gypsies must have trained it to do so, using I can't bear to think what methods).

That monkey's smile, and perhaps its wandering eye too, has become my wife's.

I go over and open the window. Wipe the sweat from my upper lip and lean out. When I hear quick light steps outside on the gravel I pull myself back in, because I don't want her to think I've gone to the window to spy on her.

I sit down on the leather-covered chair by the window, facing the room so that if she does glance up she won't see me and I won't see her either, and I think about the muddled tirade I've just fired off at her, about all the people running out into the streets because for one reason or another it's unbearable indoors.

I might also have mentioned all the women who've grown tired of their husbands and have ventured out in search of new adventures.

Now that the footsteps outside have crunched away in the direction of Badstugatan and been absorbed into the general noise of clatter and shouts and clip-clops, I can look out.

I see a young family, a wood-carrier called Lagerström and his young wife with their two children, a boy of about five and a girl I've just recently christened Svea.

They are slowly crossing the churchyard. Fru Lagerström is saying something and clearly hoping her husband will agree; he's walking with his hands behind his back, and every so often he looks at her to encourage her to continue.

Suddenly she notices me up in the window and abruptly falls silent. Herr Lagerström follows her gaze; they nod to me and I nod back, and I realise as I do so that I have automatically assumed a pensive, elevated expression, as if deep in thought about some sermon I'm planning.

The young couple's conversation is over, and Herr Lagerström is pointing towards a corner of the churchyard. His earnest listening expression has changed to one of appreciation and optimism, as if he's praising some new building or waxing lyrical over some beauty of nature.

I wonder when Fru Lagerström will go on with the story she was telling. If she ever does.

Perhaps her husband really has seen something that delights him. It's not long since they moved here, from some hole in Västergötland.

I remember the first time I met him; there was something about him that made me uncertain. He was carrying an entirely unnecessary letter of introduction from the firm that employed him. The gaze of his cornflower-blue eyes was steady, his handshake was a trifle too firm, and he repeated several times in his stolid dialect that he'd be happy to help if I ever had a problem, or if I 'needed a strong pair of fists', as he put it. The corners of his mouth were black with snuff and he cleared his throat at regular intervals, as if to imprint himself on my memory, and there was nothing about him to suggest shyness or a sense of inferiority. He looked at me as he might at an ordinary farm labourer. I'm sure this didn't imply disrespect or contempt, just that he looked on all men – farm labourers and pastors, boozers and barons – with the same honest blue eyes.

There are men like that, convinced they're destined for something great and important. What's unusual about them is they can see this greatness and significance in everything, even merely carrying logs in order to earn a living and be able to care for one's wife and two children.

Sometimes I think this attribute or view of life, or whatever one might call it, is the most important thing of all, and that people of this kind are capable of going as far in life as anyone can. I'm sure that if they chose this wood-carrier to be king or prime minister, he'd have a cup of coffee, sort all the tasks before him into separate piles and then deal with his tasks one by one, and it would be obvious to him that if there was anything he didn't understand it was up to him to ask other people for advice, and this realisation wouldn't embarrass him in the least.

You could take it for granted he'd do his job brilliantly and be remembered as a great prime minister.

Now the Lagerströms are out of sight. Other families are bound to appear soon.

Suddenly my heart gives a double beat. Blood rushes to my

face. I hurry over to the big mirror. Look for a sign. I don't know what.

A definite double beat. The sensation resonates through my body in a strange and disagreeable way. Like when a stone lands in a mirror-smooth lake causing strong ripples at first and then progressively weaker ones.

I stand resting my hands on the chest of drawers, fingertips on Aunt Anna's lace cloth. The figure before me in the mirror, red as a lobster, looks like a squashed insect on the high white walls.

I must start keeping a diary, and I must keep it accurately so I can know whether this double beat is coming more frequently now. I want to be able to fish out a piece of paper when I am sitting with Dr Glas and tell him exactly when the double beat happened. Perhaps he'll repeat the date and time of day aloud to himself as he makes an entry in his own notebook...

Or perhaps that would seem strange. I might catch an amused glint in the doctor's eye, as if to say: Well, well, Pastor, are you really so monstrously afraid of death?

Yes indeed. That's a thought that would cause him a great deal of pleasure.

I swallow. I become unpleasantly aware that the movement is spreading through all the loose hanging folds of creased skin on my throat. Like a curtain rising.

Or falling.

I'm on tenterhooks. Sometimes the next double beat comes after only a few minutes. It can happen at any time.

It's as if an animal was waking inside my ribcage. I usually think of a mink. I don't know why. A mink that has long been hibernating. Now it has woken and is frisking about with its little feet. Feet with sharp claws. It isn't malicious. It doesn't have a soul as we do, or the same kind of consciousness.

The mink has woken and doesn't understand why it should

lie there, shut inside my ribcage. That's what makes it kick so violently. The horrible thing is, it doesn't understand how badly it could injure me. It just wants to get out at any price.

So it struggles and scratches. Its movements spread through my body like a heavy, painful pulse.

It can come back at any time.

I search for signs of change. Is my face going back to its normal colour? Is my breathing quieter? I have a detached clinical eye.

Then suddenly it's clinical no longer.

I'm just standing there staring at an old man scared out of his wits. A bizarre apparition. There's nothing at all familiar or domesticated in his features.

Clearly I'm watching an organism in a state of disintegration. Hair beginning to turn grey and fall out. Skin beginning to shrivel and sag.

Another image brings me up short: if the man in the mirror was a flower, it would merely be a matter of time before the gardener would stop, frown, put down his watering-can, and bend to nip it off: a withering growth beyond saving. That's how it is with nature. New flowers need to grow and they're going to need light and space.

My nightmare is that this is precisely what Helga's realised. She's noticed what's happening to this once magnificent plant, once a source of pride and confidence to her, a plant she admired for its luxuriant splendour when it stood a little higher than all the others. But now everything points one way, the plant's dying and at any moment the gardener will bend down, pull it up by the roots and casually throw it on the compost heap, so she must try to escape before she's contaminated by its decay.

She must escape from me in accordance with this implacable law of nature. In order to survive.

So here I am, in a world where everything I believe in,

everything I hold dear, is collapsing and will be trampled into the mud by dirty hoofs.

A world where the only thing that matters is survival. A world where concepts like conscience, consideration and affection rattle emptily, and I'm struck by the bleak insight that these concepts are merely something we've hit on to make bearable this vale of tears. A comforting sweet to suck during our long journey to the black empty grave. Nothing more than that.

A world where humanity hardly ranks above the insects, and my wife's trying to escape me by rushing out into the din of Stockholm to find a fitter mate to couple with.

Look at the bright red face, look at the pathetic attempt to comb hair across the shiny crown of his head, look at the blood-shot whites of the anxious, restless eyes. Almost like the monkey on the roundabout.

I must go out. I should be working, but what's the point.

That much I have learned. I've often been sitting at my desk and woken as from a trance to look at the clock and see how much time has passed. How long I've been away. How long my thoughts have been wandering the lanes a few metres behind her like a mute attendant, quivering with dread and curiosity in equal measure. Who is he? Perhaps he's there, in a doorway near Järntorget. Perhaps he'll give a low whistle to attract her attention. And her mute follower, fascinated, will lean forward to detect a feverish gleam in her eyes. He'll see her red lips open in an involuntary smile. She'll slow down and her body will give an involuntary jerk as if someone's trying to stop her and get her to turn around, but her feet will draw her irresistibly towards the man.

No, I've got to go out.

I go down the back stairs so no one will see me. I don't want to have to explain myself to Märit or Sivert or anyone else.

At the same time I realise I'm only making things worse. If anyone comes looking for me... I can hear voices. The exact cadence of the words. No, the last time I saw him was up in the salon... Ah, then he must have gone out by the back way. I wonder why he should choose to go out by the back? And so the gossip starts.

When I come out into the street I slow down. Clasp my hands behind my back and look straight ahead. Now and then I notice people nodding to me, curtseying or raising their hats. But if I have a sufficiently resolute expression on my face no one will stop me with their troubles. I know that from experience.

It's oppressively hot. The sun's still broiling over the rooftops. It'll be a little while yet before it goes down. People are keeping to the shady side of the street. There's hardly any wind. Clothes have been hung out to dry in backyards; stockings and shirts droop motionless on their lines.

I'm already beginning to regret this adventure.

Perhaps I have a more sensitive sense of smell than other people. In this kind of weather it's as if someone's spread a cloth over us, just above the treetops, pressing every stench and miasma down to earth, cramming it all into a broth festering with bacteria.

The stink from long-unemptied privies wafts into the butcher's, where animal corpses hang in rows and little clouds of flies are busy vomiting and laying eggs on the meat and whatever else they do. Sweat and dust from passers-by, a puff of cheap perfume, puddles of horse-piss in the gutters and a dustbin, brimful, outside an alehouse... All a filthy, infected mixture. There's no escape.

Still I go on. There's always a possibility – however small – that I may run into her.

That, of course, is why I'm here. The hope – and fear – that we may end up in a situation where masks will fall and everything will be revealed.

'Excuse me, Pastor?'

A man's voice on my right. A woman's voice trying to hush him.

I walk straight on. But I know I should have stopped, if only to fix my eyes on him. It's perfectly acceptable to look determined and sunk deep in your own thoughts. Especially if you're a priest. But you mustn't overdo it, or your parishioners will think you're behaving oddly.

Really, I'm not well suited to being a priest. I wonder if I'd have chosen the same profession if I'd been able to peer into the future when I was twenty. If I'd been able to go for a walk then, wearing the clothes of the man of nearly sixty that I am now, if I'd been able to experience this torment of hearing lively conversations die away when people catch sight of me, and tittle-tattle start as soon as I'm only a few steps further on when they think I'm out of earshot... How horribly well I've learned to ~~recognise that combi~~nation of vowels: 'eeoo...' with an 's' at the end. 'Eeoo... s'.

Gregorius.

Wherever I go, at every step I take, conversation's hushed around me and I hear those sounds.

I wish I could pass unnoticed through the streets. I haven't the slightest wish to attract attention.

But of course I'm no shrinking violet either.

When I was a boy I liked attention. I learned to read younger than any of my brothers and sisters. My brother Egon would never admit this; to him it was like a red rag to a bull. It was almost touching to see how seriously he took the question of whether I'd been three years old or four, or possibly five, when I learned to read. He seemed to suspect everyone in the family of being cunningly engaged in rewriting history. As if we were always busy taking several years off the age at which I learned to read, and in Egon's case adding several on.

He would have been seventy-two this autumn. He had a long

and successful life. He lived on the interest from investments on a small island off Väddö, where he fussed about on his stick and made the servants' lives a misery as he went in for one eccentric project after another. During his last years he tried to have the moss scrubbed off the rocks after going on a trip to Marstrand and admiring the "austere and powerful" appearance of the bare cliffs there.

Oh well, let Egon say what he liked. I have an early memory of how I used to sit and read the Gospels aloud in the evening.

It can't have been an accident that I was the one reading, and not him. He would naturally have been given the job if he'd been capable of reading, just as he was always the one called in when someone was needed to wield saw, scythe or axe. There was never any doubt about it: if anything needed doing properly, it was best to get Egon to do it.

Yes, touching is the word. As I saw it, everything came to Egon, while I was always dismissed as a bit too lightweight, too sensitive, not tough enough.

But clearly it was the case that if there was a single area where I was Egon's superior, where for once I showed myself to be competent and bold, it left him no peace.

Let him say what he liked, the old goat. That was where I came into my own. That was where I could sense I had power. Power to impress other people, and influence them.

I put my whole self into every line, every passage and every story that crossed my lips. For me it wasn't enough just to read aloud, I also wanted to understand what I was reading. Not the easiest thing for a seven-year-old.

When I read from Holy Scripture my surroundings vanished. The sticky dining table, the heavy smell of paraffin, the howling wind from the ill-fitting window.

I was transported to another world. A world of deserts and

shepherds and animal sacrifices, a world of incense and saffron and gold and silver. A world where kings went to war, captured slaves and took prisoners. A world without the insinuations and allusions and rapidly exchanged glances I was so used to, and above all without the painful silence I grew up in – a silence that wrapped my childhood in endless November gloom… in the Bible everything was sharply lit, clearly defined and uncompromising, all the difficulties of being human; envy, spite and that desperate longing to be destined for something great and beautiful, or at least meaningful…

When I read these stories I felt a claim was being made on me. It was as if I'd been admitted to share in a great trust, stemming from events that people had experienced thousands of years before I was born, but which were still as relevant as ever.

The tale of how Joseph's brothers threw him down the well wasn't just a thrilling and horrible story. It also cast a bright light on much in my own life. It was as if a voice was speaking to me, warm and benevolent, even if it sometimes told of unpleasant and shocking things.

When I'd read about Joseph and his brothers I looked on my own brothers with new eyes. Nothing was the same after that. Now all our quarrels had an explanation and made sense and seemed less frightening, less incomprehensible.

I enjoyed the attention. But most of all I liked asking questions that my reading suggested to me, and I would ask them straight out, at the kitchen table, in a loud clear voice – and I noticed that these questions were as new for all the others, even for Mother and Father, as they were for me.

I realised that they'd always read their Bible as though it was just any old verse, without reflecting on what they had read.

They certainly tried to belittle me and make me look ridiculous – 'precocious' was a term of abuse they often used – but I still noticed how my questions sank into their minds and stayed there, when the cottage was dark and silent and the body ached after the day's labour… and still sleep would not descend as it usually did. Yes, that was obvious. Something had been set in motion. I remember several times when I looked up after reading a long passage and looked from one face to another, and a tense silence would fall over the room. Egon and the others were tempted to shrug off everything I read to them by muttering scornfully or mimicking some word I'd mispronounced… but something more powerful had been passing through their minds during those sleepless hours.

For a time, perhaps for several months, we had lively discussions around the dinner table.

I remember Father and Mother glancing furtively at one another and laughing, and I remember what a strange new experience it was to talk to my brothers about big and important things without feeling tense and shrinking defensively in anticipation of the malice and sarcasm that had previously been bound to follow sooner or later.

We tossed words and thoughts freely backwards and forwards between us and each looked at the others with bright and enquiring eyes, listening with respect to what was said.

It was a giddy time, it was as if the whole family had suddenly learned to speak another language: Persian or Greek or something that had earlier seemed impossible but now clearly was possible, with everyone having a miraculous aptitude for this unfamiliar new language. Without having known!

Then one evening, I remember, we were having problems: some cows had been taken ill and were coughing and snorting and moving about unsteadily, and the vet had come from the market town and spoken to Father in a worried voice, but none of us knew how things really were, or if the others did, they said nothing to me.

During the evening Father gave a roar, which wrecked everything. He roared in the middle of an exchange of words between Egon and me. I'd just started our discussion in a light tone and with a happy heart, but we must have done something that irritated Father. Perhaps we'd both been talking at once, or perhaps Egon had been laughing too loudly.

Suddenly everyone went silent and looked in terror at Father, at the insane whites of his eyes, at his red forehead, and the drops of saliva in the corners of his mouth.

He got up, went out and slammed the door, which normally we all closed with great care as one of the glass panes was cracked. Then we heard an ominous tinkling sound from the hall.

And I discovered something terrible: everyone was ashamed. The foreign language we'd learned, that had brought us so much joy, already seemed strange and incomprehensible, something no sensible person could have any use for. Absurd too, if you listened closely to it.

It had been the work of a moment.

And there'd been something in my father's face when he got up from his chair and went out.

It took me many years to understand how deeply he'd hated himself at that moment.

He knew exactly what he'd done. He knew evenings around the dinner table would never be the same again. But he still had to do it. He couldn't help killing our happiness. He couldn't bear to sit there watching his children grow. Perhaps he understood that very soon we'd have overtaken him. Perhaps it had already happened.

The sun's about to set. The roof tiles are glowing mellow red in the dusk. I pass a piece of waste ground where several street urchins are throwing dry clods of earth at the wall of a house and are cheering every explosion of dust. A mongrel's watching with interest; a little boy who goes towards the dog with outstretched hand is told off brusquely by his older brother.

I cross the square, Brunkebergstorg, which is virtually deserted and lined with empty droshkies. A coachman is sitting drinking a pilsner. He wipes his mouth on his shirtsleeve and says something in a loud drunken voice to two young women standing below who nod and mutter and giggle. All three fall silent when I pass. The coachman seems to be holding his breath. Colour rises in his face and his eyes are bulging. I look straight ahead. When I've gone about ten metres the coachman says something in a low voice and the girls break out in a rippling laugh.

Even so I feel more at ease. I've been out a long time. Perhaps she'll manage to get home before me. She knows I've a lot to keep me busy. Perhaps she'll wonder where I've got to, perhaps she'll ask Märit. Perhaps she'll be standing at the window looking out when I cross the churchyard...

But even so I decide not to turn for home.

The clock at Klara church strikes nine. As I go over Tegelbacken hill I feel a strong wind coming across from Riddarfjärden water. A passing woman presses her hat to her head with a little cry. She smiles at me as one does to strangers when the weather changes and I smile back even though I can barely manage a grimace.

I've just started crossing Vasabron bridge when I catch a glimpse of something from the corner of my eye, a familiar combination of colours that makes me look left, towards the other side of the bridge.

It is Helga.

I stop and follow her with my eyes, but she doesn't see me. She's moving with rapid steps, her eyes fixed firmly on the ground. I open my mouth to call to her, but no sound comes out.

It's all over in a few seconds; I catch a quick glimpse of her red mouth, lips pressed together, before she hurries on, hair flying above her neck. She is moving as if hunted, but no one is following her.

Loud voices approach, a drinking party in high spirits. I stand by the rail of the bridge and look out over the water while they pass. Someone with a Danish accent is talking about something with fantastic prospects for the future that is going to change our lives, but I don't manage to catch what this fantastic thing is.

My blood has rushed up into my head, roaring and pressing. I open my mouth several times to lessen the pressure on my ears, but it doesn't help. I daren't move. It might come at any moment, that floundering sensation in my chest. Perhaps this will be the worst attack of all.

But while the fear of death paralyses me and I cling fast to the rail of the bridge like a sailor on a rolling ship, I can still lose myself in oddly comforting fantasies.

I look over to where Långholmen island lies like a black snail, and think of all the men in prison there. There's something in their predicament that I can relate to, even though I'm a respectable citizen with a beautiful home and a young wife.

My prison's worse because I carry it with me wherever I go.

My prison is that everyone knows me as someone different from the person I really am.

My prison is all the desires I've never been able to articulate; when I open my mouth to speak of them, to my astonishment I hear something entirely different come out.

My prison is all the sorrow and despair I've hidden away in ingenious places where I can never find them, even when I try.

I inhale the sour smell from Mälaren water and find I feel distinctly peaceful, despite the fact that I'm writing a remarkably sombre, not to say tragic, final chapter of my life.

I can state that I'm carrying my own prison around with me, and I know it's true.

At the same time I can believe that this is a beautiful picture. Nor can I avoid feeling a certain sense of satisfaction in the fact that I am the one who created it.

And my feeling of satisfaction at the picture's beauty is stronger than the tragic element in the picture. Thus my vanity has a more powerful voice than anything else.

It's as if this image of a man carrying his own prison around with him has nothing to do with me.

I'm like a man who is shown his own death sentence but who, instead of being horrified at the thought of his own imminent end, is overcome with admiration for the magnificent handwriting in which the sentence has been written.

Another beautiful picture.

Not as beautiful as the first, but good enough.

Yes, I know I'm a hopeless case.

But at least I can still laugh about it.

As I can when I think of my overheated state of mind just now, when I was drifting aimlessly about the streets and fantasising that Helga would appear in front of me, preferably in some compromising situation. And then there she was, on the other side of the bridge. But alone. No young lover at her side.

I can only interpret this as a sign. It must be the Lord's way of lovingly shaking his head at my restless imagination, just as my mother used to when I couldn't get to sleep in the evening.

I was afraid of most things, both those that existed and, perhaps in particular, those that didn't.

Mother would sit by my bed stroking my head while she listed all our reasons for thinking ourselves fortunate. She would speak in a low voice so no one else could hear about my warm bed and soft nightshirt, about how the roof shielded us from cold rain and wet snow, and how the walls protected us from biting winds, and she'd remind me that yet another day had passed when we'd been able to eat till we were full and drink till we felt no thirst, and that I had parents and brothers who were fond of me and cared about me.

Listening to her catalogue used to make me think my unease and fear were both unjustified and ridiculous.

All the threatening spectres of my imagination, ghosts, werewolves and madmen on the loose, faded before my mother's sturdy cheer: fire in the stove, food on the table and walls and a roof enclosing us.

At least that's how I remember it.

In the same way I now feel the Lord's hand on my head, as if He wanted to show me: look, there she goes, out for a walk alone, exactly as she said. She's troubled, hunted and driven, and she needs your help, your support and your warmth.

She shall have them, Lord. I promise I'll give her all I have.

At last I can stand tall and look on my world with a love that knows no bounds. Puffs of steam from the ships on Riddarfjärden, wisps of smoke from the factories on Kungsholmen, the glitter of lanterns on black water, the hoarse voices of distant oarsmen.

Behind me pass horse drawn vehicles, some with a sharp clip-clop, some slowly and as if gout-ridden, with loose planks rattling and banging, a baby screaming and a drunken farmer scolding a farmhand about something he 'never' manages to remember, while the farmhand in turn seems just as determined to have the last word in the quarrel.

Life's easy for some and difficult for others, but I feel that suddenly I'm standing in a river surging with life, determined to be able to pass on the valuable gift of life to someone else, a life a little better than the present.

I stand in the midst of the stream of water. I'm part of it. A moment ago I was sitting on the bank watching it run by. Now I'm standing in the middle of it.

I'm just about to start for home when I catch sight of Dr Glas, standing about ten metres away looking down into the water while stroking his little moustache with rapid, nervous movements. A strange thought comes to me: perhaps he's trying to see if anything's going to float up to the surface.

I must go over and greet him; it'll seem strange if I don't.

He turns away towards Riddarholmen, and the thought lingers that perhaps he's seen something drifting with the current towards the Royal Palace.

I could have turned for home. I don't think the doctor saw me. But I wanted to make an appointment for him to listen to my heart and find out whether its condition has changed.

If I'd been a different man perhaps I could have laid a hand on his shoulder and discussed the problem of my agitated and irregular heartbeat with him. Perhaps if I'd been able to do that he'd have been able to help me.

Instead I stop at an appropriate distance, my elbows on the rail of the bridge, and stay there, despite the fact that I realise that by doing this I make a much odder impression than if I'd simply continued on my way home.

Eventually the doctor notices me, greets me with a forced smile and asks me how I am, and, while speaking lightly, I give an account of the irregular movements of my heart, I'm also struck by the thought that perhaps the doctor, like me, has been going about the streets longing to be left in peace, hoping no one will recognise him and that none of his patients will disturb him and heap their infirmities on him.

Perhaps we should both have chosen other professions, the doctor and I.

'Come and see me in a day or two, Pastor, then we can see how things are.'

'Thank you, I will,' I say.

Silence. A cart passes behind us. Someone on the cart is singing a ribald song that sounds more bitter than cheerful.

I think I detect a little expression of triumph on the doctor's face. It's not the first time I've seen it. Far from it, it's depressingly familiar. It's the malice of the godless towards the believer. As if he'd like to say: look, that's what the world's like. There are your lost sheep. Why not run after them and bring them home? Or are there perhaps so many of them it would be too much for you?

The doctor's young and unmarried, but I've a feeling he's not going to stay in that state much longer. He has his little practice, he's esteemed and respected in his profession and he gives the impression of being modest and unassuming, with no sign of being greedy for advancement and apparently no ambitious plans for the future.

Even so, I know he has a glittering future ahead of him.

He'll marry a reasonably pretty girl and they'll produce a reasonable number of children, and he'll continue to work every day in his unpretentious surgery.

His colleagues and friends will all come to grief, one after the other. Their sure-fire investments will fail and their cast-iron projects come to nothing. In the evening they'll sit in their fat armchairs and drink a large whisky to help them unwind after the pressures of the day, then a second because the first has made them feel so much better, then a third because they've already knocked back two so why not have just one more.

And the ravishing society girls they married will begin to suffer from nervous attacks. At first their husbands will see this as adding a touch of spice to their lives and as evidence of their wives' sensitivity – a charming character trait, after all – but then the wives' attacks will happen more and more often till finally they end up in Konradsberg asylum, or drown themselves in an inlet out at their summer place one morning while the birds sing and the bumblebees hum in the long grass.

But Dr Glas follows a steady course and proceeds at the same even, careful pace.

To begin with he can hardly be seen for the noise and bluster of all the others who are shouting and swearing and elbowing their way forward. But after twenty years he'll be the only one still on the road. His colleagues and friends will stick their heads out of the ditches they've ended up in, beaten black and blue, exhausted and badly knocked about, and cast long, astonished looks after Dr Glas as he disappears in the distance.

I try to keep the conversation going. I don't want him to think I only went up to him to complain about my health.

I try the weather.

Dr Glas hums and smiles.

I try the parliament building they're going to build on Helgeandsholmen island.

Dr Glas hums and frowns.

I try Helga's tiredness in the evenings.

Dr Glas hums and assumes a faraway look. Perhaps he sees her before him, and can't see enough of her.

A flock of gulls has gathered on the north side of Helgeands-holmen, where a man is scraping out a wheelbarrow, throwing blood-red scraps into the water. Some of the scraps stick to the scraper. The man shakes it in irritation. Some gulls come flying from Strömmen water, passing just above our heads and launching themselves forward like projectiles.

I steal a sideways glance at the doctor; the sight of his smooth cheeks makes me feel wretchedly unshaven, and I wonder what it is that makes me so anxious to win this man's approval, perhaps even his affection, when it's so obvious I shall never succeed?

Probably my efforts make it all the more difficult.

But then that's how it's been all my life.

I say goodbye and set off for home. I can feel the doctor's gaze on my back. I think of my wife waiting at home, entirely alone.

I have a friend in the cathedral chapter called Halvar Sternelius. He's a few years older than I am.

As I walk I think of a conversation we had. It was out on Dalarö. It was late in the evening and Halvar and I were sitting on the veranda, him in the rocking chair and me on the sofa, both with blankets over our knees.

Halvar was telling me how it was sometimes when he was walking the streets on his way home. He'd find himself longing intensely for his wife. He would begin to think the most tender thoughts of her and formulate the most considerate and loving words about her.

'On these walks,' said Halvar, 'it seems as if it's being revealed to me how things are supposed to be...'

'You mean...'

'The love between a man and his wife, when it's... you know,

22

made perfect. After, what is it now, twenty years together, when you've avoided the worst obstacles, kept yourself as whole and pure as possible, and lived your days in a spirit of trust and respect… and that all these years have strengthened your marriage instead of weakening it…'

'Sounds enviable,' I said.

Halvar laughed.

'Yes, doesn't it? What I've never been able to understand is where all that solicitude and tenderness disappears to the moment I'm home. It flares up so strongly during my walk. But the nearer I get to our garden, the less of it is left. When I wipe my shoes on the doormat I wipe off the remainder of this warm, intense feeling too. And when I step in through the door it's as if it never existed at all.'

I sat there dry-mouthed and couldn't think of any response. With me it's the opposite, if anything. Walking home I sometimes see myself as harsh, cold and energetic. The sort of man who never gives in to pleading. I fantasise about how I will enter the room with resolute steps and use my whole hand to point with, because I'm a man who knows what he wants and doesn't hesitate to insist on it.

At the same time I know that the moment I stand at my own door this decisiveness will be as good as blown away.

I will sit on the edge of her bed and listen attentively to everything she says, I will commiserate with her and smooth her brow, I will sit with a worried expression while tears pour steadily down her cheeks, and when she snuffles and gropes for something to wipe her nose on, I will offer her the handkerchief from my trouser pocket. And when I lift my head I will see myself in the mirror above the fireplace. The crimson face with slack jowls.

I don't know how often I've looked at that face with distaste and contempt. But this evening I find that I feel sorry for him too.

There was a time when he felt himself loved. Not all that many years ago. When she would look at him with a steady gaze, warm and inquisitive.

I liked to think of us as two industrious people. As I looked at her I liked to think of phrases like 'young and strong'. 'Busy bee', I remember thinking once as I watched her sitting in a corner darning stockings, and she stopped and looked at the thread as if she couldn't tear her eyes away from its bushy little end, as if she'd never seen anything like it before.

Now she's given up. I'm trying to remember how it happened, to detect a few milestones on the way. But it's like they say, ruin comes slowly. You don't notice it coming.

I'll be home in a minute. The outside lanterns of the taverns have been lit, and their dirty windows have been thrown wide open. Men sit puffing on their pipes in their shirtsleeves and watch me warily as I go by. The windows of houses facing inner courtyards are wide open too, and resound with shouts and laughter. Mothers scold children who hope to stay up late. Hordes of residents are sitting outside in their yards, waiting for peace and quiet to descend indoors.

As I cross the churchyard I try to visualise Helga just as she looked on Vasabron bridge. Grey, shrunken, a lost soul. I try to recapture the feeling that she needs my help, that she's about to go under.

Above all I try to get it into my head that something has to happen this evening. Something decisive. And that if I throw away this chance and let this be an evening just like any other, then everything's lost.

There are some people outside the door to the parish hall. From a distance I can make out Georg and Märit, and a thin, lanky man who's looking out over the churchyard. When this man catches sight of me a spasm goes through him. He turns to the others and points in my direction.

Georg lays a hand on his arm as if to tell him to stay where he is, then hurries up to me, his steps crunching loudly on the gravel.

'What luck,' he says, still about ten metres away.

'What's happened?' I say.

'That man there,' says Georg. 'He's extremely insistent. His name's Höglund, and he has a boy at home who... I mean, Höglund says he won't survive the night. I offered to go with him, but it seems they lost their youngest daughter some years ago, and it was you, Pastor, who conducted the burial, so...'

I keep walking. Georg is still talking, but I'm not listening to what he says. Höglund is pacing nervously and spinning his hat round and round in his hand. I study his deeply lined face in the light of the doorway but I don't recognise him.

We shake hands. His is large and warm.

'Good evening, Pastor. I don't know if you remember me?'

No, I still don't. Höglund's rough black hair looks dusty.

He's lost several teeth from his upper jaw. I usually have a good memory for faces, but some people can age so quickly they become unrecognisable in only a few years.

'How can I help?' I say.

'When little Margareta left us,' says Höglund, 'it was like a bolt from the... It went so quickly. There were so many things we should have thought of. We didn't remember to send for you, Pastor. But this time, with Olof, we thought...'

I nod to Georg. We set off. Georg, Höglund and I.

The street Höglund lives in is Norra Tullportsgatan, and during the short walk there I ask after the boy's condition, and whether he's had a proper medical examination.

Höglund hesitates in his speech, which I find strange, since people usually make a point of remembering such things. Parents so often rattle off expressions like 'confined to bed', 'convulsions' and 'copious phlegm', with a desperate look in their eyes, as if simply repeating these unfamiliar phrases again and again gives them strength.

We go through a gateway and come into a yard full of smoke thick enough to make one's eyes smart. Both Georg and I cough and turn our heads away.

An elderly woman is sitting by the wall stirring a large pot, the source of the smoke. She seems to be roasting something. She nods to us. A little girl standing near the pot brightens and takes a step forward, but the woman grabs her arm and pulls her back so sharply that the girl loses her balance, sits down on the ground with a thud and begins to cry. The tears streak her dirty face with black.

The woman picks her up, sets her on her knee and hushes her. Her movements suggest considerable physical strength.

I turn to look at Höglund, who's heading for a narrow staircase on the side of the house.

We go up and find ourselves in a cramped, shabby room where it's so dark I can barely make out Höglund's figure ahead of me even though he's only an arm's length away. I stop to take several short breaths so as not to start coughing, and wait for my eyes to get used to the dark. Suddenly the mother is standing before me, her face at chest level, weatherbeaten, suspicious and furrowed by sorrow.

'Thank you, Pastor. It won't be long now.'

Her words are like short, bitter lashes.

I step past her to a sofa against the wall. To begin with all I can see is a pile of blankets. Pieces of cloth seem to be hanging all around the room with heavy sombre fringes covering every table and chair.

'The doctor said he's not infectious.'

I turn half around. Fru Höglund is bent forward, waiting impatiently for me to sit down by the boy. There's a stool by the sofa. I pull it towards me and sit down.

Olof's lying with his face turned to the wall, under a blanket pulled up so that only the top of his head is visible. It's impossible to see whether he's breathing.

'The pastor is here now.'

The mother again. She has sat down at the foot of the sofa. She shakes Olof gently and pulls down the blanket a little. The boy doesn't move. He has the same matted dark hair as his father.

I have the strange thought that I'm looking at something not fully developed. Presumably because the father's head is still so fresh in my memory. This similar but much smaller head makes me feel warm and sad at the same time and I think: let it grow, Lord, let it grow big.

I pull the stool a little closer.

Fru Höglund edges up the sofa, strokes the boy's cheek and speaks to him in a low voice. She turns him till he's lying on his back. His eyes are still closed. If I listen carefully I can hear a light, sobbing sort of breathing. I've heard this kind of thing before. It's the breathing of someone who has coughed till his lungs can cough no more.

There's a pungent smell of urine from the blankets.

I lean forward and rest a hand on Olof's brow. No reaction. His brow's cool, as if life has already begun to leave him.

I look at him, at his little nose and thin lips.

I try to imagine him before he was ill: playing with friends who are throwing stones at something; Olof is running up and down a small rise in the ground to fetch more stones, I see wild happiness in his face and I hear his voice giving a running commentary on everything that's passing through his mind and happening around him.

I see him busy with everyday work: helping his father to shovel snow, and struggling when his spade gets caught in the cobbles, a spade that looks as big as an oar in his hands.

I see him on the sofa after the evening meal, following his mother with his eyes, interpreting her movements and the expressions on her face as she shuts a cupboard or goes over to the door and looks out, and I can see thoughts forming in his head, perhaps a vague perception of how vulnerable he is in the hands of these two people.

All this time I keep my hand on his forehead and study his face, his long dark eyelashes, the freckles on his cheeks and the bridge of his nose, and try to form an idea of everything that must have moved inside his head, barely a thumb's breadth below my palm.

All his thoughts and hopes, light and dark, all the memories he has stored away, light and dark, all the experiences that have affected him, light and dark, all the things he has studied and learned, light and dark.

All the faces and human figures he has grown to be fond of and can't help needing, and who in their turn have come to be fond of him and can't help needing him...

In short, everything that has come together to make him a unique creature, a being whose exact likeness the human race has never seen before and will never see again; I try to grasp all this.

It can't be done. This much I do understand. But at least I try.

I turn around.

Fru Höglund is standing with her hands tightly clasped over her breast, staring expectantly at me. Her husband's sitting at the table, utterly defeated and exhausted. Georg's standing by the door with head bowed and hands together.

A steady soporific sound can be heard from the yard where the old woman's still stirring her pot.

'Does Olof have any sisters or brothers?' I say.

Fru Höglund nods mutely, almost in irritation.

'Her down there,' her husband explains, gesturing with his thumb towards the yard.

I turn back to Olof again.

I recite the Lord's blessing over him. He doesn't even open his eyes. Just continues his light tormented breathing.

A light spreads through the room. Fru Höglund sets a lamp on the table. Her husband reaches for it, perhaps to screw up the wick. His wife moves it away from him, as from a meddlesome child. Herr Höglund slowly withdraws his hand.

'Which doctor have you seen?' I ask.

'My sister works for one,' says Fru Höglund. 'They live in Nyköping. So we've been there.'

She checks herself and widens her eyes at me as though expecting me to commend her. I smile and nod at her to continue.

'He said it's gone too far. Just a question of God's will now. That's what he said.'

I nod.

'But Pastor, you do understand what's caused all this?'

Fru Höglund holds up her hand and rubs the thumb hard against the index finger.

'What do you mean, Fru Höglund?' I say in a friendly voice.

'Greed. That's a deadly sin, isn't it?'

'Indeed it is...'

She brightens, nodding vigorously. It's as if some tension in her has been released. Now she radiates peace and wellbeing. All her wrinkles seem to have been smoothed away and everything that was mistrustful and ill-humoured in her has vanished.

'Exactly. Exactly so. I know you understand that, Pastor. But it's not something everyone's able to accept. Look at us. What did we have? Nothing special. I worked as a washerwoman down at Norrström. He worked in Nylén's store. He had friends there. You need to choose your friends carefully. Not everyone has the sense to do that. You can have friends who set up their own businesses. Become wholesalers. Strut about. New waistcoats and shiny shoes. And women. Let's not even mention them! Some looking for work and some just… there, among the sacks and shelves. They get a praline chocolate, they get several, they're promised one thing and another. And – you can imagine it, Pastor – there's such a thing as weak souls who want a particular waistcoat, or a particular pair of shoes. Not something their own resources will stretch to. They think all they need is to be near those who have waistcoats and shoes. That if they do nothing more than open beer for them and laugh at their jokes, they will get what they want…'

Fru Höglund savours the pleasure of her story like a chocolate truffle.

'Just look at him, Pastor.'

I look at her husband, who's smiling in embarrassment, like a scolded schoolboy. But there's something coquettish about his smile, as if the schoolboy knows that he can take the scolding with a pinch of salt because he's going to escape punishment yet again.

'I had to go and fetch him in the evenings. He would have stayed there otherwise. I had three children to care for already. And now I had a fourth, a grown man. If I'd had any sense I'd have let him go.'

Silence falls in the little room.

The boy's breathing, almost inaudible a few minutes ago, can now be heard clearly, like a small painful clicking behind my back. I find this extremely disagreeable, like the ticking of a clock that may stop at any moment, and I want to be far from here when it does.

I do my duty. I ask some questions about Olof. I offer Fru Höglund a way out of her bitterness, but she returns again and again to the days in October when Olof grew increasingly listless and she had to leave him on his own in the evenings since 'some people' liked to linger at the wholesaler's on Storkyrkobrinken hill.

I ask them to get in touch with me again if Olof's condition changes for the better or for the worse.

The Höglunds see us to the door. The yard's empty. Now only a few wisps of smoke are rising from the pot. Suddenly Herr Höglund touches my arm with the back of his hand.

'Look…'

He points at the dusty maple tree. It takes me a moment to realise that it's a bird that has caught his attention. It looks like a blackbird, but it's impossible to be sure.

'It's completely tame. It comes here every summer.'

I glance sideways at him. His eyes are shining with rapture, and he's smiling so broadly that he shows the gaps in his teeth in a way I haven't seen before. He clicks his tongue a few times to attract the bird.

*M*ost children don't see us. We're just one unfocused authority among many, and they are fully occupied with those of their own age, with securing and defending their place in the flock and pushing aside and, if necessary, destroying all who threaten it. As an adult you're merely one of the many it's important to keep sweet so as to avoid detentions and boxed ears.

And that's of course how it must be.

But there are some children, even if you seldom come across them, who look you straight in the eye, not out of insolence or defiance but because they're curious.

To them you're simply a human being. A grown-up human being, certainly. But these unusual children have grasped the fact that one day they themselves will be grown up. This insight makes them curious.

I'm not talking about the primitive sort of curiosity that makes children ape adults and soullessly mimic their words and gestures.

I'm talking about a deeper understanding, a curiosity that relates to the human condition, rather than just learning how to knock in a nail or darn a stocking.

Helga was such a child.

She was ten when I first saw her.

It was during a reception at her home. I'd got to know her

father, Birger, when the parish buildings were being renovated. It was his wife Eva's birthday. They lived in a house with a view across Brunnsviken water. It was the middle of May. Birger had a garland of flowers on his head.

I remember an awkward circle of men of a similar age who were standing fingering crystal glasses with some sort of clear red aperitif in them. They all knew each other, but only superficially. I already had a suspicion, the truth of which would not become obvious till many years later, that Birger liked to develop contacts in as many different fields as possible.

One might have come close to feeling exploited, but I could see the boy in him so clearly. I knew who his father was. I could see how well Birger had learned that if you have ambitions to advance in this world, you have to have a particular set of colours on your palette. You need contacts in the arts, politics, law, the church and business.

So there we stood, carefully selected: a writer, a civil servant, an appeal judge, a wine wholesaler and a clergyman, all reasonably young and with a future before us.

I don't know if the others saw as clearly as I did that they were nothing but colours on Birger's palette. I expect they did. I suppose they also realised that this was a gathering that could do something for everyone because it also served to increase the range of colours on their own palettes.

It might also be pleasurable, if they were lucky. Time would tell.

It was easier for Lydia. I looked in her direction now and then. She was showering our hostess with serious questions about her children, her house and her garden.

It used to amuse me to watch my wife from the far side of a large room. On one occasion it occurred to me that the changing expressions on her face were like the ancient Greek theatre with its grotesque masks. After that I couldn't get away from the idea. Watching my wife from a distance of up to a hundred metres I could tell whether our hostess was describing something calculated to awaken sympathy, loathing, surprise or indignation.

This may make it seem I had little respect for her. On the contrary, I felt full of tenderness since I had also seen the other side of the virtuoso struggle that a social life demanded of her.

I knew what would happen when we got home, once she was sitting on the edge of the bed and had taken off her evening gown and tight shoes and had combed out her hair, and I was standing there, looking at the helplessness of her fat, drooping shoulders.

Either a migraine would come on, making her obstinate and capricious, and needing tea and headache powder, and I would have to tiptoe about in silence, or she would burst into tears and weep for hours on end, and if I asked her how she was she would turn towards the curtain blowing in the breeze and simply shake her head.

But at this moment Lydia was displaying her Greek masks, and there we were standing, a bunch of influential handpicked men in our forties, with an almost unbearable understanding; a knowledge that each member of our little circle knew what it was to wield power over the simple souls living and working in the conglomeration of rotting, tumbledown hovels and noisy workshops and smoke-belching factories outside, and that we were all initiates who shared the same dearly-bought experience of the blessings and curses of power.

After a bit I began to find the situation rather ridiculous, so allowing myself the pleasure of feeling gratified that I had done the good Birger a service by merely turning up, I gave the company a little nod and withdrew to explore the house.

I passed through a drawing room in which a woman was playing Haydn to several happily twittering female friends. It was clearly a piece she'd only just learned, for she repeatedly stopped to apologise and was repeatedly urged to continue, while a young officer with curly hair offered a stream of well-informed comments on her playing.

Beyond the drawing room was a library, and it was there that my life took a new turn.

There was a girl standing in front of a window. Long blonde hair that had been washed and combed till it shone like silver. White dress, stockings decorated with lace, and small black shoes.

The tips of her fingers were resting on the window-frame as if she'd just started playing on it, and she was moving her heels up and down impatiently, causing a knocking sound on the parquet floor. There was a rhythmic clattering coming from somewhere further off in the room, and I saw it was coming from a porcelain figure on a small table, of a galloping horseman dressed for fox-hunting whose little brass stirrups were endlessly drumming against his porcelain horse.

The girl was looking out over the grass slope and budding fruit trees, the grey-gold reeds waving in the wind, and Brunnsviken's glittering waves, and she seemed to be tapping her little heels ever more impatiently, as if a steam engine inside her was working under increasingly high pressure.

I could hardly help laughing, but pulled myself together and took several steps towards her.

When she heard the floorboards creak she turned her head. She had blue-green eyes. At the sight of my clerical dress most children of her age – I guessed her to be ten or eleven – would stare and then look down and begin to flap about nervously as if my office was something that towered threateningly over them. But after a quick glance at my clothes this girl looked inquisitively at me straight in the eye and held out her little hand.

'Good afternoon, Pastor.'

'Good afternoon to you. I'm Pastor Gregorius.'

'My name's Helga.'

'A beautiful name.'

'Thank you.'

'Of course you'd expect me to like it, since I'm a priest. You know what it means, don't you?'

'Yes, it comes from "holy".'

'Holy, yes, that's right.'

I clasped my hands behind my back and looked out of the window. I became aware of tension in my face and realised it was because I was smiling so broadly, and that I didn't know how long I'd been doing it. And that it was perhaps an unusual smile, a smile making demands on many unpractised facial muscles.

We spent a while in small talk. I told her she was a lucky girl to live in such a beautiful house, and have such nice parents. She told me she'd been collecting frogspawn down in the bay with her father, and that she was keeping the frogspawn in a large glass jar under the steps. And that some of the tadpoles were already growing little arms and legs. And that Persson, the gardener, had told her that we humans developed in the same way many millions of years ago. That we had started as fish and then began to crawl on land, and that it took several more millions of years for us to learn to walk upright!

'Then we must've been very slow learners in those days,' I said. 'Just think. A million years to learn to walk upright! You must have taught yourself that in one summer!'

Helga studied my face, then smiled uncertainly.

'Now you're joking, Pastor.'

'I'm not so sure…'

'It sounded like it.'

'I know. But, Helga, you must understand we can sometimes joke and be serious at the same time. We can say something really serious, lightly. Put a funny hat on, if you like.'

Then she laughed. It was a laugh that made me feel dizzy inside, like when I was little and my father took me by the hands and swung me round and round like a hammer-thrower. When she looked at me I felt privileged. As if I'd won her confidence, and we'd become good friends.

'Why would we want to put a... a funny hat on?'

She laughed again, but she held me with her eyes.

'I really don't know.'

But I did know very well why. The answer made me both ashamed and sorry. The answer was I didn't feel I needed to discuss theories of evolution seriously with her because she was only a child. Obviously I thought I could dismiss the whole thing with a few cheap witticisms.

'Perhaps one might just feel light-hearted. A bit skittish, you know.'

Helga nodded, but I had a feeling she knew I was keeping back the real answer.

She was the sweetest child I'd ever seen.

The rest of the day I went around in a daze.

I have vague memories of cake being served in the garden, a brass quartet playing and a famous baritone singing... But already, after our first meeting, I was in the same stunned state as when one suddenly falls in love. I avoided her parents because I was afraid I wouldn't be able to stop myself once I started talking about her; it would all be too obvious.

I wished I could at least have talked to Lydia about it. But that was naturally impossible. We'd been trying for a child for fifteen years. Lydia was reaching a point where she hardly dared have children anywhere near her any longer. Some embarrassing situations had occurred.

At first it wasn't too bad. It can take several years for children to come, that's nothing unusual.

But then so many years passed that women in particular began to look at Lydia with a sort of reserve, as if they were standing near the bottom of a volcano and looking up at its crater. They knew there was no immediate danger of an eruption, but they still liked to be on the safe side and keep at a slight distance.

Lydia felt their eyes on her, but while she had her own sorrow to bear – and mine – she was still struggling to present herself as a woman who faced the future with unshakeable confidence, and knew that with God's will we would have children soon.

But no sooner was she near small children than it was as if those close to her could hear a rumbling from the volcano. Something watchful came into their eyes, and the conversation around them faltered and they became distracted… or wasn't this really happening? Weren't we rather imagining things?

In her attempts to be easy-going with children, Lydia was caught in a vicious circle she couldn't escape.

I saw it myself several times. Talking non-stop, a sort of forced babble in which normal words followed each other so closely that they seemed to snap at each other's heels, she would bend over some three-year-old, passionately stroking the child's hair, and the child would stare up at her with tears beginning to tremble in large frightened eyes, and soon the mother would come to the child's rescue and lift him or her up, and a heavy silence would fall over the room, in which all that could be heard would be the mother's soothing whispers in her child's ear, while Lydia tried to say something to smooth things over and I slipped an arm around her shoulders to lead her away.

When I remember these events it is like standing close to the source of all human pain. It has occurred to me that if one wanted to inflict the maximum possible inner suffering on any human being, one should give her the same life as Lydia.

With the emphasis on 'inner', of course.

I'm well aware that many childless women also have other torments to endure. Cold, hunger, illness. But with them, it seems to me, a woman's inner pain may find an outlet by means of her outer pain.

Lydia, on the other hand, had nothing to complain of on the surface. She had all the food she needed every day, she was in excellent health, and was married to a man who was good to her and in marrying her had brought her respect and esteem. There was nowhere for her inner sufferings to find expression.

So I hadn't the heart to tell her anything about Helga, or admit what a deep impression the girl had made on me. It was something I must keep to myself and banish to the world of daydreams and fantasies.

And that's how it was.

Helga was with me when I went to bed and when I ate breakfast… it's pointless to list all the situations in which she came to me in my thoughts. She was with me every hour of the day and night.

I liked best to think of her in the evening when I was ready for sleep.

I'd sit on the edge of her bed and hold her little hand and talk about the day that had passed. She would have combed out her hair and would look up at me with a big white pillow under her head. Her eyes would be so wide open when she looked at me. I'd hold her hand and we'd talk about anything under the sun. Of big things and little things, easy things and difficult things.

What was so absorbing and – I have no hesitation in using the word – 'religious', about these fantasies, was that I could feel something inside me expanding and being made use of; I was like a hot-air balloon experiencing for the first time what it's like to be filled completely, with every crease smoothed away by a determination to do good and to wish well, to protect, care for, and even, if necessary, offer one's life for the other person.

Love, quite simply.

But these fantasies would never have gained so much power over me had I not felt them streaming back from Helga to me, just as strongly, just as stubbornly, just as obviously.

Fantasies are dangerous. I didn't realise it then but it's clear to me now: fantasies are the beginning of everything.

Sometimes I fantasised that Birger and Eva died and that I conducted their funeral, and that then, if not earlier, it would seem an ideal solution for Lydia and me to adopt their daughter since everyone knew how close we'd been to the family. Even Helga's maternal and paternal grandparents – who in my fantasies lived far away, somewhere like Skåne or, better still, Lapland – would approve of this arrangement.

Naturally I can try to persuade myself or anyone else, that it was purely by accident that we gradually started to see the Waller family socially, at first occasionally and tentatively, then more and more regularly and on increasingly familiar terms.

Was this something I planned? To gradually win the confidence of the parents, to make myself such a good friend to Helga that she would think it was obvious that she should eventually become my wife?

It seems absurd. But I also notice that I avoid going more deeply into the matter.

But I don't accept any charge of falsifying the truth or being guilty of any other reconstruction after the event when I say that both Lydia and I gained greatly from their company.

Birger, above all, was a fascinating person. Quick on the uptake, unpredictable and with a flashing wit. Handsome, too.

Someone with whom people liked to be on good terms.

He reminded me of childhood, of going to the forest to play with friends. Among the children there were some who would automatically attract more attention than others. It was as if one knew that in their company one would not only have the most exciting adventures, but one would also survive those adventures unscathed. With them one would have the wildest laughs, find the best wild strawberries and have the best stories to tell coming home.

But naturally I came to have a more nuanced picture of Birger over the years. You need to associate closely with someone for a long time to be able to distinguish what is fundamental and unalterable in them from what is mere polish.

Birger had a superficial side to his nature that could seem almost alarming. He could only involve himself deeply in topics of conversation he'd introduced himself. He could be almost pathologically insensitive. He was capable of interrupting anyone in the middle of an account of something deeply personal to them, in order to begin to talk about something entirely different.

I should make it clear that he didn't show this side of himself till you knew him well. Only then did you realise that the impression of the attentive listener that he was capable of giving when you first knew him was nothing but a lure. Then you'd find yourself fast in his net together with other helplessly struggling insects and when you looked at them you'd realise, as I hinted earlier, that his prey revealed a remarkably wide range of varieties; there would be a poet floundering here, an appeal court judge there, a government official somewhere else, and so on.

Oddly enough, every time you sat in his company and experienced this lack of interest in what you wanted to talk about, you'd still think it was worth it. It was the price you had to pay for the privilege of associating with such a winning personality. It was as if, deep inside, you were giving him credit for being right, for doing the right thing when he swept aside your own story and took over the conversation himself.

It was worst for his wife, Eva. He scarcely even bothered to be polite to her. But she responded like everyone else. She would sit in silence, admiring his charm, intelligence and good looks, and living for the rare moment when he would tire of talking and could give her his full attention.

When this happened, exactly like the rest of us, she would be so flattered that she wouldn't know what to do. Words would stick in her throat, and she'd blush and not know where to look. Sometimes this rare attention seemed to make her so happy that it became too much for her, even downright painful, so that she longed to return to her familiar peaceful place in the front row of the stalls.

I can afford to reflect on these things now that a good twenty years have passed since the events I'm describing.

It's like so much else in life. Insights seldom come when you might have some use for them, but only when everything's sunk away into the past. The good Birger has long since disappeared from this world.

In fact, this was a question Birger used to like to put to me: what can have been God's purpose in letting wisdom only come to us when it's too late?

... I have to smile, seeing him so clearly before me, like a conductor rapping his baton on the music stand, enjoying startling everyone: he dares to put such a question to a priest!

The others didn't know Birger and I had often had that conversation so that the comparison with a conductor is unusually apt.

I used to answer that I agreed the question was well put, but that the conclusions we came to were different.

God has never intended us to be omniscient. That's my deepest conviction.

Birger aimed for perfection. I've never done that. The idea that one day we should be able to look at our lives and see nothing we would want to change or improve is horrible for me. It's then, I imagine, that real world-weariness would begin.

As long as we can strive for perfection our lives have meaning. We're like a gardener who cultivates his seedlings and waits for the results. But what happens if one day we walk through our garden and decide we've reached our goal, and that nothing can ever be better than it is now? In that case what's the point of getting up in the morning at all?

Birger liked to suggest that our imperfection and slowness to perfect ourselves was a sign that God had been a bit negligent when He created us.

I used to answer that it was precisely these defects that made us human, and that God knew exactly what he was doing when he provided us with them.

Birger had an answer to this too. But I've forgotten what it was.

I'm sitting on the edge of her bed. Or, more accurately, of our shared bed. But I'm not holding her hand, and we aren't talking of everything under the sun, big things and little things.

I think she's asleep. She's lying still, turned in my direction, with the cover pulled up to her shoulders and she's breathing through her nose with small even breaths. It must be nearly three in the morning, and it's so light in the room that I can see an eider-down feather on her right arm trembling every time she breathes out.

But of course one can't be sure. I've often pretended to be asleep myself. Most recently only a few days ago. It's not difficult, as long as you don't get an itch. Though even then you can make a hesi-tant movement with your eyes closed, perhaps groan a bit for effect, give yourself a sleepy scratch and then go on 'sleeping'. The trouble is itches seldom come singly, and if you scratch yourself too often it'll soon be quite obvious that you aren't asleep.

On that occasion a few days ago, she came and sat on the chair by the window. She sat there peaceful and still, watching me, and I felt an icy conviction that my pretending to be asleep was the only thing protecting me from the abyss, and that if I opened my eyes she would say something that would destroy my whole life.

Strangely enough that's exactly how it feels now, with the small difference that it's her sleep or pretended sleep that's preventing everything from crashing down.

I get undressed and creep into bed. The window's half open, the curtain's moving slightly and I see the sun's about to rise. Outside the birds are singing, shrill, harsh trills that roll backwards and forwards across the churchyard.

It's been an extremely eventful day. I try not to think about my heartbeat, and notice my thoughts are drawn in that direction precisely for that reason.

I have to conjure up my usual fantasies to find peace.

Fantasies about a little child. A boy. He's only eight months old, and sometimes he's called Bengt. But usually Ernst.

He's lying in a little bed beside ours, so Helga can easily lift him over when he wakes in the night and wants the breast, and when he's asleep he looks as severe and determined as only small children can. And Helga's sleeping deeply, since her days are filled with responsibilities to do with our little son. Of course we have a nursemaid at hand, but Helga doesn't find it easy to entrust Ernst to her; she's never satisfied with the nursemaid's efforts, some detail always catches her attention, and it usually ends with Helga sitting on tenterhooks listening to Ernst wailing in some neighbouring room. Then she gets up with a little sigh, rolls up her eyes to me to express exhaustion and makes her way with weary steps to the door, while I put down my book and say something to the effect that she must occasionally hand over responsibility to someone else, and that the nursemaid's experienced and sure to know what to do, and sometimes I shake my head in resignation and tease Helga about being a real mother hen.

Sometimes I get to hold him. Sometimes he lies in my arms and weighs so little that I have the dreadful thought that a puff of wind could blow him away, and when I look at his little face I see myself and I see my beloved Helga, but I also see something that doesn't come from either of us, but is altogether his own.

God. There, right in front of me. He has never before shown Himself so clearly. And when I hold Ernst this streams through my head: all the times I sought for God, all that long life, all that reading and analysing the Gospels and Old Testament, all those hymns and psalms, all those church halls and pulpits, all those visits to the sick and christenings and burials... all that time I was searching for God.

And there He suddenly is, in my arms, in what comes neither from Helga nor from me but makes this little boy unique, one of a kind and not like anyone else, either before him or after him.

Then I hand him over to Helga. And he is just there. And we do things together, the three of us. We take a carriage to Djurgården park. Ernst likes to sit and look out at the buildings and trees we pass. Sometimes the carriage lurches violently, but Helga holds him firmly. We sit on a blanket under the chestnut trees. We eat food we've brought with us. We drink a good burgundy. We look at our son and at each other and talk about his progress and laugh at things he does and sounds he makes and we know nobody else would think these things as comic as we do. And we look at Ernst, and we know – even if we don't say it aloud – that through him we've become one, and that we shall never be separated...

No, my fantasies aren't managing to lull me to sleep as they usually do.

Soon I'm going to begin worrying about how I feel, and directing that fearful attentiveness to my heartbeat. Soon I'll be getting myself ready to feel that struggling movement in my ribcage again, and I know it'll wake me from my rose-tinted fantasy world, where Helga and little Ernst and I are the happiest people on earth, as mercilessly as a box on the ear, and the struggling movement will remind me that I shall soon be dead; perhaps in a month, perhaps in fifty, but soon.

In a ghastly moment I see myself on my back, exactly as I'm lying now, but with my mouth half open and my eyes staring and dull, and my face a purplish colour like a rotting plum, and I'm dead. Helga's sleeping peacefully beside me, breathing with healthy even breaths. She still has a long life before her. She'll love someone else, and give birth to a lot of strange-looking children with features not the least bit like little Ernst's.

And the birds will sing, just as before.

I raise myself on one elbow. With my left hand I pull down Helga's cover, so I can see her shoulders.

She moves slightly. Sighs.

I pull the cover down a bit further, lean over her, breathe in her scent.

I look at her body outlined under her white nightdress, all soft rounded shapes, and I think of everything that's soft and round about her, and which fills me with such pleasure, and I think of everything that's soft and round about me, which fills her with such disgust.

Sometimes I wish she could look at me in the way I look at her; absorbed and almost solemn with desire.

I climb carefully on top of her and ease apart her legs. She is too dazed to protest. She lies half asleep under me while my movements make the bed shake and creak. A few sweaty strands of hair are stuck across her mouth, and she grimaces weakly, as if in pain but too tired to do anything about it.

I could be anyone. She would lie just like this, her young body quivering in the same way under the same hard thrusts. In a month, or fifty, this is what she'll be doing, with another man on top of her.

The thought intoxicates me. I can't describe where it takes me.

But despite the bolting and exploding of my heart in my breast, I am no longer afraid.

I wake to the sound of loud knocking on the door. I lift my head. Helga's not there. I mumble something half-stifled straight out into the room.

The door opens jerkily and clumsily and Märit sticks in her head and says madam has sent her to say that breakfast's ready.

I nod, imagining I can detect a malicious glint in her eye, and once more I have a sense of all the gossip that flows from this house and out into the city, like an overturned latrine barrel sending filthy water rippling into every nook and cranny.

It's enough to remember all the gossip when Lydia was alive – a time when there was nothing to gossip about! Just think how much gossip there must be now, when to be honest there are things to gossip about.

At least I don't grudge Märit the pleasure it would give her if I asked her where Helga was.

I find her in the garden. I stand in the doorway and watch her for a moment. She hasn't noticed me yet.

She's put on a thin yellow linen dress that looks unpretentious, so long as you don't notice its white hem – the very latest fashion from Paris.

I laugh when I remember how delighted she was when she discovered I'm rather a connoisseur of women's clothes; I have a 'natural talent' as she put it. That was during our first year together. She respected my eagerness to learn new things, laughed lovingly at my questions and said it was a side of me she'd never been aware of even though she'd known me as long as she could remember.

I watch Helga going about the garden with dawdling footsteps. Now and then she stops to examine some rosebush or other.

A deafening noise can be heard from the other side of the wall; it sounds as though they are breaking up paving stones and throwing them into a cart, but Helga seems undisturbed, as if isolated inside a bubble where nothing can reach her. The harsh, violent noises and the rough male voices are in such stark contrast to the dusty greenery of the garden and Helga's sleepy movements that they seem unreal.

When the noise stops for a moment I can hear that she's humming something.

I can't remember her having done that for a long time.

When I go out into the garden and make my way over to her I remember the events of the night. Perhaps I should feel embarrassed, perhaps I should try and pretend it didn't happen. But that's impossible. It's singing through my whole body.

I hurry over to Helga and plant a kiss on her cheek, and for a moment the sweaty feel of her cheek against my lips makes me feel dizzy.

I look at her and lift my eyebrows in a humorous expression, trying to meet her eye in the hope that perhaps we can make light of the night's events; that I lost my head, but that it's something that happens in even the best marriages, something one should be able to accept with, I don't know, tender indulgence, perhaps.

But Helga looks away.

'I don't feel...'

She shakes her head, looking for words. Her voice is weak and slightly embarrassed.

'... quite well.'

'How?'

I lay my hands on her cheeks. Try to catch her eye. But the more I try, the more she looks away.

'It's a pain that...'

'A pain where?'

'That…'

'Where?'

'Leave me alone!'

She knocks my hands away and finally meets my eye, but her look flashes fury. It really looks as though she hates me.

She mumbles something about needing to go to the doctor, and hurries into the house. I stay where I am.

I look up at the sun, a white piercing light through the leaves of the chestnut. An evil sun. Blindly shining down on a day in which every bodily movement, every attempt to do anything is a torment.

A little further off, on one of the gravel paths, Byström is standing with his rake. As soon as he realises I've noticed him he hurriedly starts raking twigs and rubbish from the gravel.

*I*t took me several years to reach the point of no return. We became good friends with Birger and his family. Helga passed her eleventh birthday, then her twelfth. I was a little worried our social connection would prove painful to Lydia, but I was rapidly reassured. The older Helga became, the more she fitted naturally into our group. Besides, I believe I've noticed that single children, with no older siblings to struggle against and no younger ones to be responsible for, are often accepted in the family as if they were full adult members. It seems natural to ask their advice, listen to their objections and let them share the privileges of the adult world.

With Helga, luckily, none of this went to her head. I have seen dreadful cases of single children turning into family tyrants. I've seen their parents transformed into cringing slaves who obey the child's slightest gesture and happily let their conversation be interrupted by commands to do this or that. Occasionally such parents throw appealing glances to those around them, as if desperate for company in their senseless servility; indeed, they beg you to reassure them that their child's a real charmer, when all you can see before you is a little monster who has been allowed far too much authority.

Helga understood early on that it was as a favour that she was allowed to sit up with us in the evenings and talk a little about all kinds of things, while the toddy steamed in our glasses, the wind sighed in the maples outside and the fire crackled and spat in the open fireplace.

It would have been easy to say that this was because she was well brought up. But that would give a wrong impression, as if Birger and Eva had succeeded in imprinting blind obedience in her.

No, it was a result of what I mentioned earlier: that we were real people to her and she was curious. But she'd also understood that you have to be careful with grown-up people who excite your curiosity.

We often discussed religion, Helga and I. Among other things, she wanted to know why there were so many gods in the world, and how we could be so sure that our own God was the right one. She asked me many questions about my profession, and I was conscious that my answers were stamped with a gravity and frankness I seldom allowed myself. I trusted her. I knew she wouldn't embarrass me by repeating my answers in front of other people.

Helga was the kind of child one observes with a certain sadness. One knows that one day the brightness in her eyes will dim and begin to turn inwards. And her body will begin to change and weigh on her and cause her suffering.

Naturally I had no wish to stop her development. But I can state confidently that I didn't want to hasten it either.

I was very fond of Helga's mother. She's one of the most silent people I've ever met. Silence can spread social unease. It's easy to begin wondering what it may indicate. You can persuade yourself that she's bored, or that she doesn't like you, or that she's not intellectually capable of joining in the conversation. All three assumptions can lead you to feel hostile.

But Eva belonged to the rare category of those who only open their mouths when they have something to say. She never seemed to worry what the rest of us might think about her sitting silent so long. Perhaps she simply enjoyed listening. There was nothing in her silence to indicate that she was unhappy that people didn't speak to her, or that she was shy. Eva radiated calm and harmony, and a firmly rooted sense that it was right for her to be exactly as she was.

One tradition we had was to gather in their garden to pick blackcurrants. Like all good traditions it started spontaneously. One Sunday in July Birger and I had been for a walk down by the water, and as we were going back up towards the house he stopped in front of the row of blackcurrant bushes, muttered something in irritation and bent over a sprig that was hanging down almost to the ground because of lack of proper support.

We both picked a few berries and ate them and decided, with our mouths full, that it was difficult to stop eating once you'd begun. Then, with blackcurrant juice running down our chins, we burst out laughing. We made so much noise that Lydia and Eva heard us and hurried out to find out what it was that was so much fun. All of a sudden we each had a jug in our hand and were running about among the bushes. We filled our jugs and sat down on the ground to clean the berries and fight off insulted wasps.

For some reason I took it upon myself to carry several full jugs up to the house, which as I now look back, seems a little odd to me. I can't remember ever running a similar errand to the kitchen on any other occasion during our acquaintance. In some moods I can have the disagreeable thought that in some obscure way I must have had some presentiment of what was waiting for me inside.

But I'd like to add that when I'm not in that sort of mood, this idea of presentiment seems to me just superstitious nonsense, like fortune-telling in the coffee grounds.

Let me try my hardest to remember that short walk to the

house. I remember looking down into the mass of blackcurrants bursting with juice in the jugs. I had a jug in each hand and was humming a tune; at the same time I noticed that my hands were so sticky I could hardly separate my fingers and I began fantasising that webbing was about to grow between them.

Trivial rambling thoughts: should I wash my hands in the rainwater barrel at the corner of the house… or would I get germs all over my hands if I did that?… Perhaps it would be better to take a scoop of water from the kitchen…?

And so on.

I put the jugs down in the kitchen and poured a little water over my hands from a pail I saw on a bench.

Then it struck me that Helga might like to join in the currant-picking so I decided to look for her.

I went through the rooms on the ground floor. In the drawing room there was a tea tray on the delicate little table, and various pieces of needlework spread on the sofa. I touched the teapot: it was still warm. In the library flies were happily relaxing in a broad sunbeam that extended across the floor. They fled to the window when I walked in, but quickly went back to their old places after I'd passed.

I could have called out. But I didn't.

I remember how a surge of unease passed through my body, because it was so extraordinarily quiet in the house, and I remember that a certain contentment was linked to this unease, a singular warmth, since it had become for me a sign of how close Helga was to me now, that she had come to hold a significant place in my life, and that, however one looked at the matter, any unease I felt as I walked through the silent house was the unease of a father.

But I didn't call her name. I think it would have seemed a bit too domesticated, rather as if I weren't content with Helga having become like a daughter to me, but also as if I were making claims on the house where she lived.

There was only one more room on the ground floor to look into: Birger's and Eva's bedroom, which lay next to a dark hall. It was a beautiful room, with white walls and big windows that overlooked the courtyard. I'd never actually been inside it, had only stuck my head rapidly in and out again.

I took a step into the hall which contained rows of waterproofs on hangers and overalls of various kinds.

The door to the bedroom was ajar. I stopped about a metre from the door and stayed where I was.

In the egg-shaped mirror on the beautifully carved wardrobe I saw Helga. She was naked. She was feeling her breasts with both hands, pressing carefully up and down.

Her eyes were half-closed. She had an expression of great concentration, perhaps with a touch of melancholy.

It was as if she had deceived us all.

What I saw in the mirror was a fully-grown woman. Yet Helga was only twelve years old. I wondered how she'd managed to hide that woman's body from us for so long.

Of course I'd noticed that she'd shot up in height. But I'd still thought of her as a long-legged little girl with freckles on her cheeks and restless little hands.

I don't know how long I stood there. But I've never stood before a sight that had such a hypnotic effect on me.

Her hands wandered over her body in wonder, over hips, buttocks, belly and thighs, returning time and again to her breasts as if these remained the greatest miracle of all.

It struck me long afterwards that there was something in Helga's movements that indicated that she'd only recently discovered she'd become a woman, however strange this may seem; as if she had gone to bed the evening before with the thin, flat, calf-like body of a girl and woken the next morning with the full and rounded figure of a woman.

If any of us, for example myself, had been transformed in the night as in a fairy tale, and woken up as a completely different person, as a woman for example who could conceive and give birth to children (and not only could do it, but had a body that was intended for doing it, and expressly demanding to do it), I would have reacted in the same way as Helga.

I would have gone to a room where I wouldn't be disturbed, and I'd have taken off all my clothes and stood in front of a mirror to study this new body in minute detail, as if to be able to take in that all this was mine, my mind floating in speculations and fantasies about what this body could be used for.

And in time my hands would have moved over the new body so that they too could understand that all this was mine, and that it would be there for me whenever I wanted it, and that all these changes were there to serve the highest of all purposes, a purpose that was even divine: the creation of life.

Big words. A little frightening, of course.

But when the big words frightened me my hands would have searched for what was round and soft; the soothing warmth of a breast, and no doubt my hands would have moved in the same solemn, disbelieving way as Helga's hands exploring her body that afternoon.

My mouth had gone dry. My temples were pounding. Everything was silent and still.

I can't remember feeling the slightest trace of lust or sexual desire. That came later. So far everything was merely so vertiginous it was like a dream.

In the end it became so unbearable that I hurried away. I don't know if Helga heard my footsteps. I expect she did. But I just wanted to get out into the garden again.

I have only the vaguest memories of the rest of the day.

I know we went on picking blackcurrants. I suppose we went on chatting and babbling as before. I can see myself bending forward to get through the undergrowth and collect one cluster of berries after another, and I can feel my mouth moving in its usual way and a voice answering me from a nearby shrubbery.

At the same time I feel myself moving as if amid the ruins of everything that existed till then. And I know everything has changed. That something important has been taken from me, or at least that it looks entirely different. And I dread Helga coming out to us and seeing all this in my face, and that I shall see in her face that she knows it too.

I soon realised my reaction was quite natural, and that it's what most parents feel when they realise their children are about to turn into adults – and how fearfully fast this happens.

It must be one of the most bewildering times in anyone's life.

For parents it means that their work in bringing up their children is over, and they won't be needed any more. Instead they must get used to meeting their children as adults, and accept that they make their own decisions. Sometimes they will make foolish decisions, and their parents can only stand there powerless and look on, which must be infinitely painful. Sometimes they will make sensible decisions, and show by this not only that they can get on fine without their parents, or perhaps even better, which must be no less painful.

Even so, I think adjustment must have been easier for Helga's parents, since they were able to follow developments from day to day. As for me, I peeped into their bedroom and was presented with a *fait accompli*.

All my daydreams of us adopting Helga, and of her becoming our child, vanished from that day. The memory of her naked body before the mirror was altogether too strong. It burned away everything else. There was no room for anything else. Slowly new daydreams developed. Daydreams in which I was no longer her father, but her husband.

I would still sit on the edge of her bed and hold her hand and talk of everything under the sun.

But our old conversations were over. And she would slowly lift off her bedclothes and push them to the floor while an acrid and alluring scent I'd never known before would come to me, and she would look at me with eyes so heavy with desire that I almost felt threatened.

$\mathcal{H}$elga doesn't come out. Perhaps she's gone to the doctor. Perhaps she really is ill.

Perhaps death's going to take her from me too.

The thought feels bitter and strangely peaceful.

It's as if the bare thought of it makes me grit my teeth in response. It's as if the thought of losing Helga and what it might do to me is a temptation I must resist at any cost. And I know I shall succeed.

At the same time a thought comes to me from nowhere: that it's precisely this steadfastness that's my curse. That it's this that obstructs my happiness. The core of my loneliness.

I'm so tired. Hungry too. I haven't had any breakfast yet. I've sat out here for far too long; there are a thousand things I should be doing.

Yet I can't tear myself away. It's as if this place has suddenly become the most wonderfully beautiful place in the world. The dreary, withered roses on the trellises. The cracked earth. The bees buzzing so sleepily. When I look around me it's so clear to me how I used to think life at the vicarage should be.

For example, you can't help noticing the rich abundance of garden furniture for sitting on. Beautiful furniture too. Benches and chairs.

Once some foundry worker put his whole soul into the arms of these chairs.

Once I evidently used to think we were going to be a small company that sat out in the garden in the evenings. At least it was important to furnish the garden with that possibility in mind. A little group. A family.

You could say I laid the table for rather a lot of people. But not so many came.

It's a thought that ought to rip through my paralysis. I really do know that. It ought to make me howl in torment like a wounded beast.

But I can't leave the fantasy alone. Can't stop fingering it, reshaping it, manipulating it.

I paint a picture. It's beautiful. Up to the standard of the most famous works of the Impressionists. The harsh, evil light in the leaves. The arid garden with its mass of empty seats. And the black-clad figure alone in the middle, bent forward, hands clasped and elbows resting on his knees, as if in a desperate prayer for someone he can embrace to come hurrying through the garden with arms outstretched.

The picture will be hung in a museum and people will stop before it. Clever, educated people, people who could be my friends.

But as it happened they didn't become my friends. Rather they stopped before a picture and saw me in the empty garden, and they stood a long time in front of the picture and carried on mumbled conversations with those who were with them, and they moved a few steps nearer to the picture to point out particular details, at which others nodded in agreement, and they were all agreed that this was a masterly study of loneliness.

As for me, I float about suspended in the room listening to their comments. I'm no less taken by the painting than the people visiting the museum, just as gripped and depressed as they are… At the same time I feel my heart swelling with pride, since I've not only painted the picture but supplied the subject, more, I am the subject. My life is the subject. My loneliness. And they all clearly understand that it would never have been such a gripping picture if there hadn't been such a long lonely life to fill it.

Depressing, I know. But it turned out to be quite a good picture, didn't it?

This is how I hold the roar of the abyss at bay. This is how I can get through life on my own without it having any particular effect on me. And however much I disgust myself by the coquettish way I make pretty little pictures of my misery, I can't stop doing it. I'm stuck.

But if we had a child... how different everything would be.

It's become fashionable to say we can find paradise even here on earth, and that it's up to us to find it ourselves.

This naturally clashes with everything that's sacred to me. But what indescribable happiness it would be to be able to forget oneself!

When I come into the office, work's in full swing. The shelves are so crowded now I have to turn sideways to get in. I'm worried someone might notice this, as I feel it's more likely to cause spiteful comments on the condition of my body than on the expanding population of the parish.

The silence is deafening. Nothing can be heard but the scratching of pens. It sounds like insects about to chew their way through the walls.

Georg and Sivert are sitting at their desks. They put down their pens. It becomes disagreeably quiet. The insects have heard me come and are holding their breath as they wait for me to go again.

We say good morning. Georg gets up ceremoniously and bends short-sightedly over all the papers in front of him. Sivert watches him groping about with a little smile, as if he knows something

Georg doesn't know, perhaps where the right paper is, and he makes a casual movement towards his left ear but stops himself. Sivert has reddening and flaking skin around his left ear and inside it too, which looks bad. The doctor says it's caused by overwork and has written a prescription for an ointment that smells of fire-ants for Sivert to rub on every day.

'You should open a window,' I say. 'It's stuffy in here.'

Georg stops moving and stands stock-still with his body in its curved position.

'We've tried that. But the papers get blown about.'

He continues to keep still. As if he daren't move unless I give the word.

'Aha. Strange. I thought there wasn't any wind. Oh well…'

I clear my throat meaningfully. Georg slowly begins to move again. It looks as if he's found his piece of paper. He straightens and holds it up to the window. When he pushes his glasses back on his brow I see he has large sweat-stains under his arms.

'The most important thing today…'

Georg's voice dies away in a confused mumble, and he brings the paper still closer to his face and his eyes search up and down it. Sivert quickly turns away and pretends to look out of the window, presumably to hide his malicious smile.

'A certain Lieutenant Daniel Henriksson died yesterday during manoeuvres in Strängnäs. His superiors at the regiment have informed his next of kin, who would like him buried within two weeks.'

Georg looks up.

'Would this Sunday be…?'

I nod. Georg reads on.

'Then Professor Johan Wallgren and his wife would like to talk to you, Pastor. It sounded urgent. I made an appointment for two o'clock.'

I nod and go out. Out through the door, a walk of some ten metres along the gravel path, in through the next door. As recently as two years ago I used to be able to reach the office by a door in the hall, but that door took up almost three metres that were needed for shelf-space. That's where we've put the files that contain the parish accounts.

I can hear Märit's voice from the kitchen, and there's something in her tone that rouses my curiosity. It sounds as if she's trying to make someone laugh.

I look in. The firewood-seller is standing with his arms held out from his body like a bear, nodding eagerly with his mouth half open at everything Märit's telling him. When she sees me she pauses in her story. The firewood-seller greets me hastily and begins unloading wood from his boxes. Märit stands still looking at me, her mouth neutral and eyebrows slightly raised.

I say I'd like a cup of coffee. Märit curtsies without taking her eyes off me. There's nothing strange about that, since I'm still standing there.

I imagine I see something in her eyes. The heat of passion. Not directed at me of course but at the firewood-seller, a large, noisy type, the sort who enjoys female company and moves from one woman to another as if they were wells in a desert, always getting what he wants and deriving his strength from that.

I go upstairs. Drawing room, dining room, bedroom. Helga's not there. I open the window and look out over the garden. Byström's under the big chestnut. He's propped his rake against the trunk and is standing, hands on his hips, looking inquiringly at one side of the churchyard; then he slowly turns and looks equally inquiringly in another direction, like a general waiting for the start of an offensive. He is a master at giving the impression he's working, I have to acknowledge that. I was like that myself once, in the days when I was supposed to help my father with various jobs.

I remember once at haymaking I was worried about lifting the heavy hay up onto the cart and felt as if something in my back was about to break. Apparently I thought there'd be no point in telling Father because he'd never take me seriously. Instead I pretended things kept getting stuck in the rake, so that I had to keep bending over to clear it. Thus by constantly stopping work I was able to reduce the number of times I had to do this painful lifting, doing as little as possible without rousing Father's suspicions.

I remember how I tried to do a bit of convincing acting, uttering irritated little cries every time I bent down to pick up the rake. It also brought a new sense of excitement to the work: would I manage to fool Father or not?

Yes, I not only fooled Father, but I fooled myself too. In the end I put so much imagination and acting ability into my 'broken' rake that I honestly did begin to believe there was something wrong with it. It became a new reality I'd got used to, and I'd have found it most unjust if anyone had suspected me of trying to dodge work.

I feel an impulse to call to Byström to allow himself a bit of a rest; there are lots of seats he could sit on, he can choose any he likes, no one ever uses them.

Instead I shut the window and go through the rooms as I often do, collecting signs and clues like a detective. I want to establish what her frame of mind was when she left the house.

Sometimes, if there are books and newspapers lying open and the light by the window is still burning, I know she's been searching for some system of thought, any will do, against which to lean her own thoughts.

Sometimes a tangled pile of clothes has been flung on the bedroom chair, and this tells me she's been standing in front of the mirror rejecting one dress after another, as if her real reason for searching had been to find a Helga she could like, and that she'd been in too much of a hurry to hang up the clothes she threw aside.

Sometimes the white dress is missing.

It's made of some kind of artificial silk I've forgotten the name of. The cloth falls around her throat and wrists in a way that makes one think of small water lily leaves. It's neither light and fluttering, nor heavy and rigid, but billows silently and follows her movements as if she were moving in water.

The first time we saw this dress was at Halvar Sternelius's house. He was giving a dinner for New Year, and his brother Viktor had brought his family over from America. Viktor had married an emigrant like himself; her name was Sara and she'd come from a small village on Öland. They had three children, and this was the children's first visit to their parents' old homeland. They ran through the rooms and cried out 'so old, so old' in English at everything they saw, that it had clearly become a sort of joke between them.

I won the children's acceptance at once because I bent forwards, pointed to my face and repeated 'so old, so old', which made them laugh till they shrieked. But I could also see that, in the midst of their fun, it had given them something to think about, particularly the eldest boy, whose name I've forgotten. It was as if it had never occurred to him that people too grow rusty, yellow and cracked.

Anyhow, Sara had a pretty white dress, which Helga so obviously admired that a similar one reached us a few months later.

Even when Helga unpacked the dress from the parcel I couldn't remember that I'd ever seen Halvar's sister-in-law wearing it.

I asked Helga whether she didn't think it a bit eccentric to send a dress halfway around the globe, particularly to someone one hardly knew, but she shrugged her shoulders and assumed that secretive set of the mouth that means we're discussing something only a woman can understand.

Then she put on the dress. She stood in front of the mirror and adjusted something around her neck. She pulled the cloth a little around her hips. She gathered her hair together on her neck and fixed it up with some hairpins. I stood behind her and looked in the mirror.

It revealed rather more of her collarbones than usual, but there was nothing sensational about that. All the same it did something to her that made her look almost indecent.

It was something to do with the way the cloth fell across her breast and lay over her stomach and, above all, how it drew attention to her legs all the way from calf to groin. When I saw her legs in that dress it was as if I could smell the most intimate scents of her body; indeed, it was as if they spread themselves through the room as self-confidently and distinctly as newly ground coffee.

I took a step nearer. I stared at her neck, shoulders and throat, then lifted my eyes and looked at her in the mirror. Our eyes met. And we understood each other, without either of us having to utter a word. I grabbed her waist with burning hands and kissed her neck with a greediness I'd never experienced before. When I think back to it, it was as if I was eating her rather than just kissing her. As if it was more a matter of satisfying an aching hunger than of expressing love.

I practically threw her onto the bed and we were together. Helga met me with a shamelessness I'd never seen in her before. It was as if she was opening herself to a force of nature. Something it's pointless to try to resist.

It hurts me to think of it. That a word like 'shamelessness', for example, has such a thoroughly bad sound. But if you remember that Helga and I are husband and wife, two grown-up people who love each other… There should be no shame between us, shame is irrelevant here.

Even so that moment has assumed such a place in our life that I cling firmly to it and cherish it, since whatever else it may be it's still evidence that such a thing does exist.

It's just that it's something so desperately difficult for us to rediscover.

After that it was a long time before she put on the white dress again.

I remember on some occasions asking her to put it on, but if I know myself, I must have done so in an uninvolved tone of voice, with a sort of unimpassioned irony, which would have made it easy for her to get out of it by answering with a sort of light irony herself, and so the subject was dropped.

When occasionally she did wear the dress, I would seek feverishly for a glance or a smile from her, anything, to show that she hadn't forgotten that we had once been exposed to one another in liberating shamelessness.

But in her, that was closed and sealed. When we dressed to go off somewhere, and she stood before me in the white dress, she was always at her most resolute. We were never more anxious to go off quickly than on those occasions, and never so sad or quarrelsome, and she was never more likely to have a pain somewhere, as when we got home again and found ourselves alone.

A few times it so happened that she came home from some errand – some trivial everyday occupation like delivering a letter or buying a pair of gloves – dressed in the white dress, and if I then said anything humorous or ambiguous, or asked if she didn't have a whole queue of admirers after her when she went out into the streets in that dress, she would look at me with an expression of boundless boredom, and say something matter-of-fact and corrective; that the dress might perhaps have been modern five years ago, but now could be seen in every drawing room and wouldn't even cause a newly released convict to raise his eyebrows.

I go to her wardrobe and push the clothes aside systematically from left to right. And though a hasty glance has already told me that the white dress isn't there, I think I may have been wrong, and search through first one cupboard then another, till I'm forced to accept the fact.

Then I stand before all these evening dresses, skirts, petticoats, bathing costumes, stockings and boots, and it feels as though they're sneering scornfully at me. As though their voices are united in humming some tiresome jingle over and over again.

Fury rises in me, I can't hold it back. All these expensive garments... She certainly isn't satisfied with just any old thing, my dear wife... All this trouble and thought and, not least, money that has been invested in her beauty – and for what purpose?

Nothing to my advantage. That's one thing that's certain.

I feel a wild impulse to tear something to pieces. To grab one of these delicate, fragrant pieces of clothing and rip long, jagged gashes in it. But at the last moment I stop myself, and yield instead to complicated deliberations as to which garment to choose, how best to tear it, and where to put it afterwards, and should I wait in the room to see her reaction, or would it have more effect if I stayed away from home and let her make the discovery on her own... and so on, endlessly.

And by the time I've pondered all these possibilities my anger has dissipated, and I'm forced to realise that destroying any of her evening dresses would be nothing but an empty gesture, a sort of overstrung attempt to make an impression.

Why is it seemingly so hard for her to love me?

I think I've done everything. I've been very tolerant of her melancholy. I've tried every imaginable method of dealing with her coldness. I've tried being gentle and listening. I've also tried being as chilly as her so she'll understand what it's like. Well, not exactly chilly... but at times I've tried to push her aside, which perhaps doesn't sound very noble, but bear in mind that my days are full of demanding work responsibilities. If I never stopped thinking about the problems of my marriage I'd never get any work done.

It's all theatre and dissimulation anyway. All my manipulative attempts to get her to love me lack weight and conviction. And if I see this so clearly, is it surprising she does too?

When I was younger I had no difficulty believing in a God who punished people for their sins.

But this was not always an easy belief to maintain. The sceptics' arguments were always the same. They pointed to a person near them; often they used their mother as an example of human goodness, and asked what she had done to deserve an early and painful death.

And if it wasn't a mother who was held up as an example, it would be some little child: a boy or girl taken seriously ill during the first years of their life, or who fell into a stream and drowned.

But I was unshakeable. To me it was obvious that human beings were sinful creatures, and that anyone who denied this was to be deeply pitied, because it implied a degree of self-knowledge that was virtually non-existent.

All those people who held up their mothers as free from sin... They seemed to think 'sin' was everything the judicial system, the law books and the police are already trying to stop us doing. Like stealing, lying and killing. Which is a grotesque misunderstanding.

Of course it's a matter of deliberate misunderstanding. Deep within themselves, everyone knows that if they understood 'sin' correctly, an accusing finger would point to their own breasts, tear open an abyss before their feet and force them to make many difficult reassessments.

No, it's more comfortable to cherish the hardwearing old mis-understanding that says if you've kept yourself clean and proper and refrained from swearing, drinking, stealing and seducing your neighbour, then you've lived a life free from sin.

But in that case what you expect of yourself is no more than what you'd expect of an animal.

I'm sure you can train a dog to live life without 'sin'. You shout angrily at it when it does some things and babble lovingly and dish out bits of meat when it does others. Eventually it'll behave perfectly.

But it's not the capacity to respect certain common rules of behaviour that separates human beings from animals. It's the capacity for love.

Natural science prefers to talk about other things: the unique ability of human beings to press thumb-tip against fingertips, to think on several levels and all that kind of thing.

I'm no scientist. For me it's enough to look at an anthill. I've the greatest respect for the ability of ants to organise their work. To trudge backwards and forwards carrying food and building mate-rials. To build their anthill in a sensible place, pointing in a direc-tion favourable to their survival.

But I very much doubt that any ant can make another ant feel loved, with all that would imply.

But humanity does have this capacity. And it's the greatest thing on earth. Something given to us by God. And it is exclusive-ly in our capacity as loving creatures that He has allowed us to rule the world.

What, then, is sin?

My definition of sin is when you deprive yourself of the oppor-tunity of being a loving person.

This doesn't mean I have no understanding of how difficult this is. The road is long and painful. It demands high courage. The courage to see and understand oneself as one really is, and through this to see and understand others.

Naturally this is not granted to all. I'm the first to admit that I still have a long way to go myself. But you have to start somewhere. You have to make an effort. And you have to understand that the goal is precisely this: to become a loving human being.

But it is also possible to be satisfied with being an ant. You do your work. You find someone to live with, another human being to keep your bed warm, put food on your table and bear children to look after you in your old age. And if it's not the woman with red hair called Birgitta, then the one with black hair called Magda will do just as well.

You do your duty but you're living your life in a state of indifference towards yourself and the people around you. So you might just as well be an ant.

That is living in sin. That is turning away from God. Shrugging one's shoulders at all the opportunities He has given us.

And when I think of all these people who have held their mothers up as evidence that beings exist who are able to float suspended in what is in fact unattainable freedom from sin...

It occurs to me that not one of us can think of his mother without being stricken by guilty conscience, and sometimes I wonder why this is.

I don't know how many times I've sat and listened to people describing mothers who've sacrificed themselves, never thinking of themselves and always being available... and sometimes the thought has struck me: is this an accident? Why do I suspect that the real reason for all these sentimental paeans to motherhood is to draw attention away from something furious, dark and frightening?

I too could preach a sermon on the thoroughly good mother. Someone who toils and drudges from morning to evening, fetches water and prepares food. Washes clothes and sweeps the floor. Someone who cleans your wounds when you've hurt yourself. A warm hand to wipe tears from your cheeks, a soft knee to sit on and a soothing word in your ear.

That's a good mother.

I had one of that kind myself. She's eighty-three now. She lives in a well-kept nursing home in Ersta. Nurses and deaconesses look after her.

It's nearly five weeks now since I last saw her. That was on her name-day. Helga stayed at home and I didn't criticise her for that. Not much sticks in my mother's mind any more, and sometimes I'm not sure she even knows who Helga is. On the other hand she often mentions Lydia's name, and asks anxiously after her health. When I answer that Lydia's been dead for more than seven years she gets depressed, shakes her head and says what a pity, she was such a good wife to me.

She never said that when Lydia was alive.

I took a cake with me. We sat in the day room and ate it. Mother took as long as possible to sit down. She stood behind the arm-chair anxiously fingering its back, and kept making little gestures towards helping the nurses with the cups and plates. They kept telling her it wasn't necessary and that she could sit down and relax.

But she seemed not to hear. Nothing torments my mother more than not to be able to be of use. She watched the nurses' work with an expression that radiated gratitude and enthusiasm, and a broad smile that showed all her teeth.

In the end she sat down. One of the nurses was allowed to help her. My mother moves with short tottering steps, groping in front of her with her hands as if she might lose her balance at any moment. Some years ago she had something wrong with her hip and the problem hasn't left her.

The nurses withdrew and closed the doors, and we ate the cake. Cream, custard and marzipan.

'What a good cake,' said Mother after a pause that had gone on too long.

I agreed. I told her where I'd bought it. Mother nodded, and silence fell again.

I looked at her out of the corner of my eye while she ate. The trembling spoon on its way to her mouth. There was something about her mouth as she swallowed the mouthfuls of cake, I don't know what, but I couldn't take my eyes off it. Perhaps it was just that she looked serious for once. And the disagreeable thought came to me that this was all that was left for her now, shovelling in food.

And that she knew this.

Vagueness, they call it at the nursing home. They also say it has a tendency to run in families.

I've come across this illness many times. It's common among old people. Halvar Sternelius's father was gaga too. But I remember it as something quite different in his case. Halvar often used to describe how his father misunderstood things and mixed them up, but they were merry tales, with nothing condescending or ashamed in them, only a great warmth, and Halvar wasn't embarrassed to have his father with him at dinners and receptions. Every time his father said anything a bit mixed up, or plain wrong, Halvar would raise his eyes and make a joke of it so everybody relaxed and laughed.

His father's reality was different from ours, but he seemed to feel safe inside it. He stood firm with both his feet in it.

What makes my mother's dottiness so much more difficult is that she finds no foothold either in her own reality or in our healthy reality. Instead she floats suspended somewhere in the middle, and seems painfully conscious of her shortcomings.

During the first years I tried to talk to her as usual, asking her questions about how she was feeling, and what she'd been up to. Her eyes would roam backwards and forwards while she opened her mouth and fumbled for the words she wanted, but for the most part all she could get out of herself was:

'Yes…! I'm fine.'

Her tone was happy and brisk. But I could also see how she sometimes tightened her lips and how they moved silently, so that it looked as if she was whispering curses to herself.

There was an occasion, very near the beginning, only a few weeks after her illness had been diagnosed, when I asked her how she was feeling. And she answered 'Fine', her tone was friendly and she looked as gentle and kindly as ever. Yet somehow I had the impression she'd really said:

'That's nothing to do with you.'

I stopped asking questions. Instead I told her things without expecting any response. Then I stopped that too.

Now I say nothing more than what's absolutely necessary.

I still imagine it does her good to see me.

She hasn't yet reached a state in which she doesn't recognise me. That's what happened with Halvar's father. He often mixed Halvar with one of his brothers, and sometimes didn't even realise they were his own children. Which didn't make Halvar any less cheerful.

Mother ate two pieces of her name-day cake. An organ could be heard playing 'The Blessed Day', and individual shrill voices singing from a neighbouring room. I stared at her mouth. Occasionally our eyes met and she burst out laughing as if we were sharing a secret.

I've always believed Mother and I were very close. She has often said that even as a boy I was unusually mature and sensible, that she could speak to me as to an adult. I can remember often turning to her with my worries even when I was grown up, and she would listen and give me good advice.

Nevertheless I could sit before my empty cake plate, while Mother opened her mouth in that mechanical manner for the last spoonfuls, and I no longer asked her how she was or what she was thinking about, nor told her anything about what I myself felt or was thinking about… and I couldn't get rid of the thought that there was something icily familiar about the whole thing.

That it had always been like this.

Oh yes, I can certainly tell the tale of a good mother.

A good mother sits in front of a plate with two jam tarts on it. A good mother sees your greedy eyes on the cakes, and despite the fact that she hasn't had a single one, while you have had more than your fair share, she pushes the plate towards you and says: You eat.

So you cram your mouth full, and while you greedily suck every last sweet, sticky crumb from your teeth, you look in wonder at her hunched back while she carries away the plate, and you ask yourself how such goodness can be possible.

And while you're spoon-fed from earliest childhood with this unbounded goodness, you can't help seeing what a poor figure you cut yourself. What a selfish, egotistic and narrow person you are.

Again and again you look at your mother and wonder who she really is behind all that goodness. But you get no answer.

If she would step forward as a human being, with everything that that involves… as somebody with her own dreams, her own wounds in need of being cared for and her own desires, even if they involve nothing more than jam tarts… then we would be able to love her, instead of merely worshipping her.

But this is the price we pay for growing up enclosed by boundless goodness: we never break free of our mother. We keep her portrait on the mantelpiece and dust it and polish it and no bad word about her is ever allowed.

The years pass. Then she dies. And worship takes over from love, which is a pity and a sin in every meaning of the word.

At the same time, when I hold little Ernst in my arms, and watch him growing… I feel the same boundless goodness well up in me. And a powerful longing to be able to forget myself for a little while. Or, best of all, for ever.

Yes, we certainly are sinful beings. I haven't changed my mind on that point.

But just as I've never believed in a concept of sin that coincides with the legal concept of crime, so I don't believe that God hands down 'punishments' like an ordinary High Court judge: if you've stolen a horse, I'll make your daughter blind; but if you've only stolen an apple, I'll be satisfied with making your son lame…

On the other hand I do believe God tries to make us aware of our sinfulness. That he gives signs for us to interpret. But I no longer think of Him as an angry avenger who sends out flashes of lightning. Rather I imagine a troubled father who again and again taps us on the shoulder and urges us to stand up and reflect and take the road that will make us into loving people.

Most people need to be humbled. I'm quite sure of that. Some struggle against it as long as possible. They cling firmly to their self-sufficiency, they don't need other people and they create their own gods out of themselves.

These people have hardened themselves to such an extent that they have to be cracked, broken into small pieces, crumbled into fragments. Every escape route must be closed to them till in the end they have no choice but to reach out a hand and say: help me. I've lost everything. Please be kind and help me.

This is the first step on the road to becoming a loving person.

To need help, to ask for help, and to be capable of accepting it.

As for me, I've gone astray somewhere along the way. If I've ever even started on it. I don't know any longer. But it's in the light of this that I see my trials. God tapping me on the shoulder, time and again, and trying to get me to understand something.

All my adult life I've longed to have a child. First with Lydia, then with Helga. We submitted to one medical examination after another. We were found to be entirely healthy. No one has ever been able to explain our childlessness.

God knocks and knocks.

Sometimes I think there must be something in me that He doesn't want to pass on. Some undesirable inheritance I would give to an innocent little boy or girl that he must want to prevent.

Sometimes I try to widen my view and see childlessness as an expression of something bigger, perhaps a certain lack of love.

Lydia. Did I love her? I don't think I did.

I was an ant. She was kind to me. Utterly loyal. Denied me nothing. In my mother's words: she was good for me. But was I good for her? I never thought about that.

When I saw a cloth she'd embroidered, or a letter she'd written in her clumsy handwriting, I'd be overcome by sentimentality, like when you see a misspelt swearword on a wooden wall, or a crudely carved bark-boat in a clump of reeds. But I never came nearer to her than that. My heart was as firmly closed to her as it was to everyone else.

And Helga...

God knocks and knocks.

Perhaps I'm like a child you daren't entrust with a box of matches. Perhaps God is unwilling to let me possess the power of love because He knows I would misuse it.

I'm sure He acts from the basis of His unbounded goodness and wisdom.

All I can hope for is that one day I'll prove myself worthy. But I'm in a hurry. There's a mink inside my breast that won't let me forget. I should thank God for that.

I don't tear up any clothes after all. I sit on the bed for a while and pull myself together. An angry light is falling diagonally across the bed. Flies have gathered in the warm sunbeam. They clean their legs and wings, walk a few steps, take off, land, copulate, take a short flight and land again.

In three hours I'm due to meet Johan Wallgren and his wife. I get up and go to the mirror. Polish my glasses and pull a comb through my hair. Then I go down to the office.

Georg and Sivert have left their desks and are sitting on the low chairs, each with his packet of sandwiches on his knee. Georg pauses when I come in, and after an initial moment of paralysis he moves his jaws a couple of times and swallows a mouthful so large that the effort brings tears to his eyes.

'Just one thing,' I say. 'Have we heard anything from the Höglund family?' Georg lowers his gaze, his eyes flickering from side to side. He tries to get to his feet. I see the little malicious smile on Sivert's face.

'Hög… Höglund?'

'The family we went to see last night. The sick boy. They were going to let us know if there was any change in his condition.'

Georg shakes his head.

'I'm going to see them,' I say. 'I'll be back by two.'

I turn and go out. I quickly slow down when I realise I'm not sure which way we went, even though it was only a few hours ago. The streets have had time to change: so many shops have had time to open their windows, so many maids and domestic servants are streaming in and out with their baskets. They catch sight of someone they know and stop to chat for a minute, making exhausted gestures towards the angry light and wiping the sweat from their brows with exaggeratedly demonstrative gestures.

At regular intervals a tram cuts like a knife through the throng of people hurrying to cross the street. Everyone stops and waits at a respectful distance while the passengers get off; some, blasé and perhaps puffing nonchalantly at a pipe, leave casually before the tram has completely stopped while others emerge with difficulty backwards as if struggling to descend a not altogether trustworthy ladder while hampered by a collection of baskets and bags.

I feel infinitely old when I remember how quickly the time has passed; but it seems only yesterday that the trams first appeared, first as a newspaper item at which one shook one's head distrustfully, calling into question the practical usefulness of the whole venture and imagining the whole thing to be so far off in the future that one could barely visualise it, and wondering how it would actually work but feeling too embarrassed to ask questions… and now here it is, this tram, part of our everyday life, and now, ironically, it's hard to remember how things were before it existed.

Carts and wagons clatter and screech on the paving-stones; when I cross Stora Badstu I see as many as four family carriages obviously on their way to summer homes. The fathers are sitting on the coachman's box with inscrutable and resolute expressions, while the mothers at the back with the children are frowning, hands moving constantly over their baskets and bags, as if all the shirts and boots and bottles they contain might jump out and run away at the first possible opportunity. Only the children seem expectant and cheerful; they point at every exciting thing they pass, though there are always some who fail to grasp what the others are pointing at, quarrelling about what was actually seen. An older sibling says something spiteful to a younger one, causing the younger to start crying or attack the older, provoking their father to turn abruptly and hiss something at them, or their mother to box their ears. Then the disturbance stops, and both children sit sullen and surly for several minutes with tears in their eyes, both considering themselves unjustly treated. But soon something new catches their attention, and they start pointing and shouting again and so on, all the way out to Danderyd or Edsviken or wherever they're heading for.

Finally there I am standing outside the shabby entrance in Norra Tullport. Two street-boys pass me, so close that we bump into one another, lightly it's true, but without question. The manoeuvre is so impudent and calculatedly aggressive that I'm struck dumb and stand staring helplessly after them. Which is clearly exactly what they wanted, since one of them turns half around and looks satisfied to see how annoyed I am.

I walk through the gateway and stand in the yard. It looks smaller in daylight. There's the large pot, with a grating over it. The fire has gone out. Beyond a fence stretches a patchwork of other yards, some light and well looked after, others neglected and overgrown with weeds, while one of the yards, buzzing with flies, contains a rotting mountain of refuse presumably thrown over the fence by neighbours.

In one corner there's a little building I didn't notice the night before. It looks like a storehouse, and outside it there's a miscellaneous collection of rusty scrap iron. The maple tree in the middle of the yard provides blessed shade. Its branches almost reach the windows; you can imagine how they've been cut back time and again and nonetheless are still struggling on. A family on the second floor is using the tree as a place for hanging flannels and handkerchiefs out to dry. Under the tree some boxes serve as seats and also for storage; I notice several empty bottles in them, and smile as I imagine the men quickly disposing of them when their wives call out that dinner's ready.

I look up; the Höglunds' door is wide open.

I begin to regret the whole venture. No one asked me to come, and no one's expecting me.

Suddenly I realise how disappointed I was that Georg didn't try to stop me calling on the Höglunds again; indeed, I probably hoped he'd suggest the errand wouldn't be a good use of my time.

I'd been looking forward to the chance to give him a lecture. The whole thing was ready prepared in my head; all I'd had to do was deliver it.

But of course the real intention of this lecture hadn't been to develop in Georg deeper insights into the nature of human kindness, but rather to impress on a nearby but invisible ear what a fine person I am, winning me points towards yet another little gold star.

I am overcome by despair so powerful that my eyes fill with tears.

This is followed by anger and defiance; I want to shout straight into this deafening tempest of self-contempt that, yes, I may well be a hypocrite of the highest class and a master of self-deceit.

But even so I am standing here now.

When I have pulled myself together and climbed the stairs I hear a child's voice singing from the darkness. I stop and listen. The song is 'The Priest's Little Crow'. Someone's singing it over and over again at breakneck speed, breathless and snuffling.

I continue up the steps and stop in the doorway. A few shards of sunlight have found their way into the room through the leaves of the maple. They reach nearly as far as the sofa, where Olof is still lying.

His little sister is the one singing 'The Priest's Little Crow'. She's curled up on the pallet with her legs under her, her little hand hopping over the bedcover and slipping this way and that and down into the ditch as she goes through the action of the song. Then she goes through it all again.

I take a step into the room and gently clear my throat. A sound from the left takes me by surprise. The old woman from the previous night is standing by the fireplace. She's drying something with a dirty rag, and a clinking sound from under it suggests she may be cleaning some tools. Meanwhile she stares at me with a lack of expression that seems almost threatening.

I turn to the girl. She's stopped singing, but her hand does a few more hops backwards and forwards over the bedcover from sheer impetus.

'I've come to see how Olof is,' I say.

My voice sounds unnaturally loud in the little room, and my tone is awkward and defensive, as if I've been caught in an embarrassing situation and am trying to talk my way out of it.

The old woman turns her back on me, which reinforces my feeling that I must have done something wrong and that she's finally lost patience with me.

The little girl jumps down from the pallet and goes over to the old woman, and as she passes me she looks up and says something I don't understand. Her intonation seems Swedish, but the words aren't familiar. I fumble for various languages I've heard, wonder if it can be Norwegian, perhaps some impenetrable dialect from Sörland? Whatever the case, it's a shame not to be able to answer the little girl, since she seemed so friendly.

All I can do is nod and smile. I must look like a big fat idiot, and now the girl is standing beside the old woman and holding on to her dirty apron. She looks at me and produces another harangue in her strange language. But her words seem to be directed at the old woman, who is keeping her back obstinately turned towards me and rattling on with her work on the bench.

I go over to the pallet and sit down on the stool.

I see no movement from the boy.

Someone's changed his shirt and dressed him in something light-blue and freshly ironed. The collar looks big. Perhaps it's his father's shirt.

My eyes don't want to study him too closely. I don't want to discover that he's dead and has been left alone with the strange old woman, while his little sister sings 'The Priest's Little Crow' over his lifeless body.

I see a movement from the corner of my eye. The girl's standing at the foot of the bed with her hands behind her back. I manage a smile.

She nods to me with bright eyes, as if we share a secret, then bends over the pallet and hits the boy's feet with her hands, at the same time shouting in her strange language what sounds like: Motchik! Motchik!

I try to catch the girl's hands, and at the same time feel an impulse to get up and rush out through the door, since this is so clearly a situation that's beyond me and for which nothing I've learned before is of any use.

Then I see that Olof has opened his eyes. He blinks drowsily and lifts his head a little, and when he recognises his little sister he lets his head sink on to the pillow again. I raise my hand firmly towards the girl. She nods, crawls down to the foot of the bed and draws up her feet under her.

'Olof?' I say.

He turns his head and looks at me. It's all I can do not to laugh wildly. It's so clear that this is no dying boy. That he's turned the corner and come back. When he gives a little yawn I can control myself no longer, I've always thought it's so sweet when little children yawn, and I burst out laughing.

Olof gives me a quick look. Then he fastens his eyes on the ceiling. Perhaps he's already dismissed me as one of many strange emissaries from an equally strange grown-up world, someone there's no point in trying to understand. Perhaps he's just too tired to take any interest in me.

'Good morning to you, Olof. My name's Gregorius, and I'm the priest of this parish.'

'Good morning.'

'I came to see how you are. I was here yesterday evening, but you were asleep.'

Olof nods. His eyes are fully awake. He even looks a little afraid. He starts to dig into one of his nostrils with his thumb, and picks out several bogeys, which he puts in his mouth.

'You seem much better now. I'm glad to see it.'

He nods again.

'How d'you feel?'

'Tired.'

'That's understandable. You need rest. Get your strength back. That's important. You know that, don't you?'

Olof looks up at the ceiling and continues digging in each nostril in turn with his mouth wide open.

Soon I feel how my smile is beginning to pull at my face, causing little spasms at the corners of my mouth, a particularly disagreeable feeling.

The silence in the room seems almost unreal.

I look around me, as if searching for someone to share my happiness with, but the old woman is still bent over some activity at the other end of the room; she seems to be sorting something out. All I can see is her curved back and small arm movements, like those of a great insect. The girl is kneeling on the pallet, rocking backwards and forwards absent-mindedly and looking down, lost in her own world. Her lips are moving slowly, and suddenly it strikes me that there's something of a contradiction in the fact that a moment ago she was singing 'The Priest's Little Crow' in impeccable Swedish, only to start speaking immediately afterwards in incomprehensible gibberish, and I'm seized by a vague suspicion that she was poking fun at me.

Voices can be heard from down in the yard. An excited male voice is speaking with another, interposing 'Yes of course, of course', and a woman is laughing loudly.

The voices come nearer and the stairs begin to creak.

I get up from the stool and turn to the door. The light's blinding. Several silhouettes crowd the doorway. Herr and Fru Höglund, and with them a short suntanned man in shirt and waistcoat with a well-cared-for grey beard.

'Pastor!' exclaims Herr Höglund.

'Has he... Has the pastor...?'

Words fail Fru Höglund. In any case it sounds as if she has something in her mouth. I would guess it's some sort of sweet, which clicks against her teeth as she hurries over to the pallet and points at her son with over-explicit gestures.

Her arms flail like the sails of a windmill. She rolls her eyes. I nod and smile cautiously, at which she closes her eyes and shakes her head, and the malicious thought comes to me that someone seems to have set her to mime such concepts as 'happiness' and perhaps also 'gratitude' for the benefit of a slow-witted listener.

She bends over her son and kisses his cheeks again and again while he feebly tries to defend himself, and even lets out a nasty hollow cough so loud it's hard to believe such a big cough can come from such small lungs.

Fru Höglund ignores Olof's cough. She takes my left hand,

kisses it and talks of God's miracle. Meanwhile Herr Höglund takes my other hand and shakes it clumsily, again and again, mumbling in agreement. I notice he's breathing fast, as though he has been running.

'He seems a good deal better,' I say, but my voice sounds weak and absurd and is drowned by Fru Höglund's overheated cries and her husband's monotonous expressions of thanks.

My eyes wander to the newcomer who carefully puts a small cloth bag down on the floor.

I stand indecisively between the two Höglunds, my arms jerking with their kisses and handshakes; I imagine I must look like a puppet on a string and I feel like one too. My face goes red all over, and I can only hope it's so dim in the room that this can't be seen.

The newcomer's watching me with a little smile, and I think I see a challenging glint in his eye.

Fru Höglund suddenly lets go of my arm and begins to wag her finger at me instead.

'I prayed, Pastor, you understand, I did pray…!'

But her power of speech deserts her again. She disappears into a corner of the room and comes back with a prayer book. She leafs backwards and forwards through it impatiently and mumbles to herself.

'A miracle from God.'

This is the first time the stranger has spoken. He nods emphatically. Then he takes a step forward and holds out his hand, introducing himself as Johan Laurén.

'No one can persuade me that it's a coincidence,' he goes on. 'What with your visit last night, Pastor, and the boy's recovery… which clearly came like a bolt from the blue… You'd barely managed to get to the corner, Pastor, before…'

Johan Laurén produces a few more abrupt sentences in the same tone of wonder while bending down to take a couple of bottles of schnapps from his bag. He puts the bottles on the table and holds out his hand to the old woman, who's wiping her fingers on a rag with a clairvoyant expression on her face. It's only when he waves irritably that she realises he's waiting for glasses. She smiles and nods, but instead of fetching several together she gets the glasses out of the cupboard one at a time and carries each to the table separately, setting it down before going back to the cupboard again for the next, and so on.

'A drink for you, Pastor,' says Johan Laurén.

I shake my head.

He nods, as if realising it might indeed not be such a good idea, and makes a movement towards Herr and Fru Höglund as if to apologise. Then he lays two fingers across his mouth, thinks for a minute, and begins to speak again.

'We're all simple people. We haven't much to offer. But do allow us, Pastor. Allow us this modest little…'

Johan Laurén is articulate and expresses himself in correct Swedish. There's even something aristocratic about him. He clearly has both healthy teeth and well-ordered thoughts.

But he seems to have an unhealthy influence over the Höglunds, who look at him with reverence and expectation, as if they can't make themselves understood without him.

It would be easy to make certain assumptions about the relationship between Herr Höglund and Johan Laurén. They could simply be drinking mates. Herr Höglund is clearly drunk, his face is as red as a lobster and he has a glassy smile. He's learned never to make an unnecessary movement or say anything unessential, for fear it'll betray his condition.

But with his wife it's something else. She seems to look on Laurén as a beloved son just home from a long and adventurous stay on the other side of the globe.

In the midst of the excitement my eye falls on little Olof. He has his hand under the bedcover and is scratching himself under the armpit with careful, preoccupied movements. One might have expected him to be cheered by the return of his mother and father, and with a family friend as well. By his home being full of people excited by his own miraculous recovery.

But the boy seems remarkably indifferent to all the fuss. As if he can neither see nor hear.

'Pastor? A little, symbolic…'

Laurén holds up an empty glass and swings it slowly backwards and forwards.

'No thank you. I have certain demanding…'

Laurén's smile hardens a touch at the corners, but he nods and turns around. He fills three glasses, giving one each to Herr and Fru Höglund. All three face me with their glasses raised and I have the oddest thought: they seem to be taking aim at me.

'I think…' I begin, then sit down on the edge of the pallet and lay my left hand on Olof's head.

'Don't you think Olof has deserved…?'

Sudden silence. Fru Höglund puts a hand uneasily to her throat and looks sideways at Laurén, whose smile has hardened even more, indeed all cordiality has vanished from his face and he's looking at me with an indifference that threatens to tip over into loathing.

Herr Höglund is standing with his mouth half open, gaping like a fish for his needlessly delayed schnapps.

'Isn't there anything he could… Something to celebrate a bit?' I say tentatively.

I take a few coins from my purse and offer them to Olof's little sister.

'Here!' I say. 'Be a good girl and run and buy your big brother…'

I stop short. Well, what can one buy? Peppermint rock? Or is that seasonal, something you can only find at Christmas?

'Something tasty! A bag of sweets… Perhaps a little lemonade? They say it's good to drink as much as you can when you…'

I gesture towards the trio still standing with their schnapps glasses raised and venture a little laugh, but no one seems inclined to join in.

The girl jumps down from the sofa, stands in front of her mother and holds out the coins to her. The mother makes a violent movement of the head and grimaces with irritation; she looks like a hissing snake, and the girl hurries out through the door.

It isn't until I see the mother's irritation that I realise my mistake. All I achieved when I took out my purse was to make the mother look greedy and selfish, quite simply a bad mother, while presenting myself as thoughtful and generous. And the bad mood this arouses in her will perhaps in the best-case scenario extend over herself and her husband, and through them to the children, but more probably it will go straight to the children.

Laurén clears his throat and turns first right then left in a servile manner. All three empty their glasses. They swallow and stand still a moment.

Then comes a great silence. As if the whole room takes a deep breath.

Herr Höglund pulls up a chair, sits down and begins drawing invisible doodles on the table. His wife puts her glass down and goes over to her son. She bends over him, straightens his blankets, strokes his brow and whispers a few words I can't follow even though I'm sitting less than an arm's length away.

Johan Laurén has also sat down. He lifts his right foot onto his left knee and begins to unlace his shoes.

'Funny,' he says. 'We planned to meet here to prepare a surprise for the Pastor. And then…'

He shakes his head.

'It's almost as if the Pastor could read our thoughts.'

'My powers don't stretch that far,' I answer.

I feel extremely tired. I suppose the night's broken sleep is beginning to claim its due.

I look at Olof. It's wonderful. Even though he does no more than lie there blinking his eyes, it's quite clear he's out of danger, at least for the time being.

But while silence falls over the room I gain a melancholy insight into my own limitations.

Everything that has seemed mysterious or threatening or incomprehensible to me in this home, is domestic and everyday for Olof. He doesn't know anything else. He thinks this is how life should be. He would be just as bewildered and uncertain as I am here if he came to my home. He'd long to get back to his own. 'Home' is exactly what I see before me now.

He's helplessly stuck in his home. Like a little twig on a great tree.

However much I would like to break off the twig and plant it somewhere else, in better conditions, that would be idiotic. Naturally it would die. I can't help the twig unless I help the whole tree. And how do you help a tree? Especially one that's grown so high and is planted so firmly in the ground, with roots that stretch in every imaginable direction.

'Your wife can count herself lucky, Pastor, to be in such good hands.'

Johan Laurén leans back in his chair and contentedly stretches the upper part of his body, like a seal on a rock.

He chews on a splinter of wood, then pulls it out of his mouth and spits out several fragments with delicate little movements of his tongue before continuing:

'I saw her not long ago; she was coming out of a nearby doctor's surgery. It was strange, because I'd just heard the news of Olof's miracle and I was, indeed, you must forgive me, Pastor, but I was nearly shouting for joy and I was so happy I nearly rushed forward to Fru Gregorius to thank her, and it was only at the last moment that I calmed down and realised that your wife and I don't know each other, and that it would have appeared extremely forward of me. Isn't that funny?'

I manage to force a smile. I'm so tired. And the day's barely started yet.

I let my head drop. It's time to go home. But first I must empty my head of all the irrelevant stuff that has collected inside it.

I know perfectly well that something important happened here during the night. I know God's tapped me on the shoulder. And tapped Olof's shoulder, and his parents', and his little sister's and even Johan Laurén's. But if I'm to help them understand this I must first understand it myself.

So I stoop and look at Olof. His pale face and his chapped lips, his bristly hair and his smooth brow. And I'm slowly filled with great warmth when I think of what has happened during the night.

First I think back to everything that happened on my first visit, when I tried to get an impression of what his life must have been like, how he had played with his friends and shovelled snow. When I tried to reach an understanding of everything that was in the balance at that moment.

Now Olof's come back, and I look at his face and try to visualise it at twelve, nineteen, thirty-four.

I let my mind fill with bright images: he's learning a trade – for some reason I imagine him becoming a typographer – and standing listening attentively to some old master teaching him a handgrip, who then gets Olof to try it himself. Olof's face is tense with concentration, and the old master typographer is unable to hold back a smile, but when Olof's finished he pulls himself together and contents himself with an austere nod... And there's Olof with a thick moustache resting on his oars in a skiff, which is gliding slowly towards Djurgårdsbrunn; it's late August and he's wearing a white suit with dark stripes, and the trees are beginning to look a little brittle and exhausted, and a plump young woman with lively eyes and honey hair is sitting in the stern with a little girl in her Sunday best on her knee. And the little girl, who has a string of saliva running down her chin, is thrilled to see the water slipping by. Olof's wife is chattering happily about something of importance to Olof and herself, perhaps something to do with obstinate neighbours or relatives, and Olof's listening with bright eyes and it's quite clear that at this particular moment he has everything he could want.

And Olof reaches forty, then seventy, and if anyone asks him if he was ever close to death, he answers that apparently he was once in a very bad way when he was six or seven, but that he can't remember much about it. His mother, on the other hand, does remember; she says he was so ill that the old parish priest came to read over him…

'Goodbye then Olof,' I say, laying a hand on his shoulder.

He looks up at me, terrified. His shoulder is so thin under the shirt. It'll be stronger soon.

Coming out into the street and closing the gate to Höglund's yard behind me is like being born again.

The air feels fresh and clear, and people look so dependable and good-humoured that I want to smile at everyone I pass. Even the midday heat tickles my body pleasantly, like when you've been feeling cold for a long time without being fully aware of it.

I hurry home with such eager steps that my heart soon reminds me of its existence. I stop, go into a shop and ask for a glass of water. I find a good place by the window, between two large pots and drink my water in small mouthfuls, watching the people pass by.

The manager comes forward and asks if I'd like some more, and indeed I would, and he brings it and for a while we make small talk about the heat, and everything goes swimmingly. Then some new task demands his attention and he goes off, and I am able to think over the morning's events in peace and quiet. It's as if I've been given a valuable present, and this is the first moment I've been free to go off and open the parcel.

This time God hasn't knocked in vain.

His love's streaming over me like a blessed shower of rain, great heavy drops that soak right through my clothing and run into every fold of my skin, while I stand helpless out in the open with no chance of shelter anywhere. I'm exposed to God's mighty power and it is a liberation since I know – not only in my mind, but with my *whole body* – that He wishes me well.

And if I make a little narrative from what I've experienced – as I have a certain unhappy tendency to do – even so, it won't be the usual thing. I won't end up outside myself, an indifferent spectator. Instead I shall be taking part in a story about my own life; simple, pared down and uncompromising, just like when I read the Bible stories as a child: I feel myself taken care of, and made use of.

But then again this is not a story I've created myself. It's a narrative I've received from God. He's given me a narrative so clear, and so uncompromising towards the most sensitive and painful aspects of myself, that the smallest child could interpret it.

It's the story of the childless old priest and his young wife. Of a life in which emptiness has nibbled away at them in small mouthfuls – every fruitless embrace, every time a doctor has taken off his glasses and shaken his head in defeat, one more little bite – and the old priest and his young wife have become ever more torn and transparent, ripped full of long, gaping holes, till it doesn't seem to matter how intensely they gaze at one another;

their eyes are still lost in the distance, they still end up somewhere else: on the spine of a book, a clock on the wall, or a stranger's white teeth.

Then a little boy crosses the priest's path. The boy is severely ill, beyond all saving. The doctors have shaken their heads and turned away. One night the priest pays the little boy a visit and then goes home, leaving the boy lying alone like a sacrificial lamb. Only God sees him.

And God gives him back his life. The doctors leaf feverishly through their books, but no one can explain how it happened. It shouldn't be possible for such a thing to happen. But all the same, it did happen.

That's what it looks like, the story God has given me.

Can it be a coincidence that it runs like this? And, above all, that God gave it to me at this particular moment?

Hardly.

When I was little I'd sometimes be out with Father, and we'd see something along the way. I remember one day in late summer we were walking along a ditch; on our right rye was growing so high it almost came up to my chest, and on our left pasture stretched away for miles.

We heard a distant snorting, and we saw a long way off a tired stallion hanging his head and a young mare trotting about and grazing, and suddenly the stallion made a rush and tried to mount the mare, but she sprang away with an elegant movement, and when the stallion tried again she kicked him off with her rear hoofs.

Then the tired stallion was even more tired, and snorted even more desperately than before as he began trying yet again to find new strength.

I looked up at Father, and he looked at me, and we smiled quickly to each other and walked on. Nothing was said. It wasn't necessary. We'd seen the same thing, and drawn the same conclusions from what we'd seen. We'd both thought it a comic and rather pitiful sight. And it had been good to have someone to share it with.

*H*elga's lying on the bed with the back of her hand against her brow. I can see she's been crying.

I hurry over to her. She smiles at me. She's wearing the white dress. She grimaces slightly when I sit down on the bed beside her. I bend forward and kiss her cheek.

'I just asked for something to drink,' she says.

'Have you been to the doctor? What did he say?'

She shakes her head. Her eyes fill with tears. She takes my hand between both her own and squeezes it cautiously, up and down.

'He wanted to speak to you. He'll be here any minute.'

'With me? What about?'

'About my... I mean, my condition, how should I put it...'

'But...'

'Please forgive me, darling, but... I can't speak about it.'

'Is it something serious?'

'No, I don't think so.'

Helga lowers her voice.

'Let's talk about it later. Agnes is here. I met her outside, and she asked if she could come in with me, and I didn't know what to say, I felt so confused...'

Steps and voices can be heard from the stairs. Someone is talking in a hushed voice, someone else is answering 'Yes, yes'.

Märit comes into the room with a tray; there are two glasses on it, and a carafe containing something that could be elderberry cordial, with a few slices of lemon floating in it.

Agnes hesitates a moment on the threshold before coming forward to greet me.

We exchange a few words about the heat. Her voice is carefree and cheerful, but there's something strained about her, and it strikes me that this is exactly how I must look when I talk to people who sicken me: I can speak lightly and easily, but not even the most strenuous effort can ever make me look warmer than *neutral* at such times.

'I hope I'm not intruding, Pastor, but you need to know... how she looked!'

I mumble a few words to thank her for having come to Helga's rescue, and I also hear myself return to the subject of the heat, and how it's hard on us all.

An idiotic remark. Agnes nods in agreement, but she does not make a secret of the fact that she is well aware that Helga is suffering from more than the heat.

I don't like her and I never have, and our feelings are entirely mutual. Agnes is the sort of friend of which all women seem to have at least one specimen.

She's been around as long as I can remember, and since she's the elder by several years, she imagines she always knows what's best for Helga. She enjoys all the advantages of a big sister — power and influence — without any of the duties and responsibilities a blood relationship would impose, such as sending Christmas cards, helping rescue derelict family estates and looking after ailing parents.

Of course Helga should never have married me, Agnes has never had the slightest doubt about that. I've never heard her say it straight out, but I'm sure she sees me as a ruthless profiteer who stuck his claws into her poor friend before she was fully accountable for her actions, and got her to sign a bond to which she has been enslaved ever since.

And since Helga committed the sheer madness of becoming my wife, Agnes has been permanently ready to sally forth to comfort her and commiserate with her. I'm sure it's no surprise to Agnes that Helga is sometimes melancholy and depressed; more likely it's a wonder to her that Helga doesn't feel like this more often.

When we're discussing the most everyday matters Agnes can give me reproachful glances and make comments that imply I've no idea how lucky I've been, and that I don't appreciate all the sacrifices and efforts Helga makes for my sake.

Of course there are others who would've been more appreciative, Agnes hints, time and time again.

Her whole being lights up and she twitters with enthusiasm when she talks of various elegant young men known to our circle and how charming, kind and well-behaved they are, and yet at the same time somehow exciting – not to mention the brilliant future that lies before them in the civil service, law courts and government departments.

When these elegant young men are mentioned Agnes is careful to keep me out of the conversation. Every sentence she pronounces raises spines like those of a hedgehog – warm and comfortable for those inside, and spiky and impenetrable for those outside, and she likes to add comic little allusions that make herself and Helga choke with laughter, while I sit there with an idiotic smile and raised eyebrows, waiting in vain for an explanation.

Agnes loves making sure it's absolutely clear to me that no one knows Helga as well as she does, and that there are nooks and crannies in Helga's personality to which I will never have access, but where she herself can move freely.

If she hadn't been so domineering one might have been able to sit down with her and reason about the matter, and get her to understand that every human being is a puzzle, and that no one can have control over all the pieces of the puzzle. Not even Agnes. No matter how much she might like to.

Well, Agnes is unshakeably convinced that she's Helga's great support in life.

But I wonder if she realises how often Helga comes home in tears after being with her, and then sits all evening with lifeless eyes. And when I've been wrangling over something with Helga it always turns out to go back to something Agnes has said. Some comment on Helga's figure, skin or hair, or a correction of some name Helga has mispronounced, or some discussion to do with politics that has left Helga speechless and made her feel like a silly goose.

Sometimes when I've been sitting with her in my arms trying to comfort her, I've wondered whether Agnes can really be entirely unconscious of the effect of her comments.

Perhaps she's only too well aware that Helga is one of those people who can never have enough of seeing herself through critical eyes. It's like a kind of drug to her, and so long as Agnes takes care to deal out the poison in small, carefully measured doses, she will always have unlimited power over Helga; indeed, to the very end of time Helga will come knocking on her door begging for more.

A disagreeable thought. But I can't get rid of it. When I look at the friendship between Helga and Agnes what I see before me is a treadmill, or a machine for perpetual motion; something that continues under its own steam, so well constructed that it can never stop.

This has never been clearer than during the first year of our marriage, when I was bold enough to question their friendship.

I still shiver when I remember the hostility in Helga's eyes on that occasion, and it took several days for us to recover our equilibrium. It was as though I'd suggested she should shave off all her hair or amputate a leg.

Since then I've realised my wife finds a sort of perverted sense of self-confidence in thinking badly of herself. It's what she is used to. She believes she doesn't deserve any better. Agnes is ready and willing to supply her with this addictive poison, and all I can do is patiently keep the serum of love ready, and occasionally remind her that she will do very well exactly as she is.

'Excuse me, perhaps you'd rather…?'

Agnes's index finger waves backwards and forwards between Helga and me, as if to ask whether we'd prefer to be alone, and I shake my head and feel my lips moving, and a few polite remarks passing through them, and as if from the far side of a great sea I hear Agnes asking Märit to bring another glass, and I pull out a chair, and it strikes me that Agnes clearly has a strange influence over me too. With her I always feel I'm making a succession of serious blunders. I brood over things I've just said and feel sorry I didn't say something else.

For example, when she wondered if we wanted to be alone, I automatically shook my head, because I didn't want her to think we had anything to hide from her. But a few seconds later I was regretting it because I saw myself as having provided Agnes with confirmation that I'm an insensitive lout with no interest whatever in devoting time to my wife.

Those hot-blooded young men Agnes talks of so greedily would of course have driven everyone else out of the house to guard the holy bond between husband and wife.

(At the same time I'm helplessly aware that I would have regretted it just as much if I'd chosen the other alternative and told Agnes to leave.)

So Agnes pours out elderberry cordial and goes to stroke Helga's hair and asks if she'd like something to cool her forehead, while I sit on my chair with my hands drooping between my knees and fret over the fact that she has pre-empted me with all these gestures of caring.

When she goes off to get a cooling cloth I have a short moment alone with my wife.

I move nearer to her, take her hand and caress her cheek. And although I know time's short, and that there are urgent matters I need to talk to Helga about, I still can't help thinking that all this is something I'm only doing to make my mark in one way or another with Agnes, that I'm busy arranging a scene I can triumphantly demonstrate to her when she comes back — *and that it's so hard for me to grasp that there are other, infinitely more important reasons for me to hold Helga's hand.*

'Tell me,' I whisper. 'What did he say? Was there anything... Is there anything serious? If so, I'm sure you understand I'd rather hear it from you.'

Helga smiles weakly and shrugs her shoulders.

'"Serious?"... I'm not dying, if that's what you mean. It's just... like any other complaint. There are things you have to be careful with so they don't get worse. The slightest cold can easily develop into something serious if you don't take proper care of yourself, can't it?'

'But I don't understand... Cold?'

'I've got a dreadful pain here...'

She lays her hand below her stomach and looks at me appealingly.

'And when I told the doctor... the symptoms... He warned us against... Under the circumstances...'

She falls silent. Bites her lower lip.

'Yes?'

'Well... he meant a certain abstinence might be necessary.'

'But why? What did he think you...?'

'Please, I can't…'

She shakes her head from side to side on the pillow and tears rise in her eyes. I panic: Agnes must in no circumstances come in and see Helga in this condition.

'You talk to the doctor; he'll answer all your questions…'

Helga is wailing and her voice is getting louder, slowly but surely. I recognise the signs.

If I don't go now the violent crying will soon start. Sometimes this is followed by an outbreak of rage, when she can say the most horrible things. Then come more tears, after which she normally quietens down and lies apathetically on the bed staring straight ahead without blinking. And after that it's best not to remember any of the horrible things I've just heard, because if I repeat any of them, everything will begin again.

So I speak soothingly, say everything will be all right, draw her fingers across my mouth and kiss her fingertips. Her hand smells of metal.

Abstinence? Was that what she said?

I can't understand why she should take it so hard. If abstinence is all that's needed, I think, it can't be all that serious. Perhaps it's no worse than when you pull a muscle and have to rest it for a few weeks.

That's what it must be.

Suddenly I feel light-hearted. As if nothing's too much for me.

It happened when Helga showed me where she was feeling pain. How her white hand shyly sought out that particular place.

I suppose it made me feel a little virile. However idiotic that may sound.

My eyes don't leave her face for a second. Her wide red mouth. The microscopic white down on her cheeks. Her dark eyebrows – I think of them as 'noble' – that arch so generously over her glistening eyes. The blonde hair coiled above her forehead.

Something runs through my body, a dizzy feeling, like when you stand before something tremendous and imagine it to be really true. Like when I was little and looked up to the stars and understood, or at least tried to understand, that they all actually existed, in reality, every one. Or when I stood on a rock and looked out over the sea and tried to understand how much water there must be in it.

Or when I was older, standing in front of a painting of the battle of Lepanto, how I began to see it with new eyes, as if I'd never seen a painting before, and all the clouds of gunpowder smoke over the deep-red twilight sky, all the torn bodies, all the broken masts and lacerated sails... In an instant I realised that it had probably looked just like that.

My head was spinning.

I often feel like that when I look at Helga. Such a beautiful young woman – and I'm the man allowed to be with her!

But you are not allowed that.

I stiffen. The voice runs through me like an escaping echo.

I glance uneasily to either side, as if to see whether anything has changed in the room. But there's the same bed, the same chest of drawers, the same slack, lifeless curtains and the same scent of starched linen. Helga's lying with her eyes closed and her mouth half open. She swallows a little saliva, a thick unpleasant sound, and her breathing sounds more laboured than before.

I try to think somewhat ironically that things must have gone far with me. Hearing voices is a reliable sign of madness, they say...

At this point Agnes comes into the room. She pulls up a chair; the sound makes Helga start. Agnes begins to bathe her forehead, seemingly with deep concentration, and gives Helga alternate worried and loving looks, before turning to me to say:

'Märit sends word that Dr Glas is here.'

★

He's standing in the hall looking at a picture with his hands behind his back. It is a portrait of my Uncle Daniel. It's hardly more than a modest sketch, and it usually goes unnoticed. I've only kept it because it evokes a certain melancholy in me.

Daniel was the eldest of my father's brothers. He ran an inn in Örebro. He was large and red-faced, noisy and jovial. Uncle Daniel was the silver lining of my childhood, an intimation of the good life. But he was careless with money and died bitter, destitute, and alcoholic.

The portrait's careless brushstrokes strike me as eminently suitable. Even the painter clearly felt it wasn't worth paying Uncle Daniel much attention...

He spent his life somewhere in the background uncorking bottles and shouting out jokes to heighten the atmosphere around the table.

When Dr Glas turns from the portrait he has a little smile on his face, and when I shake his hand he becomes one of the distinguished gentlemen in Uncle Daniel's inn: a thin figure commenting sarcastically on the roast veal he's just eaten, but in such a low voice that Uncle Daniel doesn't hear.

We go up to my study. It's disagreeably stuffy in there.

The doctor looks around; it's his first visit to the vicarage. I imagine I detect a certain greed in his eyes, as if he's committing certain details to memory, and has already caught the scent of a collection of excellent anecdotes.

Of course he's sworn a vow of professional confidentiality. But you know how it is. Everyone has something they pass on in confidence to someone else, sometimes against their better judgement. This makes their vow of professional secrecy worthless, because their confidant also has a confidant, and so on.

Dr Glas clears his throat to speak; his eyes are still travelling around the walls.

'I shan't keep you long, Pastor. I know your time is precious...'

I shake my head firmly, hold up my hand and assure the doctor he may take as much time as he needs.

The doctor gives me a look as if I've just said something incomprehensible. And his mouth, which had just opened to say something, shuts abruptly.

I get an awful suspicion that there is something in all this that's obvious to everybody – Helga, Agnes, the doctor and God knows who else – except me. That something very important must have passed me by. There must be something I should have grasped a long time ago: either things must be worse with Helga than I realised, or perhaps the opposite, that it's something quite trivial, and that it's ridiculous to worry about her.

During the silence that follows I search the doctor's face in vain for any sign that might point one way or the other.

He takes out a little blue handkerchief and presses it against various points at the edge of his scalp. Then he folds it, and it's all I can do not to break into insane laughter, since the little movements he makes with his thumbs and index fingers remind me of a housewife folding a freshly mangled sheet, though in miniature, as in a puppet theatre.

Then he puts the handkerchief away and sits expressionless with one leg over the other and his hands clasped on his knee.

'Helga's told me about her pain, and about your... recommendations, doctor, but I have to ask, is it anything serious?'

He pulls in the corners of his mouth in an ambiguous grin, giving him an almost mischievous expression. He looks as if he'd like to say something in the style of: 'Serious? Well, I don't know about that...', but something's stopping him. Consideration for Helga, perhaps. Perhaps he doesn't want to present her as some sort of malingerer.

One thing is certain: he would never have assumed such an expression if she'd been seriously ill.

This suddenly makes me feel his advice must be open to nego-tiation, and that if I can argue powerfully enough on my own behalf, perhaps abstinence will not seem so necessary.

So without beating about the bush I tell him we've long been hoping to have a child – apparently news to him, since both Helga and I went elsewhere to be examined – and I also give a few hints of my age, so that he'll understand I haven't got all the time in the world.

Thus I lay all my cards on the table.

I go more deeply into his recommendation of abstinence, I go into concrete details, try to see the whole picture before me, go through everything aloud and invite him to see the arrangements from every point of view, so he'll be fully aware of the difficulties.

Should Helga and I have separate bedrooms? Encouraging not only the servants to gossip and speculate, but virtually every sin-gle visitor to the house too?

When I've finished, I'm in a better mood, since by now it should be crystal clear to the doctor that he'll have to think of a different solution. A holiday at a cure resort, a pill, anything.

Every discerning doctor should not just trumpet out recom-mendations any old how over his patients' heads, like imperial edicts, but first listen to what his patients and their families have to say, and form a picture of what their lives are like, so as to be able to adjust his cures and medicines accordingly, to the greatest possible extent.

But the doctor seems not to have heard a word I've said.

'I see,' he says. 'Naturally I'm in no doubt whatever, Pastor, that you rate your wife's health above all other considerations. Added to which, we have high hopes of being able to restore her to the best of health.'

I stare at him. He stares back. All my arguments dismissed as nothing more than mentally sick babble.

But he does touch one sensitive point, no matter how much it costs me to admit it, when he says that naturally he's in no doubt that I put Helga's health above all other considerations. I thought I heard something sharp in his voice. And suddenly I feel unsure of myself.

I ask him how long it'll be before we can live normally again.

'It's difficult to say. But six months' absolute abstinence is certainly necessary. After that we shall have to see.'

I nod.

Six months.

Half a year.

Don't six months usually go by rather quickly? Besides, the doctor said 'certainly', that it's 'certainly' necessary. Which might mean a full six months, at least six months, or perhaps even more than six months. But it might also mean probably six months, perhaps less.

The doctor gets up from his chair. He pats his jacket pockets discreetly, notices that one of his lapels is not quite as it should be and straightens it with an embarrassed movement.

We shake hands, and I watch him disappear down the stairs. I force a trusting smile and stand ready to raise my hand and wave if he turns, but he doesn't.

I go back to my desk and try to breathe calmly and empty my head of thoughts.

God is tapping me on the shoulder. That much I do realise. But God, I don't understand You.

*I*s it as the doctor says? Do I really put her health before everything else?

Or was he being sarcastic? Did he mean that I clearly *don't* do that?

I see now that I've had a tendency to belittle her mysterious pains in the lower abdomen. But is that so strange? I can't remember any part of her body that Helga has spared from her sometimes highly-strung attention.

To begin with I used to find it quite charming. (But in those days I thought everything about her was more or less charming.)

I remember one evening finding her in the library; she'd turned the reading lamp up to its brightest and was holding her right arm at an unusual angle, staring as if bewitched at a point on her upper arm. She asked me to come and feel a point she was indicating, and didn't I think the skin felt suspiciously rough?

I remember I found it hard to tear my eyes away from her face. There was something about it that moved me and that I found attractive. It's not until now that I realise what it was. There was fear in her face that was pure and unclouded, and it was the fear of a child. She'd forgotten everything an adult knows about restraining fear or perhaps simply controlling it. She was still as close to her childhood as that. It was a moment when fear ran freely through her and controlled her, and there was something in this I found beautiful.

On that occasion I managed to calm her worries by saying I couldn't feel any roughness at all, and that her skin was as smooth as velvet at that point as everywhere else. She laughed and we exchanged a quick kiss, and I was able to leave the library with a light heart.

It seems like a thousand years ago.

This pattern came to be a permanent feature, in the way that habits and routines grow in all marriages: she would worry about something, and I would wave her worries aside with a compliment or sign of love, even if I'm the first to acknowledge that these compliments and signs of love became increasingly mechanical.

So the years passed, and sometimes she'd get worried about something and I would wave it aside, and this became an almost cosy feature of everyday life...

Then suddenly one day there she was standing in front of me with something black in her eyes, accusing me of not taking her worries seriously, and this has naturally led to the argument that I don't take *her* seriously, and in fact never have, and she's suspected it for a long time but now it's quite obvious to her.

Since then she's never been able to claim that she has a pain (or burning feeling, or soreness, or ache) anywhere without me hearing – or thinking I'm hearing – a challenge in her voice. It's as if it's a test: will I take her seriously or not?

I do the best I can. But things get very tense. I expect I often fail the test.

Nor is it only her body that's the object of her attention.

She's at least equally vigilant when it comes to her spiritual wellbeing, or, to be more accurate, lack of spiritual wellbeing; whether she's experiencing sadness, grief, despair, disgust, frustration, emptiness or apathy, and to what degree and for how long and for what reason.

I've got used to it. One gets used to everything.

But sometimes I look up from this reality and imagine how it might be if only she were capable of enjoying all the advantages she has.

I've never seen a more beautiful woman. And beyond that she's clever and quick. She has a rich imagination. She has insight and empathy.

But once again it seems she feels a paradoxical sense of satisfaction in finding things in herself to worry about, things that give her a troubled frown. At such times everything else becomes alien to her, perhaps even unpleasant or frankly menacing.

I often rack my brains over where it comes from, this critical gaze.

I knew her parents, of course. Helga was their only child, and they worshipped her. Nothing was good enough for her, and nothing was left to chance, whether to do with her schooling, her appearance or her circle of friends. In the evenings, after she'd gone to bed, they would often sit together and go over things that had happened to her, or were going to happen to her.

I wouldn't go so far as to say they worried about her. But their conversation was permeated by the firm determination that Helga must have only the best, and that nothing was more important; indeed, that this was the main purpose of their lives.

Sometimes I was present at these conversations. It might perhaps be considered a touch tactless in them to persist with a subject of conversation that excluded their guest. But when they started talking about Helga it was as if they'd been sucked into a world so wonderful they couldn't stop. Which I understood better than they could have imagined.

I was sucked into their conversations even though I didn't take part in them. I listened attentively while they discussed Helga's various interests and crazes and which ones should be encouraged and which discouraged, and whether the children of the family that had just moved into the old pharmacist's house might be suitable company for her.

The tone of the conversation would be light, but there would be no mistaking the fact that it dealt with the most important subject they knew; it was there, endlessly, like a warm undercurrent. And Birger, who could be so unfeeling and lacking in empathy towards his wife, was at his best where Helga was concerned, listening attentively to everything Eva had to say, and showing clearly that he accepted that in this area Eva's authority was absolutely equal to his own.

I so enjoyed dipping my feet into this warm undercurrent.

If Helga and I should have a baby, we'd sit up in the evening just as her parents did. We'd be no less concerned than they were that our child should have the best of everything. Just as certain that nothing was good enough for our little one.

But there's something in those words that leaves me no peace: that 'nothing was good enough'.

I'm faced with the disagreeable thought that Helga grew up to be a woman in circumstances in which the phrase 'nothing's good enough' became so firmly implanted in her head that it still echoes there endlessly, even when she looks at herself, or worse: *above all* when she looks at herself.

Nothing's good enough.

In Birger and Eva it was an expression of their love for her, exactly like everything else. And it brought her nothing but misfortune.

The doctor may be right when he insinuates that I don't take her health seriously enough. But at the same time he's wrong. I know her better than he does. Who can blame me for wanting to give her something big, important and concrete to occupy her, when I see how she constantly loses her way among things that are small, unimportant and illusory?

And if I'm gripped by feverish eagerness since I believe the solution of our difficulties to be within reach, and this eagerness makes me a bit less sensitive than I might be to her lamentations – who can blame me for that?

I must be careful not to get gloomy and bitter. It's so temptingly easy to let oneself be smothered in clouds of dark, injured feelings.

I don't know how often I find myself thinking that if they only knew Helga as I know her – and by 'they' I mean the ill-natured little troop led by Agnes – they wouldn't look on me with such disapproving eyes. And Dr Glas would understand why I don't automatically accept his advice.

Or would he?

I've imagined it to be obvious that he too longs to start a family. But how can one know? I don't know him.

He's certainly young, but he's already achieved a good position and he should be careful not to wait too long. If a man has everything in place, but nonetheless stays unmarried, people begin to think something's wrong. They begin to get ideas. They gossip and speculate. And I'm convinced speculations have an unhappy tendency to become self-fulfilling, and that a man people speculate about will himself become increasingly convinced that there must be something wrong with him… completing a vicious circle.

We could have discussed all this, the doctor and I.

But I've seldom met such an inaccessible person. Everything I say is followed by silences that seem to last for ever. The consequence is that my words seem to remain hanging in the air, without being either dealt with or returned, and of course it doesn't take long before my words begin to sound ridiculous. I myself come to feel that everything I say sounds empty, pretentious and superficial.

I suspect the doctor and I live in different worlds. Or more accurately, that he's living in a world I left behind long ago.

I've seen him in the company of young men-about-town from the newspaper world. Though I should add that they're no longer quite as young as they think they are.

I know that sort through and through. They're still cultivating the sort of world-weariness and indifference that most of us take so much trouble to affect in our twenties. They remind me of what parents sometimes say when their children pull faces: be careful, you might get stuck like that. Which is exactly what has happened to Dr Glas's friends, and perhaps to the doctor himself too.

As schoolboys we try and impress girls with physical achievements like throwing the highest, spitting the furthest, or balancing on the rail of a bridge. When we're older we try to impress them with our intellect, and if we have none we content ourselves with giving the *impression* of having an intellect. What can be more tempting than to appear like somebody who has read everything, understood everything, and seen through everything, after which one can turn one's back on the world with an indifferent shrug of the shoulders?

As I've said, some get stuck at that point.

Unfortunately they forget that there's something a twenty-year-old may have but a forty-year-old may lack, namely charm.

A twenty-year-old may be guilty of any piece of madness you like, but his youth excuses him most things. He can gamble away his money or get the maid pregnant or mess up his studies or his business affairs while those close to him allow themselves, at most, a sentimental smile, since we calculate that sooner or later he'll find his balance.

But no one smiles indulgently when a forty-year-old makes the same mistakes. In him such actions are merely tiresome, tragic and in bad taste. At forty it's too late. Everyone knows that and the forty-year-old should know it too, and we are deeply depressed to see him so careless with the short time available to him.

When I see these gentlemen sitting wrapped in cigar-smoke on the veranda at The Grand, staring at the pavement and uttering their poisonous comments, I remember being twenty, when one pretended to be so weary of life, so despondent, and it was all of course because one was afraid of other people, particularly women, and one longed for them so intensely that one was forced to keep them away.

Hence these well-dressed gentlemen, entrenched behind their smoke-screens with their lifeless eyes, and their mouths, just as their parents warned, locked in an ironic grimace that betrays the fact that they're sitting in death's waiting-room, having seen through everything as being meaningless, and especially the impossibility of loving and being loved in return and thus making life happy for themselves and those closest to them...

Yes, their grimaces have become fixed. And they have held women at arm's length for so long, and so stubbornly, that they have never learned how to let people in.

I'm overcome with longing for Dr Glas's predecessor, old Dr Morén.

For a moment I can see him before me, his glaring red fuzz of hair, only faintly grizzled at the temples, his searching, clear, blue eyes, his wolfish smile.

With him you could talk about everything between heaven and earth.

He was capable of asking the most unexpected questions. He

might interrupt me in the middle of describing a persistent head-ache to ask about something entirely different; about some new assistant pastor I wasn't getting on with, perhaps, or whether I'd visited my father's grave lately.

To him the practice of his profession was a passionate research project, and he was always prepared to look for the solution to a riddle in unexpected places.

We often discussed religious questions. He used to say the more he learned about the human body, the more humble he became, and that a doctor who didn't believe in God must be either incred-ibly naive or pathologically lacking in imagination.

He was especially fond of fever. Can you imagine anything more ingenious, he'd say, than that the body has been provided with a built-in alarm clock, through which virtually all illnesses announce their arrival?

It was there, in the human body, that Morén found God.

Where will Dr Glas find Him?

When I saw him recently, with his thin lips and fish eyes, I saw an awkward young man who may not wish for anything more than that his patients should have faith in him. He must have heard a good many sentimental tirades about Dr Morén from his older patients. But perhaps he just doesn't know how to behave.

I can't help feeling a bit sorry for him.

It's almost impossible to maintain eye-contact with him for any length of time. His eyes flicker from the window to his desk to the ceiling; he's as restless as a house-fly.

I should perhaps tell him a trick I learned from Pastor Bauer when I was working in Linköping: if you fasten your eyes on the spot between a person's eyebrows or on the tip of their nose, it will give the illusion that you have a firm, penetrating gaze. (I use it myself, so I know it works.)

If on the other hand you look a person straight in the eyes, maintained Bauer, they will merely find it unpleasant.

My thoughts are interrupted by a sudden monotonous, long-drawn-out sound from down in the churchyard. Like a steam whistle. Or a ship's foghorn.

I go to the window and look out. The sound is coming from a little girl, perhaps five years old; her mother has just lifted her up to comfort her. I can't see the girl's face, only two blonde plaits hanging over the mother's shoulder, which is so damp with sweat that the thin linen of her dress is sticking to her skin. A convulsion passes through the girl's body and a mass of pink vomit spreads down the woman's back.

The woman squats and places the girl stomach-down over her knees, at the same time stroking her head. Flies have already begun to gather around them.

A few young office workers pass; they give the mother and child a wide berth and, casting amused glances back over their shoulders, they continue on their way towards Stora Badstugatan. After a while an elderly woman passes by; she has a small child on her hip and is holding a boy by the hand. She stops near the vomit-covered mother and says something, but the mother shakes her head. The boy demonstratively pinches his nose between thumb and forefinger and pulls at the older woman, and they go on.

After a while the girl gets to her feet and the mother gathers up two large bundles that have been dropped on the ground, she swings them up on her back and takes the girl's hand and they go on their way.

I was just about to go down to ask Märit to make me some sandwiches, but I've lost my appetite.

I don't know whether it is because of the heat, but recently I've often felt hungry, only to be overcome by lack of appetite, even distaste, once the food's actually in front of me.

I decide anyhow to make the attempt. I go to the stairs and call Märit. I ask her to make some sandwiches, preferably with the good cheese, if we have any left. She says we have, and wonders how many sandwiches I'd like.

'Three,' I call out.

Just when I'm about to turn I change my mind and call again to say that two will be enough. I go back to the study. No sooner am I behind my desk than I wish I'd stuck with three.

In a basket on the desk a pile of papers is waiting for my signature. I skim through them to get an idea how long they've had to lie there waiting. This is something I usually avoid; I can usually manage by quickly passing my eye over the date on the letter or certificate. Anything else would be self-torment.

The pile of papers amounts to five centimetres of concentrated human misery.

There is a certificate to the effect that Mr X of Tegnérgatan is hereby awarded custody of the three minors Å, Ä and Ö, since their single mother, as well as Mr X's sister, have been committed to Långholm prison for vagrancy. Another certificate states that Mr F of Malmskillnadsgatan has been allotted a place in a temperance institution. An official communication informs the R family that their lost daughter is now living in Sköndal, in a newly-opened home for delinquent children.

In other words, nearly a hundred distressed people who have had to wait several weeks longer than necessary for help because I haven't yet added my signature.

This was never my wish. I've done everything in my power to change the system. I've complained again and again that we're short-staffed. I recently calculated that if the parish administration had kept pace with the increase of population, there would be nine of us working here now! But as it is, each of us is expected to do the work of three men.

It's obvious we're overworked, causing unfortunate poverty-stricken people to have to wait an unnecessarily long time for help. Which makes it all the more important for us to avoid anything that can delay us further. For example, if I started wondering what's happened to Mr F during these three weeks during which he has been left to his own devices when he should already have been having help in his battle against alcohol, I'd end up paralysed with self-reproach.

I've only managed to get through about half the pile of papers when there's a knock on the door. It's Georg, bringing Professor Wallgren and his wife.

I ask them to come in. I've never met them before. I can't remember that I've seen them in church either.

The professor's something of a celebrity. He has travelled widely in South America and lived with head-hunters and has studied primitive people at such close quarters that he has almost become one of them, and he writes columns in the papers that are highly regarded in some quarters. I myself have tried to read them several times, but there was a streak of manipulation in his style that I found irritating.

He's quite young, not much past forty I should guess, and he makes a compact impression. He has small hands and the short, muscular arms of a labourer. He's clean-shaven, with sparkling blue eyes. His dress is slightly eccentric and reveals sunburnt skin – a rather over explicit indication, it seems to me, that this is a man who has travelled widely and seen fantastic things, and experienced such hair-raising adventures that he imagines himself to be above such provincial conventions as wearing a tie when calling on the Pastor.

Naturally the professor is not unconscious of what is expected of a professor. What irritates me is not that he neglects to fulfil these expectations, but that he enjoys the neglect.

The professor's wife is tall and dark and almost alarmingly thin. Her hair is tied in a hard knot on her neck. Her face is beautiful despite cheekbones so high that her eyes disappear into small slits when she smiles. She gives an impression of being nervous and rather haughty. In contrast to her husband she's strikingly pale, but the clothes she wears are as unconventional as his. The sleeves of her dress are so wide that one can almost see into her armpits, and several bracelets in glaring colours jingle around her wrists.

Both sit quietly for a while. Both are smiling, but while the professor seems to be rather enjoying the situation, his wife is clearly collecting herself to say something. And I let her collect herself.

I need the silence as much as they do. It gives me time to review my first impressions of the Wallgrens systematically, and I soon realise our conversation may degenerate into a pointless power-struggle.

Of all human weaknesses none is more often inflicted on me than arrogance.

The worst is when I meet, or think I meet, arrogance in others. That causes a rumble in me like a force of nature, taking control of me before I even notice what's happening.

When the Wallgrens cross my threshold, and I know in advance that he's something of a celebrity, and I see their smiles... in a few seconds I begin to imagine them looking down on me and gossiping about me, dismissing me as an absurd figure; it's just that since they've now suffered some trouble they need my help with, they're forced to condescend and call on this ridiculous person.

These fantasies become like a red rag for me to wave in front of a large bull. The animal is snorting and getting ready to charge, just as I'd hoped; soon I'm sitting there watching the Wallgrens with a sort of malicious triumph, chuckling inwardly and think-ing: oh yes, look at the two of you, cap in hand, before this ridicu-lous figure.

Even as a child I knew you can't fight pride with pride. But there are forces in me that it takes more than common sense to get the better of.

I let my gaze wander between Professor Wallgren and his wife.

Meanwhile the professor does a little play-acting – he gives a laugh, turns up his eyes, and shakes his head – clearly to let me know that he's waiting for his wife to make a statement, and that he thinks it's pretty pathetic that she's taking so long about it.

Finally, her eyes lowered, she says quietly:

'I want a divorce.'

'Ah,' I say. 'Why?'

'There's no love left between us.'

'I see. And the professor…?'

He snorts, shrugs his shoulders, looks out of the window. But this time I leave him no time for his ham acting, but ask at once, sharply:

'Am I to take this to mean that the professor doesn't want to divorce?'

The professor stiffens and becomes serious.

'That is a correct interpretation, yes. You must excuse my inad-equate engagement with the subject, Pastor. But this is a wish my wife has returned to with a somewhat soporific regularity, for many years. This, on the other hand, is a new manoeuvre from her side: that we should look up the… Pastor.'

He sighs lightly through the nose.

'I only wish I could get away from the feeling that this is just the usual drama played in slightly different costumes.'

The professor's wife hasn't looked at him once. Her smile has faded and she's gripping the arms of her chair firmly.

Suddenly she raises her eyes and looks at me with an expression of the deepest despair. It's as if she's appealing to me about something, but I can't put my finger on what it is.

I turn to the professor.

'It's high time you understood that you are not acting in a play. Far from it. This is as real as anything can be. You have entered into a holy union. You have done it of your own free will, and with your eyes wide open. And let me say once and for all, professor, that the frivolous attitude that you've brought here with you today is both depressing and upsetting.'

He stares at me with hatred. But he makes no quick riposte, and spares me any more amateur theatricals.

I let him stare, and ask his wife if anything in particular has happened to make her decision more urgent.

'No, not really,' she says after a while. 'But Pastor, can you imagine how it would be to live in an atmosphere of arctic cold. Can you imagine that?'

'Yes, I think I can imagine what that would be like.'

'You get used to it, of course. But if at the same time you can still remember a time when you lived in... in flowering gardens, where the sun always...'

'Excuse me, Fru Wallgren. I'm happy to listen to your story. But please try to omit the metaphors.'

She nods in bewilderment.

This time it takes her longer. But in the end she begins speaking again. Slowly and tentatively to begin with, and she's obviously making a great effort to avoid metaphors, but she soon gathers speed; her cheeks gradually take on colour and something begins moving in her eyes. It's like seeing the shadow of a great fish in unfathomable grey-blue water.

'I've seen how people can treat each other lovingly. I see it everywhere. They speak tenderly to each other. They help one another with little everyday things. When she returns, after being away for a while, for a shorter or longer period, he shows both that he's noticed she's come back, and that her return makes him happy. And if she's troubled or anxious or distressed in some way it troubles and distresses him too, as if the two of them were connected, as if they were one and the same person. And this way they come together to do something about what's troubling her.

'That's how it was with us once. During the first years. Every day was full of little signs of his love. Then, one after another, they disappeared. Even so, I've managed marvellously well to be happy with the little that was left instead of lamenting what was lost. I've also tried to be more generous with my own small signs of love, hoping they would awaken some response in him. But all it seems to waken in him is… is…'

She bursts into tears and says no more.

After a while I begin to be afraid she may become hysterical. She's shaking as if with malaria and gasping for breath like a landed fish.

Professor Wallgren is sitting with his hands clasped and his eyes lowered.

I could get up and go over to Fru Wallgren and try to calm her, but the years have taught me that if you want to understand the life of a married couple, the best thing to do is to sit attentive and still, watching how they behave towards each other, without any involvement whatsoever.

Eventually she begins to recover. She sits hunched over, breathing in deep tremulous sighs. Then she straightens, picks up her handbag and starts looking for something, presumably a handkerchief.

The professor takes a handkerchief from his pocket and holds it out without looking at her. She takes it, dries her tears and wipes her nose carefully, and I find myself following the handkerchief closely with my eyes, as if it's an important witness to something.

When she's finished with the handkerchief she rolls it into a little ball, which she keeps enclosed in her wax-pale hand. And however far-fetched it may seem, there's something about that handkerchief that gives me a feeling of confidence.

'Go on. All it seems to waken in him is...?'

'Disgust.'

'Disgust?'

'That was the word I was looking for. Indifference or disgust. Either the one or the other. So long as I keep away from him and don't speak to him, it's indifference. But if I try to approach him, if I speak to him in a tender or friendly way, caress him or kiss him, or if I've done something to my hair and ask what he thinks...'

She goes silent. Slowly shakes her head.

'Then he looks at me in a way that... yes, if I'm to be honest: in a way that frightens me. As if he hates me.'

The professor, who's been sitting still and expressionless through his wife's narrative, now turns slowly towards her and shakes his head. But she is not looking, so she doesn't see that all the scorn has left his face. He just looks sad. I almost expect him to reach out his hand to her.

Instead Fru Wallgren starts speaking again, and the professor takes his eyes off her, almost ashamed it seems, and resumes his earlier attitude.

'Obviously you become more cautious about... about giving these small signs. Since they seem to arouse such disgust in him. You end up living in a world where perspectives are completely distorted. Where you watch yourself in case you might lose your head and accidentally let slip some friendly word to the one who...'

Fru Wallgren's voice thickens, and she turns her head and looks straight at her husband. Her lips pull apart, her face crumples and seems for a moment like an exotic mask, and tears again begin to glisten in the corners of her eyes.

'... who swore to love me for better or for worse...'

Her body shakes with silent tears.

The professor looks straight ahead and doesn't move a muscle.

I'm beginning to feel uncomfortable. It's certainly quite normal for conversations of this kind to arouse feelings of sadness, anger and bitterness. But there's something about the strength of Fru Wallgren's feelings that worries me. It's like hearing a rumbling from deep beneath the earth, and realising that one is faced with forces one has hugely underestimated. If she should suddenly get up and launch a physical assault – and I have experienced such things in past interviews of this kind – I'm not at all sure that even together the professor and I would be capable of overpowering her.

I realise I sound extremely frightened as I throw in a question:

'Have you talked to your husband about this?'

'Yes, she has.'

The professor intervenes so quickly it takes me unawares. Then he looks at his wife and asks, this time in an utterly sincere tone, without irony or sarcasm:

'If you'll allow me...?'

No answer from Fru Wallgren.

The professor moistens his lips and grimaces. Then he begins speaking in a thin, uncertain voice, and I realise he's as uncomfortable as I am. Perhaps even frightened.

'There's something in the way my wife has spoken that may give the impression that at home she cringes in the shadows like a timid little ghost, quaking for fear in case this... monster casts one of his hate-filled glances at her. I can't recognise myself in this description. It's not my wife's habit to leave me uncertain as to what my marital shortcomings may be. On the contrary, she's more likely to issue little 'lists of things she would like'. And scarcely to give me time to read through one list before I find the next in my hands. Embellished, I must add, with miscellaneous pronouncements on the effectiveness or otherwise of my response to the last list. This sort of thing: On Monday I may be ticked off for never saying anything affectionate to her. Then on Tuesday I'll be ticked off because such affectionate words as I did manage to extract from myself - on Monday evening that is - didn't sound as if they came from the heart, or were unconvincing in some other way. Then on Wednesday I'm in the wrong because Tuesday evening's revised and improved assurances of affection were forced out in response to a command rather than issuing from me spontaneously...'

The professor interrupts himself. Perhaps he's realised that the pattern and tone of speech he's landed in here is only too familiar to him, and perhaps this routine is repugnant to him. He turns to his wife.

'I don't hate you. I never have. I can promise that much.'

For a brief moment they look at each other, perhaps for the first time since they came in. Then the professor turns to look straight ahead again.

'There remains the question of whether or not I love you. I wish I could say yes. But if I'm to try to be honest... You must understand, Pastor, I don't think many people have the capacity to love another person. I believe that those who do form an exclusive group who have been granted a happy gift, comparable perhaps to, well, to having an exceptional talent for mathematics, or perfect pitch in music. Enviable talents... all of them, but not something to be taken for granted as a universal quality or something we should be able to expect in another person. I think many happy circumstances must coincide before one can belong to this happy and fortunate group. No one would be happier than me if I were such a person. But I've realised I'm not.

'Perhaps at one time I believed that I did. Well, in the beginning that was the case. During our first years, as my wife's so fond of recalling. The trouble is she seems to believe the man she was married to at that time was the real me, and that since then I've lost my way and strayed ever further from my true self, and that it's been her duty in life to lead me back again. But the reality is the exact opposite. For a number of years I decked myself in borrowed feathers. Words of affection poured out of me ceaselessly and I wrote verses and poems in her honour. I wanted to be sure she never lacked for anything. The mere suspicion that she might do so was enough to cause me panic. Looking after her in this way was like a holy vocation to me. Everything else – work, friends, family – seemed ephemeral and insignificant.

'In fact I was enjoying a sort of summer holiday from my true self and was sure I'd never need to return to it. But the borrowed plumage fell out, the holiday came to an end, and now here I am, and it's painfully clear that every time my wife looks at me she wishes I was somebody else.

'But even if it's true, as she says, that "there's no love between us any more", and that this is all we now have left to live with, does it necessarily follow that we must divorce, with all the consequences that will bring not only for ourselves, but also for the two children we have produced and brought up, and whom I haven't heard mentioned even once during this discussion? Is there nothing in our joint life worth holding on to?'

The professor has been gripped by rhetorical frenzy. He gesticulates wildly and leans this way and that in his chair. But he doesn't expect answers or objections. He just enjoys our attention. He can't get enough of that.

'One doesn't need many days' travel from here to reach cultures much superior to our own, where they would think us mad if they could hear our arguments. What we call "love" and which my wife never tires of demanding from me, is a relatively modern concept. By that I don't mean it's illusory, or an empty invention. Absolutely not. But if we've now established that it's lacking, not because of mean-spiritedness or ill-will, but because the prerequisites for it quite simply don't exist, then I think we can ask ourselves: does anything else exist? I think it does. There is companionship. The two of us get on, as they say. We know each other better than anyone else possibly could, and what we know could fill a whole library!'

Now he smiles. It's an infectious, boyish smile, as if he's only just realised what an amusing thought has just occurred to him; his eyes move eagerly between us as if seeking instant confirmation of how funny it was.

Fru Wallgren bursts out laughing, and even I venture a smile.

But in the middle of my amusement I get the feeling that a heavy door has just slammed shut, and that the key has been turned in its lock.

It's a strange conviction that what's just happened has happened many times before, and that if at an earlier point in our conversation there might have been a sort of quivering uncertainty between the couple, and an opportunity for change, then that opportunity has now escaped them.

'... don't you think so? I mean all those little components, each of which can seem meaningless and interchangeable in itself, but which taken together form something that for better or for worse is both large and impressive and utterly unique, namely our life together. Just think of all the knowledge ploughed into it, knowledge we have procured for ourselves during this strenuous expedition, in which one day leads to the next. We have good days, we have bad days, it doesn't matter, we trudge on, and the next morning is always yet another new day. In our house, with our family, we have shared our little look-out post on the outside world. What you have seen I have seen too, and what I have seen you have seen. Forgive me if I'm getting a bit sentimental, I can hear that clearly myself, but I can't help becoming just a trifle moved… I just want to give you a sense of the endless fine small threads that bind us together. And no one can persuade me to think otherwise than that this is something…'

He gives a great sigh, blood rushes up to his face and he presses his knuckle against his eye.

'… that there is something *valuable*…'

Fru Wallgren shows signs of getting up from her chair and going to her husband, but stops herself and sits watching him uneasily as if perched on tenterhooks. But he seems fine. He blinks in bewilderment a couple of times, then clears his throat, sits up straight in his chair and nods at me.

'You must excuse me, Pastor. It would be interesting to hear your view of the matter now that both parties have had their say. That's why we're sitting here, of course.'

He clears his throat again and assumes an almost stern expression, as if to show that they are now ready to receive the Word of God.

I'm just about to speak when there's a knock on the door and Märit looks in. When she sees the Wallgrens, she stares, excuses herself and shakes her head humbly.

'I didn't know… so sorry… just wanted to say your sandwiches are ready when you want them, Pastor…'

The door closes.

I make a comic grimace, as if to invite the Wallgrens to laugh at the interruption; they need no persuading. The professor thumps his knee and wipes his eyes, and fires off one howling salvo of laughter after another, while Fru Wallgren looks up at the ceiling and laughs with her mouth wide open and her shoulders heaving. I join in as best I can, but soon the laughter begins to sound a little different in my ears.

After all, Märit's my housekeeper, I employ her, it's my roof she lives under, and it becomes increasingly clear to me that I'm the one being laughed at.

When the laughter has finally stopped the professor asks my opinion of divorce, and I explain it. Both nod solemnly, and then I finish with my usual harangue, to the effect that the mere fact that they sought me out for a private interview is evidence that there is still good hope of married happiness for them…

After this we take leave of each other. Fru Wallgren encloses my hand in both of hers, and I get the disagreeable feeling that her long fingers are about to slip in under my shirtsleeves and rush up my arms like rapid little snakes. She pauses a moment to look deep into my eyes, presumably to express the deep sincerity of her gratitude… And yet, I sense all the time that they can both hardly wait to hurry out into the street, and that the reason they're so impatient is that they're still reverberating with barely suppressed laughter. Once outside they'll be free to set off for home hand in hand, laughing at the ridiculous figures up there in the vicarage.

When they've gone I can't stop myself peeping out of the window to see whether my misgivings were accurate. But they don't come into view. They must have gone another way.

While I stand there burning with shame I recall some of the qualities that have been attributed to me. All the times I have heard that I'm ambitious, painstaking and dutiful. Diligent, I've heard too. Vainglorious, someone said once.

Sometimes I think there is only one thing that has driven me on: the dream of eventually reaching a high enough official position for me to command enough automatic respect to ensure that I'll never again feel paralysed by shame.

Seen from that point of view my life appears so unbearably meaningless.

It's like watching someone hurrying through the desert, chasing one mirage after another and never stopping for a moment to reflect or draw any illuminating conclusions from his experience. Just hurrying on tirelessly with the same burning commitment.

In the same way I've incessantly set myself new goals, managing with considerable success to persuade myself that if only I pass this exam, or if I can just manage to become an assistant pastor in X diocese, or a full pastor in Y diocese, or a principal pastor in Z diocese... then I'll have risen so high that I'll be sufficiently content and gratified for shame to have no power to bite me any more. And no matter how often I've discovered that this is an illusion, I've always managed to deceive myself yet again.

It's endless.

I can live with the shame. At least, I think I ought to be able to. But shame is only one of the two faces of Janus; the other face is pride.

$\mathcal{T}$he slices of cheese have developed little pearls of sweat. The sandwiches are warm, and the plate too; I suspect Märit's left it in the sun.

I hurry up to the bedroom to see how things are with Helga. But the bed's empty and has been made, and the chairs have been placed neatly against the wall in their proper places. Everything that happened in the room only a few hours ago could just as well have been a dream.

I begin to be aware that it's been an exceptionally strenuous day. Tiredness and hunger have caught up with me, and suddenly I seem to be hearing a well-meaning voice telling me to slow down.

I do something I very seldom allow myself: I fetch the pile of papers I was forced to put aside when the Wallgrens knocked, and carry the lot to the bedroom: paper, pen, inkstand and all and put it on the bedside table. I call Märit to bring me up some coffee, then arrange the pillows to support my back, take off my shoes, stretch out on the bed and waggle my toes.

This is the other side of solitude. The good side. Such a thing does exist.

You can go around for days on end brooding on how lonely you are in your work and your marriage, on how your responsibilities are so heavy and your workload so great, and how nothing ever gets done if you don't do it yourself. You can become bitter with longing for someone to say: that looks heavy, and you look so tired, let me help you.

But these simple little gestures: the pile of paper on the bed, the sandwiches on their plate, a cup of coffee... No one else arranged this for me. I did it myself. And it's as if someone's peering in at me through a chink in the wall and smiling.

I must have nodded off.

Helga's sitting on the edge of the bed. She's changed her dress. She's smiling at me and holding my hand. Her hand is soft and cool. It's darker in the room now. The papers I'm supposed to be signing have spread into a pool between my legs.

'Poor dear.'

She leans forward and embraces me with slow and carefully balanced movements, making her action almost ceremonial.

'You need to rest,' she whispers.

'Where have you been?' I ask.

'Agnes persuaded me to go for a walk. She was sure it would do me good. You know how she can be...'

Helga raises her eyes to heaven. I laugh, and sit up on the bed. My head's aching. When I straighten the pillow I notice a spot of cold damp and I realise I must have been dribbling in my sleep.

I try to collect the papers together; Helga whispers something and helps me to put them in order.

I look around and see the coffee pot and cup and the plate of sandwiches, which has several flies wandering backwards and forwards over it. I remember how pleased I was to have arranged things so cosily for myself. Then I fell asleep, and now I'm seized by colossal self-pity.

I turn to the wall and close my eyes, and everything comes back to me: Helga's white dress, Dr Glas's visit, abstinence, all the things that for a moment were blotted out and surrounded by a shimmer of unreality now emerge from the mist.

Helga rustles the papers hurriedly, then takes a few steps around the bed and lies down beside me, shifting herself nearer still to stroke my forehead, and I hear her whisper something, I can't hear what, but her tone is tender and troubled, and I daren't open my eyes, daren't look at her, not when she's lying so near me.

The sight of the coffee pot, the sandwich plate and the spilled papers has burned itself into me and is dancing about before my eyes. I hug Helga hard, burrowing my nose into her throat. I want nothing more than to be able to weep and I'm sure I need to, but all that comes out is a few dry sobs.

'There, there,' she whispers.

I open my mouth several times to ask what she's thinking. Does she secretly blame me for the fact that we've never had a baby? After all this is my second childless marriage. Does she think this can hardly be a coincidence, that it shows clearly where the fault lies?

Does she dream of a future when I shall be dead and buried, and when, after a suitable year of mourning, she'll be free to meet someone perhaps poorer and lower in social status, but also younger and more carefree; someone whose strong arms will lift her across some humble threshold, and who'll then get to work on her and give her so many babies she'll scarcely be able to keep count of them?

But each time I stop short. The room seems full of these strong young men with broad shoulders and large hands, but so far they've remained as motionless as statues, and I'm the only one who can see them.

But the moment I prepare to talk of them they will slowly begin to move and gain life and colour and odour, and Helga will lift her head, look inquisitively at them, and wonder who on earth they are...

Outside the sun's going down, the houses and trees cast long shadows, I cling to Helga with all my might, and when I become still I feel her ribs heaving inside my arm, and her narrow waist, and it's as if her breathing is somehow defying me, somehow reminding me, every time she breathes out, of my own insignificance, and that her world is moving inexorably forward while I stand by with my eyes wide open, gaping foolishly.

She is so good to me this evening. So kind, gentle and considerate.

Every time I try to get up to fetch something or attend to something she holds me back. She pretends to be stern, and teases me to make me laugh.

She opens the window wide and draws the curtains, then goes downstairs to get supper, and meanwhile I lie watching the curtains, how they are sucked outwards as if in convulsions, or perhaps struggling to escape, pressing themselves outwards with all their strength, only to give up and hang lifeless again, collecting themselves for their next attempt.

Helga brings up a tray, grouse with dauphine potatoes and lingonberries. Helga often teases me about my weakness for sugared lingonberries, and when she sets down the tray I see she's arranged the mashed berries to look like a trace of blood winding from the meat across the plate and over the tray as far as the teeth of the fork.

When I've finished eating we lie silently side by side, and I give in to my tiredness. And it is a blessed tiredness.

Normally I'd probably be worrying that she must be bored in my company, and that she'd rather be somewhere else, and I would ask her what she'd been doing during the day and what she had planned for tomorrow, and I'd make an effort to seem carefree and relaxed so she wouldn't suspect anything, but in fact I'd be lying there examining her answers from every possible angle and not be satisfied till I'd hit on some really ominous interpretation of what she said.

But this time I'm too tired.

The shadows in the room thicken. We can hear Märit carrying things backwards and forwards in the kitchen, opening cupboards and shutting them, and later her voice is right under the window, in abrupt conversation with someone a little further off, presumably Byström who will be wandering about the churchyard waiting for someone to send him home at the end of his day's work.

I put my arm cautiously under Helga's neck and caress her arm while we look up at the ceiling and giggle at Märit's and Byström's yelped exchanges.

I squeeze her shoulder carefully. Usually this is enough to make something thicken inside me, to make everything that is volatile and restless coagulate and become sluggish, while I'm filled with an almost insane lust.

This is normally enough: that I touch her shoulder or hand, or any other part of her body and when I hug it, it resists, it objects - in a word - it *exists*. And I'm allowed to touch it! No police will come to handcuff me for assault. She's my wife. She has stood before God and said to me 'I will'.

… but this evening I'm so tired even this is too much.

I can feel her young body resisting my hands. I must be strong. For the time being we must be content to be friends. For at least six months. (If it will really have to be so long.) And this – being friends – is the unspoken agreement we enter into as dusk falls, as we lie silently side by side in a harmony we haven't experienced for a long time.

At last Helga has found an occupation that gives her pleasure, so much so that she hurries out of bed in the mornings.

Agnes has started spring-cleaning the boxroom in her attic, and Helga is helping her. They carry down old boxes and go through the contents. Many old memories are rediscovered. Letters, portraits, tickets and pressed flowers. They throw some things away and sort others into piles.

Helga says she thinks she's about to enter a new stage in her life, and that working on Agnes's spring-cleaning is helping her to close the books on her own past so she can leave it behind her.

Of course I have my views on Agnes, and feel no reason to reconsider them. But this time I decide to disregard them, since keeping company with Agnes is so clearly doing Helga good.

She's almost unrecognisable. She's begun enjoying jokes and pranks. Nearly every time we meet something happens. Sometimes, when we meet in the hall or on the stairs, she surprises me by pulling a funny face as she passes. Sometimes she sneaks up behind me and pokes her fingers into my waist. She knows what effect this will have since I'm very ticklish.

Once I lash out so awkwardly with my elbow that I accidentally hit her on the bridge of the nose, making it bleed. She hides her face in her hands and her whole body shakes, which worries me, but when she takes her hands from her face, I see a laughing mouth, with blood running in two furrows down either side of her Cupid's bow.

At every mealtime she's full of little stories and things she's noticed on her walks to and from Agnes, and descriptions of old teachers and schoolmates, and accounts of Agnes's amorous entanglements, and I sit for long periods with my knife and fork resting in my hands while she gives all the details and laughs and gesticulates, and I try not to stare too hard at her since I don't want to embarrass her.

But I do allow myself a thought that seems as vulnerable and brittle as a butterfly on a banister: this is the woman with whom I once fell in love.

And if I can be sad that that woman faded away and I forgot I'd ever found her, I can be no less achingly happy that she's come back.

Naturally I spend ages trying to puzzle out what can have caused this. What kind of memories does helping Agnes with her boxes rouse in her? But so long as I see no signs of her sinking into melancholy, or starting to look at me coldly or bitterly, I let it be.

The most noticeable change in Helga undoubtedly happened on the day Dr Glas was here.

Though I'm none the wiser for knowing that. I remember so well how I reacted. How the thought of having to keep my distance from her dug a moat between us. But for Helga this moat may have been liberating. It may have dispelled fear and unease in her.

Perhaps we'll have to start again from the beginning. Rebuild our old friendship from the ground, block by block. And perhaps we shan't have the peace to do this so long as that image of the twelve-year-old Helga carefully exploring her breasts has such power over me.

Perhaps this six-month chastity, which first divided us like an abyss of painful uncertainty, will be our salvation.

During morning service I notice a familiar face in one of the pews. It's Halvar. A ray of light's falling across his face, and I only just manage not to smile at the sight of his powerful nose and sunken eyes.

Something about him is forever apart. However much he may want to blend in with groups something always separates him from those around him. He can't help sticking out like a carrot in a field of cabbages in the midst of the sparse summer congregation and its shrunken old ladies. After the service I hurry to change. He's never before turned up in church in this manner, and I'm worried in case he's in trouble.

He's waiting for me in the church porch. He bursts out laughing when he sees my anxious expression.

'Relax,' he says. 'I just thought it's been so long since we saw each other. Do you feel like a walk?'

We decide to go to Skeppsholmen and sit there for a bit on the benches by the water. Halvar laughs again.

'I remember a time when we weren't so precise about stating our destination,' he says. 'But these days of course we have to make sure it's a place we're likely to be able to get to, that it won't be beyond our range.'

'At least nothing seems wrong with your mood,' I say.

'It's just that it's such a relief to be able at last to talk to someone with a little sense,' he answers.

We walk slowly along Hötorgsgatan. The morning dew's lingering on the shady side, and the air's a pleasure to breathe.

Halvar tells me they should really be out on Dalarö, but that only a few days before they were due to leave they heard that his sister-in-law's husband had left her, like a bolt from the blue, after nearly forty years of marriage. The poor woman had sunk into such a severe depression that she was barely capable of eating or drinking unless spoon-fed like a child. She'd never make it as far as Dalarö, so there was nothing for it but to unpack the trunks again and get the guest room ready.

Since then they've been tiptoeing around the house, putting down cups and plates with great care and opening and shutting doors as noiselessly as they can, with their whole lives focused on the sister-in-law and whether she's taken a whole cup of gruel or only half a cup and whether she's answering when people speak to her or not. And Halvar sits all evening with his wife analysing the fragments of information about the errant husband gleaned from the lady during the day.

Halvar's wife says it'll be fine if he goes to Dalarö on his own.

'But I've learned enough to know that if I jump at this offer, I'll have to live with it till the day I die.'

'But she did offer, didn't she?'

'The sort of "offer" the devil made to Jesus on the mountain. The usual term for such offers is "temptation".'

'Aren't you being a bit cynical?'

'Wish I was. The point of her "offer" was to see whether I'm capable of being loyal and unselfish. Going off to Dalarö on my own would have proved the opposite, according to her logic.'

'Well, well. But I'm sure it won't do you any harm to show a little unselfish consideration for your sister-in-law.'

'The trouble is there's not much unselfish consideration left in me. No matter how much I wish there was. I've reproached myself in every possible way. But recently I've begun thinking there isn't much to be done. Everything else is drying up and withering away. My memory's failing. My legs don't carry me as far as they used to. My hands shake so badly, especially in the morning, that I can't even write letters. My optic nerves or whatever they're called, the ingenious little membranes over the eyes, are getting weak and drying out and losing elasticity. I haven't much imagination left either. I think of something I want to say and I say it, and then afterwards I find myself shuddering at how badly I expressed myself. But it was the best I could do.'

'Nonsense, you're expressing yourself as well as you ever did, I can hear that quite clearly!'

'Only because for once I'm in stimulating company. Anyhow, why shouldn't compassion wither in the same way? No matter what I do, I can't summon up any sympathy for the old lady. She's just an object that needs turning over and feeding at regular intervals, nothing more or less. She might just as well be a potted plant. I try to bear in mind all the misery she's suffered at the hands of a man who, according to the latest rumours, has run off to be a sort of patron to a young female opera singer from Norway. But not even these disturbing circumstances can wrench me out of my useless ruminating state of mind. I just rattle my false teeth, stick my feet into my old man's slippers and believe everything'll work out for the best.'

'At least no one can accuse you of lack of self-knowledge,' I say with a smile.

Halvar shakes his head.

'Don't try to cheer me up. You know as well as I do that self-knowledge is useless if it doesn't lead to change. I'm one of the worst sort, and sometimes I suspect you are too – the sort who think developing profound self-knowledge may excuse them from being expected to be responsible for their actions.'

'How would that add up, do you mean?'

'I've no idea,' answers Halvar cheerfully. 'I haven't got that far yet.'

We fall silent for a minute. A brewer's horse is standing wheezing at a street corner. A handsome old mare, blinking, her muzzle white with foam; presumably her driver has driven her to a stand-still. A group of people are standing watching curiously while a man in a dirty white coat feels his way forward under the mare's chin.

Halvar stops near the group and asks questions about the horse, where has she come from, how old she is, but gets nothing but irri-table and monosyllabic responses, since no one wants to take their eyes off her.

He turns to a young officer, and I can hear him explaining how when he was a child a horse bolted right through a potato stall, and a six-year-old girl nearly got trampled, but an old woman snatched her away at the last moment. Instead the girl had her ribs crushed under a sack of potatoes. The officer nods politely. For my part, being near the horse depresses me, and I want to get away as quickly as possible.

Finally we continue our walk. There's a blue-black covering of cloud spreading over the horizon. We try to work out which way the cloud's going and decide, not without disappointment, that it seems to be heading for the Åland Sea.

Halvar's not his usual self. As we go through Berzelius Park I notice he's making strange movements with his arms, not at all typical of him. He looks as if he's walking along a narrow, bend-ing plank, struggling to keep his balance. He looks worried, espe-cially when we have to stop to let a droshky or tram pass. I've often seen this expression before in old people; they look as if they've forgotten something important but can't remember what it is.

But I've never seen it on Halvar's face.

Normally I'd make some comment. Halvar and I can talk about anything, and we've never had secrets from one another.

But what starts as no more than a vague feeling that Halvar's anxiety has deeper causes than usual focuses into the paralysing realisation that, in his deceptively light-hearted manner, he's already told me everything.

What he's been telling me is that he hasn't long to live. And thereby he has driven a wedge between us.

For as long as I can remember we've been a support and comfort to one another. We've helped each other through grief, doubt and world-weariness. But now I realise for the first time the gulf between talking about small, manageable, worldly things, and talking about things so vast that one is struck dumb and knocked back; between what's transitory and repetitive like the changing seasons, and what's irrevocable and final.

It's desperately clear to me that Halvar's about to start on a journey he'll have to make alone. And that I shall be left behind.

Everything has suddenly changed.

A moment ago we seemed to own the city, as we advanced along the pavement side by side like stately old galleons. But now each footstep hammers the ground as if we were on our way to the gallows.

I become sharply aware of all the smoke-belching ships pressing around Blasieholmen, and all the passengers crowding their gangways and collecting baskets and cases and pointing at the quayside and waving to acquaintances standing there waiting.

Halvar and I pass through a cacophony of raucous steam-whistles and excited shouts, of clattering hooves and calculating seagulls. I walk through the din wishing it would get even louder so that it would drive away my gloomy thoughts.

We cross the bridge in silence. There we find an empty bench under some ancient willows. Halvar sweeps it clean of dust and pollen with his handkerchief before we sit down. A young couple are sitting on the next bench. She has curly red hair and is simply dressed. There is something sun-bleached about her, as if she has been hung out on a clothesline and accidentally been left there for too long. The young man has a newly pressed Sunday suit, and when Halvar and I sit down he twists his body away from us at an unnatural angle as if to hide his face.

Soon he gets up and begins to walk away and the girl follows him, watching him anxiously as if trying to understand how he expects her to behave; whether they should turn right or left, whether they should walk side by side or whether she should keep a few steps behind him, whether they should hold hands or not, and I notice she's always a little slow in following his example.

The last I see of them they're climbing the hill towards Kastellholmen; he's scattering gravel with his walking stick, and she's trotting after him like a strictly trained mare that has just incurred her trainer's displeasure.

'You know how it is with all successful swindlers,' says Halvar suddenly, smiling happily when he sees my bewilderment.

'All successful swindlers use a cloak of concealment. But not just any old cloak will do. They have to take enormous trouble over it and put their heart and soul into it. If you're printing fake banknotes in the cellar, and at the same time are running a hairdressing salon upstairs to conceal your criminal activities, then you must devote at least as much commitment and passion to your hairdressing salon as you do to your banknote-printing business. The more you think of yourself as a hairdresser, the more successful you'll be as a forger. In other words, the better you are at deceiving yourself, the better you are at deceiving other people.

'I believe that's how it is with what people call self-knowledge. I don't believe in it any more. That's not how true self-knowledge expresses itself. When I think back over all the conversations you and I have had over the years... well, you know yourself. We've turned over many stones, and seen things which would make anyone turn pale. But I can't remember ever having felt anything but curiosity, and even a certain delight. Then we've changed the subject, and I've never had the slightest difficulty in shaking off the memory of the revolting creatures that crawled from under the stone, and starting to discuss something entirely different instead... But you're not saying anything!'

I give a hollow laugh, but no matter how hard I try I can't find anything to say.

I can't bring myself to tell my old friend that I'm watching him walking towards death, that I've seen his anxiety and fear, and that it grieves me not to be able to stand with him, at his side. I can't say this. And anything else is bound to seem a lie. That's why I remain silent.

'I know I'm long-winded and perhaps incomprehensible,' says Halvar. 'But if this so-called self-knowledge takes on the character of a party game or amusing pastime... won't one then suspect that one must be dealing with an illusory activity?'

His words ring out. Silence creeps nearer. I can't stand it any longer. I know only too well what my own silence contains.

I start talking about Helga's illness and the unexpected changes it has brought. About the work she's helping Agnes with, and how tender and good-humoured she's become.

After a short time I notice Halvar's attention wandering, and his gaze vanishing into the distance.

'You must forgive me,' he says. 'I was thinking about all the times I've come home to Maria a changed man.'

He goes silent and grimaces, as if he's noticed a nasty smell.

'Oh yes. I've been a vessel of plenty, full of consideration, friendliness and tenderness. I've seen her astonishment when she looks up from her book or her needlework, and it's been so obvious that my warmth awakes warmth in her, and fills her greyness with colour and life and laughter...

'What she's never realised is that my transformation has always been the result of me having a guilty conscience about something.

Various flirtations and relationships, some more or less serious, others more or less meaningless, and then I've come home and found her, most often in the drawing room with one of her many pieces of embroidery, and I can hardly move. All I can think of at such times is how easy it would be to smash everything, turn her whole world upside down. How eerily easy! All I'd have to do is open my mouth and say what I've done, or what I've nearly done. Indeed, not even that. Sometimes it's occurred to me that all I'd need to do is say a single name. "Ellen." Just that.

'We have that power over each other. I don't know how many times I've abused it. But when I see her sitting there with her needle and thread, always making the same movements, a sort of sticky, sentimental tenderness rises in me and overflows all barriers. And I hurry to her, treating her essentially like a little child who has tumbled down and hurt herself and needs comfort and warmth and rest.

'I don't know how many extravagant presents I've given her that have derived from this state of mind. It's like being drunk. When I buy all those presents and embrace her tenderly, then at last I'm an ideal husband. And that's the only thing that means anything. That I shall be a touch less contemptible in my own eyes, and become a man who deserves respect, and preferably admiration. In this connection, Maria is both inessential and replaceable. I'm transformed from a miserable liar to an ideal husband. And this fact intoxicates me to such an extent that I tend to forget its origin and find myself brimming over with love.

'Once I happened to hear Maria telling some of her women friends about one of my exploits, I forget which, but I'm sure it was some ingeniously arranged surprise. I heard how proud she sounded. As if she was conscious that she was boasting but couldn't stop. And I promise you, her women friends were so touched they wept. I saw myself how they dabbed tears from the corners of their eyes.'

Halvar gives a laugh. But there's no happiness in his laugh, and he doesn't expect me to join in. He reaches out a hand and pats me reassuringly on the arm.

'Once again, I ask you, please be indulgent with my egocentricity. I do really see how happy you are, and you understand that it wasn't my intention to spoil your happiness. But this is one of the curses of getting old. Other people's purity makes the filth in oneself stand out all the more clearly. When you tell me about Helga I think perhaps I was once as pure as that too. I wonder how it felt.'

I utter a few objections, but I hardly know what I'm saying. I drop into the role I'm expected to play. The words come automatically.

Our conversations always follow the same pattern, with one asserting something and the other opposing it. The assertions are often pessimistic; gloomy statements about the possibilities of love, or the place of the church in the new century – so that it's up to the opponent to speak well to defend his own point of view.

Halvar doesn't seem to be listening very carefully either. He's sitting silent and still with folded arms, looking at me with a little smile as if my words are a well-known piece of music... And I have the impression that, like me, he's been struck by an earth-shaking vision of all the times we've sat and talked in this manner, and has realised that all our conversations fit into this conversation, and that this has made him sad but at the same time has warmed his heart.

I must write him a long letter before it's too late.

I've begun to take various precautionary measures. In the evening I let Helga go to bed first. Then I wait for nearly an hour before I go to bed myself, to be sure she's asleep.

I've had new curtains put up; stiff, prickly ones made from material that has a slight smell of tar. They darken the room so completely you can hardly see your hand in front of you.

When I go to bed myself I like to carry a candle, and force myself to keep my eyes on its fluttering flame. Once I'm near the bed I put the candle down on the floor, undress and put on my nightshirt. Then I creep into bed with my back to Helga, lift the candle to the bedside table and blow it out.

The new curtains ensure our sleep's deep and pleasant, and both Helga and I are very pleased with them.

Since my hearing is worse in my left ear I usually lie on my right, so I can't hear Helga's breathing or her slow movements under the bedcover, or the moaning sound she sometimes makes when she has a nightmare.

But it's been several nights now since I last managed to get to sleep easily.

There's nothing unusual about that; I've had this problem for as long as I can remember, and I recognise the symptoms. But it's harder to cope with insomnia when it's black as a sack all around, and when I can't have a light to read by, and must remember always to lie on my right side.

When I was a child insomnia was a torment. My parents and brothers took it as evidence that, if I hadn't exactly been lazy, at least I'd been hoarding my strength during the day, and thus making a heavier burden for them. So, to avoid their sneers and reproaches I did my best to look as if I was asleep. I would try to breathe heavily and evenly, and lie as still as I could. Egon and I slept head-to-foot on the kitchen sofa; he was a light sleeper and very ready to make comments – if possible loud enough for Father to hear – about how I'd disturbed his sleep with my floundering about. He knew perfectly well that this would make Father more dissatisfied with me than ever: not only was I idle during the day, but I also wrecked the night's rest of those who'd done an honest, hard day's work.

The worst was when the bedbugs got to work. I knew I couldn't scratch myself too much, at least not if I'd seen any movement from Egon, because this would mean he'd woken up or that he would easily do so. I got good at moving so slowly that it couldn't be noticed, a millimetre at a time. The drawback of this was it often took so long that the itch had stopped by the time my hand reached the place I wanted to scratch.

When I was a bit older and had a bed of my own I could scratch myself as much as I liked. But I was still plagued by insomnia every few weeks. I learned to know the signs. The tiredness would slowly run out of my body, and I'd start worrying that I was due for a night of lying helplessly awake until the room grew light.

On one occasion I told Dr Morén about it, and asked if he could recommend any medicines or household remedies.

He shook his head.

'There's always a good reason for sleeplessness,' he said. 'Everything goes so fast these days. The moment we finish one piece of work we have to hurry on to the next. We collect in our heads a great deal we need to think over in peace and quiet. Most of us don't have a chance to do that until we're lying in bed.'

I remember I couldn't help smiling. Morén smiled back.

'The wisest thing you can do, Pastor, is to respect your insomnia. There's nothing unnatural about it. To be quite honest it surprises me more that some people do manage to sleep well at night.'

So hour after hour I lie on my right ear with my back to Helga and try to remember the old doctor's voice. It had such a calming effect on me at the time.

Sometimes I wish everyone had a Dr Morén. During a long life one acquires many aches and pains and peculiarities, and one easily comes to think of them as enigmatic and unnatural.

But for Morén everything had a natural explanation, and if it wasn't clear to you what it was, well, you should still calmly assume that an explanation did exist somewhere. He was unshakeable on that point.

There were times when I came to his surgery, when both my body and soul felt like one, single, great trouble spot, but he always managed to persuade me that I couldn't have been any different than I was, and that being as I was both logical and natural, and, above all, that I had no reason to blame myself for it.

In this respect Dr Glas is the opposite of Dr Morén.

Tell him what you like, without any ulterior motive or hidden agenda, and you'll soon discover that with him everything becomes ambiguous or, worse still, takes on sinister overtones.

If while sitting in Dr Glas's surgery I happen to observe in passing that it was raining on my way there, it won't be long before I find myself wondering why I've mentioned such a thing, or what I must be trying to conceal in this clumsy way by mentioning it, and then all at once I find myself doubting that it ever rained at all.

With Dr Morén you felt you were finding an explanation of who you were, and that who you were followed naturally from a number of circumstances that you couldn't control and never would have been able to control.

With Dr Glas you constantly discover new aspects of yourself to cause you torment and shame.

There's a millimetre-wide slit between curtain and window-frame. Earlier you couldn't see it at all. Then it became just visible as a light-grey line. Now it's turning milk-white.

I think about the little baby we're going to have. I think how happy the last few days have been, and how I wish we could conceive our baby in this happiness. Begin his existence in precisely this atmosphere, and no other.

Suddenly Helga laughs. I lift my head from the pillow and listen. She laughs again, once. Then she hums as if in quizzical agreement and laughs a third time, and I smile to myself and think, these days she's even exhilarated in her dreams.

When Helga wakes me she's already dressed and on her way out of the house.

With a great effort I manage to drag myself out of bed, and no sooner have I had my breakfast and got dressed than Georg comes to tell me that two appointments I had for that morning have been cancelled, one with a builder who wanted to go through the arrangements for his daughter's wedding but has suddenly been taken ill, and one with a cantor from the Maria church congregation who wanted an interview but has now called it off without explanation.

In other words, I could have slept all morning. Poor Georg doesn't understand why I look at him with such exasperation.

I go upstairs, fall on my knees by the bed, clasp my hands, close my eyes and collect myself for morning prayer.

I think of all the people I shall meet during the day, and conjure up several faces, some known and some unknown; some helpless and despairing, some hardened and scornful, and pray to God to grant me strength, love and humility to be able to help people and listen to them and show them a glimpse of His goodness.

For a short moment I feel God's presence, and I stand before Him in my pitiful anxiety and aching exhaustion, and He turns to me with a look that in my confused state reminds me of the alert blue eyes of Dr Morén.

I feel God's love streaming towards me like a firm hand on my shoulder, exhorting me to lift myself out of my exhaustion and self-pity, and reminding me that I'm a valuable instrument in His work, an instrument I must take good care of.

I open my eyes and get up. I decide to go to the public baths. This puts me in a better humour at once, as it's a long time since I was last there.

I pack swimsuit, soap and towel in a rucksack, and on the way out I stick my head into the kitchen and tell Märit I'll be back at eleven. She half-turns and opens her mouth to reply, but I slap the doorpost cheerfully and hurry off before she has a chance to say anything.

That's the way to do things!

I walk quickly. I pass a newly-dug grave and note that as usual Byström has spilled the earth left and right over the grass without raking it up afterwards. I've told him time and again that this isn't the churchyard at Blattnicksele, or wherever it was he worked earlier, where you can happily wait for weeks till the rain has blended the spilled earth with the grass. No, this is a place where hundreds of people pass every day, and we have good reason to suppose that they come with a particular purpose. Either they're looking for a few minutes away from the noise and dust of the streets, or they want to be near a grave into which someone close to them has been lowered to their final rest, and it's negligent and inconsiderate of their feelings to let the churchyard take on the same slovenly and ephemeral appearance as the city beyond the gates, where everything is a mishmash of wheelbarrows, mortar and dirty buckets hauled up and down the walls.

Time and again Byström has stood there and nodded, his eyes fixed on my chest, and promised to keep my words in mind, but, as the proverb says, you can't teach an old dog new tricks and time and again I've been on the point of insisting that this is completely wrong: of course you can teach old dogs new tricks, you can teach them anything, but you have to use methods with which I don't think either Byström or I would wish to have a closer acquaintance.

I could find him, but that can wait.

I hurry on down the roads, and as I'm crossing Tegelbacken it strikes me that I've felt no irregular heart movements for several days now. The thought fills me with a sense of wellbeing, as if I've been given a totally unexpected present, and for a moment I feel entirely invulnerable.

I walk with the sort of long firm strides I normally find disagreeable, since they cause a certain heavy vibration in my overweight body, a sort of lingering wobble, but today I associate these quivering feelings with strength, as if my voluminous body might even inspire respect rather than ridicule.

I think of myself as big and strong, as someone who'll live a long time.

On the railway bridge I'm forced to fall into step with everyone else. Nor can I stop, because of the inexorable pressure from the stream of people behind me.

A shiver runs through the bridge, a growing thunder, a goods train rushes by enveloping us in white steam, grey dust and black soot. Sparks fly from its wheels, and everyone slows down, and I have the wild thought that I too, and all those around me, are tumbling forward, imprisoned by the same shining rails that wind so monotonously onwards, through the next curve, and the next, and the next...

The train thunders on towards the south, stabbing and throbbing in my ears, and inexplicably I find myself thinking of my father. Of the day I heard agitated voices from down in the forest, and of what happened afterwards.

It all comes back, in the same order as usual.

How I come out of the privy, fumbling to straighten my braces so they won't ruck up my shirt; I'm still a child.

Looking down at the forest I hear a jumble of rough voices, like the barking of dogs and apparently close at hand.

But the forest lies as it always has, rising like a roar from the hill below, an inscrutable lattice-work of rain-drenched tree trunks, of tall, scaly pines, stretching as far as the eye can see. The voices seem so near. It's incomprehensible, it seems almost supernatural; I shudder and a cold shiver goes down my back.

Then they come.

My three brothers, I recognise them by their clothes.

They're carrying something, it's obviously heavy, they're in a hurry and they look as if they're in pain and out of breath with their mouths open, leaving behind what looks like little puffs of smoke, and a comic detail in the midst of all this is that Egon's cap has slipped to a ridiculous angle, but is in some incomprehensible way still clinging to his head. I ought to run and meet them, but I stand as if nailed to the ground.

Now I can see two hands sticking out, and two arms my brothers are holding clamped in a firm grip, the hands floating lifelessly, palms uppermost. As they hurry past I see that it's Father they're carrying, and my first impression is that it's like when they played wheelbarrow with me and said it would give me strong

154

arms, which no one needed more than I did, and me with blood collecting in my face as I walk on my palms over dew-drenched grass with my child's wrists creaking as I shout to them not to go so fast, but there's a wild laugh I can't get out of my voice, and I know that in a moment I shall end up on my nose in the wet greenery. Once I cut myself on some sharp blades of grass and when we came in my mother scolded my brothers and bathed my wounds and I felt everyone was looking at me in a new light and I felt quite heroic in spite of everything.

Two of my brothers are each holding an arm and the third is behind and holding Father's calves, exactly like it was when they played wheelbarrow, except that Father's lying face-up, looking as helpless as a beetle on its back. As they pass he turns in my direction, and his face too, gives the impression that they're playing a game. Can that be my Father's face? It looks grotesque, with staring eyes and mouth twisted in terror.

Can that really be Father?

They rush into the cottage; they are like an upset flock of crows. Then the door closes and all's as quiet as before, apart from occasional bumps from inside.

The world I'm standing in, the world outside the cottage, was transformed into a world of horror the moment the door slammed shut, and I want nothing more than to run inside.

But the cottage too has been transformed into a world of horror.

I run towards it nonetheless. I've just managed to open the door when one of my brothers rushes past. He shouts something at me, I don't hear what clearly, but I do understand I must keep out. That I can't come in. And when you're little you do what you're told. Especially when someone shouts at you in a voice like that.

I sit on the steps; I don't know for how long. But the steps are a good place to sit. I know that at once. They're a borderland between the horror inside and the horror outside. A sort of limbo.

They have a lot to do. I hear thuds and voices. One of my brothers rushes out and the door strikes me on the left arm, but I've put myself in a position that has taken into account the possibility that someone might rush out through the door; if I hadn't, the door would have hit me in the back and my brother would have stumbled over me. He goes on down towards the carriage-house and a moment later I see him riding away. Then Dr Wibjörn arrives.

I assume I've been forgotten. I blame no one for this. In some respects I'm better off than those moving about inside the cottage.

There is enough time for it to dawn slowly on me that my Father is soon going to die and enough time to free myself from my paralysis, and enough time for me to turn to God.

I can't remember ever having turned to Him in this way before. I look down at the forest and up at the sky. It's a grey, windless day. The sun sparkles through a few golden-white cracks in the grey clouds, then it is blotted out, then comes back again.

And as the hours pass I sit as if bewitched by all the great things before me, and I no longer feel I'm sitting in a world of horror. Everything's quite simply great, beautiful and impressive.

I feel that God's looking down on me in all my misery and nodding reassuringly, and I wish I could explain the warm and all-embracing feeling of being chosen that sinks over me. But perhaps you have to be a child to understand that.

It's like standing in a great crowd of people, as you sometimes do when you're little, with your face waist-high compared to all the people around you, and you're helplessly lost in an anonymous herd of muddy boots and coats and skirts and linen that smells of sweat and dirt and horses, and you pay careful attention to all the currents in the sea of people, because you know if the crowd starts moving in a particular direction, you'll be faced with the choice of either going with them or being trampled to death.

Then to be noticed, to achieve eye-contact with someone, perhaps to be lifted up by a pair of strong arms… That's almost indescribable bliss. Like being rescued at the last moment from the jaws of death.

That's how it is. God's watching me, and it's as if, almost a little ostentatiously, He's swept his arm out over all His works, over everything He's created, over sky, sun, earth and trees; it's as if He wants me to understand the range of His power and the extent of His love for us, and when He sees that I've understood He looks at me and says wordlessly: I know you understand that I'll take care of your father.

Then I'm no longer afraid.

I know God has seen everything. He doesn't need me to convince Him that Father's a good person. I shan't need to recite everything Father's said and done, everything he's *been*, everything that makes me think tenderly of him. God already knows all that. He's been there all the time.

I must have sat out there for hours.

Mother's hand on my shoulder seems to wake me from a slumber. I look up at her. She signs to me to follow her in. Keeping her hand on my shoulder all the time, she steers me in the right direction. I'm not sure where I'm going. Normally I'd hear a noise somewhere, or voices, and go in that direction without a thought. But now it's so quiet.

We go around the corner, and Father's lying there. My brothers are standing around the bedhead. Someone's sitting on a chair. Father looks at me. He's swallowing, and his breathing is rapid and troubled. Mother takes me forward to him. I stand beside the bed. The light in the room is painfully bright.

Father reaches out his hand to me, and I back away. On reflex, I can't help it. But I take his hand. It feels larger than usual. It is dry and warm, as it always is. Normally when I hold Father's hand an expectant and rather solemn feeling pours through me, usually a sign that something amusing or exciting or perhaps frightening is about to happen, at all events something above the normal, and that's just how it feels now too.

That's why it's so bewildering to look into his face. It's white with terror. His eyes are roaming about, he swallows and clears his throat incessantly, his mouth is twitching and quivering, and I don't want to think it, but I do: my Father looks like the idiot we often see in the town square.

He can't get out a word, and I look up at my brothers, but their faces are a row of closed doors, no help to be had from them.

Suddenly it's clear to me: Father hasn't experienced anything of what it was granted to me to experience when I was sitting out on the steps. He hasn't seen God's smiling face. He's imprisoned in a world of horror, and he can't get out of it.

This is where I betray him.

I could tell him something of what I experienced when I was sitting out there. I could calm him and drive away his bottomless terror of what lies ahead.

Perhaps if I'd been alone with him I could've summoned up the courage. But surrounded by all those expressionless faces I shrink into myself as usual and daren't open my mouth for fear of being ridiculed or mocked or seeing someone roll up their eyes to heaven. I can't bear the thought of my face going red with shame, especially at a time like this, and I know I can easily blush to the lobes of my ears, which can glow like rowanberries in the October gloom.

Only too often I've offered some thought, observation, fancy or desire, only for them to knock it out of my hands with a single sarcastic remark or, even worse, to leave it in my hands but make even me think it ridiculous, empty and pompous.

As I stand there, I can myself hear how arrogant it must sound for me to suppose I could have anything important to tell Father. How could I have anything important to tell him? How could *I* help *him*?

So I leave him alone in his anguish. My own fear of being ridiculed is stronger. I never saw him alive again. Mother's hand patted my shoulder lightly, and I understood Father needed to rest.

The next time I saw him he was dead. I can't remember much about that. Just that his eyes were closed and his hair had been combed and obviously someone had shaved him too. And it seemed to me that there was a trace of disappointment in his face.

Since then I've seen countless numbers of dead people.

People often say how light, calm and pure dead people look. There may be some truth in that. But I've also often seen on their faces an expression similar to the one on Father's face that day. Disappointed and resigned, as if they've been told off. Or as if something has been promised and then not given to them.

My thoughts about Father's death follow the same pattern as they usually do. With the passing years they have been chiselled into a story with a given beginning, middle and end.

This story has followed me through life, and I've noticed that every time I listen to it, an explanatory light falls on certain decisions I've made, and I feel I can trace the origins of some of my own character traits, both good and less good.

The powerful feeling that I failed my father, for example, was presumably a vital factor in my choice of profession, not least for the devotion I've brought to the job.

In this way I have from time to time occupied myself with the narrative of my father's death, trying to analyse and interpret it.

But when I think about it, it seems almost like a 'parlour game', as Halvar, so disagreeably apposite, put it. It reminds me of women amusing themselves by fortune telling.

But this time it's different. The story holds me in such a strong grip that I feel myself floating a little way above myself, while in the lower corner of my field of vision, so to speak, I watch myself turning away from the bridge, going down to the baths, patiently waiting my turn at the entrance, buying my ticket, changing into my swimsuit, and with reluctant steps climbing down into the black water.

People are crowding all around me, romping and splashing each other, ducking and pulling each other's legs, and sometimes everything stops and they shade their eyes, looking up at the diving boards, where a slim young man solemnly walks forward and collects himself for a moment before launching himself artistically into a dive; when he hits the water all you hear is a controlled plop, followed by a general sense of exhilaration and a murmur of appreciative comments.

I swim about listlessly in the midst of all this, an old grey seal ignored by all, and not even the feel of the cold water shimmering beautifully against my white arms can dissolve my paralysis.

My mind is a blank. I draw no daring new conclusions. The story of my father's death merely gives me a panic-stricken feeling that something irrevocable has happened, and the strangest thing of all is that it seems only just to have happened.

It's as if I've just missed an opportunity to save him. As if Father was standing at the rail on a boat that has set sail from the quayside, travelling with terrifying speed, and I remain on land watching him disappear. And gradually a certainty spreads through my body, that all this grief and consternation is something I have to adjust to from now on.

I get out of the water and go around looking for a free chair, but there are far too many people, so I sit down rather laboriously on the edge of the bath. Even though I can't see clearly without my glasses I realise people are looking askance at me and can't easily take their eyes off me, and I know only too well what this means: they know they've seen me before but they can't remember where. Soon it'll dawn on them, and they'll have difficulty controlling the amusement that begins to bubble up inside them.

I suppose there is something comic about a priest in a swimsuit. No one can have any idea that I'm sitting grieving for my father, who's been dead for nearly fifty years.

Perhaps the story of his death, and my habit of taking it out at regular intervals to analyse and interpret it like the grounds in a coffee cup, has been my way of keeping him alive. But if so, I can't think why it didn't work this time.

When I go to get dressed it's as though he's following me with his eyes. And I feel he wants passionately to come with me.

On the way home I lose myself again in dreams and fantasies that centre on the little child I so ardently hope Helga and I are going to have. It's as if my recent experience and thoughts about my father have given new nourishment to my daydreams. Just imagine, to be able to mean so much to another person! A little boy or girl.

I walk with my hands behind my back feeling pleasantly relaxed after my swim, indeed almost drowsy, and I look at all the people hurrying past and wonder whether they're all constituted as I am, in the sense of having their own special daydreams that they take out and taste like a sort of stimulant from time to time.

I remember a story Halvar used to tell many years ago, about a man called Zeinetz, a timid little man, whose job was emptying privies in Halvar's part of town. It was rumoured that this Zeinetz had been saving up for decades to buy a cottage near Ronneby, in the archipelago. No sacrifice was too great for him. He put up with his disgusting work for years, struggling up and down narrow stairways with splashing buckets in the company of the most alcoholic and brutalised fellow-workers imaginable. Zeinetz worked harder than any of the others, refusing all the drams and bottles of pilsner he was offered since he knew these would have a detrimental effect on his work capacity. The years passed. By the time he was fifty-five he'd reached his goal and bought the cottage. He gave up his job, packed his furniture and household goods on a cart, helped his wife up onto the box and set off for the south. They'd only got as far as a resting place just south of Nyköping when he suffered an apoplectic stroke and died on the spot.

'There's a happy man for you,' Halvar would say. He had a goal in life, and achieved it. He was spared from sitting there on the front steps wondering why on earth he'd chosen this extremely ordinary cottage as the be-all and end-all of his existence.

'Pastor?'

The voice seems to be coming from a long way below me, or at least from no higher than my chest. I turn.

It takes me a moment to place the face. It's Johan Laurén. He looks smaller and slimmer than I remember. He's informally dressed in shirt and waistcoat, but his clothes are neat and clean, and his shoes well polished.

He raises his hat and we shake hands. I'm a trifle nonplussed, being just about to cross the road. Johan Laurén gives an interrogative nod towards the other side, as if to ask which way I'm going, and we fall into step.

'I'd like to take the opportunity to thank you again, Pastor.'

'Not at all,' I answer. 'How are things with Olof?'

Johan Laurén shakes his head and is so slow to answer that I have time to begin worrying whether the boy's fallen ill again.

'Can't keep still for a second. Fit as a fiddle. You know how it is with small children, Pastor. Their memories are short. When his parents warn him to take it easy it means nothing to him.'

We walk along the quay. I notice he's slowed to a stroll and clearly expects me to do the same. He obviously wants to talk to me about something, and it irritates me that he's taking so long to get to the point.

To cap it all he stops by the quayside to exchange a few words with a fisherman, whom he clearly knows, and the fisherman starts going on about some adventures he's had in Skurusundet, and even if Johan Laurén doesn't exactly egg him on to spin out his story to the greatest possible length, he certainly makes no effort to hurry him either.

After a while I clear my throat, but the only result is that Laurén begs me to excuse him for his rudeness and introduces me to the fisherman, who wipes his fists on his scaly trousers before shaking my hand.

The fisherman then continues his story, this time including me in his audience. There's something apologetic about this suspiciously long-winded tale, as if the fishing boat is their common property, requiring him to give an account of everything that's happened to it and how it happened.

At long last he reaches the end; we say goodbye to him and continue on our way, and I fix my eyes on a street corner where I plan to stop and tell Johan Laurén I'm in a hurry to get home, and if he hasn't got to the point by then, too bad.

He seems to be reading my thoughts, because he slows down even more, pinches his lips together thoughtfully and drops his eyes. Finally he speaks.

'We're all so extremely grateful,' he says.

I take a deep breath and begin to say something polite, but Johan Laurén interrupts me almost rudely. Now he's started his monologue, and he's in no mood to be interrupted.

'Extremely grateful. I'm not only speaking for the boy's parents, but also to a great extent for myself. It's true Olof isn't my own son. But he's near enough, or how should I put it…'

He stops, interrupts himself and observes a mysterious moment of silence before looking up at me.

'I have no children of my own. No living relatives, in fact. I grew up in an orphanage in Skövde.'

I nod expectantly. Johan Laurén starts walking again, with the same expression on his face as if screwing up his eyes against the sun, and I listen to his story with greater attention than before, and can't avoid an irritating feeling that he's well aware of this.

'So naturally I've given a great deal of thought to the question of what it can mean for a boy to grow up without any... roots or branches in any direction... Over the years I've met many who've grown up in similar circumstances, and I've been able to observe certain similarities between us. We come to have a good knowledge of people. We gain the ability to judge quickly if the people who cross our path are trustworthy, loyal and honest. We're good at forming close relationships with those who are, and we keep well away from the rest. Perhaps this sounds crass and calculating. But we had no choice if we were to survive.'

I tell him I know what he means, and that I myself have made similar observations.

There's an anxious edge to my voice, probably because I think I can detect an undertone in his story. It's as if he's walking with a tightly clenched fist in his trouser pocket, waiting for me to express in word or action anything that could be interpreted as insulting or disparaging.

'I've also noticed,' he goes on, 'that we tend to create small families of our own to compensate for the families we've never had ourselves. The Höglund family is an important branch of my own little home-made family tree, and I daresay I'd have grieved for Olof at least as much as his parents if he'd died. Of course they have an advantage in that he's the offspring of their own flesh. But there are also points at which *I* have an appreciable advantage...'

I nod thoughtfully, though I've no idea what he means.

We've reached the street corner. I stop, flash a sunny smile and hold out my right hand.

'I can't tell you how happy I am that little Olof...'

Laurén stiffens. His eyes narrow and he clasps his hands demonstratively over his stomach.

'I'm sorry,' he says, 'but there's something I need to talk to you about.'

I take out my watch. It's nearly eleven. I tell him I'm expected home and I'd rather arrange a mutually convenient time a little later in the week. But Laurén shakes his head and looks cautiously to left and right.

'It's a sensitive matter. Strictly speaking, it couldn't be more sensitive. In fact, it was out of consideration for yourself, Pastor, that I decided to approach you in this way.'

I stare at him. He meets my gaze calmly.

I have an uncanny suspicion that he's been following me ever since I left the house this morning. How else could he have known where to find me? I never told Märit I was going to the baths.

I nod again, trying to gain time. I begin to wonder if he's mentally disturbed. There are some signs to suggest it. An obsessive expression I think I see in his eyes, that wasn't there earlier.

I've seen that metallic expression of detachment many times before.

I've been sought out by people who have got stuck in a mental rut, often connected with some injury they imagine has been done to them, or a sum of money they think they've been swindled out of. But usually their obsession goes round and round in their heads so obsessively that there's no room for anything else, and it doesn't take long for them to state their business.

I almost hope Johan Laurén will reveal his business, and give some clear sign that all is not well with him. Then I shall know how to proceed.

'I know a place where we can talk in peace.'

He gestures in the direction of the Jacob church, and we begin walking, despite my whole body protesting and my head resounding with warning cries. I try to think calming thoughts, to remember to be sure we go to a place where I'll be able to summon help if the situation gets out of hand. I even find myself glancing sidelong at Laurén in an attempt to get some idea of his physical strength.

A few blocks from the church he lays a hand on my arm and stops. He looks around before going forward to a glass door, which looks like the entrance to a café; someone's stretched a lace cloth over the window, it's greasy and discoloured, and there's a cracked wooden sign hanging over the door, though since I'm standing immediately under the sign I can't see what's written on it.

Laurén opens the door and nods at me to go in.

I take a few cautious steps into the place, which is surprisingly light and pleasant. It contains half a dozen well-worn tables, but only one is occupied, by a young man with a fuddled red face who puts his bottle down carefully, his Adam's apple moving up and down as he swallows his pilsner.

He watches us closely. Strangely enough this doesn't disturb me. Instead I feel enormous relief at not being alone in the room with Johan Laurén.

'Just a moment...'

Laurén goes behind the service counter and opens a door, nearly colliding with a young boy carrying some long article at arm's length. The boy's attention's entirely concentrated on what he's carrying, so he only stops when Laurén presses a hand against his chest.

Laurén and the boy exchange a few quick words that I don't manage to catch, and it's only when the boy passes the counter and continues towards the exit that I see that the object he's carrying is a large cat with mottled red markings, which he's holding by the scruff of its neck. The boy is dressed in a green waiter's jacket a couple of sizes too big for him, and his black hair is shining with brilliantine. This solemn-looking figure passes without giving me so much as a glance, the cat strangely still in his grasp; it makes a sleepy movement with one back paw, but otherwise seems resigned. Presumably it's the tightened skin of the cat's neck that seems to give it such a broad smile of pleasure. The boy opens the door and throws the cat out into the street, at which it gives an insulted peep.

Laurén holds open the door behind the service counter and I feel a good deal calmer despite the fact I've no idea how the boy in the waiter's jacket and the pilsner-drinking young man feel about me, or whether they would come to my help in a dangerous situation.

We pass through a little room stacked up to the ceiling with boxes and buckets and go up a short staircase; then Laurén finds himself in front of a door that gives him a certain amount of difficulty – its heavy old key doesn't want to turn, and the lock refuses to click back until he pushes it with all his strength.

He prises the door open and a blindingly bright light shines over us; once our eyes have adjusted to it I see that we're standing in front of a little tobacco plot, long and narrow in shape and enclosed by a mustard-coloured wall.

Laurén closes the door behind us. Several small birds rise into the air in agitation and hop around up on the wall.

'Just a moment…'

He opens the door again, disappears back down the stairs and soon returns with two chairs. He presses the chairs' legs a little way into the earth to make sure they're steady and offers one to me.

I sit down cautiously, feeling the chair sink into the soft ground. Outside the wall, a cart passes below, with rhythmically squeaking wheels though it sounds so close as to be right next to us.

Johan Laurén looks out over the tobacco plot. He's breathing with even, regular breaths and looks worried. When he finally begins to speak his voice is muffled and monotonous.

'It wasn't just out of politeness that I wanted to express my deep gratitude to you, Pastor. As I said, there's something I want to tell you. Something that's come to my notice. If you wonder why I want to tell it to you, the reason is the deep gratitude I feel to you. If it had concerned anyone else, I'd probably have let the matter rest. But since it concerns you, and you have been such an invaluable help to people very close to me, I felt I couldn't just sit there with my arms crossed doing nothing.'

I notice he's looking at me. But I avoid his gaze.

The conversation has taken a new and unpleasant turn. I've waited impatiently for him to deliver his message, and taken it for granted that it would concern only him. That perhaps he needs my help in some worldly matter and hopes I might be able to exert pressure on his behalf, or that he's suffering pangs of conscience for something and wants me to supply rapid relief. That's the way it usually is.

But I'm completely unprepared for the matter to concern me.

'It's to do with your wife,' he says quietly.

I slowly sit up straighter in my chair. It moves, and I nearly lose my balance.

And somewhere inside me I know exactly what's coming. And everything that's being said between Laurén and me takes on the character of a kind of slow liturgy. Meaningless words passing backwards and forwards, their only purpose to fill the time until something of immense magnitude has sunk in.

'Helga?' I say.

He nods.

'I saw her a few days ago. In one of the alleys near Stortorget. I'd gone to see an acquaintance of mine, a tailor, and was just about to leave. Then I saw her. She was coming out of a doorway.

I've written down the address. Soon afterwards a gentleman came out of the same doorway. Perhaps I wouldn't have suspected any connection between them if they hadn't both acted in a similar manner. They both looked around carefully in exactly the same way when they came out into the alley and walked away quickly, looking down.

'I won't weary you with details. Nor do I want to waste your time with guesses and idle assumptions. I must emphasise I'm only telling you what I know for certain. I won't say anything about how I went about collecting information, unless you particularly want to know. I'll just assure you that I used the utmost discretion.'

Laurén takes a scrap of paper from his waistcoat pocket and hands it to me.

'This is the address where they meet. They arrive in the morning, several minutes apart. After an hour or so the man comes out of the doorway and walks north, then towards afternoon he comes back and stays several hours. Then they leave, again several minutes apart.'

Laurén is silent, gets up from his chair and goes down to the café.

I look at the piece of paper in my hand but don't read it.

I try to see the whole thing before me, but it isn't easy. Helga and another man. A room near Stortorget.

I sit as if stunned.

At the same time I have a rare feeling I've been here before. Thousands and thousands of times. Those were of course figments of my imagination. Horror scenarios. I have also on occasion used such images to stimulate myself, since, in the midst of all the horror and humiliation, something has emerged to drive me to Helga with a passion and decisiveness that has astonished us both, and been a source of great pleasure.

Now it's the real thing. Now it's really happening. That's what I try to tell myself, again and again. Like trying to wake someone out of a deep sleep.

But he won't wake up. At least it seems he won't. Perhaps he's been woken too many times, too often jerked breathless from sleep, only to find it's all a fantasy that can be dispersed by the slightest breath of wind.

Laurén comes back and hands me a little glass, full of a golden yellow liquid. Perhaps whisky.

I hear him sit down. I hear him swallow his spirits. I can't induce myself to empty my own glass.

It warms my heart that someone cares about me. That I don't have to sit here alone. It fills me with a sense of wellbeing I can't defend myself against. But the glass in my hand would be a step too far. If I empty that something dreadful will happen. So I keep telling myself, my thoughts whirling faster and faster in my head.

'I can't find words to describe the pain this causes me,' says Laurén. 'But I may be able to suggest a way out of all the distress. And now I want you to listen carefully.'

I nod to him to go on.

'I've done a certain amount of research. In the greatest secrecy, of course. I know his name. I know where he lives and where he works. And not only that. I've discovered his weak point. I don't know that I need to go into details. In a way, probably the less you know about it the better. But I will say this: all you need do is give me the sign, and I'll get to work immediately. And I can promise that if I do, this man will break off all relations with your wife.'

I turn slowly and look at him. He nods energetically. He is deeply serious.

It was something that happened a moment ago. I think it was when he said 'his weak point'. It was something in his voice, perhaps greed or delight, I can't describe it exactly.

But when I look at Johan Laurén I realise that weak points are precisely what lie at the heart of his business activities. He knows exactly where to find weak points, and how best to make use of them.

'How do you mean?' I say.

He gives a little laugh, and holds up his hand as if to ward something off.

'Don't misunderstand me. I'd never allow myself to do anything that would make difficulties for you. I'm no harbour thug, if that's what you're worried about. I hate violence as much as you do. Not only because it's morally abhorrent. It always works against one's own interests. I learned that early in life. That those who live by the sword will also perish by the sword. Truer words have never been uttered or written down… Anyhow, I want you to know that ever since these matters came to my knowledge I've been looking at various ways in which I might help you. I didn't want to look you up just to tell you what I saw in that alley. If I did that I'd be nothing but a common gossip. No, I wanted to offer you a way out of your difficulties. And, as I've said, it didn't take long before one was revealed to me.'

There's a soft humming coming from behind the wall, it sounds like girls' voices. I raise my head and for a moment I can see them before me, two or three little girls walking side by side singing something, quietly keeping time, as children do, and a little out of breath.

The voices pass like birds, like distant cranes, and then they are gone.

I think about the man, and I wonder what he looks like, and I wonder if he is young, and I wonder what they talk about.

I wonder what they do together after they've passed through the doorway. Perhaps they kiss and hold each other. Perhaps she has that wild hunger in her eyes when she looks into his face.

Strangely enough a wave of compassion sweeps over me. I feel endlessly sorry for her. It is as if I've just discovered that she's the victim of serious delusions. That she's not accountable for her actions. That she needs help.

And the mysterious man has crossed a threshold in my head, he stands in a corner, a somewhat timid figure, and for a few short seconds he steps forward into the light, and in my imagination I can give him various advantages. I can make him young, slim, handsome. I can give him velvet eyes and shining black hair. I can conjure up Helga from another corner of the room, I can let them fall into each other's arms, I can let her caress his sleek white face.

It doesn't matter, I don't feel any the less sorry for her. It's like hearing a small child chattering about all the things she'll be able to buy with her penny. A castle, horses, boats and a hundred sweetshops.

I can admit myself defeated by him on one point after another: he's young, slim, in good health, and certain to be extraordinarily virile and able to give her many children.

But his love for her isn't greater than mine. Not by a long way. On that point I can never give way.

Poor thing. How could she end up going so badly astray?

'Tell me to do it and I'll do it. This very afternoon.'

I shake my head. I make a gesture to stand up, and find I still have the glass in my hand. I don't know what to do with it. I can't really put it down on the ground. It would fall over.

I hold it out to Laurén. He takes it. His movements are slow, and he is frowning. He looks disappointed. Perhaps dismayed as well. He's clearly unwilling to let me go.

'I do understand this must have come as a shock to you, Pastor. I may have proceeded too quickly. It naturally takes time for something of this kind to sink in. I think the Pastor should go home and think the whole thing over in peace and quiet. My offer remains. You are free to contact me whenever you wish. And you have my guarantee. I shall proceed with discretion. I'll make sure none of those involved will come to any harm. But I can assure you he will leave her alone, for ever.'

I stand up. I hold out my hand to him.

At the same instant I feel a blow strike my heart. Like a violent attack of cramp inside my ribcage. It stabs and cuts and I have time to think: now I'm dying. On the edge of a tobacco plot, a stone's throw from the Jacob church, in front of a stranger.

And for a short moment I look at Johan Laurén in a way I haven't looked at him before. As if I want to make some sort of appeal to him, to support me. Perhaps hold my hand, perhaps get me a glass of water and whisper a few comforting words. And then to say bright things about me to those who are close to me. Write me a good obituary. Because now there's only him.

I don't think he's noticed anything. I hide it in an attack of coughing. My eyes fill with tears. Sweat breaks out on my forehead and temples. I quickly take off my glasses and wipe my face with my handkerchief. I laugh and shake my head. Laurén doesn't move a muscle.

An embarrassed silence follows. I daren't move. Not yet. I don't know if the attack's over, or if there's more coming. I have to say something. I must try my best to talk slowly and thoughtfully.

'I attach the greatest value to your efforts,' I say. 'But I don't want you to take any action. I must respond to this myself. I hope you can respect that.'

The words come easily. There isn't even a tremor in my voice. The movements inside my chest have stopped, leaving behind a slight pain rather like a bruise.

Johan Laurén wants to help me with the door, perhaps come out into the street with me too, and I even believe he's offering me his arm to lean on. As if I were an old man with a weak heart.

Again I come to think of the words 'weak point', and it's a great consolation to me, in the midst of all my distress, that I don't think I have exposed a single weak point to him. *Not even now*, I think, and it's like receiving a reward or a certificate; indeed, a testimonial to the fact that I am somewhat superior.

I need a little peace and quiet. I must have a moment to myself. I walk back the way we came.

I continue over the bridge to Kungsholmen. Unusual winds are blowing. They are warm and powerful, dying down as quickly as they get up.

I cross the road and turn into one of the small paths that wind over the little hills by the shore at Kungsholmen. I pass a multitude of decrepit shops, and workshops with large skylights made dark and impenetrable by dirt and dust; I pass factories with chimneys spewing out thick yellowish smoke, which makes my eyes and throat smart, and now and then I meet expressionless workers who push clattering wheelbarrows or are helping to carry great troughs full of boards or brown coal, and sometimes I see men in the distance on the hills stare at me, then turn to others to make comments.

After a while I become aware that my clothes are stained with dust and soot, and I beat furiously at them till I've got the worst off, but soon they look just as bad again, so I let them be.

On the other side of the hill I see a large crowd, workers lounging on the dusty grass, eating sandwiches and drinking water and milk and pilsner, and I slow down but realise I can't easily turn back. Some of the workers are lying in the middle of the path, among them an elderly bareheaded man with silver-white hair and bare arms sitting proudly on the grass while a dirty half-grown boy presses himself against his chest and caresses it with curved, claw-like fingers. The boy smiles senselessly, he looks cretinous;

strings of saliva run from the corners of his mouth. The man, who's perhaps his father, looks angrily, almost aggressively at me when I come near, and makes not the slightest effort to move out of my way. Perhaps he thinks it's my fault he has a retarded son.

All the workers are sitting silently except one, who is talking in a heated and monotonous voice, and suddenly he breaks into a rapid stream of obscenities; I do my best not to listen, and succeed, in fact, above all expectation. I notice that some of the workers are only just managing to hold back delighted smiles, and that one man is trying to shut his comrade up, while another tells him he'll end up in Långholmen prison.

My legs are shaking with fear, and when I leave the workers behind me I notice I'm on tenterhooks as if I'm expecting someone to throw a stone at me, or run after me.

Far off in the distance I see a bridge and I am overcome by great despair. It's like being lost in a great forest. All the roads seem equally hopeless and I have an unpleasant premonition that I'm never going to get away from here, and that if, contrary to expectation, I do succeed, I shall have to pay a high price.

My panic increases in a crescendo and I stumble helplessly on over roots and rubbish. I look up at the sky as it flickers in pale blue streaks behind all the smoke and steam and I think, beloved, good, God...

Then suddenly it's over. I give up. I deliver myself to His will. I can be mocked, spat at, persecuted. If that must be, so be it. God will look after me. He's stretched out His arms to me.

I no longer feel alone.

I go down to a rock by the water and sit there. The water's thick with pollen and twigs and black fibrous lumps. I see a rapid tremor among the rubbish, something shiny making its way in among the protecting branches, perhaps a grass snake.

A fishing boat glides by. A man bare above the waist is standing at the rudder. He's hairy as a ewe; grey curls cover his chest, stomach and shoulders. He looks at me, smiles, and nods; I nod back, he looks up at his sail, then at me again. The boat moves on towards Karlberg.

I don't know how old I was when I began to say evening prayers. Three or four perhaps. An age from which I remember nothing. When I was a little older and had learned to read, I wrote out a prayer I'd found in the hymn book. I suppose I was no longer satisfied with *Our Father*. Perhaps it had dawned on me that one could reach God in many different ways and through many different words. Perhaps I wanted to find a prayer I could feel was my own.

What makes me a bit suspicious, when I look back on it, is that I simplified the prayer a bit, gave it more 'childlike' language, if you will – despite the fact that I had no difficulty whatever understanding the words in the hymn book.

Thus it seems feasible to believe that I wanted to use a little persuasion with God. As if I was hoping He'd be a little more loving if I pretended to be less skilled in language than I actually was.

This suggests a degree of cunning that I find rather depressing. It's generally more common for a child to burn with eagerness to show the world how proficient he is. Obviously I'd already discovered at an early age that there were benefits to be gained from the opposite course of action.

But I took the prayer just as seriously as I do today. I never allowed myself to be satisfied with soulless gabbling. I never went on to the next sentence before the one before it had become entirely meaningful to me. I could wait any length of time, letting a sentence roll backwards and forwards in my head, while I patiently waited for understanding to dawn.

One of the sentences in my evening prayer was: 'I pray for those I find it difficult to like.'

I used often to lie in bed trying to visualise the features of someone who'd done me harm during the day. I wouldn't give up till I hit on someone so contemptible, despicable and detestable that they turned my stomach.

Sometimes it would be one of my brothers. Sometimes my thoughts turned to a local horse-dealer, who in a frenzy had murdered his whole family – a sickly wife and two small children – with an axe.

For many years I would think of a boy called Sven-Åke who lived close by.

Sven-Åke lived with his parents on a bigger farm than ours and had no brothers or sisters. I once asked my mother how that could be, and I remember how silent and embarrassed she became.

On another occasion I heard Father say Sven-Åke was a bit 'different'. I didn't know what he meant. Before it was explained to me, I thought it sounded like something enviable, like floating suspended above everyone else, with the privilege of being fenced off, unlike the other, more 'ordinary' part of the population, who were freely accessible to anyone.

Later I understood that being 'different' was also a form of imprisonment. A loneliness you were born into and couldn't leave. I had assumed that being 'different' was voluntary. Later I understood that it could also be something that hindered you from being with others, and that you were then helplessly stuck in your difference, like a little island in the middle of a great sea.

Sven-Åke and I sometimes played together. But there was an

unpredictability about him that frightened me. One minute we'd be chasing each other and playing tag or hide-and-seek or aiming things at a target. But when we were at our most excited and helpless with laughing at all kinds of things, he could slowly get serious, and I'd realise I'd said something that had made him angry.

It never helped if I tried to explain I hadn't meant anything, and that I was so confused after all the laughing that I had hardly any idea what I'd said. Sven-Åke's fury seemed to grow out of nothing, and once it started nothing could stop it.

It was one of those occasions. We were squabbling about something, the way boys do, and bragging and boasting and trying to get the better of each other. He pointed out that their farm was bigger than ours, which stung me, and I said something about having more elder brothers, and that my family was so much stronger than his.

At that Sven-Åke went quiet. He got up from the floor, where we were sitting, and began sauntering around the room as though looking for something.

I was unprepared for such a reaction, and I'd just begun to blame myself for having really hurt him, and had even started to think up an apology, when he suddenly reached up to a shelf and pulled down my herbarium, which was my dearest possession at the time.

Sven-Åke knew that. I'd once shown him the thick album. He'd been the first person outside the family who'd been allowed to see it. I'd been happy to show it, since he seemed to have noticed that it was something of an honour to be allowed to glance through its pages of pressed plants, which I'd found with my mother and father in meadows and glades and ditches.

But now he opened the album and slowly began to take flower after flower and pinch them to dust between his thumb and forefinger.

I attacked him furiously, hitting and kicking and spitting, but being a few years older than I was and much stronger he had no difficulty at all in holding me off at arm's length.

When I bit his hand hard he boxed my ear, shoved me out of the room and shut the door, and presumably blocked it with the weight of his body, since I couldn't move it.

All the time, in a loud, scornful voice, he shouted out the name of each plant as he crumbled it to dust. I was crying and pleaded with him to stop, but he went on calling out the names – yellow bedstraw, cat's-foot – and finally I heard a thud as he threw the album to the floor, pulled open the door and went out.

I opened the album. A grey-green powder with occasional yellow or lilac fibres was all that was left of my herbarium.

I never dared tell Mother or Father what had happened. I couldn't have borne seeing their dismay. I couldn't cope with the thought that my grief for what had been lost should also affect them. I preferred to bear it alone.

That was the last time I played with Sven-Åke. Some years later the family emigrated to America. But Sven-Åke remained in my prayers for most of my childhood. 'I pray for those I find it difficult to like…' Then I would see his face in front of me. Sometimes with my ruined herbarium lying at his feet. Sometimes he laughed.

Even as a child I knew what God wanted of me: to go up to Sven-Åke after he'd deliberately destroyed the dearest thing I owned, and embrace him.

I could have struck him, or thought out ingenious methods of revenge. But it wasn't for me to punish Sven-Åke. That was God's domain.

It's the same with the man Helga runs from home to meet every day. The man for whose sake she's lied to me in the most underhand way. Time after time. Straight to my face.

I must love him.

★

She's slightly late for the evening meal. Barely ten minutes, to be sure, but even so. Usually she'd be with Märit in the kitchen keeping an eye on the cooking. She once read an article in the papers with advice on diets for people with disturbed hearts. She's put the article up on one of the kitchen cupboards, but she doesn't trust Märit to have learned all the instructions properly by heart.

Helga is in a radiant mood this evening. She comes and kisses me on the cheek. Her skin feels cool and damp.

'How strange you smell,' I say.

'Really?'

I look searchingly at her as she goes to her place. She sits down on her chair and unfolds her napkin. She's a firework display of energetic movements. She meets my eye; I can see no uneasiness in her face, no sense of guilt, only happiness and curiosity.

I wait as long as possible before saying anything. I wrinkle my brow, pretend to be looking for words. In the end she bursts out laughing.

'What do I smell of?'

'I don't know. Smoke from a fire, perhaps…?'

She takes a lock of hair and sniffs at it. She puts on a strange expression.

Then she tells of a waste-site she passed on the way home. Of two men standing by a barrel that was belching out thick black smoke with an atrocious smell. Suddenly she interrupts herself, and says the rest of the story isn't suitable for the dinner table.

I nod and eat a little mushroom omelette. Silence reigns. And at some point, during the brittle clinking of our cutlery, I begin to wonder whether she's just made up this story about the men and the barrel. If it was something she'd fumbled after in desperation, and that perhaps she interrupted herself because she couldn't think how to go on.

I put down my knife and fork, wipe my mouth and ask her to go on with her story.

She chews, looks at me, raises her eyebrows.

'Go on,' I repeat.

She stops chewing, her eyes take on an amused glint and she shrugs her shoulders.

And she tells of some small boys who were out in the street watching the men from a suitable distance and excitedly telling everyone who passed that the men were rat-catchers, and that if you listened carefully you could hear the screams of the dying rats when they were thrown into the fire.

I nod thoughtfully.

No one says anything for a long time.

I keep my eyes on my omelette and watch it growing smaller on my plate. And the asparagus. I cut them into exaggeratedly small pieces, push them into my mouth, one by one, chewing each mouthful for a long time. I take a piece of bread and slowly wipe up the remains of the egg. The piece of bread inexorably gets smaller too.

I sense Helga's searching gaze, it burns my head like the rays of the sun. I think how I've met this moment. One could even say I've enjoyed it. Longed for it, like a holiday. The moment when I would make her answerable.

… oh yes, it's odd, how poorly one can know oneself.

Instead of laying my cards on the table and quietly waiting for her reaction, I sit silent and introspective and feel the paralysis spreading.

All I need do is open my mouth and tell her what's come to my knowledge. What'll happen then I can't predict. But one thing should be absolutely clear: nothing will be again as it was before.

I daren't take the leap. It's as simple as that. And as unbearably difficult.

Paradoxically enough, of the two of us Helga has always been the one who has given evidence of a devoted, even virtually fanatical passion for truth. The least deviation from truth has often given rise to a long-drawn-out depression, and searing self-reproaches. Not even in her social life, where the demand for good manners makes it more or less inevitable that one occasionally does mild violence to strict honesty, has Helga's conscience allowed her to compromise with what she conceives of as the truth. On such occasions she's preferred to stay silent, or changed the subject in a manner that has often seemed brusque.

Yes. Truth and honesty. They've been her most prominent virtues. Her most holy guiding principles. If she perceived the slightest deviation from them she would strike hard and merciless-ly, like a bird of prey, and she wouldn't easily let go with her claws.

How many nights has she not kept me awake because she has heard – or thought she has heard – some change in my intonation that has made her suspicious. How often have I not feared her voice in the darkness beside me, when all tiredness has vanished, little by little, and then her voice is right up against my ear, wide awake and sharp. I know then that she's raised herself into a half-sitting position, and one question follows another, and with every answer I give the atmosphere between us becomes more and more ominous, and the silence more and more fatal.

And what could it be about? In what areas did she imagine she'd caught me being dishonest?

One evening, during our first year as man and wife, she made a largely incidental comment on Lydia. I don't remember exactly what she said, only that it was some mildly condescending obser-vation on Lydia's physiognomy.

It was the first time Helga had referred to my first wife in that manner. I found it unpleasant, and I think I made some objection in the same light tone as Helga had used.

That was enough for her to fall upon me with questions. She wanted to know how often I thought about Lydia. If I still grieved for her. She wanted to know whether Lydia had had any good qualities she herself lacked, and if there were occasions when I wished I was still in my first marriage.

She immediately took the least hint of hesitation in any of my answers as a sign that I was dishonest and trying to wriggle out of something.

It naturally didn't take many minutes for Helga to decide that I had been deceiving her, and had concealed important facts from her.

For this I was punished with several days' silence and gloom, and it wasn't until I made a sacred vow never again to compromise with my honesty or shut anything up inside myself that she opened her arms to me again.

Then she was tender and loving.

Later, in the evening, she met me with wide-open eyes. She looked at me incessantly, up and down, as if she'd never set eyes on me before. Her hands wandered over my body, and I was both embarrassed and depressed when I noticed that they tended to stop on the parts of my body I was most ashamed of. There are places where the skin is particularly loose, and I always avoid looking at the rolls of fat. Helga's hands lingered precisely at these places, and she fondled, fingered and squeezed them, kissing them passionately and greedily with an open mouth.

Afterwards while I lay on her breast, exhausted and happy to have been restored to favour again, she talked of how important it was for her to know if love had anything to offer her, and that the question was vital and she couldn't be satisfied with a few half-hearted attempts.

I think I felt like a schoolboy who had just been caned, and who, when the punishment was over, was told that the blows had been administered with the best will in the world, and that the whole thing had been done out of love and kindness.

Everyone who has ever been in this situation knows how thankful one is for such an explanation, not because it's a particularly good explanation, but because one's despair is so bottomless that one clings to the first hand that offers to pull one up out of it.

The more I think of Helga's passion for truth, and the ways in which it has expressed itself during our years together, the more frightening does she appear, this woman on the other side of the table, the one laying down her knife and fork and sticking the end of a finger into the corner of her mouth to pick some scrap of food out of her molars.

'What's the matter?'

As if in a dream I see her coming towards me, a figure in a blue dress with honey-coloured hair, and I hear the careful tapping of her heels on the floor, slower and slower, and now they've stopped, just beside me, and suddenly her face is close to mine, and I look away, and she smells of the rose water I once bought her in Strängnäs, a large and beautifully shaped bottle, and the glass was matt and a weak reddish colour and nice to hold, and I remember how she looked when she held the bottle under her nose and closed her eyes, and how she said it was a scent she'd keep for special occasions, because it'd be a pity to let it become associated with ordinary days.

And one thought leads to another, that she's been going around smelling of rose water, and I wonder if he complimented her on smelling so good, and above all I wonder what she answered.

I should be furious. I should smash all the furniture. Married men have murdered their wives for considerably less, and it wouldn't surprise me if a court took a lenient view, if it got to hear the whole story.

But things have gone so far that the only thing that bothers me is an almost senseless fear that she will notice something. That her penetrating gaze will find something in my face to arouse her suspicions, and that she'll begin to attack me with questions. It wouldn't take long for her to drag it all out of me.

And then it would be over. I know that. And however contradictory this may sound, it would be linked to her passion for the truth.

First she would be devastated. She would weep floods of tears. She'd wander from room to room whimpering like a wounded animal, and I'd worry that her whimpering could be heard out in the churchyard, and in no time at all I'd be blaming myself for indulging in such trivial speculations when my wife was so heart-rendingly unhappy.

When she had recovered to some extent she would begin to speak, in a dull, toneless voice, and tell me how difficult things have been for her lately, for one reason or another, but that I've been so taken up with my own concerns that I haven't noticed anything, or worse still, I haven't *wanted* to notice anything, so she's been feeling lonely and neglected and virtually invisible.

Then this man appears on the scene. He's kind, thoughtful and attentive, and discusses her spiritual needs with her for hours. What should she do?

I'm pretty well convinced that by the time Helga had finished her presentation, she would have succeeded in convincing me not only that her fall from grace was inevitable, but that I had more or less driven her to it.

And she might be right.

Then she would state that this constituted the death blow of our marriage, and that the only way to resolve the situation is to divorce.

I can see her before me saying it. I can even hear her voice – quiet and firm, with a touch of sadness.

Panic is spreading. I've got to say something.

Without meeting her gaze I tell her about my visit to the baths and my thoughts about my father's death. I take my time, and at some point in the story Märit comes in to clear the table, so I assume one of us must have rung the bell, and I think I detect an amused glint in Märit's eye, and I wonder if the little tableau Helga and I are presenting as she stands over me stroking my head depicts a happy marriage or a disintegrating marriage; then Märit clatters out through the door, and as her steps die away I stumble on with my story, and get rather gripped by it myself. While my mouth talks on a triumphant warmth spreads through my body when I realise how many times I've managed to frustrate Helga's sharp-sighted gaze, and with this very course of action.

She does notice something's the matter with me, and that I'm in a strange mood.

She'll take my account of my father's death as a natural explanation of my gloom. So she can't easily accuse me of lying. I've most certainly been thinking a great deal about my father's death during the day.

The trick is to surround the story with enough serious weight to prevent it occurring to her to ask whether I've got anything else on my mind.

So Helga's got what she wanted: a husband who never lies. (Though clearly this hasn't been enough for her...)

But she's never gained enough power over me to be able to control my choice of what I decide to reveal to her. I've kept that power to myself, and I've used it with all the understanding, restraint and sensitivity that are the most prominent hallmarks of a consummate fraud.

By the time I've finished my story the danger is past. She hasn't noticed anything.

*I*t's like waking up in a new world. Everything must be reconsidered. Not only in the present, but even more with respect to the past.

In the evening I take refuge in the library. I prepare my way carefully. I take several substantial volumes down from the shelves and as I walk past Helga I hold them up so she'll see them; then I give a weary grimace before climbing the stairs with deliberately resolute steps.

I go into the library and shut the door behind me. I light the reading lamp and throw open the window. I breathe in the scent of the chestnut tree, and become aware of all the birds, insects and squirrels that look on that mighty tree as their home.

I watch several people going past below. There's a young man carrying an elegant briefcase with brass mountings that glow in the lantern-light; he's walking slowly, and just before he disappears under the foliage of the chestnut it seems to me that he casts a few searching glances towards the house... and I'm immediately lost in fantasies of how next time they're together he'll tell her how he became so sick with longing he couldn't stop himself taking several turns around the house in the hope of catching a glimpse of her at one of the windows. Perhaps she'll warn him not to be so careless, and he'll hold his hands wide apart and say if only she could have seen with her own eyes what a state he was in every moment she wasn't near him…

Here comes another man, this time walking with rapid steps; he has a wedge-shaped beard over his shirt-front and plunges his walking stick into the gravel with military regularity while a plump little dog trips passively in his wake.

This too could just as well be him. A staid, mature man, but still young enough to be able to acquire an impressive brood of children.

Perhaps he's a big fish in the financial world. Able to provide a bit of worldly stimulus for her. Perhaps he's my absolute opposite in practically every way. Perhaps he's an extrovert who drinks cognac in the evening and presides over noisy dinner parties. Perhaps he sweeps away any objections with a cheap joke and a deafening salvo of laughter… and perhaps Helga finds this is just what she'd been longing for, even though she didn't know it herself. To be belittled, perhaps even ridiculed. Perhaps this gives him a secret power over her that almost frightens her, when she realises she'll have to follow him through fire and water, her willpower as weak as that of a sleepwalker, at the mercy of his slightest whim.

And here I stand, a ridiculous figure, who's devoted years to meeting her halfway and adjusting myself to her wishes while using one pathetic subterfuge after another in an attempt to win her love.

I see her tear her eyes away for an instant from the man with the beard, eyes as dead as the eyes of a china doll, and I seem to hear a little snort as she opens her mouth to say in the tone of a teacher explaining something to a fretful child:

'I want a man. Not a lapdog.'

I sit down in my favourite armchair. I open a book. I hold it so that it looks as if I'm reading.

A knock on the door. I think I see a movement at the keyhole, something white fluttering, is someone peeping in?

'Yes?' I call out.

Helga stands in the doorway holding some newspapers.

'Would I be in the way if I sit here?' she asks.

'No, not in the least,' I answer.

She pads into the room and lights the lamp by the sofa. She stretches herself on the sofa, opens a newspaper and shakes it impatiently several times to straighten a creased page. She lies turned away from me; she could equally well have rested her head on the other arm of the sofa and faced me.

I've lived quite a long life and I've met people of many different kinds.

I've known people who've done remarkable things and endured difficulties most of us can barely imagine. I've also known people who have done the most atrocious things imaginable, not just once but again and again; people who've been severely punished for their evil deeds but who have also been offered love, warmth and understanding and a chance to live in settled circumstances, but who have obstinately turned their backs on everything and thrown themselves into the filth yet again.

In a word, I should be hardened.

But this is something I can't understand.

She lies there carelessly twisting a lock of hair around her finger and twining it between thumb and forefinger. She rubs her bare feet together slowly. She looks up from the paper and over the back of the sofa towards a corner of the room. Perhaps she's looking for a rug to put over her feet. Then she looks down at the paper again. She seems to be reading. Sometimes she raises the paper against the light and sometimes she turns a page. She seems to have found peace in which to concentrate on reading the paper. To think about what's printed there and nothing else, as if there were nothing else in the world to think about.

Recent events wash over me in small painful waves. Apparently insignificant details emerge from oblivion.

A tune she was humming one morning sitting in front of the bedroom mirror, brushing her hair, and how I stopped what I was doing and looked at her, and laughed when I heard the contrast between the peacefulness of her humming and the vigorous sound of the brush through her hair.

Or one morning at the breakfast table, reading aloud from a letter that had just come from her mother. I remember struggling with mild irritation as I'd just taken a mouthful of crispbread when she began to read and so had to sit motionless with my mouth full as the noise of my own chewing made it impossible for me to hear properly. I compensated for this by chewing at high speed at places where she was forced to pause briefly as she struggled to decipher her mother's handwriting. As she read, Helga sometimes looked up at me and we smiled together a little indulgently, for her mother tended to dwell rather feverishly on episodes and events from Helga's early childhood, telling us that she was astonished not only to be able to remember things that happened more than twenty years ago, but to remember them with such sharp clarity and richness of detail, while in contrast she would suddenly find that she had only the vaguest recollection of things that had happened the evening before. Helga read out some recollections of her childhood, and I noticed that she would sometimes glance at me, especially when her mother related things that tore at the heartstrings, and it may be that Helga wanted to find out if I was as moved as she was... and then she broke off her reading abruptly and lifted her arm to study the lace hem of the sleeve of her blouse; perhaps she'd noticed a spot, though it can't have been particularly eye-catching as I couldn't see anything, but she put the letter down and sighed crossly before leaving the room with a furious clattering of heels while I went on sitting where I was, and I can well remember that I smiled that she could be so fussy about her clothes, particularly when she was only going out to meet a friend and help her do a little spring-cleaning...

And then I followed that train of thought no further.

Voices can be heard from downstairs. Märit's voice, servile and anxious, and the voice of a man. Someone not used to keeping his voice down. Someone who has an urgent errand, or at least thinks he has.

Helga and I exchange a glance.

The stairs begin to creak. Helga gets up quickly. I follow her with my eyes. I'm so fixed in my train of thought that I immediately begin to wonder if she thinks it's him, or that it'll be about something connected with him.

Helga doesn't seem to know what to do with herself. She goes to stand behind the sofa, and I realise she's embarrassed to be seen barefoot. For an instant I feel sorry for her. Standing there with her hands on the back of the sofa, white in the face and with red streaks on her throat and cheeks, she presents a miserable illustration of the drawbacks of lying, of everything one didn't think of and couldn't have foreseen when one started lying.

Lying is like an intoxicating drug. As if by a stroke of magic, it cancels all the rules one usually lives by. Lying lures you into an enchanted world where, contrary to the saying, you can have your cake and eat it too.

But when the lies begin to fall apart and the intoxicating effects wear off, you begin to look like Helga behind the sofa: thin-lipped and with the whites of your eyes flickering with panic-stricken suspicions that someone is on to you.

I close my book and put it aside. Someone bangs on the door, so loudly that both Helga and I jump. The door opens and there's

Märit, and beside her a policeman. I know him; his name is Emanuel Tjäder. He nods self-consciously to me. I presume it was him banging on the door.

'Come in,' I say.

Tjäder comes into the room with long, careful strides. We shake hands.

'Please excuse me for…'

'That's perfectly all right.'

He lowers his eyes and sticks his thumbs in his broad belt. He gives a start when he sees Helga.

'Oh, forgive me, good evening, Fru Gregorius…'

Helga hurries forward to greet him, moving in a jerky, nervous way. It's as if, between me and the policeman, she's expecting a sign and, I can't help it, I stand still and enjoy her confusion, and can't even stop myself from turning a demonstrative glance towards her bare feet, treading there so helplessly beneath her.

'I should perhaps… Perhaps you'd like…'

She makes fluttering movements with her hands. Tjäder looks expressionlessly at her. She leaves the room, and when I see how slowly she closes the door behind her I think she would probably have preferred to stay, to settle her unease. This must be the liar's fate. This permanent unease.

I invite Tjäder to sit down. He's breathing heavily. He strokes his moustache and slides his nails up and down a seam in his uniform trousers.

'We've found a man up on Observatory Hill,' he says eventually. 'He'd rolled down the slope a bit. Shot himself with a revolver. Some foreign make, I think.'

'When did this happen?' I ask.

'Not more than a few hours ago. The shot was heard all around. A young couple reached him immediately afterwards, but there wasn't much they could do.'

'Who is he?'

Tjäder looks up, and I look into his steady brown eyes.

'We don't know. But since it happened so near here, Pastor, we thought perhaps you could... He's lying covered up on a cart out here in the street. The gossip's already started, so...'

I nod. We have no time to lose. It's surprising how many people seem to find some sort of satisfaction in bringing news of a death. Perhaps it's just that they feel it makes them important. On more than one occasion overheated gossip has travelled so fast and given rise to such complications and misunderstandings that news of the death has ended up reaching the wrong family.

I know from experience that the police, perhaps because they're short-staffed, are less meticulous when the dead person comes from less well-off levels of society. So I feel able to assume that the man who shot himself up on Observatory Hill isn't just any old tramp.

I go into my study and put on my coat. Tjäder waits for me on the stairs. We go out.

It's an exceptionally dark evening. The wind is sighing through the trees, as if whispering that summer won't last for ever. It wouldn't surprise me if it rained.

The cart's outside the gate, by the street-lamp. An inquisitive crowd has gathered. Tense white faces; a pipe lights up in the dark. A constable is slowly patrolling around the cart, his sabre in his belt and his eyes fixed on the onlookers. A farmer is holding the horses, staring greedily at the constable and the cart behind. He points and turns to someone sitting near him on the box, but then another wagon comes clattering up and wants to get past, and a number of angry words are exchanged before the farmer lashes the reins angrily and moves forward.

'If you would come this way, Pastor...'

Tjäder goes through the gate and stands at the end of the cart, which is covered with grey-green sailcloth, under which the contours of a human body can clearly be seen. I can to some extent understand why the crowd are finding it so difficult to tear themselves away.

The constable keeping guard on the other side has seen us. Tjäder and the constable remove two large stones, which have been holding the cloth in place. I stand waiting with my hands behind my back. The crowd has taken the chance to move a few steps nearer while the constable's back is turned.

I clear my throat, catch the constable's eye and nod discreetly towards the inquisitive crowd, who, studied more closely, reveal themselves to be Stockholm people of every imaginable class: street urchins in frayed clothes, old women from the market with narrow mouths, bright-eyed women rocking children on their hips, red-cheeked students swinging the arms of street-girls who look like withered orchids, distinguished gentlemen glaring through pince-nez and monocles, and a group of society ladies, perhaps on their way home from a soirée, one carrying a pop-eyed little lapdog.

'Now then! Move on, before I arrest the lot of you!'

This time the constable stays where he is, turned towards the crowd with his hand on his sabre.

Tjäder lifts a corner of the sailcloth. I take a step forward. Tjäder lifts more of the cloth, so that the light from the street-lamp falls straight onto the dead man.

First I see the face. Then the wound. Like a crater in his temple, faintly pink with a meaty shine inside, where so many thoughts, memories and hopes once collected and circulated.

I look once again at the face.

There can be no possible doubt. It's Professor Johan Wallgren.

He is barely recognisable. I only met him once. Then his face was full of life. It's true he was trying to hide most of what was going on beneath the surface, but that's life, too.

Now everything in his face, every muscle, has relaxed and gone to rest. His eyes are closed. There's a light scratch on his cheek and a hint of dirt, as if someone has stroked him with earth on their finger.

I nod to Tjäder and say I know who the dead man is.

Tjäder and his constable replace the sailcloth with noticeably careful movements as though tucking the body up in bed, and put back the stones.

Tjäder salutes. They get up on the cart and drive away.

The droshky goes off in the direction of Ladugårds-landet. The rain has still not come. There is an obnoxious stink of filth and urine inside; for some reason I didn't notice it until it was too late to change to another droshky.

I grasp a handrail with one hand and my Bible with the other. The coachman turns around and glares at several young men on velocipedes, sitting on their two-wheelers with straight backs and supercilious expressions as if to say: the future's ours, and there's nothing you can do about it.

The droshky stops at the far end of Brahegatan. I tell the coach-man I'll be back within two hours at most. He nods silently and shows no sign of getting down.

There's an expanse of pasture where the darkness begins behind a row of well-lit, newly-built, four-storey houses. A brew-er's dray passes, silence descends for a short blessed moment, and I seem to hear the sorrowful sound of far-off bells.

It is almost like standing in front of a collection of imposing theatrical props and I get the feeling that a light push would be enough to topple them slowly backwards into darkness.

The Wallgrens' home is directly opposite the new houses. It has a backyard where ivy has climbed the façade of the building like a wild beard, and before I go in through the front door I imagine how the Wallgrens must have shaken their heads in despair and anger at the din caused by the builders and the repeated explosions that must have made the ground tremble underfoot, and how they must have made condescending comments on the ostentation taking shape just across the street, but that even so, almost in secret, they probably could not help feeling excitement as they watched what was coming into existence, and satisfaction at being there in the midst of it, and sitting, as it were, in the front row of the stalls.

I cross the yard. A cat roaming about over by the dustbins stiffens and follows me with its eyes.

I go through the front door and up the stairs, which are lit from the yard outside, but when I reach the first floor it's dark and I move slowly and fearfully, as if crossing creaking ice. The Bible's heavy and sticky in my hand. No sound can be heard from any of the apartments. I climb the next stair and spend a moment collecting myself. Then I knock.

'Who is it?' Fru Wallgren calls through the door. She sounds expectant, not at all suspicious.

I bend closer to the door before answering, since I don't want the neighbours to hear.

She unlocks the door and there she stands. She has a little smile on her face, but when she sees how serious I am it dies away, leaving only anxiety.

She's wearing an elegant cream-coloured silk dressing gown with an embroidered hunting motif. She peers over my shoulder to see if there's anyone with me. How many times have I not seen that look in someone's eyes? I step inside.

We go into the drawing room. It is sumptuously furnished and full of exotic ornaments. Out of the corner of my eye I see an armchair covered in zebra skin, and on the wall something with gigantic horns that looks like the head of a buffalo. I have time to think that this must be the first time anyone has come into this room without looking around and asking questions about the Wallgrens' extensive travels.

I ask her to sit down. Then I sit down beside her on the sofa and tell her what's happened.

She takes her eyes off me. She nods slowly. Her hands are a whitening knot on her knees. She looks older than I remember.

'I know that revolver,' she says.

I don't answer. She looks at me, clears her throat a little and makes a strangely wave-like gesture with her arm towards an adjoining room.

'It was only the other day. He – we – have several, in a cupboard on the wall. Every conceivable kind, and knives, daggers… all kinds of weapons. I noticed one was missing. Johan said… I can't remember his exact words, but that the revolver had been attacked by something, rust perhaps, or… and that he was going to hand it in.'

She falls silent. She looks as if she's trying to remember the moment. To hear his voice, just as it was. She moves her lips silently and nods.

'Hand it in to some expert.'

She laughs and shakes her head.

'He could have made me believe anything.'

Then comes a deep sigh. And then tears.

I take her hands in mine. She leans against my shoulder. I put my arm around her. We sit like that for a while. I'm conscious of the scent of her hair. The warmth rising from her head.

Then she straightens up. She asks some practical questions. I answer as best I can.

I notice a light as of flames from inside the apartment. I ask her if she has any candles burning. She nods and leaves the room. The light goes out. She comes back.

'I'd prepared supper,' she says. 'Something we'd planned.

To eat together, just him and me, after the boys were asleep.'

'Were you going to celebrate?' I ask cautiously.

Fru Wallgren smiles.

'Yes, you could say that. An anniversary.'

She drops her eyes, and for a moment seems embarrassed.

'I've always been a little childish in that way,' she goes on. 'I fix certain days in my mind. Days when something significant happened. Later it doesn't feel right to let the anniversary of what happened pass as though it was nothing special.'

I say that sounds a pleasant way to add a silver lining to everyday life, and to keep hold of the happy elements in life before they are swept away by the whirlwinds of time. I say that it's really incomprehensible that we only celebrate events and people we have no personal contact with.

We sit a long time in silence. She pulls the dressing gown more tightly around her body and turns away her face.

I look around the room, at all the animal heads and pieces of cloth, all the pots and trinkets. There are several drawings hanging over a chiffonier. They show a man who looks like an American Indian. He has a stick or a bone stuck through his nose. He is smiling shyly and looks friendly and harmonious, and I think of all the journeys the Wallgrens made together, and of the journeys I've made myself both with Lydia and Helga, and I remember the particular feeling travelling brought, and which I often thought of nostalgically when we were back home and life was running its usual course again.

On journeys we had to work out new daily routines. Nothing was the same as usual. Nothing could be taken for granted. It was as if we'd been shipwrecked on a desert island. We had no choice but to help each other, we were completely dependent on each other, and perhaps for this reason became both more tender and more attentive towards each other.

'Why did he choose to die today of all days?' asks Fru Wallgren suddenly. 'We've just had an exceptionally happy time together. I can't remember when last we lived on such intimate terms. Something decisive happened between us while we were sitting and talking with you. I think it was the first time we were both able to tell each other what was weighing so heavily on our minds. We were able to speak freely from our hearts... indeed, we felt more or less *compelled* to do so.'

She laughs, then immediately becomes serious again.

'And with time I came to feel certain that I could love him again. He understood how vulnerable I felt when I showed him my little proofs of affection, and how much it hurt me when he didn't accept them or respond to them. I can't say I noticed any dramatic change in him. But I realised that it didn't matter. It was enough that he understood.

'I understood some other things too. For instance, that there are limits to what one can expect of another person. The changes I once hoped for were, quite simply, not possible for him. But I saw that he was doing what he could. And it did him good that I saw that.

'Not least I was happy for the sake of the boys. I know how it feels to grow up in a loveless home. When things were at their worst in my own marriage I used to think, this is like a curse resting over my family, a curse I thought I could break, but it caught up with me in the end. You know, when we came up to you that afternoon, I saw the whole thing mainly as a final formality, really, as if you were going to rubber-stamp a document for us.'

Fru Wallgren has more and more let herself be enclosed in the bright, confident and hopeful frame of mind that seems to have marked the last weeks of her marriage. Her voice and face show signs of sadness at the thought of the difficulties she's gone through, and of relief that these now lie behind her. She is happy to talk to me about these things since I'd actually been there when the silence inside her marriage had been broken and the bitterness dispelled, if only temporarily.

She's the recovered patient who runs into her doctor at a street corner and tells him how happy she is not to be ill any more. She's temporarily forgotten that her husband is dead, and this will not be the last time she forgets.

Grief's like a shy animal. At first you can easily chase it away. But it gradually creeps nearer and nearer, and sooner or later you find it in your house. And there it stays.

Fru Wallgren stiffens and looks me up and down as if she's only just realised that I'm sitting beside her. Impotence sinks into her like a knife and twists in the wound. She shakes her head and looks appealingly at me; her lips move, but it takes time before she can formulate what she wants to say.

'I don't know… This may sound a bit mundane and trivial on an evening like this, but… you understand… the supper we'd planned to eat together. And the anniversary I mentioned earlier.'

She pauses to take a breath, struggles to get the words out, grips my hands hard.

'I don't want to be too personal. But it was the anniversary of an event that concerned Johan and me. Something we had reason to be happy about, not least today, and that we hadn't given any thought to for several years. But today we were going to. And it was to be…'

She slumps, shakes her head and straightens up again.

'It was to have been an evening when we'd sit face to face and be happy about everything that's happened recently. I'm certain he was happy about it too. I know it! So I don't understand. Why did he do it on this of all days?'

Fru Wallgren takes deep tremulous breaths. She stares at me and makes a huge effort to hold back her tears.

I free my hands from her powerful grip, and then stroke her hands carefully with the ends of my fingers till they lie at rest.

And I say perhaps it was precisely because they were about to celebrate this anniversary and eat a special supper together that he couldn't bear to live any longer.

I try to explain that while love's something bright and wonderful, something we all search for, there are also people who can't take it and are so afraid of it they'd rather face death.

She frowns and slowly shakes her head.

'Why are they afraid?'

'For some people,' I tell her, 'love's like a place they constantly long for and search after, but once they are there, or perhaps only in the vicinity, or on the right way, then it seems they also remember it's a place where they were once deeply unhappy, or hurt deep inside. And however much they would like to enter that place again with confidence and hope, the memory of the pain they were caused that time is even stronger, and they flee, as far away as they possibly can.'

'Can nothing help them?'

I look at her and take a breath. Suddenly I feel the familiar movement inside my ribcage, and all at once everything goes black before my eyes, as if someone has drawn a veil over my face. I tremble and feel sweat breaking out on my brow and upper lip. It's as though I'm falling headlong, tumbling like a heavy stone through great darkness, while somewhere far above I can hear myself giving an embarrassed laugh and saying something dismissive about my weak heart.

And in the midst of my fall a silent howl breaks from my lips, a howl of disappointment and dismay that life passed so quickly, that there was so much I never had time for, and that everything I so persistently hoped for was never fulfilled, and that I never even had the small comfort of knowing that someone would be standing on the shore gazing after me with longing and grief as I vanish behind the veils of mist. A bitter black thought flutters by, that all I'm leaving is an unfaithful young wife who is so relieved to be rid of me that she can scarcely be bothered to remain until they have pulled up the gangplank.

'Pastor?'

'There is a way of salvation,' I hear myself saying in a hoarse unsteady voice that doesn't go well with my comforting words, and I notice how shyly Fru Wallgren looks at me when I talk of God's grace and how important it is to trust in it.

I cough and clear my throat but the hoarseness remains.

'Those who have the courage to allow themselves to be enclosed in God's love and bow before His almighty power, are also granted a sense of the splendour that love between two people can offer.

'To be able to give love to another person, and also to be able to receive it, you must dare to believe that someone's there to catch you if you fall. But you must also have the courage to be resigned to what's bigger than yourself. You described it beautifully just now when you were talking about your husband and realised there were sides to him you couldn't change, and that were perhaps beyond his power to change as well. When you humbled yourself before this you found your love wasn't cramped or diminished, but rather that it grew greater. Isn't that true?'

She nods calmly and thoughtfully.

'When you and your husband came to see me, he talked about his inability to feel love deep down in his heart. He talked about how men and women live in far-off lands, and if I understood him correctly, he meant there was so much of value in your marriage that it would have been folly to dissolve it. And it seemed as though he managed to convince you.'

'Yes.'

I sit in silence for a moment. I hesitate for a long time, wondering whether she will be able to bear my thoughts. But in the end I take the leap.

'I don't know what drove your husband to this. No one can know that. But you say you were happy together recently. Happier than for a long time.'

'Yes, we were.'

'Perhaps he realised that he'd been wrong. Perhaps he'd discovered that love had found a way into his heart. That the road lay open before him, and that there was no longer anything for him to hide behind. Perhaps it terrified him. Perhaps he realised he couldn't go down that road no matter how much he might want to. And perhaps that failure became too much for him to bear.'

Fru Wallgren has turned white. I see I was right, that she does know about this.

Suddenly she breaks into a smile.

'You speak so wisely, Pastor Gregorius. I'm so glad you're here.'

I go on looking into her eyes, as if I don't have the courage to believe what I'm seeing in them. Then I turn away.

I sit with a bright, devout expression fixed on my face, and I can't help agreeing with her. I too feel I'm speaking wisely. I believe in what I'm saying and it makes me happy that she finds comfort in my words.

Even so, I feel terribly sad.

When I go down, the stairs are bathed in moonlight. When I come out into the yard I see it, large and dazzling white against all the black. Strangely enough I can't see any stars. It's as if the moon wants all its brilliance for itself.

The droshky's waiting on the other side of the road. When the driver sees me he bends over and snaps his fingers, causing a dog to come cringing to him from nowhere. It tramples the dust in front of its owner uneasily, steadies itself and leaps onto the box.

I go to the driver and tell him I prefer to walk home. Despite the fact that I pay what I owe and more he says nothing, just clicks his tongue in irritation and drives off.

I walk down towards Strandvägen. The moonlight has blotted out all colours and painted the city silver-white against harsh black shadows. People exchange cheerful glances. Many have opened their windows; I see men in nightshirts leaning out and puffing at their pipes. Perhaps their wives have been scolding them for filling the already stuffy air inside with tobacco smoke.

'God bless you, Pastor!' someone shouts. I glance at the place the voice seems to come from, but see nobody.

When I reach the top of the hill I see Strandvägen's electric lights glittering a few blocks away, and I pass a group of men queuing outside a doorway.

As I pass I look in. A bareheaded man is sitting on the steps below the door. He doesn't see me, he has turned to open the door a little, as if to check something, and there in the dim interior I catch a glimpse of a woman kneeling in front of a man. Her hair is tousled and the light flickers, perhaps it is a torch hanging on the wall. The man towers over the woman like a tree; he's unbuttoned his trousers and is holding them up with one hand while he grasps the woman's hair with the other, and she moves her head from left to right, and her white cheek bulges.

The door closes again. The man on the steps turns and gives me a steady look. He's dressed in black, as I am, and lifts a cigarette to his mouth with what seems a deliberately slow gesture.

The men queuing outside the door watch me expressionlessly as I go by. They're wearing caps and dusty jackets. One turns around to say something to the man behind him, then faces forward again with an embarrassed laugh lingering on his face, as if finding it mildly annoying that a priest should be happening to pass by – mildly annoying, nothing more. At least, nothing to stop him staying where he is and waiting his turn.

I hurry on.

It's late now. I stand in the churchyard, in the moonlight, and look at the house that is my home. Lights off, windows closed, curtains drawn. It seems wrapped in tissue paper. As if sleeping the long sleep of the Sleeping Beauty.

I walk in, take off my shoes, pad up the stairs, open the bedroom door a crack. A streak of light has forced an entry, illuminating the contours of her body under the sheet.

I close the door again and move away a few steps, towards the library, and stop. Did I really see a body in the bed? Or was it just a tangle of sheets and covers?

I open the door again and slip into the room and towards the foot of the bed, until I can be sure I've seen her head on the pillow.

This time I stay in the bedroom. I start undressing as slowly as possible, to give my eyes time to adjust to the darkness. But I am also slow because although I'm home again, my home isn't what it used to be.

I see the roundness of my wife's body under the sheet and almost have to make an effort to remember everything that's happened. Something incredulous and somnambulistic has attached itself to me, something I can't shake off. As if the whole thing's a bad dream, or a fantasy that has run away with me, and I shall wake up from it soon, and then everything will be as it was before.

I slide under the covers. This time I don't turn away from her as I usually do. I lie with my face near hers and wait for it to move forward from the shadows. Then I regret it. As if something inside my head is whispering a warning to me. I shut my eyes, thinking I ought to be tired. I should soon be sinking into sleep. At any moment now. But I don't. At any moment now.

My thoughts have other ideas. They pull me in all directions, like playful sprites.

They pull me down the stairs, into the laundry room. There's something they want to show me. They lift the lid of the basket, and I go forward to it. There are our dirty clothes. I put my hand in among all the shirts, linen and stockings. I stir them like a cooking pot. There are Helga's soft white soiled underclothes. So much of the scent of her soft skin still lingers in the cloth that I'm holding carefully in my fingers, and the sprites nod eagerly and I run my fingers over the cloth, and inside her knickers to the most intimate place, and now I realise why: I want to know if anything has seeped out of her. And indeed, the cloth does seem a little stiffer just there. But I have to be sure. Best to breathe in the smell from her most private place, and try to find out if it smells of woman or man.

Then my thoughts let me go and I open my eyes, and she's lying there, now I can see her clearly, dark eyebrows, full lips, white hands tucked under her cheek. She seems to be smiling a little; can she be dreaming of him?

My thoughts grab me again, and put me back in front of that doorway. The black ponce has gone and this time the door glides open of itself. There are twice the number of men in the queue, no, even more, the queue winds right around the block, and the woman inside is Helga, kneeling in front of a stevedore with a greasy cap pulled far down over his eyes who takes a deep pull at a cigarette and breathes out a cloud of smoke at the damp ceiling full of waving spiders' webs, and Helga doesn't move vigorously and impatiently like the woman I saw earlier, but more slowly, with more real passion, and I stand numb and paralysed then open my mouth and say, My dear, how can you do such a thing, how can you defile yourself in this way, why are you throwing away the dearest thing you have, why let it be so carelessly trampled into the mud, and then I hear Helga's voice beside me, we're standing arm in arm, and she looks at herself there inside the doorway, and she presses my arm playfully before looking up at me and saying with a laugh: My dear, there are so many things you don't know.

And I turn to her as she stands by my side, and I ask if she's the woman we can see in there behind the door, and she shakes her head, and I'm silent for a moment, then I ask her if she'd like to be the woman in there behind the door, and she pauses before answering, then, in a teasing tone she says: Yes…?

And I say: Just imagine, I was so wrong.

She sighs: Yes, and it wasn't the first time.

I hear a movement from under Helga's cover, and stiffen as her fingers run over my cheek. They feel unnaturally large. But there's no doubt they are Helga's fingers.

I open my eyes and see her pull back her arm. Her eyes are shut. I hardly dare breathe.

I wonder if I've let out a sound, or have somehow revealed how much I'm suffering from being driven about so helplessly by my thoughts. I wonder if she can somehow hear what I'm thinking, even when I'm lying as silent as a mouse, or when I'm in another room, or at the other end of the city, perhaps that's how it is when you've known each other as long as we have and been so close. But in that case why have I been so incapable of hearing what she thinks? Presumably because she's wiser, or in some primitive way more cunning than I am.

And there it comes, like a knife in the chest, and grief wells out and drags me down: grief at being so abandoned, so much in the power of one who is so careless with, and so indifferent to, her own omnipotence.

It's hot and sticky under the sheet, and my whole body's in rebellion, especially down there, the stump rising like a blind animal, heaving itself out of its hole and standing there swinging, damp and trembling with tension like a cat about to spring.

I reach out my hand and answer her caress, and my action is so identical with hers that it has something of a ceremonial quality, and she emits a sleepy sound, heavy and warm with pleasure, and rubs her cheek against my fingers before her head lays itself to rest again, and there comes a new knife in my breast, but this time a knife of tenderness as I see again the long-legged little girl, she who was so fond of games and round-dances, she who sometimes, waiting for her turn, waiting for someone to throw her the ball, could make an unconscious little calf-like jump on the spot, a movement that she was clearly unconscious of, and that expressed nothing but her joy in being alive, like an elk leaping over a ditch.

And then the little girl stands in front of the mirror and sculpts a woman's body with her slim fingers with their sore cuticles, and no one knows her as I know her, and no one loves her as I love her.

And I can interpret the voluptuous sound that came from her in various ways and I'm paralysed between one interpretation and another: either there's something in her that understands our profound affinity and only answers to me, a voice no one else can hear, or perhaps she's so muddled and half asleep that she mistakes me for him, implying that her sexual desires are wandering rudderless over the sea, freely accessible to anyone who'd like to help himself.

And in between these interpretations I can't bear to live. I know that now.

I see Johan Wallgren's body on the cart, I see the cart creaking on its way, his body jerking and bumping under the sailcloth, and I'm gripped by a longing to be allowed to take his place, to be extinct, in bottomless darkness, in total rest.

So that is the point I've reached.

I sit up in bed. As if that could chase away my thoughts, scare them back into their holes.

Helga moves, she's woken up.

'What is it?'

I'm so happy she's woken. That I no longer need be alone.

She raises herself on her elbow and blinks sleepily at me. A bow on her nightdress has come untied. I can see a breast, white and soft, its red-brown nipple a bud ready to burst into flower. I bend over her and try to kiss her, but she sets her hand against my chest and twists her head away.

'No… You know what the doctor said…'

'Please…'

'No!'

I take hold of her chin, manage to hold her head, our lips meet. My kiss isn't entirely unanswered. Her breathing, through her nose, is agitated.

I pull up her nightdress, rub the stump against her silky smooth legs, higher and higher up. She twists and struggles under me, says I'll make her ill, asks if that's what I want.

And there's something about her struggles, I can't explain what it is, perhaps her fear or fury, that infects me. I have a feeling the woman beneath me is mad, on the way to losing her mind, and I hold her harder and try to talk to her to calm her, I get a suspicion she's not properly awake, or that she's having a nightmare, or that she's confusing me with someone else, so I kiss her again, a little harder, to make her understand it's me, her husband. The man to whom she once said 'I will', promising to love him for better or for worse, instead of as now, neither for better nor for worse.

She's still struggling under me, still trying to wriggle away, but at the same time moving her legs gently as if in sleep, rubbing her warm skin backwards and forwards over the stump and it is like fleeting caresses, and the stump wants to enter her where it is even warmer, the stump has refused to be frightened off, and the thought hisses into my brain that this is the only thing it is for. It could have created life, it could have driven away my loneliness, and it could have filled my empty rooms with laughter and bright voices, with loving responsibilities and sacred duties. But as I near the end of my life I'm forced to realise that this is all it has come to. The quivering stump that with a few strong thrusts makes its way into her warmth where it squelches about, in and out in blind animal lust, with no purpose but instant gratification, and for a moment I see the man inside the doorway, and he lifts his eyes from the tart beneath him, and he looks straight at me and nods cheerfully, as if we are on close and equal terms.

Now familiar rank smells begin to rise from between her legs, and her movements change; at times she lies limp and passive, begging me in a heartbreaking wail to stop, at times she grips me and drives her nails hard into my flabby flesh before letting go again, and it feels as though the stump is flying free through the air enclosed in warm winds, I can't remember it ever having felt like this before, and at a certain point she twists to one side as if trying to get out of bed but I take a firm grip and force her down on her back again like a sack of potatoes, and press her down, and she lets out a sound like a stifled cry, a defeated protest, but the sounds go on coming from her, louder and louder, while at the same time she begins to meet me more and more savagely and violently, almost as if making small leaps at me, and when I look at her she stares back with wide-open eyes, and from her wide-open mouth comes a bellowing sound while her lips shiver and tremble. Then she stiffens in a convulsion, as if all her muscles have locked fast. And I think: this is it, now I've killed her.

But she collapses and lies still and passive, with her head turned away and her breast heaving with deep sobs, and I go on moving inside her, almost embarrassed, till deliverance comes.

The mists disperse, then it's just her and me.

Now the curtain's edged with grey light, and outside day is dawning.

We lie silently beside each other and look up at the ceiling. Her breathing's calmer. The first carts are driving to the market with a dull and heavy sound.

I'm lost in daydreams about her voice, gentle and husky, close to my ear, whispering that I'm paying no attention to Dr Glas's orders. And for her, even if this was the last thing she should ever experience, she'd think it was worth it. She can't imagine a better way to die. Can you?, she whispers.

She whispers. And even though she's talking of such serious matters, I think I can detect something ambiguous and mocking in her voice. I turn my head and look at her. It's true, there is a mischievous glint in her eye. She kisses the end of my nose light-ly and softly. Or perhaps my mouth.

Actually, it's been silent a long time now. Silence doesn't suit me. It never has. Some people are perfectly comfortable in silence. I assume they must be equipped with some kind of feelers that I lack. They seem to be capable of judging to what extent a silence is harmonious or ominous. To me, all silences are ominous. Often it becomes clear that I've got it wrong, but by then it's too late. By that time I've already managed to destroy the silence by talking.

I don't know what happened. But I do know this much, that we've just seen aspects of each other we've never seen before. A word comes to me from nowhere: speechless. That we're speech-less, rather than silent.

I turn towards her. She's lying turned away from me, I can't see her expression. Perhaps she's fallen asleep. I reach out a hand to stroke her cheek.

First she twists herself away. Then she sits up on the edge of the bed. Harsh, brusque movements, like an explosion in the calm.

I recoil, in a reflex action, and I see her white figure on the edge of the bed, and her plait against her nightgown like a frayed, half unravelled stump of rope, and though everything's familiar she could be someone else, or a great beast that feels trapped and might at any moment rush in any direction.

'Helga?'

'Be quiet!'

It comes like a hiss.

She turns towards the window and sits frozen in this position for a moment, as if thinking something over. Then she gets up and goes to open the wardrobe door.

'What are you doing?' I ask.

No answer. She takes out a garment, holds it up close in front of herself, hangs it up again, takes out another one.

I get out of bed and go over to her. I'm naked. I take hold of her shoulders. She shakes herself in irritation.

'You can't go now.'

She tries to move away from me. I put my arms around her from behind and bury my face in her hair. She grunts at me between clenched teeth to let go. She accidentally treads on my toes, which is very painful. But nothing hurts me more than holding her and breathing in the scent of her hair feeling her trying to free her body, and knowing that these days, this is the only thing that's holding her back. The strength of my muscles.

I rattle away endlessly: you can't go now. I scarcely recognise my own voice. So miserable, so helpless, whining. Like someone who has been abandoned long ago who'd rather die than admit the fact. My lamentations pull me down into wider whirls and then I begin to cry.

She quietens down. Stands with her arms hanging and her head bowed.

There's so much I want to tell her. About the new side to her I've seen, and how it hasn't made me love her any the less, but rather more. And perhaps she sees it the same way. At least it's a possibility. It's here with us, in the room. All we have to do is choose it. But I can't do that on my own. It would be no good. Helga must do it with me.

Nothing is said. You can't speak with so much weeping in your throat. After a while I feel the weight of her neck against my shoulder as if she's surrendering. Letting herself rest. Then I stop restraining her, and embrace her. And we go and lie down.

I'm woken by the sound of heels on the floor. I lift my head and catch a glimpse of Helga, she is on her way out, she is dressed, and light is flooding in through the open door.

I call after her. She stops in the doorway. I'm altogether too dazed to focus my eyes, and I haven't got my glasses: she's standing like a blurred streak in the light, almost as if carbonised.

'Are you on your way out?' I ask.

'I'm going for a walk,' she says.

Her voice is neutral. She sounds like a schoolmistress. She pulls the door shut behind her.

I feel an impulse to get up and run after her. But I'm too tired. I open my mouth to call out something, but she's already halfway down the stairs.

I look up at the ceiling. Fragments of yesterday begin to flit past in my head.

I get up, go over to the window, push aside the curtain. And I stand outside looking in, seeing myself, the gap in the curtain, the anxious half face.

Something white passes by under the window. It must be her. Perhaps she knows exactly which way to go to keep out of my field of vision.

I fall on my knees by the bed. I clasp my hands and close my eyes. I try to take long deep breaths. I turn to God.

But I can't. It's as if I'm no longer sure who I am. It's like trying to write someone a letter to explain something you don't understand yourself. You don't even know what it was you wanted to explain.

God turns a glassy gaze on me, as if I were a stranger. As if His love has clouded over. And it's so cold without His love.

I get up and put on my clothes but the cold remains, it doesn't leave my side, and going down the stairs I feel my whole being humming with a blind, restless need for activity, and for a moment I'm transformed into an ant in an anthill, scrambling over obstacles, gathering food and fighting enemies. I move slowly in the cold and quickly in the heat, and everything's related to survival, there's never been anything over and above that. And I wonder whether this is how it is for those who deny God, whether it's with these expressionless insect eyes that they regard the world.

When Märit brings my breakfast I say 'Good morning' but she pretends not to hear. I fix my eyes on the bread, egg and coffee; I force the corners of my mouth into a carefree expression and try to look like someone facing the day with confidence, but a blush spreads over my face and mercilessly betrays me as I realise she must have heard everything, that she must have been sitting bolt upright in bed listening to the sounds from upstairs.

I look for something to say, decide on the weather, ask if it's as hot as usual today, but she drowns my words by clattering the tray and leaves the room.

My shame doesn't quite have a proper hold over me. I have other things to think of.

I can see Helga hurrying through the lanes. How she pinches her lips, chews them until they bleed, staring at the paving stones. Then she arrives at the doorway and hurries in, her chin beginning to tremble, hardly able to control herself any longer, and rushes up the stairs with skirts rustling and knocks on a door, breathing heavily, and the door opens and she falls into his arms and weeps, and he's cool and neat and smells good, and has clear dark eyes, like a forest pond, and while the sun moves through the sky she lies in his arms and tells him what's happened.

Both are serious and depressed. Especially him. Of course he's always known she's married, but to him that's nothing worse than having a demanding employer, who needs her to go in every day working herself to the bone. He can't help noticing that she goes off to work with a heavy heart and is often gloomy when she comes back, and naturally it would be better if she didn't have to go back, but things are as they are, and it'll have to do till they've managed to work out a better solution.

Now I've crashed the wall and broken the membrane of their

little soap bubble, and when he looks at her he'll think he can see the imprint of my hands like dirty stains on her white skin.

But nothing binds two people closer together than knowing they have a common enemy, and when that enemy advances and reaches the gates of the city they become indissolubly combined, and they act as though they were one and the same.

Indeed, it's like a miracle. Every time a word passes her lips, every moment she spends huddled in his arms and every time he caresses her hair it's as if he's washing her clean of my imprint, and the Helga that's his begins to reappear, and soon she belongs entirely to him.

Such is the power of love. It can mend what seemed broken beyond repair. It can heal wounds one thought fatal. But at present the power of love is not in my service.

I look down at my plate. I've shelled the egg. I have laid out the shell on the plate, and I've broken each piece with my thumb, carefully and methodically. The sort of thing you do while thinking about something else.

It's a beautiful pattern.

A moment ago it was the protective covering of something that might have become a life. Now it's been completely eaten and every bit of its shell crushed, and the plate is staring at me like a great burst eye. I let the fragments be. I want somebody to find them.

I tell Georg I've an appointment with the doctor, but I don't say when. Then I go out.

It's been raining during the night. Perhaps this is why all the colours shine so intensely and the sky's such an unnatural blue. The rain's whipped all the whirling dust and ash to the ground. It even seems to me that sounds are louder than usual.

I slowly cross Stortorget. No sudden movements in my heart, only a slight gnawing pain.

I take a turn around the square. I think about the monkey I saw that time, his desperate smile. In the middle of the square a large pile of potatoes spreads an obnoxious smell. All who pass it automatically put a hand over their noses and look around angrily. An old woman with a rough voice breaks into what sounds like a bitter defensive speech.

Then I stop and look down the alley.

It's all down there. Exactly as Johan Laurén said.

There's the tailor's. There's the doorway. It's black. The doorknob is an artistic shape. The building doesn't look shabby. That could be a good sign. Or equally well a bad sign.

I don't know how long I stand there. I've carried anger before me as if on a tray throughout this walk, moving carefully for fear of dropping it. I know well how easily it can happen. A careless movement, an impulse from some direction, an association from nowhere. Then the rage falls from my hands, and everything remains as it has always been.

I've made up my mind. This was the last lie. When she comes out through that door I shall speak my mind regardless of the consequences.

I know exactly what I'll say. The words are rolling backwards and forwards in my head. Now and then I whisper them to myself; it's as though I can't get enough of them.

She may cook up some fantastic story. Some richly ornamented tale, full of details and digressions, as she has so successfully done before.

I shall just stare at her. I know the sort of look that bites a liar best. Not loathing or reproach. Compassion. Come on out, I shall think. Leave your world of make-believe. I know how unhappy living there is making you.

That look usually brings results. Though I'm not sure how it'll work with Helga. She's become hardened. But I have my rage.

A ringing sound recalls me to reality. I don't know where it came from. I take a few steps down the alley. I pass the doorway, glance at the doorknob. Is it meant to be a snake or a dragon? I don't have time to tell. I only have time to wonder how the dragon or snake would feel against the palm of my hand. Or whether the street door makes any particular sound, or has any particularities Helga has learned to recognise. A creaking perhaps, or an awkward stone one must ease the door over. Perhaps the dragon, or snake, shows up in their letters and notes, a secret language they have in common, like spies behind enemy lines, 'The dragon longs for your warm hand...'

Further down the alley there's a spice shop with some baskets of flowers outside it, and a young girl sitting at a table binding wreaths. She gives me an embarrassed glance before going on with her work. She picks flowers from a basket, pulls a string from her apron pocket, ties up the bunch and lays it carefully on the table.

I stop to admire the flowers. She seems to have every colour in her basket, every one, it's like a thought-game. I look from one flower to another. Then I notice a certain uneasiness has crept into the girl's movements.

I go into the shop and ask for a glass of water. The rich scents are overpowering. As so often when magnificent impressions strike my senses, my thoughts turn to God's care, and the abundance and exuberance, not to say the extravagance, of His love for us.

The shopkeeper's a little man with white hair. He's very friend-ly and obliging, and before I've even had a chance to ask he's brought out a chair and invited me to sit at the table with the flowers. The girl looks confused and pulls the flowers towards her then seems not to know what to do with them, but I assure her that I don't need any space at her table.

The shopkeeper goes in. I take small mouthfuls of the water, which is cold and fresh, and feel a series of shivers as it percolates down into my stomach. From where I'm sitting I have a good view of the doorway. I'd like to start a conversation with the girl, but while I'm trying to think of something suitable to say she takes her basket, which is still half-full, and goes into the shop.

Her departure makes me strangely depressed.

I drink half my glass and look around the alley. Streams of peo-ple are passing at both ends. Elegant clothes, whites and purples, vigorous walking sticks, slowly revolving wheels, passing dream-like fragments of the city. But in the alley it's silent and dark. A reflection of the sun glides across a façade, somewhere a window closes with a sound like a furtive drumbeat.

I think of all the times Helga must have hurried down the alley towards the crowd at the end, the light and the passing voices.

I think about last night.

I still can't see it as clearly as I'd like. But I know there's something there. Something important.

All these things happening.

Helga's illness.

The man she's running to meet.

The lies she's thrown at me.

And last night too, when we met as if in a dream landscape where we've never been before, where love and hate, desire and disgust, longing and despair existed side by side, and everything struck us with devastating power.

Perhaps it would be wrong to sort these events into good and evil, right and wrong. Perhaps they have come together to place us at a crossroads, where one way will bring us closer together, and the other will drive us further apart.

I hardly think Helga will have formulated it for herself like this. I think she's mostly done what she's felt like, and then later worked out a scenario to make what she's done look less deceitful.

I can see her before me, moving through her past, and our shared past, as if through a marketplace where she can pick what suits her purpose; some heads of lettuce may be spotted and ugly, but if she tears off a few leaves a quick glance may pass them as edible, so she pushes them into her basket, and going further on sees some object that could be useful if she gives it a new coat of paint...

This isn't true only of Helga. I suppose it's what most people do. They embark on various courses of action without giving them much thought.

A happy (or unhappy, depending on how you choose to look at it) minority of us will perhaps begin to wonder much later how we ended up on this particular path. Perhaps we'll remember how it happened.

Or perhaps not.

We choose some directions through active decisions. Others, at least equally meaningful, are reached by remaining passive and doing nothing at all.

Helga has faced many crossroads recently, but she's done so alone. If I'd had the chance to be with her, I could have said yes or no; I could have gone with her, or turned off in another direction of my own. But she has insisted on rushing off by herself, lying to free herself and straying ever further away from me.

One single time we have stood at the crossroads together, and that was last night, when she lay under me, and that deep bellow rose from her, and she let me stare down into a volcano where hitherto unknown streams of lava were running together. This could have brought us closer together than ever before.

But she turned away.

I wonder why the girl doesn't come back. She's left some of her wreaths on the table. Perhaps she's lingering inside, waiting for me to go.

I wonder what she saw in me. Whatever it was, it clearly didn't arouse much sympathy in her. That, of course, I'm used to.

It's certainly strange. Some people cause happiness and curiosity simply by existing and spread a warm, open atmosphere around themselves without having to make any effort at all.

Halvar's like that. If he'd been standing before her, she would have looked up at him with eyes glittering with a kind of hunger, as if to say: Who are you? Tell me, and then I'll tell you who I am, and I know we'll enjoy ourselves!

If it were a question of looks, and of some people having more attractive features than others, I'd certainly be able to accept that. But Halvar's not much better looking than I am.

So what is it about me that causes such alarm and gloom? It must be something.

If I weren't a priest but something worldly and harmless, like a shoemaker, I'm sure I'd be completely ignored.

As a priest I do at least arouse a degree of fear. Not a fact that gives me pleasure. But better than nothing.

Soon she'll be here. Soon everything will be turned on its head.

I wonder what she'll do when she sees me standing before her. I suspect she'll lose her temper. That is, after all, the most common reaction.

There are limits to how much of themselves people can bear to see. Helga seems to have devoted a great deal of trouble and effort to concealing her deceitfulness and arranging and ornamenting it in various ways, so that by now it has presumably come to seem something altogether different.

With one quick motion, from one second to the next, I will tug it all away, and her deceit will lie there, unpowdered and hideous, staring her straight in the face.

Helga in front of the mirror. Cupping her breasts in her hands. Gazing at her naked body with lingering solemnity. Her mouth half open. Her way of turning her head this way and that as though before a work of art, which she wanted to study from as many angles as possible. The feverish glitter in her eyes.

It's the excitement of someone looking at her assets who has just realised the full extent of her wealth. And no one else in the whole world knows. To those around her she's still a child. But she knows the position. And now I do too.

I couldn't get it out of my head.

It tormented me as much as it stimulated me.

I used to think it must be an offence so great that it could never have even crossed God's mind to include it among His commandments. He must have thought it would be enough to forbid men to

225

covet their neighbours' wives, and that no one, least of all one of His own servants, would sink so low as to covet his neighbour's *child*.

I did my best to behave as usual towards her. But sometimes I glanced at her, across the room, a look that found its way through the din and murmur, and then I'd see an expression, a gesture or a movement, that revealed the woman she'd become, and how she secretly tasted it, brushing with the tips of her fingers the feeling of being a woman.

There were moments when she went quiet and her body softened, and dared to stay soft, even seeming to enjoy it, while her features stiffened into an inscrutable mask as she sat at the end of the sofa listening to a story with a little sphinx-like smile that remained on her lips as the minutes passed, and I remember thinking: now she's understood she has an inner life and that there's nothing sinful or shameful in that. Now she's understood that she can stay among people and need do no more than keep up that smiling, listening, conversing façade, and that if she does so it doesn't matter how she looks inside, and that it's what most people do.

Those were breathtaking, almost ceremonial moments. It was like seeing her look out of a room in which she was untouchable and all was forbidden, searching little by little for a way out into the same world as myself. And there was I, waiting for her.

I often thought she wasn't conscious of my glances. But sometimes she would take a step backwards when I came near, stiffening and looking at me with something mute and reserved in her eyes that I hadn't noticed earlier. She began to see me as someone she must be on her guard against. I was no longer just a friend of the family, a harmless gentleman who appeared at family parties and celebrations. I was also a man. She felt a man's eyes on her and acted accordingly.

But for every step she took away from me, her power over me grew.

The more she gave me that glassy social smile, the more I hungered to find out what was behind it.

How painful her youth was for me, and her endless capacity for falling in love. To sit with her parents, exchanging one indifferent remark after another, and suddenly Helga moves through the room, her white resolute face, her furrowed brow, and when she closes the door Birger, looking amused, leans forward and says in a low voice that our little girl is not so little any more, and she's even having a flirtation that occupies all her thoughts, and then he exchanges a look with Eva, and I play my part, laughing foolishly, and then I need to hide behind my cup, or cram a cake into my mouth to conceal the jealousy raging inside me, and I just want to stand up and bellow with weariness and frustration, since for several years I have had full knowledge of what they are only now beginning to suspect.

I kept my longing secret. Years passed. No one suspected anything. There was a price to pay, although I didn't see it at the time. One never does.

My most painful memory. I don't often think of it. But it's there all the same.

Lydia's deathbed.

I'm pacing a corridor, a nurse is talking beside me in a low voice, pouring out a torrent of medical terms the significance of which I certainly grasped though I couldn't keep up with her words, which ran into one another, and I had to depend on her tone of voice and intonation to be able to make up my mind that the news wasn't good. Then she went quiet and all I could hear was our frightened steps, and other nurses were walking behind us and no one was saying anything.

Suddenly, as if at a given signal, they stopped, and I automatically stopped too. The silence was terrifying when the sound of our footsteps stopped.

I turned and looked at each one in turn, as if waiting for an explanation of why they'd stopped. A nurse right at the back was taller and more robust than the others. Her forehead was blemished, and I remember an empty smile passing across her face. Perhaps I made her nervous. Then I noticed they'd stopped at a respectful distance from Lydia's room. I was going to have to walk the last ten metres or so alone. The mere thought of that short walk filled me with a nameless dread and bottomless loneliness.

Praying God to stand at my side, I walked forward to the door and opened it.

The first thing I saw were my flowers still standing on the table, though the ends of their petals had begun to shrivel. The rest of the room was a screaming white. I shut the door behind me. Walked forward to the bed.

Lydia's face was sticking up out of a sea of freshly pressed, dazzlingly white, shining clean linen with sharp mangled creases.

Not twenty-four hours had passed since I'd last seen her. But during the night her illness had eaten some decisive, greedy mouthfuls of her.

Her cheeks were sunken, her eyes had been sucked into their sockets. Her skin had taken on a yellowish tinge. Her cranium stood out sharply. The skin of her brow seemed tight like a drumhead. She was no longer able to keep her mouth closed, but she lay with her mouth wide open and wide-open eyes, her gaze firmly fixed on the ceiling. Her breathing was calm and even, as though there was a spark of life inside her that refused to accept that it was all over.

Someone had combed her hair. It floated over the freshly mangled pillowcase. I didn't need to touch it. My hands knew how soft and silky it was. Like lukewarm water.

I took her hand. I felt a slight pressure from her fingers, then her hand became still and slack.

Tears shot into my eyes. I wanted to sink down with my face on the bed and pray God to save her soul, and although I already knew God was waiting with open arms to receive her, my head was a whirl of things I wanted to tell Him. It was like running beside a train that has just started moving when there's so much you still want to say before it's too late.

I bowed my head towards the bed, but something made me stop, and I looked over the freshly mangled linen, and suddenly it became clear to me that Lydia had not made any movement to dis-order the bedclothes or rumple them in any way, and I saw before me how the nurses had laid her down among all the clean linen and that it was a lifeless body they had laid down.

It was several hours more before Lydia breathed her last.

I sat there holding her hand. At some point a nurse looked in to ask if there was anything I wanted, I half-turned towards her and shook my head. Slowly I began to get used to Lydia's carved face and I became increasingly composed before what was to come.

I don't know when it was that I began having thoughts about Helga. They were never far away. Always just under the surface of my consciousness. Capable of frisking about at any time, spread-ing rings on the water.

All I know is that while Lydia died, and I sat holding her hand, my gaze was lost in a possible future with Helga by my side. And I had a feeling in me so strong and fraught with destiny that I dared not clothe it in words.

It was a feeling that I was standing before something new and decisive. That soon I should open a door I had previously hardly even dared to glimpse from the corner of my eye, and enter a new room. It was the room where dreams come true.

I'd never been there before. I'd never wanted to either. At least I didn't think I had. It was a room for the intemperate, greedy and depraved, for those who fastened wings to their bodies and set off on a flight to the sun. For all those people I was used to feeling superior to. My path through life had been different. A path of moderation, humility and modesty. And I'd chosen my wife accordingly.

While she was leaving me I held her hand, and to the extent that I was thinking of her at all, I thought stray indulgent thoughts, as though thanking her for work well performed. But I was preoccupied with the future, I stared into it with a gaze that was absent and hypnotised and I thought: now I go through the door. Now I'll be able to set my dreams free. Now I will become one of those people.

And what hurts me most now is that I felt so strongly that God was with me all the time.

It was as if I'd glanced in His direction out of the corner of my eye like a timid schoolboy, my heart aching with longing, and whispered: May I? And seen God smile and answer: Yes, you may.

As Lydia lay dying I sat bewitched, as so often before, by the breathless journey of Helga's hands over her soft breasts and round hips, and all my being sang with feverish conviction: Now it's happening. Now I'm coming to you.

A scraping sound.

Someone's gone out through the front door. A man. Tall and slim. I can't make out his features. He's dressed in black and grey. Elegant, as far as I can see.

He looks about himself. First towards me. Then he turns and looks in the other direction. He shuts the door behind him and locks it. His movements are free and easy, as though he has all the time in the world. But his casual attitude seems to me studied. And when he looked in my direction he turned away so hastily it was as if something burned in his eye.

He puts the key in his pocket and sets off towards Stortorget, head bowed and one hand behind his back, then turns left and is gone. And the alley is as deserted as before. And though I never had any intention of approaching the man, I sit there feeling I've been taken in by someone who's shown himself cleverer and more cunning than I am.

'Miss,' I call out.

The girl comes to the door of the shop and takes a cautious step into the street. I hold up my glass to her.

'Could I trouble you for some more water?'

Her eyes wander. She pushes a lock of hair behind her ear. Takes the glass with her fingertips, very careful not to touch my hand. She curtsies, embarrassed.

'Of course, Pastor.'

She disappears for a while. I stare at the door and wonder why he locked it. How will Helga get out? I feel a movement in my heart. A modest one, and not followed by any more. For some reason it reminds me of an air bubble struggling through thick liquid, after which it laboriously bursts.

The girl returns. There are red patches on her cheeks. She puts the glass down on the table. She's cut a segment of apple and put it in the water, unless the shopkeeper did that. She has a funny little chin I didn't notice earlier.

I smile at her. Immediately she's put the glass down she looks up. A shy smile flickers across her face and I see that she is beguilingly beautiful. There's something healthy and unspoilt about her.

'Have you finished your wreaths?' I ask.

'I'm sorry?'

'Your wreaths. Aren't you going to make any more?'

'Oh, I see. No… I have other things to do inside.'

'I'm sorry to hear it.'

She stays where she is. I wait for her to ask me why I was sorry to hear it, but she says nothing. Her skirt billows out slowly, as if she's hopping impatiently from foot to foot.

'I'm sorry to trouble you so much,' I say. 'But I have rather a bad heart, you know. Perhaps you know what it's like?'

She shakes her head, and a soundless 'no' passes her lips. She's not smiling any more. She's standing with her hands on her hips, and when I look up at her she suddenly seems gigantic. I almost recoil backwards. She towers over the table like a monument.

'Of course I didn't expect you to know from your own experience, but perhaps you have some older relative who has the same trouble, or your father...'

Again the same rapid shake of the head.

'No, we're all well and healthy.'

I can't think of anything else to say. She's dying for me to let her go. But I can't bring myself to dismiss her with a final nod.

Perspectives become distorted as they did earlier, and a strange vision comes to me. Suddenly I'm reduced in height to a hand's breadth like a forest mouse, and I'm climbing the girl's body, hauling myself up on a thick rope I've managed to throw around her neck. She stands smiling patiently while I fight and struggle, my little face bright red, bracing my feet against her clothes, getting entangled in her blouse... and at the same time I'm standing to one side watching the fiery little priest, and I understand the reason he's climbing the girl is to reach her red mouth where he'll plant a miniature kiss on her lips, and suddenly I meet her gaze and realise we share a secret, which is that once the little priest's scrambled up the last bit and is standing with his feet on the point of her chin and his arms reaching out for the corners of her mouth, she'll open her jaws quick as a lizard and gobble him up in a single mouthful, then lick her lips with her tongue, which is long and forked like a reptile's, and it'll be as if he never existed, the little priest, who at this moment unconscious of her plans is climbing up her stomach.

No one else comes out through the door. Hours pass. I remember Johan Laurén said they usually come out one after the other, a few minutes apart.

No doubt Helga could be sitting up there, not daring to come out. If so, someone must have warned her that I'm sitting out in the alley waiting, and of course I saw the man go on his way. And he hasn't come back.

Before I leave I offer the shopkeeper a few coins for his trouble, but he won't take my money. He insists it was a pleasure to have me as his guest, and even if he sounds sincere there's a suspicious glint in his eye. I can hardly hold that against him.

I walk homewards with a burned-out feeling as if something has burst into flames and wrought havoc inside me, but now everything is still among the ashes, and I think of all the times in my life when I was sure something decisive was about to happen, that I'd trapped destiny in a corner so it had no chance to escape. But each time I was left standing there, sheepish and empty-handed.

I still manage to get to Dr Glas's surgery. The sun has climbed high in the sky and the air, so fresh earlier after the night's rain, has become heavy and sodden, smelling of decay. The streets are slippery and sticky, with toxic yellow puddles, and everyone forced to cross them has to step carefully.

The doctor lives at the far end of a wretched district. I pass one dirt-streaked hovel after another, and an empty site where a few years ago a badly constructed two-storey building collapsed. Luckily it happened in the middle of the day, when most of those who lived there were out. Some say the site's haunted, but whether that's the reason it's been left empty so long, I don't know.

Every time I stand in front of the doctor's house I wish I lived there myself, but my fantasies spark like miserable little flares against a huge background of exhaustion. It's as if I've seen someone wearing a particular article of clothing, and I am gripped by a desire to wear it myself, but at the same time I know I'll look ridiculous in it. There's something about the doctor's house that both rouses my longing to live a different life, and gives me a sad insight into how badly it would suit me. The feeling's intensely familiar, but I can't place it.

The windows of the house shine and flash in the sun, and on either side of the door are small hanging baskets of immortelles.

I go up the front steps and knock. The housekeeper comes to open the door and welcomes me in; we exchange a few words about the weather.

I walk through the long dark hall to the waiting room. Sitting there is a woman I recognise, a diligent churchgoer who usually sits in one of the front pews with her women friends, who – and I don't know if it's something they've noticed themselves or not – are more or less synchronised with each other when they come in and go out, stand to sing hymns or bow their heads to receive the blessing, but otherwise sit still and expressionless. Every time I mention anything to do with 'sheep' or 'flocks' I have to be careful not to look in their direction.

We nod to each other, and I take a seat. The woman and I have never exchanged a word and we don't do so on this occasion either. Murmuring voices can be heard from the surgery, the doctor's bass and an unknown soprano. It's impossible to distinguish individual words, but at the same time the tone is so clear that one begins to imagine what the conversation is about.

The sun is hot on my neck, even through drawn curtains. I look about for something to read, but all the papers are on the woman's side of the room and I don't want anything to do with her. I imagine I detect a lustre in her eyes, an exhilarated understanding, I've seen that look a thousand times, the malicious pleasure of civilians when one of God's servants is afflicted by physical ailments or worldly difficulties, as if they were thinking: I see, so much for the power of the Almighty.

A scraping of chairs in the surgery, the voices become light and soothing, then the door opens and an unknown town wife emerges, a beaver face sticking out above a billowing white ruffle; she disappears fussily down the corridor, the floorboards protesting under her heels.

Dr Glas nods to me as he admits his next patient, and something in his face gives me the impression he's been expecting me to come.

The door closes and I'm alone. Again a scraping of chairs and the interplay of voices from inside the surgery. I go over and pick up a newspaper. But I can't make myself open it.

Thinking back over the morning's events, I play with the thought of how I'd describe them to someone I have complete confidence in, Halvar for example. But I've no idea what I'd say.

I'm filled with a sense of impotence that makes my body feel heavy. A dreadful thought comes. That God's tapping me on the shoulder but I no longer want to know what He's trying to say to me. That I'm not up to trying to interpret His signs.

It's gone so far. God taps me on the shoulder. I feel His appealing, challenging eyes on me. But I sit here apathetic, cold and without will. Like the living dead. And I think: why, Lord, do You fill my heart with love for someone who doesn't want my love? What meaning can there be in that?

Then comes another hideous thought. It flies round in my head with quick, triumphant wing beats; hideous thoughts seldom come singly, or whatever the saying is. It's as though they know I'm incapable of offering any resistance, so they can storm in unopposed and make themselves at home.

The thought whispers so softly in my ear – I feel the warm, friendly breath. And I listen and nod, and the gruesome connection becomes clear.

Love is everything in my life. Love for God, love for those close to me, love for the world I live in.

And when I think of recent events it seems someone has purposefully and systematically done their best to undermine my belief in love itself. All the splendour I expected from love has been scattered before the wind, leaving only deceit, lies and indifference.

What reason can there be to take from me everything I hold

sacred and everything I believe in – if not to make clear that I have nothing to live for, and never have had anything to live for? That I might just as well be dead? Is that why God's tapping me so vigorously on the shoulder?

I lean forward and press my fingers hard against my ears. Of course I know I've been listening to the devil's voice. Suddenly I understand the meaning of the word 'temptation'.

I've always thought of the devil's temptations as more or less transparent lies. In other words, they seem attractive at first glance, but deep down in one's heart, and without major effort, one does understand how deceptive and false they are.

But real temptations, I now see, contain an incontrovertible logic. They always have an answer. The reality they present makes sense down to the smallest detail.

Real temptations are never diffuse or general; the devil doesn't address large crowds. No, he addresses you and you alone and chooses his words with the greatest care so that when he speaks to you a shiver of pleasure passes through you, since he can see clearly into your shadiest corners and most secret chambers...

In your weakest moments – and it is obviously only then that the devil looks you up – he appears as a reliable old man; one who, unlike your other friends, isn't afraid of uttering the most unpalatable truths.

A desperate longing spreads through my body, and I can do nothing to stop it, to give up all resistance, listen to what the devil has to say, and accept it completely. It's like sinking into a warm bath. This would explain so much that has been incomprehensible to me. Then perhaps I may be able to find peace. Then perhaps I shall be able to pull myself together and make a decision.

A scraping of chairs. The voices approach the door.

I straighten myself. My eyes fall on the paper before I push it away.

The door opens. The woman says goodbye to the doctor and trips away.

I go in and sit down on the couch. My ears are buzzing.

A ghastly moment: I look around in the surgery, among all the rubber tubes and metal basins, and can't understand why I'm here. I'm not even sure if I came on my own initiative, or if the doctor sent for me. All I know is that it's to do with my heart. But has it got worse recently, or are there signs of improvement?

The doctor sits down. He looks obliging, as if he's really curious to know what's coming. He fingers a gold pen. I fidget in a corner of the couch, and make a series of noises, as if to put off the moment when silence will envelop us like a great grey veil.

I start talking about the question of Holy Communion, which is perhaps an idiotic idea, but it was what caught my eye in the paper just now, and it could certainly be oppressive to me.

To my surprise the doctor seems interested.

He puts down his pen and looks intensely at me, with something in his eyes that reminds me of a cat in the seconds before it springs on its prey. Occasionally his features lighten unexpectedly and he makes several bold and unconventional remarks, balancing cheerfully between humour and seriousness.

I can't remember having seen this boyish charm in him before, and I feel a sense of calm, as if someone has taken a firm hold of my disturbed feelings to stop them kicking and snorting. I look at him with something close to tenderness, and note that his head is much too big for his thin shoulders.

While the doctor and I exchange witty remarks on Holy Communion, it strikes me how rare it has become for me to sit and talk with anyone in this fashion, without ulterior motives or hidden aims. Perhaps with time I've become dreadfully lonely without realising it.

Of course it's particularly delightful that Dr Glas and I have at least temporarily found a less forced tone than usual, and it encourages me to hope that in time he may come to fill the gap left by his predecessor.

He starts his examination in a way that makes me think of Morén's apparent absent-mindedness. Morén had the ability to check, quickly and as if in passing, everything visible in my body that was susceptible to being measured and weighed, a method that might at first seem nonchalant and careless, but of course he firmly believed that all these statistics were only a small step on the road to the solution of the puzzle.

Dr Glas asks me to take off my jacket and waistcoat, then returns to our subject of conversation. Meanwhile with one hand he pushes a chair right in front of me, and with the other shakes out his stethoscope, a tiny movement, but so deliberately profesional that I can't withhold a smile. He doesn't stop talking until his little metal box is pressed against my chest.

I can't remember when I last had myself examined in such a carefree frame of mind. I remember how worked up I was only a few minutes ago, out in the waiting room, and it's almost uncanny how far away that seems now. Like another world.

The doctor listens for a long time. I watch the shining metal as it sinks into my flesh, with greying hairs sticking up all around it. I try to hear my own heartbeat as the doctor hears it, and for a moment his stethoscope binds us together in an almost improperly intimate way like an umbilical cord, and I believe my heart's beating evenly and calmly, perhaps a touch more forcefully than usual, but surely that must relate to the seriousness of the moment.

I begin fantasising that the doctor's so happily surprised by what he hears that he can scarcely believe his senses, and that I've recovered so completely that it's almost a miracle.

The longer the examination goes on, the more firmly I cling to my fantasies.

I must try to think calming thoughts, trusting thoughts, peaceful thoughts, for just a little while longer. At any moment he will take the stethoscope off my chest and the examination will be over. Just a moment longer.

But my heart won't allow itself to be persuaded any longer. My calming thoughts burst and collapse, one after another. My heart begins beating with such agitation that my throat tightens and my strenuous breaths sound like small sobs from my nose.

The doctor's sitting still with his mouth half open and his head to one side. He moves the stethoscope a number of times, and each time he does so he seems to press harder than before. My fantasies change direction, and suddenly I'm a completely different kind of miracle. I'm a man with no heart. Living yet dead. I look down on the doctor's centre parting and see a few flakes of dandruff and a little group of hairs he's combed over to the wrong side.

An inexplicable fury flushes through my body.

I want to rip the stethoscope from his neck and knock him off his chair, and in a flash I see myself stooping over him, my face bright red, gripping his lapels so hard that his jacket splits at the seams and he looks up at me and blinks in bewilderment, and I shout that I forbid him to hear what he's just heard. It never happened. Is that clear? *It never happened!*

But it is happening. The stethoscope is tripping over my chest; it seems to surface for a moment from my flesh for air, then dive in again.

My head's spinning. The examination's beginning to seem increasingly unreal. I can almost see my heart pounding desperately against my ribcage, as if crying out: I'm here, can't you hear that I'm here?

But the doctor seems not to be hearing, or perhaps he is hearing clearly and has made up his mind to play my heart a nasty trick, and my heart's altogether too simple and innocent to realise.

At last the doctor eases up. He hangs the stethoscope around his neck and gets up, leaving a number of red stethoscope marks on my chest. I think: like kisses, I'm ashamed. Ashamed to be sitting here on his couch so old, fat, clumsy and helpless. I don't even know if my voice'll carry me any further. Anything I say will have to be brief.

'Is it serious?' I ask.

The doctor gets up without answering and seems lost in thought. He takes a few steps towards his desk. Then he stops and turns. Our eyes meet, but he immediately looks away.

'Strange,' he says.

He seems puzzled about something. He says he'd like to listen a bit more. But there's something reassuring in his voice and I'm sure he's brightened up a little.

No doctor would look like this when about to tell a patient that he's dying. I'm quite sure of that.

I'm beginning to smell. A stale smell from my armpits as sometimes happens when I'm troubled or subject to strong emotion. I smell like an old underground larder. I try to keep my arms pressed against my body, but I know from experience that this doesn't help. Soon sweat will be running down my sides.

This time the doctor doesn't listen so thoroughly but presses his stethoscope hastily against various points on my chest. He seems reinforced in his earlier opinion.

Then he moves the chair out of the way, puts the stethoscope on his desk and sits down behind it.

I make an interrogative gesture towards my clothes, and he nods.

'Well,' he says finally. 'If I'm to judge by what I've heard today, I can't honestly say your heart's in good shape, Pastor. But I can't believe it's always as bad as it is now. I think it must have its own special reason for being so troublesome today.'

I try not to stare at him. Something in his voice scares me.

Nothing menacing; on the contrary, he sounds almost jovial. As though he's hinting at something we both know all about. What did he say? That my heart must have a particular reason for being troublesome today.

Normally I have no problems with my memory, but now it takes me a while to remember anything at all that's happened today. There comes a moment when I turn around and it's empty, and I have to retrace my steps as though senile: walk to doctor's surgery... dilapidated houses... spice-shop near Stortorget... man who came out through door...

First my mind's empty, then everything rushes over me. Meanwhile I can't think which of these events the doctor can be referring to. What does he know? And, in that case, how does he know it? Who's been talking to him?

I must seem almost bovine. I make a vague movement of agreement with my head and pay careful attention to the expression on his face. When he gives an ironic smile I do the same, and when he gets serious I do too.

'Let's be frank with one another, Pastor Gregorius.'

The doctor has picked up his gold pen again and is tapping both ends of it against some papers lying in front of him.

He begins talking about Helga's illness. There can be no doubt he's understood that we haven't followed his advice.

'For your wife it's a matter of her health, long term or short term, but for you, Pastor, it could be a matter of life and death.'

At 'life and death' he gives a final tap with his pen, after which it lies still but menacing between his thumb and index finger. Then he lets it fall.

'Let's be frank with one another.'

He couldn't have expressed himself more clearly.

It's as if he's cursed me and turned me to stone. But it wasn't a curse. Just an invitation to be frank with one another.

Perhaps it's the same thing for me.

He talks for a long time. I can't remember him ever having so much to say before.

I hear everything he says. That from now on Helga and I must have separate bedrooms. That we must 'avoid anything that may stimulate or excite desire' because my heart can't tolerate it.

But nothing he says affects me more powerfully than the word 'frank'.

I remember how often I've compared Dr Glas with his predecessor, and longed for Dr Morén's benevolent intrusiveness.

But when Dr Glas suggests we should be frank with one another I become mute and rigid, as if something dreadful is about to happen.

That's how I am. I'm in pressing need of someone to talk to. But when Dr Glas offers himself in that role, I feel he's pointing a loaded pistol at me.

There's so much I'd like to explain to him.

Don't you understand, doctor, I want to say. There was only one single way to escape my loneliness, and it was her. I invested everything in her. Or at least, as much as I could.

Now here I am, and I have to conclude that I'm more lonely than ever before. She closed the door, locked it and went on her way. What she did with the key I've no idea. Perhaps she doesn't know either.

I try the words out on myself. To see how they'd feel in my mouth if I said them to him. But they seem mired in a sea of mud, and nothing comes out.

Meanwhile, almost exhilarated as though inspired by pedagogical fervour, the doctor lays down his guidelines.

Separate bedrooms. Avoid everything that may stimulate or excite desire.

'Helga' could just as well be the name of some newly discovered dangerous disease. Indeed, worse than dangerous. Just now the doctor said it may be fatal. But the noteworthy aspect of this illness is that it can strike only me. Gregorius.

To others 'Helga' spreads love, happiness and wellbeing. To me at best loneliness and misfortune, at worst death.

The doctor has stopped talking. He stares at me, eyebrows raised, evidently waiting for a sign that I've understood. So I give him a sign.

I get up and step forward to say goodbye. He gestures for me to wait, then writes out a prescription for digitalis. I pause and watch the gold pen travelling expansively over the paper. Like liberated leaps over a summer meadow.

The doctor makes some movements of his upper lip that I haven't seen before, pouting with what looks like a series of small twitches. Perhaps he likes to feel his moustache tickling the tip of his nose.

'Nor is it good for you, Pastor, to stay in the city during this hot summer weather. Six weeks at a spa would do you no end of good. Porla or Ronneby. But naturally you must travel on your own.'

He hands me the prescription. I glance at it, amazed there's nothing about Porla or Ronneby in it. I must have been expecting him to write me a ticket. My thoughts have begun moving in the strangest directions.

I take my leave of the doctor and set off for home. A melancholy descends. It reminds me of when I was a child and school finished for the summer holidays. I don't know why. Perhaps it was only the doctor's instructions that set my imagination going. Six weeks at a spa, Porla or Ronneby.

It's God's will.

Now everything will have to carry on without me. My parishioners will have to take their disputes and worries to someone else. There are plenty of priests in the rural districts ready to catch the first train to Stockholm. Cheerful young men, gleaming with ambition. They'll listen to all the advice and instructions I give them. They'll ask me shrewd questions. They'll give me to understand that nothing will be too much for them. As if that'll impress me. Which it won't. But that's just as it should be. They're young and ambitious, and so far nothing has got in the way of their ambitions, and they think that's how it always will be.

Helga too will have to get on without me. She'll be able to go to her door in the alleyway without having to look over her shoulder. She'll be able to go whenever it suits her and stay there as long as she likes. I'm happy for her and her fancy man to find out what's left when I'm no longer there like a menacing troll causing them to worry, fear and intrigue incessantly. I've supplied them with so much excitement and generated such a sense of belonging between them. Now they'll just have to get on by themselves.

One gives so much thought to one's own importance. That so much stands or falls depending on oneself. A profession, or a family; perhaps nothing more than a district where you light the gas lamps every day, and you're sure no one else could ever do the job as conscientiously and punctually as yourself, and even if they could, everyone's got used to seeing you pass at dusk with your pole, and they look at you appreciatively, and many greet you like a dear old friend.

But most people would be deeply shaken if they knew how quickly they'll be forgotten, and how steadfastly the world can go on without them.

One day someone else will come and light the lamps. People may wonder for a while what's happened to the other man, the one who used to greet them so cheerfully. But curiosity about the new lamp-lighter will soon replace regret for the loss of the old one, if they think about it at all.

Some people have more specialised professions. Clergymen,

scientists, and, not least, writers. People who are happy to have dedicated their lives to something meaningful, something they can, and should, mark with their personal stamp. The clergyman plans a groundbreaking reform, the scientist makes an important discovery and the writer publishes a thought-provoking novel, and all three can justifiably point to their achievements and claim that no one else could have done exactly what they've just done. At least, not in quite the same way. Their achievements are their own and no one else's, no one can prove otherwise.

But many others are waiting to take over, and the chairs of the old incumbents hardly have time to grow cold before a new minister, scientist or writer is sitting in them. The new man will be only too well aware of his predecessor's impact, but he will be just as ambitious if not more so, and if he's going to have to work twice as hard as his predecessor to make a mark of his own, well, then he'll work three times as hard, or even harder. He'll propose an even more daring church reform, or develop the earlier scientific discovery in a new direction so fantastic that people will forget how truly original the earlier discovery was. It's the same with the writer. No one's content to be categorised as a mere successor. They all want to make a great splash of their own and win honours and distinctions and magnificent headstones in the cemetery.

This is how humanity moves forward. This is the beating heart of progress. The ambition to achieve something lasting. The dream of being someone of importance.

And family? Well, I don't know. My own family, my parents and brothers, to a large extent made me what I am. Kings, inventors, and poets, none of their struggles and discoveries has made such a significant impression on me as, say, my father. But soon my time will be done, and then his memory will be lost too and it'll be as though he never lived.

I'm not planning to die, not for a while yet. I shall go away in order to live a little longer. They'll manage perfectly well without me. They'll forget me in no time at all. They'll probably be surprised, even irritated, when I reappear after six weeks.

Well, well. That's how it is. It's God's will. I've reached the turning point and now I must start again from the beginning.

I wake at the first bell and can't fall asleep again.

I go over to the window and pull the curtain back a little. Mist again today. They say it's the same every morning. Something to do with the peat-bog.

There's a nurse down there with arms akimbo; she looks at her watch, then stands and gazes towards the hospital, perhaps someone's keeping her waiting.

A family goes past, the nurse gives them a friendly nod, a man and a woman and two small children. The man's carrying the smaller child. The woman seems to be in no condition to do that. She has one arm across her face and her body's shaking with violent coughs, but though I can make out the sound of their footsteps on the gravel I can't hear the coughs. The older child, a girl, catches sight of something on the ground and squats down to study it more closely. The woman goes on alone towards the spring; the man stays with the girl for a moment and looks absently after his wife, then he makes an impatient gesture with his hand and the girl gets up and runs after her mother.

More people appear then. An old man in a wheelchair with two nurses, one pushing the wheelchair and the other walking beside them. He's wearing a white hospital shirt and an extraordinary black hat, almost like a jester's cap. He presses one hand to his forehead and starts moaning loudly. This is the first time I hear voices. One of the nurses hurries forward and bends over him and I suppose she's trying to silence him so he won't wake the important guests.

Despite the fact that I see nothing remarkable or even unusual, all these passing figures have an almost hypnotic effect on me. The mist blots out everything around them, all the trees and flowers and buildings. It's like watching creatures moving over a sheet of grey paper.

I begin to think about Our Saviour. First it's a fleeting and sleepy thought, but then it becomes almost real for me that the Son of Man is sitting over there amongst the trees, waiting for all these people. Solemn and patient, and with gentle warm eyes. I see Him open his arms to them. Tell them who He is and why He's come. Then He goes around among them and saves them with His love. The man in the jester's cap rises from his wheelchair, and the woman with the two small children straightens up and looks about in wonder, as if discovering anew the world and the people in it.

But this morning there's nothing but water waiting for them. Ferriferous and restorative. They line up in front of a doctor, who measures out the correct quantity for each. Then they sit in the pavilion, silent and tired, sucking in their water through a glass tube so it won't discolour their teeth.

Soon it'll be my turn.

My thoughts about Our Saviour persist restlessly like an unanswered question. What would I do if I realised He was sitting down there? I try to shake the question off. I'd hurry to Him, of course. But still my anxiety won't leave me.

I hear a sound from the corridor, from my neighbour's door. His name's Högström and he's an officer, a cavalryman if I remember rightly. Yesterday evening he stopped me in the corridor and introduced himself and expressed a hope that he hadn't disturbed me in any way, and I told him not in the least.

'This is my fourth year,' he told me. 'And I can assure you, Pastor, that if it hadn't been for this place I'd be dead as a doornail by now.'

Of course I could see he was drunk. Normally I don't attach much importance to confidences or assurances of friendship made by anyone in an inebriated state, but there was something about this man I found touching.

He served with some regiment outside Stockholm, and told me of the unspoken demand of his superiors to end the day with cognac and biscuits in one of the offices.

They would describe these sessions in unimpeachably professional terms; claiming that they were 'drawing up guidelines' for the regiment's future, and so on. But it always ended with him staggering home in the small hours with his clothes steeped in cigar-smoke, sometimes with wounds or scratches caused by various drunken escapades and trials of strength, with serious consequences for his health and family life.

'But that's not the problem,' said Högström, resting an unsteady hand on the wall. 'I could have said no at any time. But I can't. It's the way I am. I've tried sometimes. But not a sound. Meanwhile someone fills my glass again, and once I've emptied it there's no way back. It's like sitting in a train and feeling it start. The only escape is here at Porla. Where there are fixed hours. I have to go to bed just after nine, and that can't be changed.

'I don't know what your problem is, Pastor, and I won't ask either. But whatever it may be, you've come to the right place. Back home many things run our lives for better or for worse. But here the doctors are in control.'

Then Högström said goodnight, shook my hand warmly and went into his room.

I went into mine and sat on the bed and thought about the sounds I'd heard during the early hours from Högström's room. Sharp squeaks from the bed. Contented and demanding grunts. It sounded as though he was training a dog and expressing his approval of the animal's various skills. Then the squeaking stopped, and it went quiet. A bit later, footsteps tripped across the floor. Then the door opened and steps disappeared down the corridor.

It seems that the same procedure will be repeated tomorrow morning too.

Högström's bed squeaks and groans loudly but in an irregular rhythm, as if someone's romping about on the mattress. After a bit the sound quietens down and becomes more even.

As my father used to say: once is nothing, twice is a habit. In other words, it looks as if this squeaking of Högström's bed's going to be an everyday feature of my mornings. I wonder who she is, this woman who comes to him.

They've started taking the waters already. There aren't many free places in the pavilion, but I see an empty chair near one of the windows. There's a pleasant-looking gentleman sitting at the same table, and as I move in that direction it occurs to me that it's a good idea to sit by the window, since there's always something happening outside you can make use of to start a conversation.

The man nods when I ask if I can sit at his table, and I put my glass down carefully so the glass straw won't break and the water won't splash.

I sit down and look at the man, but his attention is directed to the room and the residents streaming into it. I'm just about to open my mouth when he brightens up and waves to someone.

A young woman comes forward. She pulls funny faces as she nears our table, putting her glass straw in her mouth and looking to one side as if to avoid looking at the man. But once she's standing before him she stops her little piece of acting and gives a ringing laugh that makes everyone turn in our direction. At first they look annoyed, but when they catch sight of the young woman they brighten up and their mouths relax, even if not altogether willingly.

I too can't hold back a smile, and realise I must be watching the man and the woman with hungry eyes, as if to ask them to include me in their high spirits.

But they take no notice of me. The man makes a helpless gesture, as if of regret that all the chairs are taken. I decide I'll offer to fetch a chair for the woman, which should be a good idea since it would more or less compel them to talk to me. But before I've had a chance to do anything the woman sees some acquaintances at the other end of the pavilion and asks the man to come over there with her.

So I end up having the table all to myself, and oddly enough no one else comes to sit with me.

At first I don't give it a thought, assuming someone will come at any moment to ask if there's a free place. I watch the residents coming into the pavilion out of the corner of my eye, all holding their glasses of water in one hand and protecting their glass straws with the other, and wonder with idle curiosity who I shall get as my table-mate.

But soon the room is nearly full and the queue of people waiting to be served with water has become appreciably shorter, so I make an effort to look out of the window instead, since it could be that there's something desperate about me I'm unconscious of, something out of my control.

I stay alone at my table, and soon notice from the corner of my eye that there's no one now at the point where they serve out the water, and that Dr Lidin is closing the register that states how much water each resident should have, while several nurses clear away the water-containers.

I keep my eyes fixed on the world outside the window. The mist is beginning to lift. The sun is shining between the trunks of the trees, sunbeams piercing the grey like honey-coloured spears. Far away above the treetops jackdaws are flying restlessly in circles like flakes of soot against the sky.

I drink my water. It's cold and bitter. I don't know what's so special about it. Lying around the room are pamphlets and brochures that describe its constituents and minerals in detail, but I can't remember them.

I doubt if many of the other residents can either. We're drinking spring water with vague ideas that it brings us tastes and smells from deep inside the earth, from forces that mystically, almost miraculously, bring health. And perhaps they do. But I can't suppress the thought that it isn't all that long ago that we believed hell was down there somewhere among the clouds of sulphur and streams of lava.

As I drink my water I try to convince myself that it does me no harm at all to sit alone. That I'm even enjoying it.

But it hurts to remember the expectations I had only a few days ago as I sat on the train watching forests, lakes and fields glide by. I was as excited as a child. I didn't give a thought to Helga and all the misery at home, or the dreadful, silent hours before I left for the station. All I could think of was that for six long weeks I'd be staying among people who knew nothing about me. I'd meet people who would look at me openly and unaffectedly and without preconceptions.

Quite simply I hoped to leave my loneliness behind and come to Porla without its dismal company. But as I push aside my water glass I have the feeling loneliness has outwitted me yet again.

I took the train. Loneliness travelled by horse and carriage.

253

That's the only difference. Now he's sharing my table again, and everything's just as usual.

Breakfast, too, I eat alone.

I'm surrounded by noise and bustle. There seem to be lots of happy reunions. Lots of people are complimenting each other on looking so fit and well. Many eager accounts of aches and pains and visits to doctors during the autumn, winter and spring. No one seems to pay much attention to what anyone else is saying. People utter little sounds as if to urge the person talking to hurry up with his or her story, so they can start on their own as quickly as possible.

I see Högström sitting surrounded by empty places and shovelling large mouthfuls of pork and scrambled egg into his mouth, then sitting still, a faraway look on his face, chewing with small energetic movements. Now and then he catches sight of a familiar face, nods a greeting and calls out something undecipherable in a booming voice. Then he gives a twisted smile, shakes his head and lifts his knife and fork again. For a moment I think of going over to keep him company, but he sees me first, and something chilly, almost ironic in his greeting discourages me. I suppose he's ashamed. Something priests often experience. People bring us their frailties then hate themselves for their weakness, and to make their lives more bearable they divert their hatred against the priest who listened to them.

As I sit picking my teeth at the end of my meal I notice a man stop near my table and glance surreptitiously in my direction.

He's small and thin, and makes a neat and modest impression. I'd judge him to be a bit over forty. He's balancing a coffee cup and saucer in each hand. I feel he's stopped because he wants to speak to me but doesn't know how to begin.

From the doors to the kitchen comes a crash. Plates smash and cutlery rings against the marble floor. Faces turn eagerly towards the noise, followed by malicious laughter and witty comments. Someone even begins to clap, then thinks better of it.

The man gives me a furtive look and smiles. His lips move, but there's so much noise I can't make out what he's saying. Then he continues on his anxious walk with the coffee cups before sitting down at a table and being swallowed up in the sea of breakfasting residents.

*E*veryone talks about Dr Lidin. He almost seems to be a bit of a celebrity. Whenever he appears he's surrounded by a swarm of residents. Everyone who speaks to him uses a rather breathless and urgent tone, and they all seem remarkably certain that nothing can ever be too much trouble for him – or too little trouble, for that matter. Dr Lidin is expected to be able to solve everything, from amorphous tensions in the diaphragm to vermin between the floorboards, and also to know the timetable for the outings to the lake.

When I see the residents flocking around the doctor all speaking at once, I'm reminded of small children fighting for Mother's or Father's attention and unthinkingly and automatically expecting answers to all their questions, whether serious or trivial. Then, having managed to exchange a few words with the doctor, the lucky ones leave the crowd and go off looking triumphant, as if they've just been admitted to an exclusive club.

At eight I'm summoned to the doctor for an examination. This should really have happened the day before, but I was told at the last moment that the doctor couldn't make it. I was unreasonably cross with the nurse who brought me the message. As if they'd already decided that I wasn't very important.

'Of course you can have your appointment at the agreed time,

Pastor,' the nurse said. 'It's just that it would have to be with a different doctor.'

It was quite clear from her manner that this was not an alternative to be recommended, and that Dr Lidin was well worth waiting for.

This annoyed me. I don't know why.

But watching the craze for Dr Lidin has made a definite impression on me. By the time I set off for the hospital I've got over my irritation and almost find myself dawdling on the short walk, as if hoping that people will gaze enviously after me, wishing they were in my place.

The hospital is a modest two-storey building, and as I go in I'm gripped by the suspicion that I've made a mistake, or even that in some miraculous way I've ended up in an altogether different building.

I stand at the foot of a big red stone staircase between high white walls like those of a prominent educational establishment.

It's so cold that I shiver. There's no one in sight, and it's so quiet that when I turn my head I can hear an unpleasant soft crunching sound from the vertebral cartilage in my neck.

I climb the stairs slowly, but as I turn on the landing to go up the second flight I'm stopped by a rope stretched between the banisters. I look around for some board or notice that might explain why the stairs have been closed off, but I can't see one.

All I can do is go down again. I'm again irritated by the capriciousness and nonchalance that Dr Lidin seems to think he has a right to indulge in, and I hiss several words of disapproval aloud to myself.

I shut up at once when I see the doctor, who's standing at the foot of the stairs looking at me in astonishment.

'So there you are,' he says.

I go down again. We shake hands, and I stammer out something about looking for a board or notice that might tell me the way to the surgery.

'No notice boards here,' says the doctor. 'I'm on the left. In at the main door, then sharp left. Didn't the nurse tell you?'

'No.'

'I shall have her dismissed at once.'

The doctor's voice is quiet and matter-of-fact. He sounds as if he's talking to himself and is only speaking aloud to make sure he won't forget what he's said.

I look at him in consternation, but see a twist of amusement at the corner of his mouth. He pats my arm reassuringly and opens a door for me.

The doctor's large surgery seems tiled all over, and he looks small behind his great mahogany desk. When I comment on this he shrugs his shoulders:

'That's how it is here in the provinces. We can spread ourselves out. To be honest, I never notice till I have to go on some errand to Stockholm. Then suddenly I get...'

The doctor performs a little charade for me, pressing his arms against his sides, sucking in his cheeks and glancing anxiously to right and left, to give the impression of someone moving in a restricted space where the walls are slowly closing together. Then he bursts out in a relaxing laugh.

I begin to understand why the doctor is so popular.

He must be my exact opposite, I begin to think, and this must be so obvious that they could use us in a scientific experiment; indeed, for a moment the laboratory experiments of my student days flash past in my head: cat-skin and ebony wands, and expressions like 'attractive' – with a portrait of Dr Lidin – and 'repulsive' – with a portrait of me.

I know it's absurd, but the thought sticks to me like a burr and I can't shake it off.

The doctor does his utmost to put me in a better humour. He asks if I'm happy with my accommodation and food and whether the electric bell system in my room is working properly, and tells me an anecdote about an elderly resident who used to bellow into the bell system as if it were a voice-pipe; I smile and shake my head and wonder how many times he's told this story before.

I sit there monosyllabic and evasive despite the fact there's nothing I'd like more than to have someone to talk to. But every attempt to respond to Dr Lidin's encouragement to start a conversation with him collapses before I've even managed to form a single complete sentence; everything seems so meagre, coarse and stupid compared to the doctor's amiability and charm.

After a while he sinks into a thoughtful silence, as if he's tried everything and been forced to give up.

He glances at me, and I think I detect disappointment in his eyes, and it suddenly occurs to me that I knew this disappointed expression would crop up sooner or later. Not just that, but that I was deliberately trying to bring it about – indeed, *that I didn't give up until I could see disappointment in his face.*

The doctor wastes no more words on me but starts his examination. He sticks his stethoscope in his ears and listens very carefully to my heart. He stays standing the whole time and moves around my chair with little steps, closing his eyes as if enjoying a piece of music every time he presses the stethoscope to my chest.

When he's finished pressing and listening all the way around my upper body he takes off the stethoscope and laughs.

'Strange,' he says.

He looks at me with a wondering smile.

'I am sure I...'

He breaks off and goes over to his desk. He fishes out a paper, runs down a column with his forefinger and peers nearsightedly at the paper. Then he straightens up slowly.

'They tell me you have a bad heart, Pastor,' he says. 'But I can't hear anything abnormal.'

I don't dare to say anything. The doctor has a little smile on his face. Perhaps this is yet another manifestation of his sense of humour.

'Are you serious, doctor?' I say after a while.

'Certainly.'

I give a condensed account of the struggling movements I've felt in my ribcage from time to time. Of how I almost black out, and feel as if I'm falling through a great darkness. I report in detail everything Dr Glas has said. I try to sound as neutral as possible, but I suspect, perhaps even hope, that Dr Lidin will find things to comment on in Dr Glas's diagnosis.

When I tell him that Helga and I have been ordered to sleep in different rooms he bursts out laughing.

'Well, I never,' he says, shaking his head.

I say nothing. The doctor pulls himself together.

'Obviously I can't comment on your wife,' he says after a moment. 'But as far as you yourself are concerned, Pastor, I'm... to put it tactfully... of a different opinion from your Dr Glas. For a start, as I said I can't hear anything abnormal in your heartbeat. And even if I had, I should have given you entirely different advice. Tell me, is he getting on a bit in years, this Dr Glas?'

'No, he's quite young.'

Dr Lidin frowns.

'The reason I asked is that there used to be a widely accepted theory that if you had a weak heart you should keep quiet and avoid any sort of undue effort. But I thought it was by now universally agreed in medical science that the opposite is the case. We do well to remember that the heart is a muscle. If it doesn't get enough exercise the blood thickens and moves more sluggishly, which in turn puts a strain on the heart. No, Pastor, you should be as active as possible, without overdoing it, naturally. And stick to a sensible diet. But you knew that already?'

I nod. I mention the article Helga saved.

'Excellent,' says the doctor.

We're both silent.

After a while the doctor clears his throat. But I can't bring myself to go.

Something doesn't add up.

Perhaps the doctor didn't listen carefully enough.

I feel I've hoodwinked him. As if I've been displaying a false heart to him and made him think I'm well, and now that I've obviously succeeded it's high time to let him listen to my real heart. But I don't know where it is. Perhaps I'll have to take off all my clothes and ask the doctor to help me find my real heart. We must be quick, doctor, you understand. It might be anywhere. It might even have left my body altogether in some unguarded moment. It's been such a dreadfully long time since I last paid any attention to my real heart. Perhaps we must contact the police to help us find it before it stops beating... My real heart may have ended up anywhere, don't you see? It could be freezing in a corner of a barn somewhere in Roslagen, or it could be gathering dust in a bowl in a cellar on Kungsholmen. Don't you realise how serious this is?

'Are you thinking about anything in particular, Pastor?'

I look up. Dr Lidin has closed his books and pushed aside his writing materials. He's leaning on the arm of his chair and watching me with his head on one side.

'I was only thinking about Dr Glas's orders,' I say. 'Separate bedrooms.'

'Yes, I can understand that. In fact, I was thinking about the same thing. I've never heard Dr Glas mentioned. Perhaps from that we can draw the conclusion that he has never made any particular mark in the profession. Which means he's probably one of the great multitude of competent doctors who do the best they can. And he's still young. Who knows, he may yet make a name for himself…'

Dr Lidin shows signs of being about to say something, but stops himself. A touch of mockery appears in his eyes.

'I shall be entirely frank with you, Pastor. I'll tell you about one of the most difficult situations doctors have to face, and the reason I'm going to tell you is that I suspect you yourself have similar experiences. Well. People come to us with their difficulties and worries. Spiritual or physical. Of the soul or of the world.'

'Or both.'

'Precisely. Precisely! But one can often feel frustrated because as a doctor one analyses the patient's worries in a different way from the patient himself. Do you understand what I mean, Pastor?'

'Yes.'

'Good. Then you will certainly also understand that one can sometimes hesitate to inform the patient of one's analysis. Either because one is a sensitive soul, perhaps altogether too sensitive, or because one has a shrewd idea that the patient won't understand, or won't want to understand, one's analysis. That he will receive it with deaf ears, and that the effect, in the worst cases, would be the opposite of the desired outcome.'

'Yes,' I say eagerly, 'I've often had similar thoughts myself. It's an intricate balancing act. People can never make important or thoroughgoing changes in their lives unless they themselves want to, or understand why they want to. The really difficult art is to give people a helping hand at the beginning, but only until they've clearly understood that they themselves must open their hearts to God. That there's no other way out.'

Dr Lidin has been sitting bolt upright in his chair with his head on his hand. But at this point he begins swinging his right hand energetically, as if he can hardly hold himself back until it's his turn to speak.

'Very wisely put. Very wisely! I notice we're capable of talking freely with one another. So let me say straight out what I think about Dr Glas and his instructions. Well, I believe he's made an analysis of your problems, Pastor, that for one reason or another he's unwilling to share with you.'

'What sort of analysis could that be?'

'That I don't know. When all's said and done, Dr Glas has greater insight into the circumstances of your life than I have. Perhaps… perhaps…'

The doctor goes silent. He shrugs his shoulders, as if he's been hesitating between different alternatives, and has now decided to choose one at random.

'Your marriage, for example. Is it happy?'

'Yes, on the whole. Why do you ask?'

'I was just trying to think of some circumstance that might lead me to issue similar instructions myself. I mean, supposing it was clear to me that your marriage was making you unhappy. Or worse, that it was a direct threat to your health.'

'I don't understand… If that were the case, wouldn't it be better simply to tell me straight out?'

The doctor smiles, as if waiting for me to see for myself what nonsense I've just been talking. He shakes his head slowly.

'And how would you react to something like that? If Dr Glas claimed your marriage was a threat to your health? If it was me, I'd make it clear to him that he'd overstepped his authority and I'd get up and walk out, firmly convinced he was stark staring mad.'

'I see. Perhaps.'

'Which wouldn't alter the fact that he might be right in his assumption. I don't know. Anyway, I've overstepped my authority too. It doesn't become me to sit in judgement over my colleagues' conclusions. All I can say is that your heartbeat's entirely normal for a man of your age and that your stay here will do you good both in body and spirit.'

With these words the doctor stands up to say goodbye. He comes with me to the door, then stands and looks after me as I make my way to the main door.

I meet no one on the way out. I open the outer door and step out into a jumble of human voices, chirping birds and barking dogs. Someone's chopping wood. Someone else is hammering in a nail.

I go out into tropical heat and deafening emptiness. I hurry my steps, tempted to look back over my shoulder at the strange hospital building, which turned out to be so different inside from what its exterior promised. But I dare not.

I remember the overheated fantasies I've just had about my real heart, and before I can protect myself a voice whispers in my ear that I've just left my real heart at the hospital with Dr Lidin, and that it's too late now to go back and fetch it.

I have time for a walk before the service. There's a path here known as Love Lane. I don't know why it has that name. It runs beside the bog, then passes the croquet lawn, the tennis courts and what they call the Firehouse.

It's a pretty walk. The mist has dispersed, and the sun's shining from a sky as white as salt. The bog lies inscrutably still. Not a sign of life, except here and there a flash of silver from some insect. Every creature is fleeing the rays of the sun, burrowing down into the cool damp moss, which seems at first glance so sterile and lifeless. But if you look more closely you see life swarming there, quivering above the ground.

Occasionally I pass residents. We nod to each other. That's what one does here. Some seem healthy and thriving. I meet a family with two small children. The man walks in front; he points across the bog and describes a hopping movement with his index finger. When the family gets nearer I see the skin on his cheeks and chin is dry and cracked, like an apple left too long on the ground. The woman's listening to his words with nervous attention, at the same time constantly casting her eyes back at her children, as if worrying they may start to quarrel or get left behind. Her unease seems exaggerated, since her sons are marching silently and doggedly in her wake. Just as they pass I notice the elder boy putting on some strange expressions. His head moves this way and that and occasionally he blinks hard, pinching together his whole face. First I think it must be involuntary muscular spasms, but then I hear a weak sound coming from his lips as if he's mimicking a bang or explosion, and realise it must be one of those childhood games that need no props, dolls or toys, only imagination and boredom, both in abundant measure.

Other residents are older and more decrepit. I meet an old lady tottering along with a stick in each hand. Her hat has slipped sideways and looks as if it will fall off at any moment. Her brow is wet with sweat. She's staring at the ground in front of her feet, whispering something and now and again breaking into bitter little laughs. Half a pace behind are her two young nurses on tenterhooks, ready to catch her at any moment if she misses her step and loses her balance.

I realise I'm ill at ease. I was so certain I'd find spiritual peace when I came here. I assumed all these disagreeable and sometimes downright nightmarish fantasies and ideas that have been haunting me were a consequence of my marriage troubles and my increasingly desperate attempts to find a solution to them.

But even though I've left all that behind me, it seems some part of my soul refuses to rest but is determined to rush on faster than ever.

I've devoted all my strength to fighting enemies who've wanted to deprive me of everything I hold dear. But it was only when I thought I'd defeated these enemies, and was sitting there so exhausted I could hardly lift my hand, that I realised my enemies weren't all around me as I'd believed, but inside me.

It isn't until one's experienced such a moment that one knows what exhaustion really is.

Because it's taught me that all the cunning and all the weapons

I use to fight my enemies may well end up in my enemies' service and be used against me.

It's as futile as trying to attack your own shadow. Or your doppelgänger. Everything I think, he has already thought. I can't keep any stratagem secret from him, nor can I lure him into any trap or ambush since we are one and the same being.

From the corner of my eye I see someone coming up alongside me.

It's the man from the breakfast room. He gives me a friendly nod. I nod back, but I'm embarrassed because I've been mumbling to myself, something I have an unfortunate tendency to do.

'Warm day,' he says.

'Yes,' I say. 'I'm looking forward to morning prayers. There'll be some shade there.'

The man nods and falls silent a moment at my side. He walks with his chin stuck out, which could look supercilious were it not that he's so small, and that the shoulder-pads of his jacket droop so pitifully.

He offers me his hand and introduces himself.

'Superintendent Hansson. I've been working at the Customs and Excise Department for several years now. Before that I was in the Navy. Not at all easy to get out of that. Had to pull every possible string. Bend my knee in every possible direction. Trouble with my windpipe. Suppose I thought my new job would make me well again in some miraculous way.'

He gives an ironic laugh and shakes his head.

'Just got worse. And now I'm here. Second year in succession. You enjoying Porla, Pastor?'

'Very much, thank you.'

'Yes, it...'

He sweeps his hand around our environment but, finding nothing to say, merely nods energetically.

I take my watch out of my waistcoat pocket, and say I must go back now if I'm to make it to morning prayers on time.

Superintendent Hansson looks at me in confusion.

'Of course, naturally. Unfortunately can't take part myself, since I have to go for an examination. You must excuse me, Pastor, but could I walk with you a little way? There's something I'd like to talk to you about.'

I give my consent. We set off in the other direction, with the sun in our eyes. Superintendent Hansson moves uneasily at my side, and seems to find it difficult to keep up with me. His exhausted and slightly prominent eyes remind me a little of a rabbit.

I try to imagine him on a warship, far out at sea, in biting winds, with the crew yelling orders to each other, but I can only see him being blown overboard and whirling away over the waves like a little face flannel torn loose from a clothes line.

'It's to do with my wife,' he says finally. 'In short, I'm worried about her.'

'Why?'

'Her brother died some time back. In mysterious circumstances, to crown it all. I've never understood clearly what happened. But they were very attached to one another.

'Since then Anna, my wife, has become more and more uncommunicative. Whole days pass when she says nothing but what's absolutely essential. Sometimes when I come into the kitchen she stands still holding a ladle in a pan, as though frozen, staring into mid-air. When I speak to her it's as if the spell's broken, and she begins to move the ladle again as if nothing had happened. Well, perhaps it sounds like nothing, but I find it frightening.'

I take out my watch again. Morning prayers are due to begin at any moment. But I don't know where I am. The path we're following seems to go on for ever. I can't very well ask the superintendent the way. Not to be able to find one's way among these paths

268

having already been here several days would be as feeble as getting lost in one's own backyard.

I walk more quickly.

'I don't think there's anything for you to worry about, superintendent,' I say, breathing heavily. 'Your wife has suffered a serious loss. It takes time to recover from that kind of thing. No two people grieve in the same way. Some weep and lament for days on end, others have a great need to be active and start societies to honour the departed... Your wife's way of grieving is far from unusual.'

'Forgive me for saying so, Pastor, but I know all that already. Of course she must be allowed to grieve for her brother in any way she likes. But I'm convinced she needs to talk to somebody.'

'Have you tried yourself? After all, you're the person nearest to her.'

He nods sadly.

'Oh yes, I've certainly tried. But I don't think I'm the right...'

'Why not?'

'Sometimes I've no idea what she's talking about. She can break one of her endless silences to say something like the world is cold and life is meaningless, and when I ask her to explain, or at least tell me how she's reached such gloomy conclusions, she either won't answer and shrugs her shoulders, or looks at me as though I'm not quite right in the head. Then she says something reassuring, just so I'll think she wasn't being serious but just expressing some whim of the moment, and then that silence sinks over her again. No, she needs to talk to someone wise and experienced. I've made a few enquiries, and heard nothing but good about you, Pastor.'

I stop.

'Made enquiries? Where? I thought no one here knew who I was.'

'Oh no...'

The superintendent sounds pained. I notice for the first time that there seems to be something strained about his breathing. Each breath ends with a groan, as if a little push is needed to get all the air out of his lungs.

At last I can see the end of Love Lane, and the trees where the Reader's Stone stands.

This conversation with Superintendent Hansson has put me in a better mood. I can of course indulge in thoughts about being here to rest, and that it's a nuisance that my responsibility for the souls of others follows me wherever I go, but however hard I try I can't feel annoyed.

I slow down and look seriously at the superintendent. He makes a movement towards his collar, wheezes theatrically and gives a laugh. Sweat has broken out on his forehead and he presses his lips together in a way common with people ashamed of having bad teeth.

'I beg you, Pastor,' he says in a low voice. 'It hurts me to see her fade away in this manner. If you could just talk to her and get some idea of how bad things are with her, I'd be eternally grateful. Perhaps you're right in your view, and if so there's nothing for it but to let time pass. But it could also be that things are worse with her than I thought.'

I look away.

'You must understand that I hesitate,' I say. 'She may very well not want to talk to me about matters of the soul. And unless she wants to, any discussion may do more harm than good.'

The superintendent shakes his head slowly.

'She would never go to a priest of her own accord. Or to anyone else either. It's not in her nature. When you meet her you'll understand why. Just trust me when I say this is the best way.'

'How do you see it happening?'

'Start a conversation with her. I'm sure the rest'll follow naturally from that.'

Over by the Reader's Stone the residents are moving slowly to the benches. Their light voices are oddly without resonance in the open air, as if embedded in thick bolsters.

The superintendent draws several deep, loudly hissing breaths, and for a moment it sounds as if, in an attack of fury over his ailing lungs, he's parodying his own wheezing breath and giving a savage imitation of it.

'You see,' he says, 'I really wanted to talk to you first, before making my request. Naturally I can't claim to have had the opportunity to get to know you particularly well. But I do feel great confidence in you, in fact I did so from the first moment, and I'm sure my wife will too. If I'd had any doubt about that I'd never have asked you to do this for me.'

I nod.

'I will talk to her, I promise. But I can't be insistent about it. If she and I are to go on talking, it must be on her initiative.'

'Thank you!'

The superintendent holds out his hand. His fingers feel damp and oddly soft.

'I can't ask more than that.'

'But how will I recognise her?'

'Come, I'll show you.'

A mischievous expression comes into his eyes and he takes a few careful steps towards the Reader's Stone. When we're near enough to be able to distinguish individual faces in the little congregation he starts walking behind me.

'See the woman to the left in the second row? White hat…'

He gets no further before being stricken by an attack of coughing. I turn and see him bent forward with his arm pressed hard against his mouth.

I look at the congregation again. I see the woman he indicated. The brim of her hat hides the upper part of her face. When she moves her head I see she has dark hair gathered in a bun at the neck.

'I see her,' I say.

The superintendent has straightened up, but still keeps the crook of his arm pressed against his mouth. His eyes are half-open and bright with tears.

He nods. Then pats me on the shoulder and hurries away with long strides, bent forward like a little wading bird.

I'm careful not to look at her as I sweep my eyes over the rows of benches. There's an empty seat a couple of rows further back. The people on the bench seem to shrink with fear at the sight of me and move closer together as if forced to make room for a large bear.

The service begins. The pale young priest nods to me before announcing the hymn, 'Season of Flowers'. I close my eyes. I've been waiting so long for this.

I keep my eyes shut for some time. Then I look around carefully, watching arrows of light pierce the foliage of the trees and butterflies and other flying insects whirling about among the trunks. The Reader's Stone towers like a monster to the left.

A wind gets up. It's mild and cooling. It rustles the leaves and turns the pages of our hymn books and I look up at the trees, thinking that the wind is like a father's playful hand in the hair of a much-loved child.

The people around me are sitting still, listening intently to the young priest with their hands folded in their laps. He's pleasant to listen to. There's something unpretentious and relaxed about his tone and phrasing.

God has allowed me to get well. Not just that, but it's possible I never was ill. At least, not in the way I feared.

It's as if the pressure on my chest has been relieved. Like being rid of a garment that has chafed and pinched for as long as one can remember.

I was in such a hurry. I thought my days were numbered. And even if I managed to forget my state of health from time to time, or circumstances forced me to, I now realise it was always somewhere there at the back of my mind.

Suddenly order has been restored. I may die tomorrow, or after twenty years, depending on when God calls me home. And that's how it should be.

God's given me back my life. Perhaps I needed to live in fear of losing it, so that I should learn to value it and rejoice in it.

When I look around among these people, who until a moment ago meant little to me, I can feel great confidence, indeed overwhelming tenderness.

We've learned so much and we've come so far. We've realised that we've been created in God's image, and we've developed ways of worshipping Him and being close to Him. It's true that powerful forces are working to drive us to destruction and to spread godlessness, self-love and greed throughout the world. But there are also strong forces resisting this that refuse to give up.

That is where I want to go. I want to join them.

I can't remember ever having seen things this way before. Outwardly, of course, I've talked about it so many times that I've lost count: from pulpits and altars, in and around church porches. But I've never felt so passionately certain in my heart as now.

I see a movement in one of the firs on the far side of the path. A squirrel jumps down from the tree, dashes down the path and disappears into the undergrowth. A boy at the end of the row has clearly seen the squirrel too; he leans over so far his father has to haul him back.

I remember something that happened when Helga was little. During the time when she was only a little girl to me, and nothing more.

She'd been given a pair of pet mice for Christmas. She kept

them in a cage under the stairs, and her happiness knew no bounds when it turned out that the female was pregnant. When I came to call a little later, I wondered why Helga didn't come down to say hello.

'She's with the mice,' said Birger in a tired voice.

He explained that there'd been complications, and that one of the young had turned out to be deformed.

We went to look, but first he made clear to me that Helga was very upset about the little mouse, and that it wasn't advisable to show anything but the deepest sympathy.

She was sitting beside the cage with her feet pulled up and her hands clasped around her small ankles. She had dark shadows under her eyes and her lips were dry and bloodless.

I got down on my knees to look at the mice, and as I remember we didn't exchange a single word, but Helga unhooked the top of the cage and opened it.

I counted four or five young lying in a row being suckled by their mother. The father stayed close to his family, watching us closely.

One miserable little creature was stumbling around in a corner. It had obviously been disturbed when the cage was opened and was looking for shelter, but one of its forepaws was shrivelled and withered, and it was getting nowhere, just scratching about ineffectively in the sawdust and for the most part slithering around in circles.

Helga picked up the little mouse and showed it to me. To make matters even worse it seemed to have a harelip, so that it was not clear whether or not the infant mouse would be able to take in any of its mother's milk, even if, contrary to expectation, it did manage to reach her teats.

I looked up at Birger with raised eyebrows, and opened my mouth to ask if they couldn't try and feed it through a pipette, but he shook his head before I managed to say anything.

Large heavy tears rolled down Helga's cheeks. I myself felt sad and I thought that surely something could be done that hadn't yet occurred to them.

'Have you tried putting the little one with its mother? It seems to be finding it difficult to get there on its own.'

'She pushes him away,' whispered Helga.

Her explanation made me freeze with horror, which might be thought remarkable since it contained nothing I didn't know already. Nevertheless it was as if I'd never clearly realised how hard and merciless the nature of the animal world was.

Helga held the little baby mouse against her cheek, caressed it with her lips and whispered tenderly to it. Then she threw her head up and looked accusingly at me.

'How can it be so different? When we humans come upon a crippled child that can't manage on its own, we take more trouble with that child than with all the others who are healthy and don't need our help. Why is it the opposite with animals?'

I hesitated before answering.

'Because they have no conscience,' I said. 'And we really can't blame them for that. They can't help it. That's how they were made.'

I talked for a long time. I found it difficult to stop. The words I was saying sounded as new to me as they must have done to her. We discovered something together.

I told her that, however painful it might be, we should perhaps be thankful that God had given us the animals to compare ourselves with, since they made visible something otherwise difficult to discover and hard to describe, namely conscience.

When we compare ourselves with the mouse that rejects her own offspring and leaves him to a certain death, it becomes so obvious that there's something in us that's divine. Something that distinguishes us from the rest of God's creation, and bears witness to the fact that God expects something special from us.

'I do understand that it hurts you to see this little mouse suffer...'

'Helge.'

'What?'

'His name's Helge.'

'Yes... I do understand that it hurts you. It hurts me too. But I'm also very happy that you and I and all other human beings have been given a conscience by God.'

Helga didn't get any happier. Not at that moment, anyway. But at least she stopped crying. And I remember that I made use of the little mouse and its harelip in a highly praised sermon.

The joy of being alive. The joy of being a human being, with all that involves. The joy of being exactly who one is.

... Yes, that's rare indeed. Sometimes you find it, then it slips out of your hands, and you think it's lost for ever. But then you find it again when you least expect it. And so it goes on.

For a long time all I can see is the white hat. Her shoulders are broad and heavy under her dress, which is the dusty red colour of dried blood. Occasionally she turns her head for a moment and looks out across the bog, and I discover she isn't particularly beautiful and has pendulous jowls, a narrow nose and a prominent chin. The sort of female face that rouses sympathy of a not particularly pleasing kind, since it is essentially compassionate.

If you watch an unknown person long enough and thoroughly enough, she soon won't seem a stranger any more, because you'll have unconsciously furnished her with qualities you'd like to find in her.

If it's someone you feel hostile to you'll furnish them with a series of unattractive qualities, so that in the end your antipathy will appear entirely comprehensible, even logical. If it's someone you'd like to be on good terms with you'll do the opposite.

As for the woman in the white hat, it seems I don't want her either as an enemy or as a friend. It seems I'd just like to feel sorry for her.

I persuade myself that she's lonely just like me, and that people either ignore her or direct worried or indulgent looks at her, and that they think she doesn't notice this, whereas she's acutely conscious of it.

Just like me.

I know no more about her than I did before. But my preconceptions get more specific with every minute that passes.

When the service is over I notice from the corner of my eye that the young priest's trying to catch my attention and that he's waving at me for some reason, so I quickly slip behind the little crowd of people and move off towards Love Lane, leaving my hymn book 'forgotten' on the bench.

I stand in the lane with a worried expression and pretend to be completely taken up with searching through my pockets for something, and when I see the woman – Anna, I think he called her – passing I give my waistcoat pocket a satisfied tap and begin to catch her up.

She's walking with slow, thoughtful steps, almost as if skiing, and takes no notice when I come up beside her.

The people bustling by on either side of us are deep in animated conversation after sitting silent for so long. Several children are chasing each other down the lane, either not hearing or pretending not to hear warnings their mothers are hissing at them.

I bend slightly towards the woman and ask what she thought of the service.

She narrows her eyes at me in surprise and stops.

She shields her eyes with her hand even though the sunlight is no longer so bright, looks me over quickly, and laughs.

'I liked it.'

She keeps her eyes on me.

'What did you think?' she asks.

I put my hands behind my back and begin to praise the young priest's voice, and talk about the difficult art of sounding unaffected and natural without doing unnecessary violence to the text or popularising it unduly. This is a subject close to my heart, and in normal circumstances I'd be ready to talk about it as long and in as unforced a manner as anyone could wish.

But I'm sounding forced and worried. Worse still, almost cross.

I could never have imagined she'd come to a halt in the way she did. We stand facing one another with people looking askance at us as they pass, and I realise that to those around us we must look like two old acquaintances in the middle of dealing with something so important that they had to stop in the middle of the lane, face to face. She seems quite unconscious of this. Perhaps this is because of her unworldly frame of mind. Perhaps it's been a long time since she last shared in even the simplest conversation. Perhaps for that reason it fills her with uncontrollable joy. Perhaps this is why she stares at me in such an unashamed and inquisitive manner and nods so encouragingly at everything I say.

We introduce ourselves. I already know her name. She sounds almost breathless when she says it: 'Anna Hansson'.

'I was thinking of taking a short walk before bathing,' I say. 'Would it be altogether too forward of me to ask you if...'

'I'd be happy to keep you company.'

Of course, I think. Poor lonely creature.

At last we move on.

We walk down one of the narrower paths that runs parallel with Love Lane. I don't know if it has a name.

We pass several villas with names like 'Bellevue' and 'Victoria' on their fences. Under a tree near one of the villas a little girl in a summer dress is swinging backwards and forwards, uttering at the same time a rich, utterly happy sound. A man in a white suit with a bristling moustache is standing behind her, still and expressionless as a post, rhythmically pushing her back to keep the swing moving. He follows us with his eyes.

We leave the villas behind. The path gets increasingly narrow. There's barely room for us to walk side by side. She's so close to me that I can hear her breathing. Perhaps she can hear me breathing too.

The vegetation's getting thicker. Shoots and young branches reach over the path and brush against us as we pass. The leaves look sticky.

The slightest false step and one would fall headlong into the arms of leathery leaves and soft twigs. The thought fills me with fear and delight.

Then the path grows wider; now the tops of the pines make a vaulted roof over us and there's a sweet smell of resin.

I glance furtively at Fru Hansson. She's walking with her head held high and a little smile on her face. She seems completely carefree, and for some reason I think she looks proud, and I wonder how this can be and feel my pitying attitude to her must be rather misplaced.

'Do you live in Stockholm?' I ask.

'No, we moved to Kapellskär several years ago, when my husband got a job with the Customs.'

Her voice is light, almost like a child's, and at the same time slightly husky, as if she'd caught a slight cold.

'They say it's beautiful up there,' I say.

'Yes, it is beautiful.'

'I didn't see your husband at the service?'

'No, he's away at the hurly-burly, as usual.'

When Fru Hansson sees my puzzled expression she bursts out laughing and touches my arm lightly.

'Forgive me. I mean the skittle alley. You must have heard it! It's dreadfully noisy.'

I shake my head.

'My husband's something of a fanatic when it comes to skittles. He looks forward to it all year. He asked Dr Lidin if it could damage his health to play so much, but the doctor said the opposite was more likely. So now he tells everyone he's playing under doctor's orders.'

I have to turn away to hide my smile. What was it he told me? That he had to go for an examination? He should have been able to work out that his lie would be detected.

We walk in silence for a bit.

'Are you very ill?' asks Fru Hansson suddenly.

I look at her in astonishment. She drops her eyes and opens her mouth to say something, and I assume she's trying to work out an apology for having asked such an impertinent question.

But no apology comes, and when I see the unconcealed agitation in her face I'm filled with strongly conflicting feelings. I'm extremely embarrassed and wish I was far away, but at the same time I'm aware that her agitation touches something deep in my soul.

It awakens a hunger in me. I can't put it better. And there's something about that hunger that frightens me.

'Not at all,' I answer in a hoarse voice. 'I thought I was ill. That I had a bad heart. But Dr Lidin has examined me and established that everything is as it should be.'

'I'm glad to hear it.'

She laughs. She sounds embarrassed up to a point, but also as if she feels great relief.

I can't think why she takes the slightest interest in my health. For a moment I'm tempted to ask. But that wouldn't sound quite right. It would sound as if I were begging.

She has small white teeth. Her mouth's wider than I first thought. When she laughs a crack stretches across her face from side to side.

It's incomprehensible that only a few minutes ago I thought she wasn't particularly good-looking.

There are so many ways in which a woman can be beautiful. Some are picturesquely beautiful, strikingly beautiful to everyone.

Like Helga.

You can see men exchanging glances at the sight of her, glances of mutual understanding, much like when a very fat person comes into the room, or someone with conspicuously red hair: everyone knows what is meant.

But Fru Hansson's beautiful too. I see that now. Evidently you have to spend a little time in her company to discover it.

That should be a sign that it's something in her that makes her beautiful. Something good and friendly.

So logically women in the first category, the picturesquely beautiful, should be transformed and become less beautiful, even downright ugly, if after a while in their company you realise they're deceitful, ill-natured and malevolent.

But I'm not quite sure about that.

We pass the croquet lawn. Some half-grown boys are leaning on their mallets with studied nonchalance as they watch a reddish-blond youth with wet-combed hair standing bent over his ball. He takes careful aim with his mallet. Several girls are standing at the side of the court whispering together in excitement. The red-blond boy gives them an irritated look, but they don't notice.

'You don't enjoy skittles yourself?' I ask.

Fru Hansson shakes her head.

'I've been once or twice to watch. Women do play, of course. But it's, how shall I put it… They seem different from me. They play with great enthusiasm, they're noisy and laugh. Some play really well. And they take it all for granted in a way I'd never be able to no matter how hard I tried. I think I'm too reserved.'

I hum and turn away. I understand very well what she means and should be able to tell her so, but something gets in the way.

We've reached the road to the bath-house.

'It was nice of you to keep me company,' I say.

She looks surprised. Then she comes to, and makes a movement towards her dress as if about to curtsey.

'Yes… Goodbye, then.'

Then she goes up towards the bath-house.

I go straight on. Everything around me has gone quiet like when something's pressed over your eardrums.

I walk past the tennis courts and greenhouses. I walk with quick steps. I hear nothing and see nothing but Fru Hansson's bewildered and unhappy face when I took my abrupt leave of her. It was so obvious, how something was extinguished in her eyes. Like a candle blown out.

Why did I do it? Why, why, why…

I board a conveyance taking people to the lake.

The journey takes us along poor roads winding through the forest.

A gentleman tells stories from earlier visits to the spa. To judge by his dialect he's from the west coast. He is in fact talking to the man sitting beside him, but he has such a rich, penetrating voice that the rest of us are forced to listen whether we want to or not. He has a bald head, cornflower-blue eyes and big white teeth that look as if they're made of porcelain. He could be a lead actor from some theatre. His voice cuts through the noise of the carriage, the clattering of hooves and the wind in our ears. He's talking about rambles with friends through the woods, about savage elk bulls who chased them over stock and stone, and about lynx snarling overhead in the trees. Of farms out in the middle of the forest where they were offered sumptuous meals by the endlessly hospitable local population. Of legends and ghost stories they listened to while darkness was falling outside.

Everyone on the carriage listens with bated breath, hanging hungrily on his words. One or two try to break in on his monologue, but if not actively hushed down, they are at least totally ignored. One or two cast uneasy glances in my direction as the bald man gives elaborate details about mysterious movements of waves out on the lake and inexplicable lights in the dark November woods. As if they're afraid I might break into some fire and brimstone condemnation of all ancient folk-beliefs.

But my thoughts are elsewhere.

I'm thinking of my home in Stockholm. My ordinary life at home. The church where I preach.

I'm trying to visualise it all. But I get even the simplest things wrong.

The door I go through every day, for example. The front door to my home. To the vicarage. It's white. I'm absolutely sure of that. But what does the doorknob look like? I summon up a particular doorknob in my mind and think with relief, yes, that's exactly what it's like! But if I then imagine another doorknob I become unsure. Perhaps it actually looks like that?

I'm looking for a firm point in my reality, somewhere to cast anchor. But instead I'm drifting ever further out to sea.

During Helga's and my first years as man and wife I could sometimes stop in the middle of something I was doing, when alone, and be aware of the intensity of my longing for her.

Then an involuntary smile would spread over my face when I realised that what I longed for was a fact. She was in truth my wife. Her name wasn't Helga Waller, but Helga Gregorius. There were papers and documents to prove it. And any number of witnesses to confirm it.

I'm the happiest man in the world, I'd think. And I'd try and visualise my happiness. How I would walk into the room. How she would get up and come to meet me. And I...

Suddenly I realised I didn't know what she looked like.

I reached my hand out to her face. But it was empty. As though someone had cut out her face and just left her hair.

How was it possible to be stricken by such mental confusion?

I shook my head, gave a nervous laugh and thought, how absurd! Helga, my beautiful young wife, of course she looks like this…

But I was groping about in thin air.

I knew all I needed was some little thing to start from, and that if for example I could visualise her mouth, the rest would follow automatically.

But nothing happened. The only thing I could be certain of was that she was blonde. That had been said so often. That, and that she was beautiful. I knew that as well as I knew the rivers of the province of Halland. Or the German prepositions. Or the Acts of the Apostles and the Fathers of the Church. But knowing she was blonde didn't get me very far. Nor did the fact that she was beautiful. 'Beautiful.' What an empty, cold, soulless word that is.

I closed my eyes. I whispered her name. But she was nothing but a mass of brittle blonde hair and a tasteful dress. Where her face should have been was a gaping empty hole.

It was like being the victim of a nasty trick. A sadistic illusion.

This woman who'd exercised such special power over me ever since she was a little girl. She who I'd seen bud and burst into flower. She who was before my eyes even during Lydia's final hours.

There's a saying: 'To stake all on one card'. I'd invested everything I possessed in Helga. I'd packed my treasure in my bag and hurried home. Eager to be alone with her. But when I opened the bag it was empty.

I experienced these eerie attacks of amnesia several times in our first years.

Finally I learned a few tricks. There was a birthmark under the lobe of her ear and a crooked canine tooth in her lower jaw. If I thought about these two distinctive features, and at the same time imagined her humming a tune, or more precisely, the moment when her contemplative humming turned into a rather more extrovert warbling... That was when I could see her before me at last.

It has clouded over considerably. Deep in the woods it's nearly dusk. The rough, harsh screeching of birds resounds through the pillared hall of pines.

We emerge from the forest and run alongside the great grey lake. For a moment the lake is a precipitous downward slope at the end of the world, while far away towering dark grey clouds billow like cool damp bolsters to sink into. Out on the lake two men floating in a skiff are taking in a net, moving slowly and instinctively, like beetles.

The conveyance stops outside the bath-house. Everyone collects their bags and gets off, all taking care to keep close to the bald man, as if they realise that if anything exciting happens here, it's bound to happen near him.

The bath-house is glittering like a king's crown, its strong electric light casting golden streaks across water the colour of expensive cognac.

Some women are sitting by the shore under a parasol which has half blown over. The wind's pulling and tearing at their hats. In their white dresses they look like dandelion seed-heads. A waiter struggles to straighten the parasol then takes a few cautious steps back and looks accusingly out over the lake. The women look in our direction. They're presumably waiting for their turns in the bath-house.

The bald man says something in an unnecessarily loud voice, someone adds a comment, and everyone laughs.

We change in small huts by the shore. Inside the floor is wet and gravelly. I move clumsily in the narrow space and constantly knock a knee or an elbow against the walls, causing hollow thuds as though I'm shut inside a cello.

I'm in my bathing costume and just about to go out when I hear voices outside the hut, and stop.

'An orange,' says someone.

'You don't say,' answers someone else in a tone of disbelief.

'Neither more nor less.'

'The going rate, you mean…?'

'Absolutely. It's generally established. You can buy them in what they call the Exchange building. I like to keep several kilos in a bowl in my room. Sort of unofficial signal.'

'Of course, they don't cost all that much…'

'You'll see for yourself. It makes them extraordinarily happy. Oranges are rich in vitamins too. Pure summer diet for some of the girls…'

Someone laughs.

'How many are you expected to give her, if one may ask?'

'One's OK. But you can make it two, if she's put a bit more effort than usual into it…'

More laughter. The voices move away.

I stand with my head bowed and a hand on either wall. My face is hot with consternation. I lift my head and look at the door.

'Filth,' I say in a low voice.

Everywhere the same thing, wherever you go. Men who want to live in filth and lovelessness. And women who help them do it.

I go out and have to struggle for breath as a cold wind sweeps over me. I totter over sharp little stones to the jetty. Some of the men who were in the conveyance with me run on to the jetty and let out happy cries when it sways and rocks beneath them.

I try to move in a reasonably dignified manner. My feet look white and unpleasant.

The women under the parasol are watching us intently. Not far from them I see a woman in a red dress at a table: it's her, of course.

She's sitting alone holding a glass. She lifts her hand and waves.

I wave back and force a smile, though she won't see it from so far away. One of the women under the parasol thinks the wave is meant for her and raises a hand uncertainly, then notices she's made a mistake. Curious, she turns to see who I was waving at, then says something to one of her friends.

The sight of Fru Hansson at her table rouses an inexplicable distaste in me. As soon as I've turned away from her I hiss out a stream of invective. I can't bear to look at her.

Alone, when all the rest are sitting in lively big groups. Wearing red, when everyone else is relaxed in white. Unhappy and gloomy, when all the others are swigging their healthy spa water and looking forward to the future with the greatest confidence.

She sits there like a perpetual reproach, with plenty of time to indulge herself in watching my swollen, shapeless body as I waddle across the jetty, one anxious hand on the rail.

Blast her. Blast her!

It's starting to rain. Heavy skies are moving over us. The rain's thundering on the bath-house roof and dripping from the roof beams. The people around me are making plans to wait till the rain passes and then eat dinner in the café. I hurry off to change. I'm the only passenger on the conveyance home.

When I reach my room I find a maid busy lighting a fire in the grate. She says something about the weather, and as I answer I can hear a weight of sadness in my voice. I sit on the bed and watch her crouching in front of the fireplace as the flames begin to spread their warm glow over the floor and along the walls. I think of the sadness in my voice and wonder if the girl heard it too, and if so whether she feels any urge to comfort me.

And if so, whether I could accept the comfort she offered.

She's sweet and dainty. She seems very young. She has the face of a little doll. Bright green eyes. Her hands are so small and child-like.

I think of the men and their oranges. I try out an idea. If any one of those men were here, he might claim his rights. If so, what exactly would he do? Perhaps go first and close the door. Look meaningfully at the girl by the flames. Go to her and take her hand. She gets up.

'A letter's come for you, Pastor,' she says, breathing out a little. 'I put it there on the table.'

'Oh, thank you very much.'

She turns away and looks into the flames. Then she looks at me again. She gives an embarrassed laugh, curtsies and goes out.

The rain seems to be easing. There is still a steady sprinkle on the courtyard, fine spray, silk threads. A thin white smoke's hovering above the ground. There's a family peering out from under the awning on the Stock Exchange building, a boy is sitting on the steps, legs wide apart and head hanging, while his father pulls greedily on his cigar and squints at the sky.

I rip open the letter. It's from Pastor Wenge, my locum. I glance through it. His main purpose is to assure me how well he's been fulfilling his duties and what warm and spontaneous confidence he's been enjoying from the parishioners. There are also several sentences in brackets, humorous observations presumably jotted down when he became aware his letter was beginning to sound a bit boastful and a bit too exaggeratedly dutiful.

In a postscript at the bottom he reports that my wife has asked him to send me her best greetings, and say she hopes my stay's doing me good.

I let the letter drop. They must have had some opportunity for conversation, and he must have mentioned he was thinking of writing to me.

Helga comes to mind in various guises and situations; I see her standing out of breath and red-cheeked at the door on her way somewhere, no doubt to the alley near Stortorget, while Pastor Wenge sits at my writing desk, a straight-backed paragon of virtue; she tosses a greeting into the room to him before hurrying down the stairs; and there they are sitting in the garden sipping a glass of cherry wine while he mentions he's thinking of writing me a letter, and it's the first thing either of them has said for a long time, and Helga, who's been sitting sunk deep in thought, looks up, suddenly awake, and asks him to send me her greetings, before slowly slipping back into her dreams again.

Which makes it clear to Pastor Wenge that I have a wife who has better things to do than send greetings to her sick husband herself, and of course Pastor Wenge has a close friend to whom he passes this news in confidence, and this friend has a confidant of his own, and so on…

I'm surprised to find these thoughts rouse no feeling in me. They try repeatedly to do so. They attack me with their hooks, as they've often done before, and the hooks have the same sharp barbs on them as they've always had.

But they scratch in vain, searching for somewhere to get a grip, then slide down and fall silently to the ground.

Instead my thoughts go back to the girl who lit the fire in my room.

I know nothing about her. Perhaps she lives on some farm in the neighbourhood. Perhaps she has older sisters who've worked here before and have told her what it's like. Perhaps she's looked forward to this summer and the spa residents streaming in, perhaps she's heard stories of girls who have married ship-owners and lawyers and found a shimmering new life.

Isn't that what we all dream of when we're young? A brilliant new life.

Either we don't get it, and go on ploughing the same old furrow as our forefathers, condemned to go about fretting for all our wasted opportunities, and walking about with it like a stone in one's shoe; fretting about how we could so easily have taken the big step and gone to Stockholm or America if something hadn't held us back.

Or else we do take the big step, in which case the day comes when we realise that unfortunately our brilliant new life didn't change us into shimmering new people, but like Cinderella in the fairy tale we shall inevitably hear the clock strike and find our silk clothes falling apart and our bony limbs peering through the holes.

For the rest of our lives we shall be incomplete, half-baked, scrambled together, and just as we never feel entirely at home in our brilliant new lives, neither can we return to our old ones, those lives we were once so desperate to leave behind, because others have now taken over that old world and they look askance at us, and the way we used to speak has become old-fashioned, and our old life is gone for ever; it only survives in our memories, if even there.

Perhaps the girl's dreaming of a brilliant new life. Perhaps she thinks she's on the point of making a decisive leap, and perhaps she's criticising herself for being indecisive, indeed, perhaps all she wants is for someone to give her a push in the right direction. Or in any direction. Rather than staying where she is and continuing to be in two minds.

Perhaps she knows better than anyone that the men who roll over her in their beds and send her out into the corridor with an orange or two never give much thought to the question of who she really is or what she might hope for from life, but that most of them are interested in nothing but an insistent bodily need, hardly different from their recurring need to snip off the hair growing in their noses or visit the privy.

But hope springs eternal. No matter how little there is of it, hope's always there. Even if only one girl in a hundred meets a man who takes a fancy to her and wants to carry her off to a new life, nonetheless she does exist, this one girl. She is real. She can't be explained away. And it should be possible to work out what her chances are, just as you can work out your chances of winning the lottery. Perhaps she thinks such a small investment is worth it.

Oh well, these things may be as they may be, and I could brood over the matter for ever. But I could never do what so many other residents do without giving the least thought to the matter. I could never take that girl as though I had a right to her.

I wish this could at least make me feel a slightly better human being. But it doesn't.

On the other hand I'd empty a ship's cargo of oranges over any-one who could bring herself to love me.

I pull my chair closer to the fire and put on a little more wood.

I can hear a carriage draw in under my window and stop in front of the Stock Exchange. I hear excited voices spreading among the buildings. I hear horses snorting. I'm tired and a bit cold, but that's all right because I have a fire to warm me, and I can lie down on my bed and rest for as long as I like.

There was a girl I was in love with during my student years. She was the sister of a friend. Her name was May. She was two years older than me. We wrote each other long passionate letters.

I've forgotten so much. But I still remember some things clear-ly. I remember insisting May's parents should meet my mother. I arranged the whole thing with great authority. I decided a date. I booked railway tickets.

I wanted everyone to know our relationship was serious. Everyone! My mother must understand it, and May's parents. My brothers too, and not least both May and myself.

They must understand, and I also wanted them to be impressed.

But I can't remember what it was that was supposed to impress them.

I breezed about as if intoxicated. Rushed to the telegraph office. The man there made a few amused comments. He wondered what could have possibly been the cause of such feverish activity. I gave him an honest and long-winded answer. I straightened my back, blushed and told him of my love for May, riveting him with my gaze till his smile faded and he dropped his eyes and mumbled his congratulations.

Then the great day arrived. I hadn't slept well the night before. It was drizzling. My eyes were smarting. I went from room to room in our little cottage straightening out creases in tablecloths, picking up chaff and pine-needles from the hall floor, sweeping the stairs clean.

My brothers weren't at home. My mother had spent several days baking, and the house was full of the delicious sweet smell of fresh baking. She cleared some things away and wiped others clean, moving slowly in that lingering, contented manner people have when setting things in order after work well done.

I stood on the porch step and felt my chest expanding. It occurred to me that it didn't bother me in the least that May and her parents would be inspecting our house. Normally I didn't like my friends to see how I lived. I'd been like that all through my childhood. But suddenly that fear had gone, as if charmed away.

I couldn't put into words everything that was going through my head. It was as though I'd been floating about for a long time with no fixed point, letting dreams carry me now this way now that. But when I stood in the porch and visualised how we'd move a little timidly from one room to another in our best clothes, then I knew I could go with them, and see everything they saw without either cowering in shame or swelling with pride, but I would see the cottage where I'd grown up *just as it was*, for better and for worse. I had come to terms with it, and with everything associated with it, and with my mother, my brothers and my dead father.

Paradoxically this intoxicated me more than ever.

We had some coffee, Mother and I. It wasn't yet time for our guests to arrive.

It wasn't easy for me to feel comfortable with the silence that had fallen between us, so I talked about the plans May and I had made for the future.

Mother had a little smile on her face. After a while she looked straight at me and said:

'You're nice to the girls, you are.'

I didn't answer.

'It's good,' she went on. 'It makes me so happy that at least one of my sons is.'

Her voice was warm. She was burning with pride. She kept her eyes on me.

She reached across the table and took my hand, and I let her. I sat watching her wrinkled thumb move backwards and forwards on the back of my hand.

She only meant well. I'm sure of that. Even so I went completely cold. Not only cold. I felt ill.

I was nice to girls.

I looked out of the window and thought of the visit we were expecting. May and her parents. They'd been travelling since early morning, and if they liked they could stay overnight. Mother had made up beds for them. Suddenly I couldn't understand why they were coming to our house at all. It had all vanished.

I thought of the boy who was 'nice to the girls', and felt nothing but contempt for him. He was a ridiculous figure. Neither man nor woman, just a spineless half-creature, wandering anxiously between one and the other.

Yes, she certainly meant well. But something in her voice made me feel inadequate. Like a squeaky, precocious little lad who's been strutting about in his dad's clothes for a while, living the game till it's come to seem real to him.

Suddenly I realised she'd never really taken my solemn speeches seriously. She'd agreed to the visit because she'd seen how important it was to me, but she never believed for a moment I'd ever marry May and build a family with her.

The visit was torture. We received them in the courtyard and showed them around the house. I kept quiet. There was nothing to say. My eyes burned with tears. May's parents were pleasant, thoughtful people. I can't remember their names. They asked a lot of questions about my studies. They insisted I was a good influence on their daughter.

I particularly remember May's mother. She was tall and dark and dressed almost like a middle-class lady. I understood from the way she spoke to me that she was taking our marriage plans very seriously. But this only made me hate her for allowing herself to be fooled by my effrontery, for having allowed things to go so far without sticking a pin in the ridiculous soap bubble I'd blown for us.

I was even hostile to May, who couldn't understand what was wrong. At first she smiled bravely and repeatedly tried to catch my eye, but I pretended not to notice. After a while she excused herself and ran off behind the coach-house. Then she came back with red eyes and the same brave smile as before.

I felt they were intruding on us. I was crushed by shame. All I wanted was that they should go and leave us in peace. The silence became more and more oppressive. They gave me enquiring looks. As though they were wondering what had happened to all my spirit and energy.

In the end Mother felt she had to take over. She told them about my brothers and Father, and remembered all the best anecdotes.

Her voice was slow and flat, and like a blind person she addressed some unspecified point in the room. At one point she almost hissed at me. As if to get me to pull myself together. But this was the last straw. I had no room in me for more humiliation. I couldn't be reached any more.

It was a relief when they left. We promised to write as soon as possible. May's parents insisted it was our turn to visit them next, and they told us about excursions we'd be able to make, and how beautiful it was down by the river when the ice was breaking up.

But we knew we'd never meet again. Our mouths constantly repeated assurances that this was the beginning of a lifelong companionship, but our eyes were saying a bitter and bewildered farewell.

Mother and I stood side by side watching them leave. May turned around one last time. I raised my hand and waved. She didn't wave back. For a short moment my bitterness dispersed, and I woke and saw her disappear. I wanted to break loose from my paralysis and run after her, I wanted to call her back, I wanted to get her to radiate happiness again. But I couldn't move.

How long ago was it? Forty years. Perhaps even longer. Now Mother's sitting in a nursing home, and she hardly knows if it's day or night.

But when I remember her words, how she said I was 'nice to girls', I feel her octopus tentacles reaching out for me, at first lightly and playfully with a soft warm touch that I enjoy, but then shooting out violently, one arm after another, grabbing me with ever greater force and energy and I am nothing like as fat and swollen as I am now, but my limbs are thin and white as a wax candle, and I sit mute and powerless, panic spreading through me, because I can't defend myself; there's nothing but love in my mother's embrace, greater than the whole world, measureless, her love endlessly gaping for more, more, and when I want to tear myself loose from her grip it's far too late, because there's no limit to the number of her arms, and she has the strength of a monster.

I wish I could intervene as the grown man I am now and help the boy with the thin arms; I wish I could prise away the tentacles or if necessary hack them off to give him a little breathing space, a chance to calm down. But he's me and I'm him.

Something's wrong. Something went wrong. Not only the day May and her parents came to call. It had been going on a long time. Perhaps ever since my life began. I just can't put a finger on what. And even now if I could walk into our cottage that day I'd have nothing to say, and I don't know what else we could have done.

I was nice to girls. I went on being nice to girls. Something to rejoice about.

At the same time it sickens me.

Everything nice, warm, good, well-meaning, everything that pours from the wrinkled hands that reach towards me across the table; in short, everything that's love. It sickens me.

I suddenly start in my chair. I don't know if I've fallen asleep. The strangest thoughts have been coming to me. Dark and frightening, but so much to the point that I can't just dismiss them as a dream.

I look around for signs that I've been sleeping. The burned-out fire would seem to suggest this. The rain's passed, sunlight's streaming in and it's unpleasantly hot in the room.

I tidy my hair in the mirror and go out.

It's stuffy and humid. I head for the spring.

A group of people come out of the salon and go towards the Stock Exchange. A gust of wind flutters the nearby birch tree and the women let out little cries when a shower of water-drops falls on them.

I hear small steps running in the gravel behind me; they pass me, it's a little girl in a white dress. Her stockings are wet and stained above her shoes, and she's holding something high above her head in her right hand. A little further on her mother's standing waiting for her. Suddenly I see the mother stiffen and start scolding the girl for running about in the grass and getting her shoes and stockings wet. The girl stands stock-still for a moment, then her hand falls slack and limp, and I think: just like someone being hanged.

Outside the music room the members of the orchestra are standing chatting listlessly, and just as I approach they extinguish their cigarettes, straighten their tail-coats and go in. I follow them on impulse.

A dozen residents are sitting, waiting solemn and straight-backed in the rows of seats. There's a smell of warm wood and the ceiling is creaking gently. A gentleman with silver hair turns towards me in irritation. Suddenly his expression softens and he smiles, opening his mouth to reveal large, horsey teeth and gives me to understand from a number of deferential gestures that I should have closed the door after me.

From the platform comes a discreet clearing of throats, a scraping of chair legs and the hollow bump of a cello knocking against something. I close the door and am on the point of sitting down when I catch sight of her.

She's in the back row, furthest to the right. She gives me a rather reserved smile and a nod. I nod back.

I feel unexpectedly happy to see her. As if she were an old acquaintance. Without reflection or asking permission, I sit down beside her.

For a while I stare at the orchestra: a cornet player licks his lips nervously, tenses them and touches them gingerly with the mouthpiece of his instrument as though it might be burning hot; a cellist restlessly rolls his shoulders.

I want to say something to her before the orchestra begins

playing, if only to smooth over the abrupt way I left her before, and I bend towards her to make some comment about the rain.

She leans a little in my direction. The brim of her hat brushes the ridge of my nose. I can smell her perfume. For a moment I feel I should say something else, anything, because the position of our bodies as we bend towards one another seems to require me to whisper something a little more intimate than a remark about the rain.

'It was... It really was too bad that...'

At the same moment the orchestra sound a long, melancholy 'A' and begin tuning their instruments.

I straighten up and shake my head in a gesture of hopelessness. She smiles and turns back to face the orchestra.

They begin to play a Bach fugue. One of my favourites. Then several more pieces, all received with respectful applause. At one point the silver-haired gentleman turns and gives me an appealing look as if to say: Not bad, was it?

I listen to the music with my eyes closed.

I remember the waking dreams I had in front of the fire, and of how the thought of love sickens me; I let the music wash over everything as if it could flush my thoughts from the rocks and sweep them down into the sea.

But my thoughts resist and become accusations: they shout that I'm an impostor who's gone to God to learn love by rote, to learn it by heart like a formula, to hammer it into my head; that I've made myself at home with all the rituals, proclamations and narratives of love as a way of avoiding looking into the emptiness of my own heart, and that I have attempted to fill its emptiness with a great hullabaloo and resounding ceremonial words.

The music is stronger than the shouting voices. It wraps them in a song of praise to all that's fine and beautiful, and it proclaims God's love to be greater still, greater than anyone can imagine, even capable of embracing a fraud like me.

The smell of Fru Hansson's perfume lingers.

I imagine her sprinkling herself with a few drops. Her solemn gaze in the mirror: what would she be thinking? Would she be feeling the same as me? That ash-grey, resigned: Oh well, that's what I look like, neither more nor less. I was never better looking than that.

And then her hand, first behind one ear then behind the other, so quickly that if I'd blinked I'd have missed it.

I've kissed women just there. I know the bitterness of perfume on the tongue. And the warmth of the skin behind their ears...

I open my eyes. Fru Hansson has turned away from me and is pressing a handkerchief hard against her eyes. Her shoulders are shaking.

I touch her arm. She hurriedly dries her tears.

'What's the matter?' I ask.

She forces a smile and shakes her head. Then faces forward to listen to the music again. I try to do the same. But from the corner of my eye I can see tremors passing through her body at regular intervals like small convulsions.

The concert's over. The orchestra rises to acknowledge the applause. They bow twice. Then relax, start chattering among themselves, and feel in their pockets for their smoking equipment.

Fru Hansson tucks her handkerchief away in her handbag and starts struggling with one of the bag's brass fittings, which has caught in her sleeve. Her movements are hurried and troubled, and there's something strained about her mouth. I offer to help. She thanks me and sits with head bowed while I work the sleeve loose.

'Did you hear the bell for the first sitting for dinner?' I ask.

'No,' she says, 'I didn't hear anything.'

'I thought I'd try and fit in a short walk. Will you keep me company?'

'Yes, why not.'

Our voices are strangely husky, as though we're planning something shameful. One of the musicians lights a cigarette and waves to someone passing outside. He gives us an ambiguous look before going out to the others.

We get up and go out. We walk past the Stock Exchange and down to the Reader's Stone. It's the same way we walked last time, like an unspoken agreement.

'Did you like the music?' I ask.

She doesn't answer immediately.

'Yes,' she says. 'I was just thinking about how to describe it. But when I listen to beautiful music it is as though it articulates something which is beyond articulation. And then all words seem so... almost pathetically insufficient.'

'Yes, I noticed the music moved you deeply.'

A shadow crosses her face.

'Were you thinking about anything in particular?' I ask.

She shakes her head. She looks straight at me, with tears in her eyes, then laughs.

'That I may perhaps tell you when we know each other a little better.'

We walk past the villa where the little girl was on the swing. We can see a woman some way off going through long grass with a laundry basket; she looks as if she's floating over the ground.

We come to the wider part of the path. The smell of resin. Fru Hansson points at what must be the biggest dragonfly I've ever seen. It shimmers gold and green and hovers for a while above her head. Then it follows us a little way and disappears.

We talk a little about this and that.

She tells me how when she was a little girl her parents took her with them to church, where the organist gave a recital every Sunday. She often suffered from ear problems and infections that disturbed her sleep at night, and when these were at their worst she was put to bed in an empty maid's room in the attic so that the rest of the family could at least sleep in peace. But when she was sitting in the church pew and the organist began playing she often fell so deeply asleep that no one could wake her, and her father had to carry her home.

Sometimes she'd wake on the way with her arms dangling and her mouth open, and would lie there rocking gently in her father's arms and looking up at the sky, hearing nothing but his heavy breathing, and she'd imagine she was lying on a camel's back and being carried to a distant bedouin encampment, her fantasies accompanied by the little music she'd managed to take in before falling asleep; it would sound endlessly in her head, and she'd feel rested and refreshed.

Other times she wouldn't wake till she was on the kitchen sofa, and then she'd sit up blinking drowsily as she breathed in the smells of dinner, which her mother would be busy preparing, and she'd feel that she'd come home after a long and laborious journey and was seeing and experiencing everything for the first time.

I listen to her story, but I can't shake off the feeling that her husband, the little tubercular superintendent, is hovering beside us like the dragonfly, but Superintendent Hansson is a small, colourless insect with nasty long legs. And thin feelers waving in front.

He asked for my help and described her as a woman in spiritual need. But no matter how carefully I study her I can see no trace of the brooding, unworldly figure he described. On the contrary!

When she talks she's full of enthusiasm, almost radiant, close to laughter. She jumps abruptly from one subject to another and seems utterly spontaneous. But there's nothing confused or vague about this spontaneity and I haven't the slightest difficulty following her trains of thought. It's as though she finds herself in a supremely happy situation that might end at any moment, so that she's in a hurry to say as much as she can before it does.

We walk quietly for a while.

I'm sorry I began thinking about her husband. It's irritated me. His ingratiating words about all the respect I enjoy tickled my vanity when I first heard them, but now they chafe and prick like gravel in a shoe. I can see his conceited little boy's face before me, disfigured by his moustache, which I feel an impulse to pull at (surely it would come loose if I did), and I can imagine his childish face taking on a cold, scornful look when he sees us walking together in happy conversation, as if he's thinking: Well, so much for pastoral care, I suspected as much…

'Please excuse me,' I say, 'but I've got the impression you're a somewhat lonely person.'

She looks at me in astonishment. I understand her surprise. My tone is both sharp and polite, and my voice is pitched higher than usual. I sound like a court prosecutor, presenting decisive evidence with ill-concealed malicious pleasure. And I realise that the irritation I feel when I think of her husband has fallen on her alone.

She forces a smile but there's a dark sadness in her eyes.

'How strange you should say that.'

'Really, why?'

'I've been thinking the same about you.'

I, too, force a smile. I don't know why. She wasn't exactly cracking a joke.

I walk beside her with my hands behind my back, her words echoing in my head.

They could have been dismissive and even aggressive. They could have meant: Keep away.

But when I glance furtively at her, from the corner of my eye, I can't detect anything like that. Her face is warm and calm. I see nothing closed. But I see something that has opened.

It's beginning to get dark. I open my window and lean out.

The dusk seems to be emerging from under the earth. Like a

mighty darkness ascending from the forests and the oceans, merging into the sharp, light-blue of the sky. But earth can contain any amount of darkness, there seems to be no end to it. One web of darkness after another stretches over the day that has passed.

I pull the chair forwards to the window and sit down. A raw chill sweeps into the room. It doesn't bother me. It cools my hot face.

I can't settle down. I get up and go over to the mirror above the washstand, a little mirror that neatly frames my head like the head on a postage stamp. My cheeks are red. My hair's a mess. My eyes have a mischievous look.

Are you in love now, I wonder.

I smile broadly at my mirror-image. At the flabby folds on my face. At the narrow slits of my eyes.

The man in the mirror isn't beautiful. He never has been and never will be. But for the first time for ages I think I see features in him that could at least waken a degree of sympathy. Say what you will, but he does look rather amusing, don't you think?

I sit down in the chair again. There's a ringing and singing in my ears. My clothes smell of tobacco smoke.

The events of the day stream over me, copious and unsorted, like in a dream.

Various situations and snatches of conversation compete for my attention, play out their piece and vanish. Sometimes I hear an unexpected question from her, but of course now it's no longer unexpected since I heard it earlier, and now I can enjoy it completely, like looking up a favourite passage in a book and feeling something of the same delight one felt when one read it for the first time.

And when I think about the day, it is indeed as though I was eagerly turning pages, searching up and down to find the place where I fell in love with her. The decisive passage.

I look up a page: she's loosed her hair, which makes her look younger; it's thick and curly and chestnut-brown and hangs in brittle strands against her round cheeks and her white neck.

We're eating almond cake and drinking coffee and cognac. The waiter stands by our table and asks if we'd like some more coffee. He leans slightly to one side as he moves, as though he's developed a list at some point and never managed to get back on an even keel; he has a little frog-face and a gigantic Adam's apple protruding beyond his shirt collar, and he peers at us through half-closed eyes, and when he's taken our order he makes a little bow slightly to one side, in the same direction as he's already leaning.

Most of the guests have already left, with occasional indifferent glances in our direction, and there comes a moment when the large company in the middle gets up, amid much noise and scraping of chairs. It's a group of red-faced men, waddling slowly towards the door; one claps his friend on the shoulder then moves his hand around in small circles as if he's trying to rub something into the fabric, another throws his hat in the air and fumbles as he tries to catch it so that it falls to the ground, then picks it up and awkwardly brushes off the dust, and suddenly I see Superintendent Hansson, standing between the massive black-clad bodies that are moving towards the exit like migrating hippopotamuses. He is standing there like the wading bird, the light from the open door falls on him; he smiles and nods to me with a strange expression on his face, his mouth forming a word and his eyes opening wide as if to give extra emphasis to this silent word, then he smiles, and I realise he's trying to say something like: Things seem to be shaping well! Keep it up!

Then he drops his eyes and disappears behind the hippos.

Once this large company has gone, silence descends over the dining room, and we are no longer just random guests who have happened to end up eating dinner at the same table. We are two people, a man and a woman, who are lingering because we can't bring ourselves to make a move.

We never mention it. We don't make solemn declarations. We simply stay at the table, in each other's company.

When did all this start?

My head is spinning.

I leaf through my book of memories and find a new place.

It's earlier. When the sun was still glowing between the tree trunks. We've spoken the short lines about each other's loneliness and we're walking on one of the narrower stretches of the path. We have been silent so long it's become embarrassing.

At this point we heard the bell for dinner. She stopped on the path and turned. She gave me a quick glance, and I don't remember how she looked, but when she turned and walked on, I knew we'd have dinner together.

It was as simple as that.

I'm not used to things being simple.

I followed her as unthinkingly as a small boy trotting after his father or mother, someone in whom he instinctively places full confidence, since he has no other choice.

And my throat tightened, and every sound came closer, all the snapping twigs, all the rustling clothes – and I could feel something fluttering breathlessly in my chest with fragile little wings. Something inside me trembled with expectation.

How could it all be so easy?

I'd been waiting for her to give some sign that she'd had enough of me. That she'd got what she wanted. That she was satisfied and content, and in her thoughts had already left me, and that the expression on her face would tell me that all that was keeping her with me were certain rudimentary requirements related to tact and good manners that must at all costs be respected.

Perhaps I've become so used to that expression that I no longer give it much thought. Perhaps it's an inevitable factor in the work I've chosen. Every day I meet people who are suffering gnawing anxiety, which can have firm and practical causes that can be solved by writing a letter or preparing a certificate, or a more diffuse and nebulous suffering demanding more subtle and comprehensive attention.

But sooner or later the moment always comes when their worries have been allayed, at least for the moment, and then I see something fading in their faces. Their voices take on a new tone, absent and metallic. Their eyes become restless and everything they say sounds servile and abrupt, almost disgusted. As if an appalling stench had spread around the room.

I never cease to be surprised at the bitterness and dark feelings that well up in people when circumstances force them to beg for help. For most people this seems to be utterly humiliating.

But there it is. It's something one must adapt to, and accept with humility, indulgence and patience.

Even so I can't help wondering what influence it's had on me, the fact that I have devoted my life to calming the anxieties of others, and in return seeing their faces close so implacably against me.

Perhaps it wouldn't have bothered me so much if I'd had other faces around me. If I'd been able to come home to children who loved me, or a loving wife.

But Helga's face is the worst of all. Not because I am forced to see it fading, but because I can't remember when it was last lit up.

But I don't want to think about Helga now.

When did it all start?

Anna Hansson. The little glance we exchanged on the path when she turned around. The dinner we ate together and lingered over. And we talk about everything imaginable. Big things and little things. One minute follows another, and before you know it an hour has passed. And then another hour.

Everything we say matters. We tell each other about our lives. But something even more important is happening behind what we say. As if we're asking each other questions with our eyes. Wondering: Will you?

Will you stay a little longer with me?

And a glance answers: Yes, I will. And you with me?

Yes, I will.

And there comes a moment when all these 'Yes, I will's seem without end. Momentary inklings that she will never have enough of me and I will never have enough of her.

There are times when it seems I'm being lifted high up, and I see straight into her, and I get a dizzying overview of her empire, which stretches as far as the eye can see, and it doesn't frighten me to discover how mighty it is, on the contrary, I feel giddying joy, and I feel chosen, I feel privileged, I realise that this is a precious trust and that I am perhaps the first to whom this trust has been given, and I see gentle waterfalls and green valleys and spiky mountains, I see fertile land and stifling deserts, and I see and understand that her empire contains everything between heaven and earth, that it contains places where life is simple and cheerful, and places where life is difficult and adverse and full of hardship and privations, but this does not lessen my excitement at having been allowed to be there and begin to explore it and make myself at home.

And I also see and understand that her empire is different from mine. I see places that remind me of my own, and I see places that remind me of nothing I know. It doesn't matter. It doesn't frighten me.

Someone lifted me up so I could look in. The air is cold and fresh. But the hands that hold me are steady and warm. And I want to go in. I want to make myself at home there. I don't want to be anywhere else.

What if she's feeling the same way? If I told her all this and she nodded and took my hand and said: That's just how it is for me too.

The very thought is enough to press me down into my chair. Something is capering about inside my chest.

I look out of the open window. I turn my face up to the evening sky, where the stars flicker in cold infinity. The crescent moon glimmers between the firs.

I take a blanket from my bed and wrap myself in it. I put my feet up on the chair to avoid the draught. Then I lose myself in the stars.

She told me about her brother.

His name was Axel. He was several years younger than her. He was the apple of his parents' eyes. Even so, ever since early childhood he'd never been much good at anything. When once in a while he was successful at something it was regarded as a minor miracle.

Axel would follow Anna wherever she went. He was her perpetual bad conscience. She could see how it pained her parents that he was so clumsy, unenterprising and generally lacking in talent.

'But he was kind,' she told me. 'He was so small and thin. He always wanted to do what was expected of him. He never gave up hope of finding some occupation where he would be welcome not only as company, like a sort of harmless pet, but where he could be of some use. He searched frantically in the hope of finding fellowship through work. And failing this, he was satisfied to make do with any sort of communal activity. If he saw that the children next door were tormenting a cat he would immediately run out and want to join in, but he was always the one who was so clumsy that the cat managed to escape, or he'd be the one who got so badly scratched that he had to rush home to have his wounds cleaned, so that mother found out what was going on, and it was his fault that the others felt the wrath of the adult world. They didn't want a boy like that with them. So he sat in the kitchen and watched them roaming in the road, and he knew it was no use going out and asking them if he could join them. So he looked at the women in the kitchen and their work with the spinning wheel and warp-beam, and soon he was offering to help them. But he was so slow and pedantic, and asked such strange questions, and made jokes when he should have been serious, and if anyone else joked he was serious and questioning. He irritated you even when you felt sorry for him. When he tried to show initiative everything went wrong, and you had to unravel what he'd done and start again, and after the second or third disaster you'd hiss at him, and then he became so cautious and timid in his work that he got nowhere, and it was as if the air began to tremble with his fear, yes, as if he knew that the inevitable would happen, that you'd clench your teeth and take the tools from him and tell him to move aside and just sit and watch instead, and then perhaps little by little he'd learn. But everyone could hear how feeble this sounded.

'I had more patience with him than anyone. I didn't dare not to. I saw how grateful my parents were that he had me to turn to. I think they'd have liked to be as gentle and tolerant with him as I was, but they never managed it.

'In time I began to have ghastly fantasies in which Axel would meet with some sort of accident, how he might be trampled by the cows in the cowshed with their feet crushing the soft bird-like bones in his chest, or climb on the rocks and not notice how slippery they were, and slide down into the water and never come up again... Sometimes when he was sitting on my knee and I was reading to him I would find myself thinking how easy it would be to slip my arm lightly around his neck as if caressing him, then tighten my grip and hold on while I felt his little body go quiet in my arms...

'Then Axel would be dead. And I'd be free. But at the same time there would be nothing left in my life.

'He had only one talent he managed to develop. He learned to be quick at repartee. He noticed the tense atmosphere would relax if he showed that he realised how clumsy and hopeless he was. And if he made a little circus number of it he could make people laugh. And people value those who know how to make them laugh. In this way he managed to turn his clumsiness to advantage. He also discovered that the more brutally he mocked himself, the more others laughed. At least up to a certain point. If you go too far it becomes more tragic than comic, and the laughter gives way to embarrassing silence. Sometimes it seemed to have become an obsession with him to get to the point where the laughter was at its loudest and tears ran and everybody looked at each other with glittering eyes. He also learned it was good to be economical with his wit, since that way he could attract attention to himself by keeping his public hungry and eager for more.

'One of my father's brothers owned a shop. Axel was taken on there as an assistant. He was never given particularly responsible jobs, but managed reasonably well at the little that was expected of him. There were always some boys there hanging about waiting for something funny to happen. When people came into the shop and saw Axel there it put them in a good mood. That sort of thing is good for business.

'One day a customer came in. My uncle has told me that he came up from the cellar where he'd gone to fetch something, and saw a woman standing at the counter showing Axel a picture postcard. They were bent over the card with their heads close together. The woman was a few years older than Axel. She spoke a foreign language. She was dark and beautiful and elegantly dressed, and wore a strong scent. She drew something on the card, then bought what she needed and went out to a waiting droshky.

'The card was from Rotterdam. She left it on the counter. That same evening Axel woke me and told me everything that had happened, and said he was thinking of going there. That he'd fallen in love with the woman, and that he was convinced that it was mutual. Otherwise she wouldn't have left the card behind, he said. Why else would she have gone to the trouble of looking for a pen to draw a ring around the house where she lived?

'I tried to talk sense into him. I suggested he might write her a letter. He said that would be no good, since he didn't know her language. In that case how did he think they could have a future together, I said. But he could see no problems at all. I can still see him before me now. He had been sitting on a chair by my bed, slumped and unhappy. But while he was describing their strange conversation over the card, he lit up and looked happier than I'd ever seen him. And he maintained that with the help of gestures and facial expressions they'd understood one another all right, and that she'd used some words that sounded almost Swedish.

'I couldn't get him to see reason. I helped him to write a letter to Father and Mother. I looked at his head as he sat bowed over the paper. The whorl in his hair that I'd seen so many times. Suddenly he was a little boy again, with dirty cheeks and a roving homelessness in his eyes, the boy who never succeeded at anything, and for whom I felt such a stifling responsibility.

'I stood in the doorway and watched him go. He left early in the morning, before the others had a chance to wake. It was a hazy, grey October morning. Crows lifted flapping from the fields as he passed. He walked with rapid steps and soon he was gone.

'A few months later a letter came, postmarked Copenhagen. It was crumpled and stained with soot, and here and there the pen had gone off the paper as if someone had been pushing him while he was writing. He told us he was working in the harbour to save enough money to be able to continue his journey. That he'd been lucky enough to make some friends who spoke Dutch, and they'd helped him to write several letters to the woman he was travelling to, and that she'd answered that she was longing for him to come.

'Several months passed before any more news reached us. Then we heard his body had been found floating in the harbour. It was swollen and had been badly knocked about, and there was a wound in the back of his head. The police had investigated but found it hard to believe he'd been the victim of violence since he'd had no enemies and no great sum of money anyone would have wanted to steal, and in fact he still had on him what little he possessed. They thought a packing-case had fallen on his head, knocking him unconscious into the water.'

She stopped, her eyes resting steadily on mine. I wanted so much to take her hand in mine.

I looked at it. At her wedding ring. Suddenly I couldn't take my eyes off it. A vision of a completely different reality was burning itself into me.

A tubercular little man with a comic moustache, standing, or sitting, or whatever he did, in front of this of all women and proposing marriage to her. He asks her to be his wife and she says yes. This is no nightmare. It's reality.

'I know you understand that I've spent a great deal of time thinking about what happened. How such a brief meeting could have had so much power over my little brother that he left his whole life behind to rush out into the world to be with this woman. It wasn't till long afterwards, when we'd had him back and buried him, that it dawned on me. You know, when the year of mourning is past and people begin to speak of him without the obligatory frown and tense mouth…'

'Yes, I know.'

'I happened to hear some men talking about him. I wasn't meant to hear. I can't remember their exact words either, but there was no mistaking their meaning: that it was typical of Axel to get hold of the wrong end of the stick even when it came to love. If he'd been able to marry some local girl like everyone else, perhaps he'd never have reached the point of being dragged out of a dock. They were talking lightly, and I could almost see them raising their eyes to the heavens and shaking their heads. Even in death, he'd given them something to laugh about.

'And then suddenly it struck me that she'd conjured all that away, the woman from Rotterdam. By a single wave of the hand. Perhaps the way she had looked at him was enough. He must have understood that with her he could be a different person. He could leave the whole of his old life behind him, just as we leave behind a pair of shoes that are too small. He could abandon all the unspoken agreements he'd been forced to make, or imagined he'd been forced to make, to be accepted as one of us. To be a certain way, speak in a certain way, think in a certain way. Till in the end it grew in him and became a part of him, however suffocating it may have felt... She could free him from all these chains.

'At least that's what he hoped.'

We sat in silence for a moment.

The service staff were moving comfortably around the tables, wiping crumbs and cigar ash and the rings made by wet glasses and bottles. Every now and then the door would open and someone would stop in the doorway, the light dying in their eyes when they realised it was far too late for dinner. One of these was Högström, my neighbour the cavalryman. When he caught sight of me he rolled his eyes as if to say: I see the Pastor has a lady companion. Usually this would have irritated me. But I have to confess that instead I felt a thrill of pride.

Anna was biting her thumbnail thoughtfully, her tongue glistening in her mouth. I must have been staring at her. She met my eyes and seemed to be reading my thoughts. But she was smiling, such a mild and beautiful smile.

'It's a beautiful story,' I said.

'Yes. But terrible at the same time.'

'Why? He found what he was looking for. The woman from Rotterdam was his salvation. Unlike most of us he was perceptive enough to realise it, and brave enough to take the consequences, whatever they might prove to be.'

'Isn't that exactly how things look to most of us?'

'How do you mean?'

'That we live a life we find more or less unbearable. Then someone crosses our path, someone we choose as our saviour, so we rush after him... or her.'

Something had crept into her voice. A new sharp edge. It seemed aimed directly at me, even if she took the trouble to choose her words so they'd sound impersonal. Her tone was almost pleading.

'Yes, well, I suppose that's probably inevitable,' I said.

She shook her head slowly.

'Axel's departure can be interpreted in many different ways,' she said. 'Some of the women thought it showed how deeply he'd fallen in love. Some of the men thought it showed how deep his confusion was. I think it rather shows how unbearable his life was. And then he chose to call it love. Perhaps it was love. But not the sort of love that can make you happy. On the contrary. It could only bring unhappiness.

'If your life seems unbearable,' she went on, 'you don't worry about what you get, you're grateful for anything at all that stops you thinking about your unbearable life. I don't think Axel was particularly interested in this woman he'd chosen as his saviour. He just wanted to be saved at any cost from the life that'd been staked out for him. But what would have happened if he'd arrived in Rotterdam? Whether or not she had succeeded in saving him?'

I couldn't answer. I assumed a worried, thoughtful expression and waited for her to change the subject. Her words troubled me, and quite honestly they also offended me slightly.

She had looked straight into my love, and she had raised a warning finger to say: Not this. Not again. We both know where it leads.

I knew she was right. Even so, I fell quiet, thinking of her as a killjoy.

I could see the irony. I'd started asking her questions about her brother for the sake of an idiotic commitment I'd made to her husband to help her in her grief. But as our conversation developed it was she who was coming to my help.

It's getting late. My temples are throbbing. I haven't heard any footsteps under the window for a long time. Night insects and moths are swirling around my lamp.

When I go to bed I think about the most beautiful memory from the day. The one I kept till last. The way she looked at me when I told her about my childless marriages, and how hope has begun to fail me.

When people hear this they usually force out something they imagine will be encouraging. They remember distant relatives or acquaintances who were childless for this or that length of time, and then they tried some household remedy, or moved to another town, or prayed intensely, and – hey presto! – nine months later they found themselves giving birth to a bonny boy.

Other people naively shake their heads and remind me that children are also a permanent source of trouble not to mention the huge expense they cause, and insist they almost envy us our childlessness.

But something happens in their eyes. A glimmer of distrust and contempt. Perhaps some of them see my longing for children as a sign of megalomania, that I want at all costs to leave little heirs behind me, or that it's just an old man's vain desire to keep death at bay.

But Anna said nothing. Not a word. She knew there could be no comfort. But she listened to everything I had to say. She understood my pain, and had the courage to receive it, with open eyes, and hold it close to her.

Her nose is very large, it throws itself forward in her face like a bird's beak. There are small wrinkles around her eyes. She has a scar on her upper lip, which I didn't notice at first. I so long to see it again.

I wake with a feeling of pressure. A dull ache in my stomach. I stagger out of bed, stumble across the floor, and only just make it to the washbowl. I vomit so violently that it splashes over the edge. Several times. A reddish-brown sludge. When it's over a sense of relief spreads through my whole body. I press the electric bell and crawl back into bed.

I shiver with fever. A girl comes. I hear her fussing around the washbasin, breathing loudly with disgust. She throws up the window and says, almost derisively, that it must be the influenza that has been around for several weeks.

Then she goes away and I fall asleep.

When I wake again it's light. More stomach pains. More vomiting.

A doctor I've never seen before comes. He doesn't stay long. He repeats what I've already been told, that the illness is very infectious and that the patient vomits and has a high temperature for a couple of days.

'The good thing is that you recover as quickly as you fall ill,' he says. 'I wouldn't be surprised, Pastor, if you were on your feet again by tomorrow evening. But till then I wouldn't like to be in your place.'

I'm overcome by a great thirst. A nurse gives me water to drink. After barely an hour I throw it up.

Then I lie still, taking short breaths. I think of Anna and feel desperate. I imagine her sitting at a table in the dining room, her eyes restlessly wandering over everybody who comes in as she sits alone.

Or perhaps someone else has joined her. Or perhaps she's with her husband. I can't decide which is worse.

I want her to know where I am and what has happened to me. But there's nothing I can do. The fever's raging in my body. The window's wide open and every sound that passes below grates on my ears. My teeth feel rough and loose, as if they're about to fall out. My nightshirt's stained with vomit. It makes no difference how often I change it. New stains constantly appear on the sleeves, the shoulders and chest.

Feeling ill's the only thing I'm conscious of. Not a thought passes through my head without feeling ill setting its bitter sticky imprint on it.

I sweat heavily. The sheets are getting soiled. At some point my lips contract involuntarily. I straighten them. They contract again. As if the heat of the fever is shrinking my body.

One of the girls who come to empty the buckets shuts the door carelessly. It swings back a little, and I can't even summon the strength to get up and shut it.

I hear heavy steps in the corridor. They stop outside my door and my neighbour Högström sticks his head in. He stiffens and grimaces.

'Oh, hell,' he says, half-choking, and pulls the door shut.

My shivers soothe me to sleep.

When I wake she's sitting by my bed.

I pull myself nearer the wall and cover myself with the sheet. I try to get her to realise she should go away. But she ignores me. I'm too weak to be more forceful. Too weak to speak.

She takes a flannel and bathes my forehead and temples, then proceeds down over my cheeks and neck.

She bathes me carefully. She's so close I can hear her breathing. She studies every part of my face as she bathes it. As if trying to fix my face in her memory, every wrinkle and fold of skin, every birthmark, every mole.

She's wearing a new dress. It's off-white and thin as a veil of mist. When she leans over me I see the cleft between her breasts. She's aware of this. Her breathing seems to be getting heavier. As for myself, I hardly dare to breathe at all.

When she's finished bathing me she stays leaning over the bed watching me in the same dreamy yet strangely searching way, and to my surprise I feel something like a sob in my chest, and an impulse to pull the covers over my head to avoid her gaze; indeed, there seems to be something in it I can't bear.

I probably managed to conceal it. It'll soon be over.

She sits on the chair, picks up a newspaper and begins reading aloud to me. Something about the unionist question. A wasp flies in through the window and circles listlessly around the cornice. Anna doesn't notice. It flies out again.

Her reading pains me. Not the content, which finds no foothold in my consciousness. But something in the language, in the very sound of it, takes me back to Stockholm, to the dusty streets, the smell of sweat and smoke, the harsh, irritable voices, the shadows of rats by the dustbins, the muggy white smogs in the taverns... Helga's hurried steps towards that door, and her tense white face.

'Your husband,' I whisper. 'What does he say?'

Anna falls quiet. She drops the newspaper.

'I don't think he says anything,' she answers, barely audible.

'You know people talk,' I say.

She doesn't reply for a long time.

I feel the nausea coming back. I shouldn't have started thinking about her husband. I see him before me in the dining room, a little figure in a mass of big dark bodies, and I hear the clatter of cutlery, and see thick, sticky traces of gravy on a plate and taste my vomit again. The thick red-brown sludge that burns my nose and throat.

'Do you remember when we were listening to the orchestra,' she says, 'and you thought it was the music that had made such a strong impression on me... Do you remember?'

'Yes, I remember. You cried.'

'It wasn't the music. It was...'

She stops and bows her head. When she looks up at me she has tears in her eyes and her voice is unsteady.

'... it was just that you came and sat beside me. That you wanted to do that. It made me so indescribably happy.'

I nod weakly. The nausea has intensified. I concentrate on her lips and listen intently to her words so as not to think about the aching movements rising inexorably in my stomach.

'I was already happy when you came forward after the service that morning and suggested going for a walk. Though afterwards I thought it must have been nothing more than a happy accident, a chance idea you'd had, and that you wouldn't want my company again. But when you came and sat beside me to listen to the music I couldn't underestimate the importance of what was happening any longer. I realised you could have sat beside anyone, or somewhere separate on your own. But I had to accept that you wanted to sit next to me and no one else.

'So many widely different feelings came over me and pulled me in different directions. I felt like shouting for joy. I was also paralysed with fear. At the same time, I realised what a low opinion I've come to have of myself. That was why I started crying. I couldn't help it.

'You must understand, I've broken down so slowly and imperceptibly that I hardly noticed it happening. That's how a breakdown can be. You can be demolished bit by bit, one stone at a time, over fourteen years. That's how long we've been married. You suddenly took me back to who I was before my disintegration began. And I felt so strongly, in every fibre of my body, that I'd reached a turning point, and that nothing would ever be the same again.'

I sit up in bed and make a movement towards the washbasin. But she stops me and holds out a bucket that was under the bed.

I bend over the bucket, my guts pulled together by cramps, but all I can get out is a little bile, and I half-lie retching over the bucket with long threads of saliva dangling from my mouth. I feel so miserable I nearly burst into tears.

But then I feel her fingers against my neck. She gently strokes my head. It's the first time she's touched me in that way. It's like refreshing rain.

I fall back heavily on the pillow. She wipes my mouth with a towel. The same light movements, the same inquisitive, searching eyes.

'Go on,' I whisper. 'Please go on with your story.'

She looks enquiringly at me.

'About your husband.'

She slowly folds the towel. She puts it in the bucket and takes the bucket out to the corridor. Then she sits down again. She stretches her neck and looks out of the window, biting her lip thoughtfully. At that moment she's the most beautiful woman I've ever seen, with her white skin, her proud bearing, and her sad dark eyes.

'It's so strange,' she says slowly with a short unhappy laugh. 'Does he ever wonder where I am all day, and who I'm with…? Perhaps he ought to. Perhaps that's how it is in normal marriages.

But not in ours. My husband spends most of his time avoiding me. It's been like that for as long as I can remember.

'I was so young when we married. Not much younger than women usually are, it's true. But I can hardly remember who I was then. I remember we had fun together. We laughed a lot. That must have mattered to me. Perhaps there was nothing more important than that. The relief of laughter. The quick turn of phrase. My husband was reliable in that respect. In his company there was always the relief of laughter close at hand.

'After a few years I was ready to be serious. Among other things, I wanted to start a family. That put an end to the laughter. He became distant and evasive. He began to frown when he looked at me. I found that beyond all those noisy jokes we had nothing. Complete emptiness. But by then I was pregnant.

'He didn't want a family. Not for anything in the world. He wanted to be free to come and go as he liked. He knew a family who could take the child, some relatives on his mother's side. They lived outside Gävle.

'So that's how it was. He managed to persuade me. I didn't want to be tied to him. I gave birth to the baby. A little boy. We'd agreed that the child would often come and visit us, and we'd visit him. I'd been promised that. But I soon understood it was nothing but lies and manipulation. My husband began to say that the boy was well off where he was, and that it only made him confused and unhappy if we visited him.

'In a way he was right. I tried to be happy during those visits. But no matter how hard I tried, the atmosphere was strained.

'One year has followed another, and my husband and I have slipped further apart. We don't meet very often. I haven't given it much thought. Sometimes I think I should feel bitter towards him. But I no longer know who he is. I don't know if I have ever known him. It's hard to be bitter towards someone you don't know.'

I hold out my hand to her.

'Come here,' I whisper.

She takes my hand. She has a big hand, almost bigger than mine. She lies down carefully, facing me.

At last I can touch her face. Nose, cheeks, mouth, the high white brow. I stroke the little scar on her upper lip with the back of my fingers.

She closes her eyes. She presses herself against my hand. She breathes heavily with her mouth open.

We put our arms around each other. I feel small movements in her body. Strong waves welling backwards and forwards. She moans with pleasure.

The door opens suddenly. I lift my head. A nurse is standing there, stiff as a poker, with wide eyes. She puts down a bucket with a bang, mumbles in embarrassment and goes out again.

Anna's body is stiff and tense in my arms as if she's holding her breath. When the door closes we burst out laughing. Immediately afterwards I fall asleep.

But a whispering voice follows me into my sleep. I don't know if it's real, or something in a dream. It's a woman's voice, and it sounds simultaneously fragile and strong. It fills my head like shattered glass. It has a cracked and distorted echo.

The voice whispers that she loves me. That she will never make any demands on me or expect anything from me, and that she'll always wait for me.

She whispers that my eyes are like a sea of sorrow, but that when one least expects it the sun breaks forth, and suddenly the sea blazes with a love so strong one has to turn one's eyes away. She whispers that my movements are heavy and preoccupied like a sleepwalker, but that she noticed the very first time she met me that she had unusual power over my body, and as soon as she came near me I woke from my trance and my movements became gentle and buoyant, as if my body had found a purpose, a goal, a reason to exist.

She whispers that I have the same effect on her body, like when the snow melts after endless winter, and all the dry branches come to life with young green leaves, and the air vibrates with the twittering of small birds that have been away so long she'd forgotten they even existed, and the streams rustle and sing in the melting snow, and snap off the ice piece by piece, playfully carrying it far away, and she whispers that her body, which for so long has been mute and anaesthetised, is now so full of warmth and hope and life that she hardly knows what to do. And she whispers that I have done this. No one else has been able to do to her what I have done.

I open my eyes. I'm hungry.

It's dark outside. A lamp burning on the table throws jagged shadows over the walls; it looks like an enormous insect waving its long legs. There's an empty space in the bed beside me. The sheets feel cold and stiff.

I'm so ravenously hungry.

Normally I'd get dressed and go out and ring bells and knock on doors and shake life into absolutely anyone to get something to eat. But when it really dawns on me that she's no longer with me I'm overcome by such despair that I forget my hunger; in fact, I'm almost grateful for it. I crawl deeper into the bed and feel the tears rise in my eyes.

Then I see the flowers. They're standing in a glass beside the lamp's dying flame. Little columbines, buttercups and harebells.

I bend over the table, turn up the flame and lift the flowers to the light. Thoughts move slowly in my head.

I'm sure the flowers weren't there earlier. It can't have been any of the nurses who brought them. In any case they'd hardly be likely to put flowers in a drinking glass when there are vases.

I don't know how long I lie looking at the flowers. I turn the glass around and around. They've been cut at the bottom with great care, all the stalks are the same length. It doesn't look as if

they've been cut with scissors. She must have pinched them off.
Perhaps with her thumbnail.

Perhaps she went a long way into the forest. Perhaps people saw
her from the path and wondered what she was doing. Perhaps she
was humming a tune, perhaps her heart was pounding. Perhaps the
only way she could find peace was to go and pick these flowers.

I put them back where I found them, blow out the lamp and lay
my head on the pillow. After a bit my eyes get used to the dark,
and I can make out the flowers in the summer dusk. They seem to
be bending over the edge of the glass to stare at me. Soon they
begin to frighten me.

I clasp my hands and pray. I want to thank God for the favour He's
shown me. For letting me meet her.

But I can't. My heart isn't full of gratitude, but unease.

I close my eyes tightly in shame.

I feel like a little boy saying thank you for an expensive present
that he knows deep down he'll never dare use. But he fingers his
cap and tries to look self-confident. As if nothing could be too
much for him.

A hypocrite, that's what I am. A hypocrite of the worst kind.

I've always felt there was a cavity inside me, an eerie echoing
emptiness, and I have complained endlessly that no one has ever
claimed it. I've begged for love, longed for love. I have prayed to
God for love.

But now I realise that every time love's come my way and
unfurled itself fully before me I've recoiled in terror, and begun to
make discreet but thorough preparations to escape. At the same
time I've outwardly been careful to seem fearless and delighted,
calm and collected and full of trust, and I've been able to fool
everyone, including myself.

Is this about to happen again?

If so I'm not a whit better than her husband. The weakling who runs to the skittle alley the moment he gets the chance. He who was so afraid of being serious that he forced her to give away her own child.

No, I fear dawn, no matter how shabby and cowardly that may be. I can't face meeting her. Everything has gone too fast, and it's entirely my fault.

I can't avoid her. She'd never forgive me that. Or rather, she would forgive me. I know she would. But she'd never get over it. It would crush her. And I can't have that on my conscience.

But even that is not quite true. I know that from experience. Conscience is more accommodating than people think. People would be horrified if they knew how flexible conscience really is.

Well, of course I'd feel worthless for a few weeks. Perhaps even for several months. Then my sense of being worthless would begin to fade. A little bit at a time.

I would move the furniture in my memory library. Carefully begin to question one or two events. Wasn't what happened the best thing, now I can look at it from a slight distance? Wasn't it in fact I who took all the necessary painful decisions, then assumed full responsibility for what happened? And was she really as broken-hearted as all that, when all's said and done? Doesn't such an assumption imply an exaggerated sense of my own importance?

And so on.

It starts like an open sore you must be careful with. Bathe, wash, change bandages. Then a scab develops. You need to be careful with that too, but not quite so careful. Then the scab falls off. You may not notice. Perhaps it'll leave a scar. You can live with that, scars don't hurt. They are just there, together with everything else.

That's how it goes. That's how we deal with our transgressions and blunders. That's how we live with the knowledge that we've

328

crushed another person. It's the same for everyone. For Anna and her husband. For me too, and I assume it was the same for Helga.

So much for that then, it should be possible for me to crush her. But I don't want to. I won't do it. I love her!

I just need a little time. I need to think in peace and quiet. Surely that can't be wrong when my whole future depends on it? Surely there's nothing deceitful about that? Surely it doesn't mean I'm about to abdicate responsibility for everything?

But I have nowhere to go to.

I can't resist a bitter smile when I remind myself how it's only a few days since I was tormented by loneliness.

Now I can't be alone anywhere. The dining room, the paths where people take walks, the bath-house down by the lake; she can find me anywhere. She might even knock on my door at any time.

What if we arrange a life together. Who could object?

Of course the little consumptive superintendent might, if anyone. I can just see him, and the expression on his face. Defiant, sullen, refined. I can hear his whining voice, and the officious high-flying language he can barely command.

The very thought awakens the same reckless anger I used to feel when I was little and playing with something that belonged to one of my brothers, a bow and arrow perhaps, and they came and snatched it from me.

It made no difference how desperately I tried to impress on them that they hadn't touched the bow and arrow for years, or that they'd let it lie out of doors and be damaged by the damp and cold.

They knew I was right, but they had one form of power only, and that was the right of ownership. When they took the bow and arrow from me I knew they weren't interested in it at all, they only wanted to be sure that *I* shouldn't get any pleasure from it.

Confronted with their malice, I was powerless. They had right on their side.

I'm sure it'd be the same with the superintendent. He's ignored his wife for years. But if she wanted to leave him to look for happiness with someone else, he'd lose all interest in his skittles and do his utmost to crush her dreams.

Who knows? Perhaps I'd be able to get him to see reason. Perhaps my name still carries some weight.

That leaves Helga.

It would be so easy to think that she would be relieved. But it hurts to think that, which surprises me.

I'd much rather imagine her astonished when told that I plan to leave her. Perhaps she'd discover unexpected feelings. Feelings she thought she'd lost long ago.

I'd like to think of her with tenderness and warmth. But my decision would hold firm. There would be a hard core of neutrality in me, a core unresponsive to all her tears and emotional storms, insusceptible to her indignation.

There's the bell for first breakfast. I sit by the window holding her flowers under my nose and spinning the glass slowly around.

Down there the residents of the cheapest rooms are passing. Soon I shall go down and have breakfast with the woman I love.

I have a feeling I'm going to do something extravagant. Make some almost exaggeratedly bold, romantic gesture.

I certainly have a bad conscience about the horror-filled thoughts I indulged in just now. It worries me that these thoughts may have left some trace behind, and that she may detect it if she studies me closely enough.

When I get home I'll apply for a divorce. I shall free Helga from the bonds she has struggled against so impatiently for so long.

I see her disappearing. There she stands outside the door with her lips pressed together while some men carry boxes and furniture, and I see her belongings swaying in their hands across the churchyard as though drifting to sea on implacable waves. A few passers-by stop to look curiously at all the articles pouring out from the vicarage to be stacked onto the cart. Their eyes turn to Helga and me, and I meet the gaze of every one, calmly and steadily, till they turn away.

And there comes Anna. Anna Gregorius.

I see us moving among the rooms, unable to pass one another without exchanging a kiss or caress. Now it's dusk, and we're sitting in the drawing room. She lowers her paper and looks at me with her mild eyes, and she says something about how happy she is to live in a great city at last.

And then someone comes leaping down the stairs. It's her son. He's ten years old. Anna couldn't believe her eyes when I led him into the room. I'd taken all the necessary steps in the greatest secrecy, because I wanted to surprise her. And so it did, I can now say calmly. She wept in my arms that evening. Tears of joy. It already feels so long ago.

He's made many friends. When he speaks you can still hear traces of dialect, but none of his friends dare tease him for that; they have too much respect for him. A few days ago he asked me if he could call me Father.

And there we are moving among the rooms. Other rooms. I see people coming forward and waiting to be introduced. They take her hand and she says her name, and they give her a forced smile and take a shy step backwards, but later in the evening they notice how much I've changed, and when we talk they think it's as though I've been through a bath of purification, yes, as though someone has swept away a thick layer of dust from me, and they find I'm no longer as grey as they always thought, but a multitude of colours has emerged, clear and beautiful, and it strikes them that my light-heartedness has become more light-hearted, and my seriousness more serious, and that all in all I've become more sharply defined. Easier to like, and for that matter also easier to dislike, but no longer someone who inspires nothing but vaguely gloomy thoughts in others.

And who can take credit for this, if not his new wife? You can see from a distance how happy they are together.

It's true that it's unpleasant and disturbing to think that even priests divorce these days, as more and more people seem to be doing... but just look at him! Faced with a look like that, all you can do is capitulate. His place is with the new and the modern. He's a standard-bearer, the fat old priest. A forerunner. Who would have thought it?

Helga – wasn't that her name? – they've already forgotten her. They have a vague memory that she was beautiful. Perhaps a little too beautiful, frankly? Well, there you are. It clearly didn't make her happy. Nor him either. There was something absent about her. Something of a lost soul. Not really reliable.

She was like the sort of horse you instinctively avoid because it lives in its own world, different from the world most of us see and understand, the kind of horse that sees deadly danger where we see something utterly trivial, and vice versa. It would be extremely unwise to entrust yourself to such a horse. So you go on to the next one.

Well said! Exactly my opinion. That's what she was like. It's good that she's gone.

The bell rings for second breakfast. I lie on my bed looking up at the ceiling. I am waiting for that blissful feeling to arrive.

I've daydreamed my way through most of my life, constructing various realities in my imagination and subsequently carrying them with me out into the world.

A common and, I must add, a somewhat unimaginative objection to such a way of seeing things, is that daydreams are one thing and reality is another, and that it's not a good idea to mix them. But I've never treated my daydreams as anything other than approximate guidelines. It's never been my intention to follow them in every detail. Daydreams strike a note. They point in a certain direction. They may be vague. But nonetheless they can be important.

But something is amiss.

Usually I'm able to reach a boiling point. I can't put it better than that. But I'm not getting there, despite the fact that the dream-images are coming one after another, and the voices are hissing ever more loudly and enthusiastically about how happy we will be, Anna and I, without a cloud in our sky.

There's something about the eagerness of these voices, and the intensity with which the dream-images are following each other, which does not particularly inspire my confidence.

It's as if someone were trying to foist inferior goods on me, while I realise with rising desperation that I've begun to detect the flaws.

I am going to go down and have breakfast, but I'm constantly finding an excuse to put it off. I look at myself in the mirror, comb my hair, wash. Change my clothes twice, three times. But it's hardly surprising I'm nervous. A decision's going to be made today, I feel it in my bones. We can't keep putting the decision off.

As I stretch out my hand to open the door I see the handle slowly turning. I pull my hand away and step back.

The door opens a fraction. Anna looks in and starts when she sees me. She's wearing the white hat. She looks down the corridor before coming in and closes the door behind her. She has a paper bag in one hand. She manages to smile.

'What a relief you're well,' she says. 'I thought you were too weak to come down for breakfast.'

She stretches her hand towards my face. I have time to think that she is stretching across an abyss. She strokes my cheek. I take her hand and hold it. It hurts me to see her so awkward. Her eyes won't settle on anything. She fingers the paper bag furtively.

I'm filled with such tenderness for her that I see black. I embrace her hard and see the white hat float to the floor, light as an autumn leaf.

'But that's not quite true,' she whispers against my shoulder. 'I thought I'd scared you away. You must think I'm awfully forward.'

I look at her. The wild despair in her eyes. Trembling lips.

I bend towards her. I feel her breath against my lips, light and ticklish as a butterfly's wing, before we meet in a kiss. She throws her arms around me. Something thuds to the floor.

'Oh dear,' she says.

I look around in surprise. Some oranges are rolling over the floorboards.

'I brought them for you,' she says. 'Of course they say you should be careful with oranges after stomach trouble. But they say they are good for you.'

'That was kind of you,' I whisper.

We kiss again.

I want to take off my clothes, and I want to be united with her. If it kills me.

Everything about her is sweetness. Everything about her smells so good. Everything about her is soft and sensuous and exciting. Everything about her is a wide open desire – for *me*. Gregorius.

I don't know what I've done to deserve it. But it's a fact, and if I turned away from her now I'd be lost. Then I would have nothing left to preach about. My heart would be empty.

Because it is for this and no other reason that God created sky and sea, animals and fish, man and woman: for me to stand here with this woman, and to be swept up with her in a deafening roar and know that we will let go of everything we have carried with us, all the qualities and thoughts and experiences we have become used to seeing as inescapable parts of the individual selves we have become – we want to give up all this to be joined together, to melt together, to become one and the same being, something new, an alloy the world has never seen before.

I press myself against her. She feels what's happening to me, releases a sound of surprise and pleasure.

All of me is here, pressed hard against her with my hands in her hair. I'm no longer thinking about whether or not this day will bring some final decision. Perhaps it will, perhaps it won't. Of my future I know nothing. Together with her I know even less.

But it doesn't frighten me. How could anything frighten me when I'm together with her? She wishes me well and that's all. It's a rare and wonderful feeling. I wonder when I last experienced it. Or if I've ever experienced it.

I take her hand and we go to the bed. I make a movement towards her dress. She catches my hands.

'Are you sure you want to do this?' she says.

'Yes.'

Something lightens in her face.

'Then I do too,' she says.

We begin taking off our clothes. I think that's when it happens. It's then that the sky begins to cloud over.

I don't know how. But for every garment she takes off and lays on the chair, she becomes more remote from me. And with every garment I take off, I feel as if I've put on two more others and become less and less accessible to her. By the time I'm naked I feel so wrapped up I can hardly move, and my skin doesn't respond to her touch.

The transformation is obvious, the work of a moment. It's as if a cold wind is blowing through the room, which is completely silent apart from the little sounds of our hasty and uneasy undressing.

I smile encouragingly as she stands there naked, but her body speaks its own language clearly, and she looks as if she wishes she could shrink to the size of a pea and disappear through a crack in the floorboards. I have no illusions that I look any different.

And everything that was previously affinity and fearlessness and the warmth of joint endeavour, two hands intertwined as though they'd always been together: all this has evaporated and disappeared, and all that's left is shame and self-contempt.

Everything that was lust and desire has vanished, leaving only a sort of dogged determination, as if we were about to do something that has to be done sooner or later, and since we've made our decision we'd better get on with it.

I know it's wrong, I know we should stop. But I can't say a word. I crawl into bed beside her. I loathe my body, I always have. During a few blessed moments with her I was able to forget this, and in the passion of her infatuated eyes I was even able to feel beautiful, and I assume it was the same for her. Now there's no passion left, not because our feelings have cooled, but because we're so obsessed with ourselves that there's no room for anything else.

When I hear the bed creaking loudly under my weight a stray thought comes to me of Adam and Eve, and the moment they first saw that they were naked. Suddenly I understand why this was painful to them, or more to the point, I understand the heavy grief God, their creator, must have felt when he saw them hiding behind fig leaves with their heads bowed in shame. Grief that something light and good had been irretrievably lost.

And still it gets worse. We lie facing each other with her hair spread over the pillow, and at the sight of her frightened smile my tenderness returns, and with the tenderness an inkling of the passionate desire I was feeling a little while ago.

I kiss her again, gently and carefully, and the feeling gets stronger, and I think perhaps this time it will last, and I push back the covers to reach her with my caresses, and she makes herself ready, lying there like a laid table, and invites me to come in and sit down and take of her what I want. Her body is smooth and warm and friendly under my hands. But it is new.

It should arouse me. It did just now.

Instead I feel sorrow. Confusion.

It starts with my hands. Everything starts there. Then it spreads inexorably outwards. That is where the sorrow begins. I don't understand it. It takes me some time to realise that my hands are looking for someone else.

For Helga.

My hands move up and down, they cuddle and caress. But they've forgotten Anna. They hunt ever more desperately over this unfamiliar body, but it's as though someone has tricked them by putting them down somewhere they've never been before, and my hands do everything wrong, they stumble and hesitate, they collide with obstacles that shouldn't be there, and they stagger on.

They miss everything familiar to them, all the curves and hollows, all the folds and bones that together form the landscape where my hands have slowly and patiently made a home through all these years; they are searching for everything about Helga's body that is particular to her, and that is difficult to capture in words, features one never gives a thought to until they are gone and replaced by something else. When my hands have finally understood that Helga's gone and may never return, I am gripped by a paralysing sense of grief.

I look at Anna, and see how beautiful she is. The friendly glitter in her eyes, the soft curve of her belly, her long shy fingers, there's nothing in her that I don't find appealing. But the moment I touch her, my hands ache with sadness that she is not Helga.

She begins to kiss and caress me, moving her hands eagerly over my body. She bends over me. I lie on my back and watch her lips gently touching my chest and stomach. I feel the eagerness of her mouth and hands. But I can't respond.

Impatience steals into her caresses. More and more. And a desperate determination. And now there can be no doubt about my failure.

We lie silently beside one another.

After a while she asks if I locked the door. I reply that I don't remember. She laughs. The oppressive atmosphere lifts a little. She rests her head on her hand and looks at me, while her fingertips move slowly over my chest. Her cheeks are flaming red.

'Now I'm happy,' she says.

I force a smile. I say I'm happy too. She says something more. She says it's not surprising we're a little shy with each other. And of course she's right.

She asks me about my plans for the day. I say I don't know. She suggests we might go for a walk down by the lake. I say that seems like a good idea. She tells me about a ramble she made along the shore, on her own. She says it can be quite an adventure. At one point she nearly trod on two adders sunning themselves on a rock.

She is getting dressed whilst she talks. She no longer seems embarrassed to be in front of me naked. She looks almost amused.

When she's got her clothes on she bends down and collects the oranges. Three of them. She puts them on the table, then goes to the mirror to straighten her dress. She twists her head in every imaginable direction and examines her mirror-image with sceptically raised eyebrows. When she's satisfied she turns to me and rubs her hands slowly together.

'So we'll meet again soon, shall we?'

'Yes, let's.'

'Good.'

She moves as if to turn and open the door, but then stops herself; her hands let go of each other and drop. She comes and sits on the edge of the bed, bending over me till we're face to face. She caresses the tip of my nose with the tip of her own.

'Tell me you're not tired of me,' she whispers.

'I'm not tired of you.'

'Say you're a little bit fond of me.'

'I love you,' I say.

Her face becomes tense and white. At least that's how it looks.

'And I love you,' she whispers. 'I love you till it nearly makes me ill.'

Then she gets up and goes out.

I lie there looking at the closed door. I hear her footsteps disappear in the corridor. I hear them hurry down the stairs.

Then the tears come. I knew they would. They've been smarting and burning in my chest like an abscess. At last I can release them.

I press my face into the pillow. I howl into the pillow. I cry into the pillow. That's all I can do. The only home I've found in this world is with someone who won't have me.

The morning passes in a mist.

Various people speak to me. My neighbour Högström. I meet him just outside my door, leaning his hand on the wall and breathing heavily. He begins speaking as I pass. Grunts and throat-clearings, a few short questions, then he comes out with what he really wants to say. He tells me a long story about some people he's spent many evenings with, who are staying in a villa down one of the lanes; he mentions the name but I forget. The villa belongs to a family with whom he shares mutual acquaintances, and the family in turn have guests from Skåne. He lets the sentence fade, he shakes his head, his eyes are red and swollen. Now he has confessed his relapse. Now his anguish lifts.

Dr Lidin. A breathless voice in the clatter of the dining room. 'Yes? Yes? Yes?'

The residents circle around him, tittle-tattling among themselves, giggling and laughing and unashamedly listening to what we say. He adjusts a pen in his breast-pocket. He's heard I've been laid low by influenza. I'm standing with a tray in my hands. From the corner of my eye, I notice someone pass in a fine green suit; it's incomprehensible how a colour can be so beautiful. I tell him I've recovered remarkably quickly. He gives a friendly answer, something with the words 'fit as a fiddle' in it; the words stick, and the pain in my chest returns, shooting and aching, and when I smile at the doctor the skin of my face feels tight and rigid, as if my cheeks were made of plaster and might split.

Someone else speaks to me as well. I can't for the life of me remember who. All I can remember is an appeal of some kind. I also remember some men unloading sacks from a cart and some guests standing in the foreground watching. One of the men very nearly dropped his sack and swore and then got a better grip and gave the onlookers a sly look as he carried the sack in, and when he was out of sight one of the residents turned to me and said something and I couldn't bring myself to answer.

Why was I standing watching something so meaningless? I don't know.

She meets me down by the shore. She's changed her clothes. Perhaps she's been bathing. She gives a little hopping movement as I come near. Bounces lightly on her heels. Her eyes glance sideways, as if she's anxious about anyone seeing us, or that she wants to make it clear that she'd prefer us to be alone.

We follow a path along the edge of the lake, stepping over roots, moss and gravelly rocks. The lake is grey. The waves are gurgling in the crevices of the rocks, like little flickering breaths. Anna keeps throwing glances over her shoulder, lingering looks at me.

After a reedy patch where the lake bends we reach marshy ground with a few half-rotten planks for us to balance on; a moment of excitement, the muddy water wells up between the planks, she calls to me, we have terra firma under our feet again.

We sit barefoot in the sand. Dig holes with our fingers while the wind tears at her hair. The creek faces the other side of the lake. We're concealed from the whole world.

She turns, with a searching look, reaches out her hand, straightens her leg.

'Come and lie on my knee.'

I put my head on her lap. Her dress is as stiff as paper. But warm, her hands too.

'Won't you tell me what's bothering you?' she says.

'No.'

My 'no' is a half-stilted sigh. Like an axe falling. I lie there on tenterhooks. Her fingers slowly stroke my head. Nothing has changed in her fingers.

After a moment I glance up furtively at her. Towering above me, she meets my eyes. Her eyebrows are lightly raised as if waiting for me to say something. Perhaps she didn't hear what I said before.

'I was afraid you'd be angry,' I say.

'About what?'

'That I don't want to talk.'

'I know I can make you talk if I want to. I could winkle it out of you or try to persuade you, or if that didn't work I could threaten you. Sooner or later I'd find out what I want to know. But I'd pay a high price for it.'

'Really? What?'

'You'd be very angry with me. Or you might begin to fear me. I know you'd hide it well. But it would be so nonetheless.'

Her tone is light, almost merry.

I laugh and raise myself. I stare at her. I'm filled with a wild feeling, something I can only just control. All I know is that I want to laugh, something in the whole situation seems almost unbearably comic. The two of us, she and I, sitting in Porla drinking ferriferous water through narrow clinking glass tubes. That we walked all the way to this little creek to sit here barefoot, that we made an unsuccessful attempt to commit adultery this morning; not to speak of the beads of sweat on her upper lip and the fine light-brown dust, perhaps sand, in her eyelashes; I want to open my mouth wide and howl with laughter.

'How do you know?' I say.

'From my own experience,' she answers casually.

I laugh. And then I laugh a little more. Then before I can stop it I'm laughing wildly. She looks at me in confusion.

'What is it?'

'I am so happy to be here.'

The words sound strange. They come with an emphasis I'm not used to. As if each word were a sacramental wafer. One wafer each for seven different women before me on their knees in the sand. At the thought of their solemnly gaping mouths waiting my laughter threatens to bubble up again.

'So am I,' she says, stroking my cheek. 'But now let's have a swim!'

She sounds so matter-of-fact. Like a big sister or a governess issuing instructions. She gets up and looks around, and then she begins to take off her clothes, facing out to the lake with her head bowed and her fingers on the buttons. Her dress falls from her naked shoulders. She turns to me with a quick movement that makes her breasts swing and strikes a rapid pose with her foot, sending up a shower of white sand that forces from me a

342

half-stifled protest. Our eyes meet; hers seem as effervescent as champagne poured too briskly into a very small glass.

She trips down to the water and I follow her bouncing buttocks with my eyes while I begin to undress too. She waves her arms and throws herself into the water with a triumphant splash.

I slowly let my clothes drop to the ground. I'm just as old as before, just as fat and ungainly. But now I'm capable of realising it's not important. It's the same for many others. When you think about it, it's really rather funny.

We swim around for a bit. Some figures a long way off wave to us. Neither of us waves back. The figures disappear.

When we come out the wind is blowing up, and we are so cold that our teeth chatter. We put our arms around each other for warmth. I rub her back and she rubs mine.

We kiss. She has the fresh smell of wind and sun and brackish water. As if she's just been wandering, slowly and purposefully through woods and lakes, over hills and bogs, and now she's reached her goal. I kiss her neck, her shoulders, her breasts. The taste of her goes to my head, I can't get enough of it.

After a while we make another attempt. We fail this time too. But the sadness in my hands has faded a little.

We have dinner together. I'm lost in my thoughts. My eyes search the room. All those furtive glances slipping over us.

If what the superintendent claimed is true, there must be lots of people here who know who I am. All those faces, all those moving mouths, all those words streaming over the tables like shoals of unruly little fish.

Some of these people must live in Stockholm; someone will go home, meet an acquaintance and tell about their stay at Porla. Someone's bound to remember the priest who was so often seen in intimate conversation with an unknown woman…

Or perhaps there's someone here who knows me well enough to describe their disturbing observations in a letter. To someone in Stockholm...

The rest'll look after itself.

Towards the end of the meal the superintendent hurries in. He seems to be in a state. I sit still with my knife and fork in my hands and follow him with my eyes. He passes between several tables with his eyes on the floor and eventually finds what he's looking for: a black bag.

As he's about to go out he catches sight of me. He seems to deliberate quickly with himself about what to do.

Then he comes forward with a little frozen smile on his face. He greets me as though we've never met before. Then he places himself behind Anna's chair and says she has talked extremely well of me, and that it's a great joy to him to be able to make my acquaintance at last.

I go along with this little charade, even though I don't find it easy.

I haven't yet told Anna that it was her husband who wanted me to talk to her. Naturally I have to do this. Before I know it they'll end up in a quarrel, and if he sees any chance of hurting her with this little piece of information he's sure not to let the opportunity pass him by.

He stays a while and makes small talk.

He tells us he left the bag with his favourite skittle ball in it under a table. He tells us it's a very special ball he ordered from a firm in Plymouth. He mispronounces the name.

I don't react, apart from nodding sagely. I suddenly feel so sorry for him I feel as though my heart is breaking.

Anna contents herself with half-turning around. She leans her chin against her fingertips and raises her eyebrows wearily, her mouth is strict and her eyes half-closed. There's something aristocratic about her posture that I haven't seen before. You might think some beggar or drunk had come to our table. Occasionally I see from the corner of my eye that she's giving me telling looks, which I don't dare acknowledge, let alone respond to.

The little superintendent is very nervous. He smiles incessantly, even while discussing the most trivial subjects. He clearly can't wait to get away, but seems uncertain how long he's expected to stay and make conversation. Finally he lifts his bag and shakes it meaningfully.

'Now I won't disturb you any longer. They're waiting for me over at the hurly-burly. I told them I'd only be away a minute or two. You see, if you don't start playing within fifteen minutes of the time you booked, you lose the alley to someone else. And between us we've worked out a little system of penalties for anyone who causes someone else to miss their turn...'

Then he begins to explain their complicated system of penalties. It's obvious that he soon regrets having started on this, and it's equally obvious that he has no idea how to make his explanation brief, or better still, stop. His face turns bright red and he begins stammering and stumbling.

Anna's turned her back on him. Her eyes are fixed on the table. Finally the superintendent takes his leave and hurries away.

Silence falls between us. After a while I begin wondering about Anna's silence. Or more exactly, I begin to imagine what would come out of her mouth if she said exactly what she thought. During one of these fantasies she looks at me intently and asks:

'If you love me, how can you let me share a bedroom a single night more with that man?'

A good question. Exceptionally relevant. It leaves me no peace.

Then it strikes me that my own wife may well have said or thought the same. And that I, too, am 'that man'.

*I*n the evening we go to listen to the orchestra. It's chilly in the open air, but they've lit torches that flame and smoke along the edge of the lane, spreading a sense of festivities and expectation. A pagan smell.

Neither Anna nor I know what's brewing. It's not unusual for them to arrange festivities of various sorts. But we have no wish to join in.

There's a considerably bigger audience for this concert than last time. Some don't even get a seat, but have to stand. Anna and I sit right at the end of one of the front rows. I can feel the eyes burning my neck. I listen intensely for any whispering that might have to do with us, but I can't hear anything.

The silver-haired gentleman with horsey teeth is here; he's managed to requisition one of the best seats, both hands resting on the handle of his cane, staring at the orchestra with shining eyes, so full of expectation that he can't even keep his mouth closed.

The orchestra begins with music I haven't heard before, several feather-light pieces suitable for any high-class hotel, and several other equally light but also artfully monotonous pieces. The musicians exchange amused glances, and sometimes the corners of their mouths twitch.

I feel increasingly irritated. I can almost see the composer, some over-sophisticated young man with a smart goatee beard and an ambiguous little smile, jotting down his bagatelles with a world-weary shrug, as if to make the point that nothing really matters. His music's decked in borrowed feathers, and he seems to take care to give each allusion a condescending tone, as if he wants above all to show how ridiculous this music is, which he so freely imitates.

I'm also irritated by the delight spreading through the hall. All the listeners seem to want is to be able to experience something unquestionably new and modern. Anything else seems irrelevant.

I'm no less irritated by the fact that I'd never dare to admit to any of these views publicly. I know how reactionary it would sound. Instead I sit like a sheep listening to one cynical bagatelle after another, and can only conclude that any sign of passion for music has obviously become hopelessly old-fashioned.

In the middle of the concert I feel Anna's leg against mine. At first I think it's an accident, but she holds her leg there and begins to make small almost imperceptible movements.

I glance anxiously at her, but nearly burst out laughing when I see a triumphant smile curl her lips. My irritation evaporates. How could I ever have given the slightest thought to that trivial composer?

During an interval between the pieces I see the silver-haired gentleman walking about, and exactly as he did at the previous concert he nods vigorously to me; I haven't the heart not to nod back. He leans forward and shouts a name through the applause; I understand it must be the composer's name and forget it instantly.

Afterwards we go for a walk.

It's even darker now. As a rule, the lanes are surprisingly popular at dusk. I comment to Anna that it's so dark now that we can't recognise the people we meet, and it occurs to me that it may be precisely for this reason that so many people are out walking at this time. The darkness lends them an anonymity they would not otherwise have.

Suddenly the paths seem full of relationships and conversations not fit for the light of day. It's both disagreeable and exciting. Shadows pass us; we keep a shy distance, distinguishing at best a silhouette against the evening sky, then they are gone. Muffled, intimate conversations approach in the dark, pass and vanish behind us.

In the distance there's a rumble of thunder. The silhouettes in front stop and stare out across the bog, then go on.

Anna's hand brushes against mine. Then, cautious and tentative, her fingers entwine with mine. Her hand is warm and safe to hold while darkness falls and thunder rumbles.

We turn off the path and sit down on a bench we've passed before. It's embedded in ferns and lilac. Anna leans her head on my shoulder and I put my arm around her. We don't say much. Mostly we just sit feeling the warmth of our two bodies and the calm rise and fall of our breathing.

A flash of lightning. More thunder.

'Like a wild animal,' I say.

'But a long way off.'

'Yes.'

'Do you think it's going to rain?'

'I expect so. Listen how silent it is in the forest.'

'Yes. As if it's holding its breath.'

After a bit the stream of people has thinned out and for long periods the path is completely deserted. The shrubs in front of us are bending to and fro in the wind, but on our bench we feel enclosed and safe.

Suddenly there's a sound, from some distance away. Almost like a laugh, but it could have been absolutely anything. Perhaps an animal.

I turn towards the sound but can see nothing but darkness. I don't want to mention it to Anna, since I can't be absolutely sure I heard anything at all. But I notice she too moves her head uneasily.

A wind blows through the tops of the pines, and there's the laugh again, but nearer. It really is a laugh, a desolate one. As if someone's laughing to himself.

I feel my skin turning to gooseflesh, and I think of the stories the man told in the conveyance on the way to the lake, about ghosts and apparitions, stories that may seem ridiculous by the light of day, but not quite so funny with thunder and rushing wind and darkness.

Then we hear men's voices approaching and calm down. When we also hear that the voices are high-spirited the situation seems to take on a soothing everyday quality. Evening revellers coming home. For a moment I worry that we may have to see my neighbour Högström and his drinking pals, but we're sheltered by lilac bushes, and it isn't easy to see our bench even in daylight.

Anna catches hold of my arm.

'Listen,' she whispers.

The voices are coming nearer, but it's difficult to make them out in the wind. A light voice is telling some sort of story while a darker one occasionally grunts encouragement.

'Can't you hear who it is?'

Anna's voice is right against my ear.

The men have stopped, almost exactly in front of our bench. Now I recognise the uncertain, entreating tone of the light voice.

'Yes, so what did you say to him then?' says the dark voice.

'That she's been terribly depressed recently and has sunk deep in introspection, and that I'm worried about the state she's in…'

The little superintendent puts on a theatrically pitiful tone which is appreciated by his companions.

'... and that I was convinced she needed to talk to someone with his wisdom and experience of life, and his... his knowledge of humanity...'

The salvoes of laughter are a trifle more restrained this time.

I draw a deep breath. Something warm spreads in my chest. Then something dry and grey. Then I feel as empty as a blown egg.

The voices have gone quiet. I hear the hollow pop of a cork being pulled out of a bottle. Then comes a voice I don't recognise that sounds more leisurely than the others.

'I don't understand. What good did you think that would do?'

The dark voice immediately goes on the attack.

'Can't you understand? Bloody hell, it's a stroke of genius! A way to stop her watching him all the time. He gets someone to give her his full attention, which gives him more freedom to come and go as he likes!'

'Oh, yes, I see...'

The leisurely voice sounds embarrassed. The dark voice becomes a bit more conciliatory in tone.

'No embarrassing questions about where he's been all evening, and...'

'Where I've been? Playing skittles of course!'

Superintendent Hansson sounds deceptively innocent. All laugh. The laughter dies down.

The leisurely voice seems to have taken heart.

'And who is he? I mean, the man who...'

'The priest! Haven't you seen him?'

'Wait a minute... Surely you don't mean the... !'

'Of course, that's the one!'

At this point one of them may have pulled a funny face or made a gesture, because they practically split their sides laughing. One lets out a wailing sound, as if he is laughing so much it hurts.

A figure flickers by in my head. A caricature I once saw in a newspaper. The drawing showed a priest. Something funny was written under it, I've forgotten what. But I'll never forget the picture. Fat cheeks, pinched mouth, malignant little eyes. And an expression of monumental stupidity and conceit.

For a moment, I am that priest. I feel it so strongly I can hardly remember what I really look like.

A mighty rushing sound comes from the other side of the bog.

It drowns the voices. It drowns everything. It should end, but it does not.

It sounds like a decisive trial of strength. Perhaps between the wind and the trees. Between what is on earth, and what comes from somewhere else. Between what is visible and invisible.

When the superintendent starts speaking again he can hardly make himself heard. He's forced to shout. The dark voice interrupts him, sounding impatient, then all the voices move on. Soon they're gone.

The rushing sound gets louder still. It is moving relentlessly towards us, and only at that moment do I realise it's the approaching rain. When the first heavy drops fall I grip Anna's shoulder and shake her lightly. But her body seems numb and lifeless.

'We ought to rush back,' I shout.

The rain pours down on us. For some time I can't see anything. Water streams into my eyes, my glasses steam up. When I've dried them I see the sky's a little lighter over the bog. The rain's beating down so fiercely that small pillars of steam are rising from the ground.

I turn her face up to me, but it's too dark to make out her features. The rain pours down on us, finding its way into my ears and collar and down my back. I get the awful feeling that I'm holding a dead face in my hands. That in a moment a flash will light the sky, and I will see that what was her face has been transformed into a mask, a grey thing, as expressionless as a tailor's dummy or a pincushion.

'Forgive me,' I shout.

At last she moves. She slowly lifts her arm, it rises like a pale-grey snake in the dark, and her hand falls around my neck.

I have an impulse to tear myself loose and run away, screaming wildly for help. It started as a grotesque fantasy, something washed up on the shore, and in the beginning it was so absurd that I couldn't see what it was. A moment ago it was something to laugh at, but now it's spread and taken charge of all my senses.

Soon her fury will strike me down. Soon she'll tear me to pieces. I tempted her love, and it was greater than I could have imagined. How vast will not her fury be now that she knows that everything grew from the shabbiest of lies?

She pulls me closer. My whole body's shaking. Whether from cold or fear I don't know. Her mouth's against my ear. Then she presses her mouth against my cheek and moves her body against me. And it feels warm.

'It doesn't matter,' she says.

Her voice is trembling. I lay my hand on her stomach, feeling her warmth through the wet cloth. It's like a wonderful reunion. A sense of relief not of this world. I feel a thankfulness that saddens me.

'We have each other,' she says. 'What's happened has happened, and no one can take that from us. What do they have?'

The morning's unreal. My flowers have begun to wither. Their water's grey and muddy. I go and change it. It's still raining. There's so much to do. Clothes to be collected and taken to the laundry. Things lying about that must be put back in their proper place. Any number of things. Fragments of firewood on the floor to be swept up.

I don't see Anna at breakfast. Nor her husband. It doesn't take long before my fantasies get going. I make sure I sit with my back to the wall.

I eat an egg. I pause, and wonder whether I'm eating faster than usual.

When I go back to my room to fetch my bathing costume and towel there's a letter inside the door.

I close the door quickly and pick it up. There's nothing written on the envelope. I wonder how long it's been lying there, whether it could already have been there this morning. If I stepped over it when I went to have breakfast. As I may very well have done.

I sit down on the bed. My fingers run over the corners of the envelope. I feel a peculiar sense of relief. As if I already know what it contains.

I open it. It's from Anna. It's the first time I've seen her hand-writing. I like it. It's intelligent.

She tells me they're going home. While she's writing the letter her husband is downstairs ordering a droshky to the station. She has told him everything. He is furious. Apparently not so much because she loves another man, but most of all because we over-heard his conversation with his friends on the path. Naturally he's utterly ashamed. And naturally his shame has been transformed into anger.

'From now on,' she writes, 'let everything have its right time and place. It's all the same to me, because you've given me some-thing I never had before: a goal, a purpose, a glimmer of hope and a dream of a life I want to live. Every time I close my eyes to see that life I see a table. Not always the same table. Sometimes it's large and grand and laid for Sunday dinner, the cloth white and newly mangled, with artistically arranged napkins and candles burning beautifully with a still yellow flame. Sometimes it's a sim-ple table, worn and unpretentious, the sort you might see in the arbour at a summer cottage, with thin legs and flaking paint. Only one thing never changes: there are always two chairs at the table. One is mine, the other is yours. As long as I live it will be there. If you already know that you will never want to come and sit there, I would be grateful if you would write as soon as possible to let me know. The chair will stay there all the same. But you know how dreary it is to wait for someone who has no intention of coming.'

I put the letter on the table and look out of the window.

I remember a story I once heard. I can't have been very old. It was about a man who cut off two fingers of his own left hand. Everyone wanted to know what it felt like. The man enjoyed the attention. He lifted his left hand and stroked the stumps where his fingers had been. To tell the truth, he said, it wasn't particularly painful, at least not to begin with. The pain came later. At first he was awed, even a bit exhilarated, to think that the little sausages on the chopping-block were his own fingers, and that they didn't belong to him any more.

Without thinking he'd picked them up and studied them. The dirty fingernails. A burst blister on the end of one finger. The white bone in the middle of all the fleshy red. The strangeness of holding two of your own fingers and having no sensation in them.

I let my hands fall. I can't help it. The first thing that comes over me is a great sense of relief.

There is nothing I can do about it. I feel relief in my whole body. As if the danger is past, and I can now move more freely and unhindered than before.

I've never been able to stand raised voices and upset emotions. When I was little I used to run and hide when the others quarrelled. If it was too loud I'd run to the forest. There was a stone there I'd hide behind.

It was no accident that I chose that particular stone. I had a good view of the cottage. I could see the kitchen window. A hole of warm light in a large darkness. I could see figures moving inside.

I'd wait behind the stone till I could see some sign that the row was over. That Mother was putting something on the table. That someone was laughing, or had lit a candle.

But I looked with no less excitement at the window in case they started to kill each other in there. In case there was some violent movement, or someone rushed through the kitchen.

I thought if there was a murder, most probably someone would rush through the house and perhaps shout to express their terror, confusion and amazement. If this happened, the stone would also be a good place to be. From behind the stone it wasn't far to the road. A slope with blueberry bushes and ferns and no stones or ditches to trip over. I'd be able to get down to the road quickly and then just go on running. That's how I'd worked it out.

If it had just been a matter of a small child's overheated imagination one could have dismissed it with a laugh and a shake of the head, merely feeling a little sad. But it's followed me through the years, fixing itself in my mind.

I was grown-up and acting as assistant minister in Falköping when a coachman lost his temper with me after some misunderstanding over payment. It wasn't my fault, the parish had promised him something and he wasn't making sense. Our exchange of views ended with him storming out of the vicarage and slamming the door so hard that a painting slipped sideways.

That evening I couldn't relax till I'd manoeuvred a large chest of drawers in front of the spare-room door. It made no difference how much I tried to tell myself calmly and soberly that the front door was locked, that the house was full of people and that by this time the coachman was presumably settled in a tavern drowning his grievance.

My imagination couldn't be pacified. In my imagination the

coachman came back with an axe, forced the outer door and murdered the minister and his whole family, just so he could get up to my room.

I wonder where it comes from, this insane self-centredness. This conviction that the world's accumulated fury glides over me like a thunder cloud, following me wherever I go and merely waiting for the chance to destroy me with a bolt of lightning.

I go on sitting on the bed. My eyes fall on her letter. I've laid it on top of the other, the letter from Pastor Wenge.

My thoughts begin to wander.

I take Wenge's letter and read it. The lines where he passes on Helga's greetings.

I remember how bitter I felt when I first read it. Now I can't understand why. I know nothing of what led up to her greeting, or what she sounded like when she asked him to pass it on, or what state of mind she was in at the time.

Now and then I've reminded myself that she can't know anything of the disturbing and crucial experiences I've been through lately. This has filled me with a sense of satisfaction, not to say triumph. It serves her right. Let her have a dose of her own medicine.

Now it strikes me for the first time that, for all I know, she may have been experiencing no less dramatic events while I've been away. Perhaps she's ended her relationship. Perhaps she's come home thinking the tenderest possible thoughts about me, counting the days till I'll be back.

Not that I think it's likely. But it could be the case.

I've always assumed nothing will have changed. Her coldness, her indifference, her lying, her regular visits to that man. Perhaps I've chosen to believe this because it answers my purpose so well. It soothes my guilty conscience.

It's an unpleasant thought. A cold wind blows from it. A raw blast of air from under the floorboards. A thought about how often I've simply *assumed* things about her, just as she presumably, must have assumed things about me, and how that's the way we have lived. How often have our assumptions been wrong? And how often have we been unaware of how wrong our assumptions were?

How would I act if I came home to Stockholm and discovered that everything was now different? If Helga were to overwhelm me with kisses and protest her love for me, and I felt she meant every word?

Would I still look coldly at her, push her away from me and tell her that her assurances of love had come too late? Would I be ready to go through all the moral, practical and economic trials a divorce would involve?

The thought paralyses me. It tolerates no obstacles. It's practical and merciless.

If my love for Anna depends on Helga being unfaithful and untruthful, it's not self-reliant. And if that's the case, then it's stillborn.

$\mathcal{N}$ot many days left.

Everything I did with her before, I now do alone.

I take long walks. Turn after turn down the lanes. I nod to those I meet, sometimes saying something friendly to the children, who drop their eyes and reach for the safety of their parents' hands. I sit on the shaky conveyances that go down to the lake, watch the scaly pines glide by; I see the dust of the road billowing up behind us, I change in my cabin, I step down into the foaming, gleaming brown water, I hear voices echoing against the walls.

In the evenings I make a serious study of the menu and try to remember what was written on the piece of paper Helga pinned up on the kitchen cupboard. Then I give my order and eat my food with great care, cutting everything into little bits; I stick a little bit of veal, a little bit of carrot and a little bit of potato on my fork and dip it in chanterelle sauce before lifting it to my mouth. If even a small piece falls off the fork I frown and go through the whole procedure again. I chew carefully. Forty times. It's something I've heard somewhere.

I eat until not a crumb is left on my plate. Then I am satisfied. As if I've achieved something important. And my eyes search the room.

All the loud groups. All the new acquaintanceships beginning.

Groups growing bigger, with waiters hurrying with chairs and arranging tables to fit more people in. People being introduced to one another and exchanging polite phrases. All the men who want to dominate the conversation and keep everyone's eyes on themselves, all the women whose eyes rest on whoever is talking, and some men evoke a hunger in their eyes, and other men evoke nothing.

And all the little mute groups, married couples with small children, grey, stiff and straight-backed, respectable people with combed hair, saying not a word during the meal from start to finish, keeping their eyes on their plates, and when they do occasionally look up, avoiding the sight of their families to gaze around the room while their jaws chomp, the atmosphere around them as oppressive as it only can be when death has long been a self-invited guest at their table.

Wherever I look I'm deeply thankful I can sit alone.

Yes, I'm enjoying my solitude, and hate myself for it. There is something slightly dutiful about missing Anna. It's like poking a dead animal with a stick to see whether there might be a last muscular spasm left in it.

I'm aware that something valuable's about to slip out of my hands. Something that could perhaps have been my salvation.

And yet: surely I'm not fully conscious. There's something missing; the last little impulse, which would inspire my hands to grab paper and writing materials and tell her I'm coming to her.

I spend time just sitting. I go for walks. I drink my water. I take part in services. Salvation slips ever further away. Mostly I'm indifferent. Sometimes it feels almost pleasant.

Thus speaks a man who's given up all hope of life. But I want to live. I don't think I've ever wanted to live more than I do now.

I often mutter to myself during my walks. Quite long discussions.

Often about Anna. I develop eloquent little arguments about why it'll be best to wait for a few days after I get back to Stockholm before sitting down to write to her. I'm certain I sound quite convincing.

I'm an old man. At least too old to throw myself headlong into some adventure. Anyone should be able to see the sense of waiting for a few days, so I can get some idea of what's been happening while I've been away.

I'm on the brink of something that could be decisive in my life. I don't want to base a decision of this kind on assumptions. I want certainty.

… yes, and so on, chiselling out one argument after another. Then I shudder with self-contempt, laugh bitterly and mutter: Well, well, old friend, behind all your lofty talk about love you're just a common old horse-dealer. Someone who wants to get by, and who adapts everything that's right and true and honourable to fit in with that.

This is my last day. I've walked a long time, at such a forced pace that I am short of breath. My heart's pounding wildly in my chest, and there's something rickety and rattling about my heartbeat that makes me think of my heart as something old. A leaky, unlubricated organ struggling to do its duty nimbly and efficiently as it always has, though it's very clear its movements are becoming increasingly fumbling and slow.

The thought moves me; I stop and look out across the marsh to give my heart a chance to rest.

The marsh is a beautiful reddish-brown in the afternoon sun. On the far side, where the forest is, a bird rises with heavy wingbeats and long legs. It could be a stork.

I draw a deep breath. For a long moment my head's empty. Then her face comes before me. That day on the little tongue of land by the lake when I rested with my head on her lap, and everything she said to me then, and the rare, almost somnolent feeling of resting close to someone who has looked deep into your soul, and still has only tenderness in her eyes.

But then comes the other voice. It has been silent for a long time. Now it can't wait any longer. It sounds tired and controlled, as if making an effort not to be sarcastic or condescending and it asks: Didn't you hear what she told you about her marriage? Don't you see that her affection is not caused by anything other than the fact that for several years she has been starved of affection? She'd have fallen just as helplessly for anyone else who paid her a little attention.

Don't misunderstand me, the voice goes on patiently. You've undoubtedly done her good. Opened her eyes, isn't that how she put it? Leave it at that, then. She's not going to waste any more time pining away at home while her husband's out having a good time. You've helped her to realise her own worth. You have even made her feel desirable. That's no small thing. Now she can go out into the world and find someone to love her. But do you honestly think that you yourself have made such an indelible impression on her? Probably she's already started looking elsewhere.

She can choose. There are plenty of men. You know how it is. You never forget anyone who's struck a certain chord in you. But circumstances force you to set them aside on a particular shelf in your consciousness; one of you may be married, or the other, or at worst both. They can stay on that shelf, and if circumstances change all you have to do is take them down. It's the simplest thing in the world.

The voice grinds on tirelessly in my head. Something inside me's spinning faster and faster. I let out a sound, perhaps one of my bitter small laughs, or a resigned invective. That's what I usually do when things start spinning, it's how I put a foot back firmly on the ground, it's how I silence the grinding voice.

Just as I let out the sound there's a noise in the bushes behind me, and heavy steps trudge off into the undergrowth.

I stare into the branches and leaves. My whole chest seems locked in a cramp.

It must have been a large animal. A roe-deer, or perhaps an elk. It must have been standing still behind me all the time, waiting for me to move on. Several feet away, by the sound. So close, breathing behind me. But I noticed nothing. I was looking in another direction.

I could have a baby with Anna. She's still of childbearing age, as they say. I can no longer remember what words I used in the days before I sat before that stream of doctors and specialists, watching their lips move and noticing the various ways they tried to hide their embarrassment.

I often sit and think about this during the services at the Reader's Stone. My eyes move to the stone itself, where it towers high above the young priest's head. Covered in damp moss. Birds land on it, peck with a preoccupied air then scatter, quick as a flash. Insects circle around it, listless and as if hypnotised, enclosed in their secrets.

The mighty stone. At some time, millions of years ago, it too came into existence. Even a stone must be born. And the birds, the dragonflies and moss.

Creating life. The holiest of all acts. I've always known this. It's never been granted to me. Now perhaps there's a chance, even for me.

I too came into existence once. Many millions of years passed without me. Then I existed. Seen in context my life's nothing more than a star that flares up briefly in the great infinite blue-black, before being extinguished again. But at least I was allowed to exist for a while.

I should feel grateful, I should feel joy. Yet I can't sit before God without looking away and bowing my head in shame.

Recently I've begun to wonder whether it is possible to live through a whole life without taking part in it. And one's life sits there, like a pair of shoes in the hall, never used.

That must be why I can't bring myself to lift my eyes. God has set out the shoes for me. Patiently, year by year, making sure they'll fit me, so I can stride comfortably out into the world and meet the people there.

But my feet flatly refuse to enter those shoes.

I don't understand why. I can't even remember ever trying to put them on. Yet I'm behaving as if I did try once, but that it was such a dreadful experience I'd rather die than try again.

Somewhere there must be an explanation. The secret must be hidden somewhere. But I can't find it.

And that expression, 'I'd rather die than try again' loses a little of its force as a persuasive slogan with every minute, every day and every year that passes, and comes closer to simple fact. Soon I'll be dead. And I seem to be utterly convinced that it's not my own life running out, but somebody else's.

*I*t's a long and dreary train journey. The country-woman opposite remarks that we've got the best possible weather for travelling. Mild and just a little grey and misty. Just how it should be: moderate. Not too cold and wet, which would be draughty, and not too sunny either, because there's nothing more irritating to the eyes than flashes of light between the trees. She points this out to me, and repeats it all again for everyone else who gets on the train thereafter.

Every time the train goes through a tunnel or a dark wood so I can see my reflection in the window, I look, and think: eight kilos.

That's what Dr Lidin said. He looked up from his tables and adjusted his spectacles, and sounded genuinely surprised.

With a powerful effort I managed to hold my face firm and assumed a matter-of-fact and almost scientific tone of voice to tell him that I was now able to go for quite long walks without stopping to rest. During the first weeks of my stay I hadn't even been able to walk the length of Love Lane without sitting down to get my breath back.

'Yes? Yes?' said the doctor eagerly. 'That… that…'

Waving his hand in front of his face, he seemed to indicate that something was radiating from my face.

'I can see that, Pastor.'

Eight kilos. I try to get a sense of the weight in my hand. An eight-kilo sackful of potatoes. Quite heavy. Perhaps not quite enough to need a cart. But heavy enough to make red marks on my hands if I walked about carrying it for long. That's how much weight I've lost. I don't have to carry that eight-kilo sack about any more.

My clothes hang much more loosely. My shirt-front looks distinctly hollow. I wonder what Helga will say. I suppose two or three kilos' difference would hardly be noticeable. But eight?

I'm healthier. Slimmer. Stronger. Have more stamina.

The hours pass. The woods pass. Fields and villages too. I have a hamper with me. I think I'm hungry. But every time I look into the hamper and see the grease-spotted packet of sandwiches, I begin to feel ill and leave it untouched.

Later in the afternoon the weather clears up. The sun shoots white flares through the window. I look around for the countrywoman, but she's obviously got off.

We pass timber yards and sawmills. Factories and workshops. Crossroads where carriages stand waiting. Horses with tossing heads and twitching ears. I see bare-chested workers leaning on fences, they point to the train and wave, wild happiness in their faces, perhaps someone said something funny.

All day I've been sitting in a state of tense expectation, as if bringing an expensive present for Helga and longing to see her face when she opens it.

But when we pass Södertälje I panic. It's all going too fast. I'm not ready. I try to think calming thoughts. It's not surprising I'm a bit nervous. But the disagreeable feeling persists.

I've been away for nearly six weeks. I've met a woman I have got attached to.

It strikes me that I've assumed I can take what attitude I like to this, and that everyone else concerned must just adapt themselves accordingly.

That it'll be fine if I forget Anna and stay with Helga, and equally fine if I decide to end my marriage and sit down on the chair Anna has made ready for me.

That both paths are there for me and I'm free to choose either.

But as Stockholm gets nearer I feel a creeping unease, an awful premonition that what happened at Porla can't be undone. That I've already chosen my path without realising it. I want to cry out that I didn't do it, I wasn't there. But of course I was there.

Nothing horrifies me more than things that can't be changed. The irretrievable isn't for me.

The last evening at Porla I wrote her a letter.

When I read it through I saw clearly that I'd balanced the scales so both sides weighed exactly the same. The letter contained enough warmth and sense of loss to encourage her, and at the same time enough reserve to enable me to abandon her with a clear conscience if that should turn out the most suitable thing to do.

I tore the letter up.

The sun has just set when we thunder over the bridge. The grey smoke from the chimneys on Kungsholmen stands out sharply against the deep red sky. The train strikes sparks from the rails, lighting up the idlers on the bridge, a whirl of fragmented images that burn themselves firmly on the retina, gentlemen biting hard on their pipes, little children on women's backs, grinning and covering their ears.

The train stops and I step down onto the platform, breathing in the smell of tar and cigars. I look cautiously around me.

A week ago I sent a short note to say what time I'd arrive. I addressed it to the office. Perhaps I hoped Helga would make enquiries about when I might be expected home.

It's difficult to distinguish the faces around me. Steam and dust have wrapped everyone in a greyish-yellow haze.

I stand with my luggage and pretend to be busy with the clasp on my suitcase and a tie-on label. I take out my watch and study it. I don't want to be the man no one bothered to meet at the station. Minutes pass. I can feel something inside me beginning to slow down. All the anticipation, all the excitement. Also the discomfort and depression that came after Södertälje. It moved quickly and lightly, like splashing water. But now it's stiffening. Now it's icing over. Soon I'll be frozen solid.

I sit down on a bench. I ought to go and look for a droshky. Let it wait. Let everything wait.

My eyes are beginning to get used to the haze. People pass, laughing. Sweaty messengers with thick pencils between their teeth like bridles. Women in artfully decorated hats, women turning smiling white faces up to silent husbands staring inscrutably straight ahead, swinging their walking-sticks mechanically backwards and forwards. A man's helping an old woman down from a carriage while his wife and children stand waiting, the little girl holding a bunch of wild flowers and nervously pinching their stalks. Through the din of the platform I can hear the old woman's anxious and reproachful voice and her son's monotonous comments.

She didn't even write one letter. Not one.

I stare straight ahead. I see blue-clad legs flitting past below the train. One person walking, another running after. Rough voices. Metal striking metal with laborious regularity, something refusing to come loose.

Then I see Georg. He is standing talking to a conductor, or to be more exact, listening to one. I recognise his greasy hair and his characteristic stooping, grieving posture.

I take my bags and go over to him. He brightens up.

'Pastor! How wonderful! Allow me to welcome you back to Stockholm...'

The conductor gives him a triumphant glance, shakes his head and moves off.

Georg takes my bags. As we pass through the entrance hall he talks breathlessly about the muddle on the platform, and how we could possibly have missed each other, and that fool of a conductor who was so unhelpful...

He makes no comment on my slimmer appearance. He asks if I had a pleasant stay. I can hardly be bothered to answer. Perhaps he thinks it would be too intrusive to comment on my appearance.

There's a pleasant golden light in the entrance hall. A clatter and hum of conversation from the restaurant. Some thrushes are flying about up in the roof.

When we reach the street Georg asks if I'd like a droshky, but I say we might just as well walk.

Stockholm is more beautiful than I remember. The evening is cool and pleasant. I breathe in the smell of horse-droppings from the road, the rich spicy steam from the restaurants and the pungent burned smell of rattling trams.

I move unsteadily on the pavements, confused by the contrasts between all the people hurrying forward with hunted looks, blind and deaf to everything except the newspapers they have to deliver, or the washing they have to carry, and the people gliding easily forward in a cloud of exclusivity, enjoying their cigars and each other's company and not least their own company, seemingly intent on prolonging their enjoyment for as long as they can.

We round a corner, and there's the church towering over us. I feel an unexpected movement.

'I really hope you're hungry, Pastor,' says Georg.

I look at him in surprise. He seems uncertain. Dutiful yet somehow teasing. He gives me a pale little smile.

'Yes, I certainly am.'

'That's a good thing, that is.'

I make no comment. We go through the gate and cross the churchyard. A family is sitting on one of the benches, near the tallest of the chestnut trees. As we pass I see it's the wood-carrier Lagerström and his family. Beside him is his young wife with her little daughter on her knee, Svea I think the child was called; she's wearing a billowing, white summer dress and is asleep in her mother's lap, her arms are so thin, her face so resolute.

Fru Lagerström's in the middle of telling her husband something, but as I pass she falls silent. I give them a friendly greeting, but Herr Lagerström limits himself to a brief nod then looks away, and neither of them bothers to get up.

I'd decided to stop and chat for a moment, but their unfriendliness makes me walk on, boiling with shame, anger and confusion.

What have I done to them, apart from baptising their little daughter?

Not so long ago the man was sitting before my desk offering his services. If I should ever need 'a strong pair of arms', or something like that. What's happened since? Has he come to know something about me that causes him displeasure, or perhaps even hatred?

There are lights on in the vicarage. We're nearly there now. The door's closed. I take a routine glance at the graves and can at least confirm that they look no more neglected than usual. I can almost say the churchyard looks unusually neat. But I may be mistaken. At least there's nothing for me to bring up with Pastor Wenge. He seems pleased enough with his efforts as it is.

As I take the final steps to the door I remember something I haven't given a thought to for a long time.

It was something that went through my head after the day I sat by the tobacco patch with Johan Laurén and he explained how things were.

On some occasions, when lying awake tossing and turning, I'd remembered Herr Lagerström's offer, and fantasised about asking him to come and see me. He'd sit before me with his sharp blue eyes and broad hairy hands, and I'd confide in him, and he'd sit listening, silent and deeply serious, and when I would finish he would look angry, and I would feel safe with him because he'd know the difference between right and wrong, and I'd see clearly that he knew I was the one who'd been unjustly treated, and that it made him angry, and he'd know no peace until he'd punished those who'd caused me so much pain.

When I call these fantasies to mind yet another wave of shame washes over me, with his tense, troubled face so fresh in my memory.

I open the door and go into the house. All's still and silent. There's a warm light coming from the kitchen. No lights on upstairs. Floorboards creak under my feet.

Mine, I think, looking around. Not hers.

I walk slowly through the hall. I think I hear sounds from the direction of the back door. A casual murmur. It's also a touch cooler than usual indoors, as though there's a door open, or perhaps a window at the back.

I pass through the drawing room. It's light out in the garden, and there's a glitter coming from the table. Strange figures and expectant grey faces.

I stand in the doorway. I look over the table, laid with a buffet of cold meats, beetroot, new potatoes and fresh bread. Expensive bottles of wine.

Märit and Sivert are sitting at the table. Märit's the first to notice me; she stiffens and adjusts her hair. Furthest off is Byström, breaking a slice of bread into small pieces and pushing them into his mouth. His wet-combed hair is shining like fish scales on his head.

Beyond the espalier lattice stand Pastor Wenge and his wife; the Pastor's explaining something with an engaging smile on his face, his fingertips touching as he shakes his hands expressively. Only the Pastor's wife notices me; Helga has her back to me and is nodding at the Pastor's words with her head on one side and a glass of wine in her hand.

Fru Wenge touches her husband's arm. He looks up and Helga turns around.

I go slowly down the steps and Helga comes to meet me. She smiles gently, casting a rapid glance over the table as if to make sure that no one is missing.

Still holding the glass, she hugs me with her free arm. She smells of some new perfume, rank and spicy. After a second or two her hand starts moving over my back as if in a hurry to get away, I watch the wine splashing near the edge of her glass, backwards and forwards, almost hypnotically, then after a few seconds more she begins patting me lightly on the back.

'Welcome home, dearest!' she murmurs in my ear.

She takes a step back and I look at her. She's done something to her hair. The knot seems bigger than usual. Her lips are redder. She smiles at me. Her eyes disappear into little slits and she looks like the child she once was. She who was so ill-equipped for growing up. She takes a deep breath.

'I thought, in honour of your homecoming, that we should... But come now!'

She interrupts herself and goes over to push the Wenges along, which is unnecessary, since they're already on the move. Pastor Wenge nods to me, almost makes a bow; he's badly sunburned, his brow and nose are as shiny and red as fire in the lamplight.

'...gather, all of us who have the pleasure of working with you...'

Helga falls silent; her eyes roam and her mouth makes a shape as if for a word that won't come; perhaps she's suddenly unsure how it should be pronounced.

'...and living with you, that we should gather together in a way that, well, that perhaps isn't so usual here, but that nonetheless could be... that I thought could be... there!'

She looks around. Everyone is watching her attentively, I see the whites of their eyes around the table. I smile stiffly.

Helga's not used to wine. She says it gives her a headache. She's not used to making speeches either, in fact I can't remember her ever making one before. She gets through it all right. I've always told her she would. She uses strong emphasis, especially at the most personal points. She also sounds a bit elusive, a trifle provocative, but only in a charming way; it's the natural privilege of every beautiful young woman.

I say what a pleasant surprise, but my voice comes out unexpectedly weak, and Helga interrupts me.

'Let's drink a toast! Märit...!'

Helga motions towards me to alert Märit to the fact that I haven't got a glass. Märit rises rather tight-lipped, but before she can do anything Helga waves her away and whirls over to the table to fill a glass, which she holds out to me.

'So! Skål!...'

All raise their glasses. I sip the wine, and nod to each person in turn.

Helga comes over to me, taking a mouthful from her glass as she goes. She spills a little and stops to wipe her mouth on the back of her hand. She says I must have something to eat. She sticks her arm under mine and leads me over to the table. Then lets go and hurries off.

I help myself to a little food.

Pastor Wenge comes forward. He asks me how things have been. I face him with my mouth full of beetroot. Pastor Wenge has a good, intelligent appearance. His wife is small, pale and red-haired. She has the powerful front teeth of a rodent. Her eyelashes and eyebrows are light, which lends her clear blue irises a rather unpleasant lustre.

I say things went very well.

Pastor Wenge doesn't take this in. He leans forward to hear better, so close that I see straight into the roots of his hair, and can confirm that he's sunburned there too. When he leans forward I feel extremely old.

I lower my voice since it's so quiet around the table, and everyone can hear what I say. But it may be that my reticence is interpreted as discourtesy. Perhaps the whole point is that everyone should hear what I say, since after all they're invited guests.

'Pastor, you've certainly... well, I must say there's a striking difference. You've become so much slimmer. Hasn't he?'

He leans towards his wife and inspects me with a look almost of concern. She nods enthusiastically. I steal a glance down the table. They're all either staring straight ahead or down into their plates, except Georg, who has stopped with his fork halfway to his mouth, and when he meets my eye he hastily nods too.

I mumble something self-deprecating. I suppose I'm meant to feel flattered. Pastor Wenge and I have only met on two or perhaps three occasions before.

I talk about the walks and the amber-coloured water of the lake, and the stillness over the marsh in the evenings, and melancholy and despair come over me. Before me I have Pastor Wenge's worried expression, the skin on his cheek bulging as he chases a fragment of food with the tip of his tongue.

Helga has come back with a plate, which she sets down on the table; it looks like sardines decorated with something green, perhaps parsley, and I hear her say to Märit, 'This evening *I'm* the one waiting on *you*', then she laughs.

I force myself to go on with my account of Porla, even if I hardly know what I'm saying. But if I stopped I wouldn't be able to take my eyes off Helga, which would make it obvious that something about her behaviour's bothering me.

Suddenly I realise she's drunk.

It's not immediately obvious. Perhaps I'm the only person who can tell, I don't know. But I stand stiff as a statue.

Meanwhile Helga circulates energetically. She is in constant movement. She moves things on the table and hums and says something to Sivert; he answers and she laughs. She stops, glass in hand, between Pastor Wenge and me, and for a moment stands absolutely still.

All this time I keep talking, my lips moving ceaselessly; I'm giving an account of a typical day at Porla or something like that. When I look at Helga her hand shoots out and grabs my arm.

'Oh, I must show you... in the paper the other day! There was a whole page of drawings from Porla by that artist, what's his name...'

She shuts her eyes and moves her fingers up and down impatiently.

'Bother! So annoying, it's on the tip of my tongue...'

She hurries off to find the paper. Pastor Wenge follows her with his eyes, then looks thoughtfully at me.

He begins telling me about various things he's done. Helga's away for a long time. At the table Byström laughs in a way I've never heard before. Märit answers in a cool voice.

For a moment I stop listening to Pastor Wenge, and when I listen again I no longer have any idea what he's talking about, except that he's irritated about something the church council has or hasn't done, and it seems from his constant pauses that I'm expected to have an opinion on the matter.

I chuckle and turn up my eyes as if to say, well, what could you expect. Then I clear my throat and, raising my voice a bit so everyone can hear, I tell him I'm a bit done-in after my long journey.

Once I'm sure I'm going to be able to get away soon I feel such relief, even light-heartedness, that I manage to say something self-deprecating about my age, and something appreciative about their having welcomed me with this little supper, and I mean every word and turn to say a word of thanks to each one of them, to Pastor Wenge and his wife, to Sivert and Georg and Märit and even Byström, and I can feel the warmth spreading around the table, and see their faces light up, and it's like breathing on a live coal in my chest: soon I'll be able to get away, soon I can be alone.

As I get near the end I hear Helga's keen steps coming through the door behind me, then stopping.

I turn and thank her too, giving her the honour of having taken this praiseworthy initiative, even if I don't know whether this was the case.

Helga slowly shakes her head, I see her lips begin to move, and a glimpse of panic behind her amused expression, and as soon as I stop speaking she will ask me to stay a moment longer, her request perhaps supported by others.

I go forward and press a kiss on her cheek, and when our faces meet I hear a sound from her, nothing more than an irritated grunt, but even so I start when I hear how harsh it sounds, as if full of hate.

I leave, and carry my luggage up to the bedroom.

I shut the door and sit down on the bed.

It's completely quiet now. The feeling of freedom's gone. Instead I begin to feel more and more like a prisoner. I can't leave the room, because I've said I'm going to bed. But to go to bed would be pointless, almost ludicrous. All I can do is sit and wait.

The disagreeable thing is that I don't know what I'm waiting for. Or who. I don't recognise the woman I married. I don't know who she's become, or if I ever knew who she was.

In the deafening silence, my fantasies from the train return. I'd forgotten them. Now they pad out from the shadows and parade before the bed. Slowly, deliberately, almost scornfully.

Do you remember? they whisper. How you were going to undress and put on your nightshirt. How Helga was going to come to you, standing so close you could feel her breath against your chest, and she'd lift her hands and let them glide over your stomach, your back, your arms, and you were going to see a feverish enchanted look in her eyes, and then she'd look quickly up at your face, to be sure it really was her husband standing in front of her, eight kilos lighter. Do you remember?

And when you were together the miracle would happen. The reward for your constancy. For coming home to her despite losing all hope and being tempted by something simpler, happier, warmer. But you were steadfast, so steadfast that everyone had begun to shake their heads in secret and see you as a pitiable wretch who'd lost his grip on reality. You didn't budge a single millimetre, and God rewarded you. Do you remember?

You were going to lie on top of her, healthier, stronger, full of stamina, and as you delivered your seed you'd know that the cause of those sterile years had always been your anxiety, but now God had rolled away the stone, now your love could flow freely, rippling merrily, and bearing fruit, and the sad, dry twigs would bud, do you remember that?

I must have had a ghastly nightmare. I can find no other explanation.

I wake with a shock, and I'm sure there's a man standing by the bed. I can see him clearly. He is tall and expressionless and he is raising his arm over me.

I throw myself out of bed and rush to the window to avoid the blow. I bump into the night table, and in my confused state I lose my balance and fall to the ground.

Despite the fact that I'm beginning to come to my senses the terror still has a grip on me, and it's so dark in the room. I scramble to my feet and pull back the curtain. Only then, when I see clearly that the room's empty, can I breathe freely.

I take my watch from my waistcoat. It's nearly one.

The bed is empty.

I put on my slippers and open the door a crack. It's silent and dark outside. There's a heavy, blue light coming in through the skylight casting dreary shadows in the stairwell. The staircase is like a dark throat. A last circle to climb down into.

I steal down the stairs. Perhaps the nightmare is still lingering. Why else should every tiny creak sound so ominous?

As I go through the drawing room I look about me, in every direction. Amongst all the furniture, clocks and flower pots, standing where they've always stood, I expect at any moment to see a face. But it is not the expressionless face from my dream. This face is white and tense, distorted by grief, anger and madness.

There's a mild light coming from the garden. I go over to the window.

Helga's sitting on the bench with her head turned away. A half-drunk glass of wine stands before her. She's spinning the glass slowly. The other hand is resting on her knee. She looks as if she's trying to get somebody's attention to come and fill her glass. But there are no waiters there, only the wall.

When I open the door and go out I see that her shoulders are heaving. She turns even further away from me, as if to hide her face. I go around the bench so as to see her better. This time she doesn't turn any more, but sits still.

I move forward, to sit beside her. But when I see her face I stiffen and remain standing.

Her face, what's happened to her face?

For a moment it's exactly the same face I shuddered at the thought of when I walked through the drawing room. White and tense. The lips are pulled apart, the eyes are wide open and staring straight ahead. Her teeth are darkened by red wine. Several damp strands of hair are plastered to her forehead. Her shoulders are trembling.

I've never seen her like this. I ought to go to her and put my arms around her. But I dare not. She seems completely out of her mind with boundless despair, her senses blown away by the wind.

'But dearest…'

As I whisper these words I hear fear in my voice.

She doesn't react. Her shoulders shake even more violently. If only I could see tears in her eyes I'd feel calmer. I begin to wonder if I should call a doctor. She moves her mouth slowly.

'Such humiliation,' she gasps.

I look at her. I'm not sure I heard correctly. She repeats it several times. Such humiliation.

'What?' I ask.

Then she raises her eyes and looks at me. She begins to speak. Short sentences about how abandoned she felt when I left her, and all the insinuating looks she's had to put up with, and how it was like a 'slap in the face' when I turned my back on her table, she who had looked forward to it for days…

I hardly listen, since oddly enough what I feel most is immense relief that her ghost-like trance has been broken.

Finally I dare to sit beside her and reach for her hand. She pulls it away with a violent movement. But soon I will reach for it again, and this time she will leave it in mine.

'Forgive me,' I whisper. 'The whole thing is just a stupid misunderstanding. I have missed you so very much. But I'd have rather met you alone. It was confusing to stand before all those faces I haven't seen for so long.'

'I see, yes, that's understandable…'

Her voice is expressionless and bitter. She almost looks normal. She hasn't got that awful grimace on her face any longer.

I move nearer and put my arm around her shoulders. Something I've done hundreds, perhaps thousands of times. But something happens.

For a fraction of a second I'm somewhere else. A grey sky, a dense forest, the sighing of pine trees. And Anna's calm, smiling face. So near my own. I feel the warmth radiating from her cheek.

The wonder of being able to put my arm around someone's shoulder *and not be afraid*.

The thought makes me gasp. It echoes and sounds in my head while I gently stroke Helga's hair. I whisper something calming. I try to get her to follow me in, to come to bed.

The fear, I think. Is that what I'm looking for? Is that what keeps me with her.

I use my tenderest voice, I kiss her cheek.

She bends forward and puts her hand over her mouth. I lean back. Her breathing's become heavy and wheezing, her upper body shoots forward and she retches.

'I'm not feeling… not quite…'

She gets up. But she loses her balance and has to support herself on the table. She leans on the edge of it with both hands and lowers her head.

I let her stand for a while. Then I take hold of her with a firm grip, using my tenderest voice and looking around carefully while we stagger towards the door. A long way off, among the gravestones, a man in a hat with a broad brim that looks like a great black globe on his shoulders is leaning against a lamp post.

Helga sobs quietly, moving like an old woman as we climb the stairs. I feel a little better, reasonably satisfied, as if I've managed to achieve something that seemed impossible a moment ago. It occurs to me that I mustn't forget to look in the calendar to check the date of my mother's name-day. I'm sure it's some time in the middle of August.

Helga sits down on the bed. I sit down beside her and try to loosen her clothes. But she removes my hands.

I go and undress. She doesn't move. Sometimes she gives a low moan.

I ask if she's feeling ill. She says yes, and she sounds like a little girl incapable of being good any longer, and who allows herself to feel immense self-pity, and discovers that it's rather nice feeling sorry for oneself.

I put on my nightshirt and get in under the bedclothes. I forgot to look in the calendar. I look at Helga's back a moment. Suddenly she yawns. Ceasefire, I think, madly. I have to laugh. It's very late. My dreams are beginning to trickle back.

I sit up and put a hand on her shoulder. Now she seems more co-operative. I manage to get her to lie on her back and gently take off all her clothes. I get her into bed properly. Her body feels cold. I murmur something about how she must take proper care of herself. That she mustn't sit outside and catch cold.

Dreams are trickling back. Of some day being able to say those words to one's child. Perhaps when it has been out playing in the first snow. Perhaps I'll be allowed this. Perhaps I'll get my reward.

I rub her belly, her waist, her breasts. At first I feel nothing. I only wanted to help her get warm. I only wanted to sleep.

But then it wakens. The stump is moving.

I press myself carefully against her. At first it feels like an almost humorous gesture. A light caress before we slip into sleep. Then I press a little harder, then I'm inside her. And I begin to move.

She lies limp and heavy under me. First I think I should leave her alone. But then I see something before me, shut in a clenched fist, and I think that I've saved myself for her. I've saved myself with such obstinacy and devotion. The knuckles are shining white, nails boring into the palm. In there, in the darkness of the hand, I saved it for her.

She's making shrill little sounds. I can't make anything of them.

Nnnnn, nnnnn.

After a while I raise myself to look at her. I smile, there is something in that sound I take for a trick of some kind, a game.

Her eyes are hidden by her hair, it has run out over her face. But I catch a glimpse of her mouth. The broad, desperate grimace. It is back.

Then I stop moving.

I lie down beside her, with a hand on her waist. After a while I take that away too.

$\mathcal{D}$uring the next few days a great many people comment on the change in me. That I look more austere, that I'm moving more briskly and freely, that for a moment they took me for someone else.

Pastor Wenge goes home. I give him a farewell dinner at a restaurant near Strömmen water. His wife's there too, so is Helga. She drinks nothing but water during the meal.

Pastor Wenge says he feels sad to be going home, and adds a number of appreciative comments about the parish and how well organised everything is, and how he often felt he was in the presence of a machine that to a large extent runs itself.

I watch his lips while he's speaking and am struck by the appropriateness of the expression: a machine that runs itself. With a human brain plotting and intriguing somewhere in the background.

Not that I suspect him of conspiring against me. But something happens to people when their ambitions come down to earth, having earlier been hovering.

Pastor Wenge's been going about in my clothes for a few weeks, so to speak, and eating off my china, and now he knows what he wants. I have a feeling this won't be the last I hear of him.

Helga's silent and pensive. She laughs when everyone else

laughs but always a few seconds after them, and her smile never comes anywhere near her eyes.

None of this is new, but for the first time I feel a stab of irritation, as if I should take her aside and shake her and say: Right, so you're unhappy, you've made that quite clear. There's nothing unique or exceptional about that. But why can't you put on a front like everyone else? Do a bit of acting?

It seems to me that Pastor Wenge sometimes speaks to Helga in a manner that on the face of it appears a trifle insensitive and this surprises me.

It's as if he's addressing a different person, someone he's got to know over the last few weeks, someone considerably more quick-witted and light-hearted than the silent woman sitting opposite him now. As if he's knocking on a door and wondering where she's gone.

Then it's time for them to go to the station. I offer to go with them but Pastor Wenge declines and we say goodbye.

I watch them make their way to the door. Pastor Wenge holds it open for his wife. Her red hair attracts a certain amount of attention among the customers. The two go out and turn towards one another; he says something. They look happy.

I change places and sit opposite Helga. My fingers move over a crease in the tablecloth. To and fro.

I feel pressure in my chest. Something that's burning in there and wants to come out.

I stare at the ends of my fingers and their slow movements. Somewhere a roaring starts up. My field of vision shrinks, blurred at the edges but almost unbearably sharp in the centre, as if I'm looking down a tube.

I lose everything that has been, and everything that will be, and the only thing left, the only thing I feel any sense of obligation towards, are those two people at our table. This man and this silent woman.

'Do you love me?' I ask.

My voice is harsher, more expressionless, more impatient than I'd intended.

Helga raises her eyebrows and presses her lips together. I think: sews them up with angry stitches. But she seems happily surprised and gives a little smile.

She nods eagerly and at the same time her eyes fill with tears.

She turns uneasily left and right, then snuffles and wipes away her tears with the back of her index finger, a little movement with something depressingly routine about it.

I reach out my hand and she takes it. I squeeze her hand hard and she squeezes back.

We sit like that a long time. Sometimes our eyes meet and we construct various facial expressions of warmth and confidence. But the distance between us is greater than ever.

Then Märit brings the letter.

I'm in the middle of a sentence. Georg is sitting making notes. I raise my eyebrows when she comes in and open my mouth to make a joke.

The letter has a red postmark. Märit says something, her tone's ambiguous and I think I hear the word 'delivery'. I make some sort of answer. I can recognise the writing from a distance.

Märit goes; I finish the sentence I'd started and add a few more. I manage to get several sentences out. Georg makes notes. We are talking about the Sunday service. We're expecting a visit from a choir from Vestlandet. Georg has made various suggestions about how we should put them up. He's not usually remarkable for initiative, and at some point in the conversation it occurs to me that this is perhaps a side of him that Pastor Wenge has encouraged, in which case it's suddenly of the greatest importance for me to be equally encouraging. I listen patiently, and make noises expressing agreement, and after a while I have the disagreeable feeling I'm treating Georg like a small child.

While Georg summarises his notes my thoughts go back to the envelope, and I can't find it.

I cautiously move various piles of papers, simultaneously nodding to Georg.

I barely notice when he leaves the room. I begin to suspect I may have stuck the envelope between a couple of sheets of paper somewhere and that it'll go astray and probably end up being read by eager eyes at a meeting of some temperance board, or by one of the members of the church council.

I don't know how long I spend looking for it. I go through the waste-paper basket though I'm sure I can't have put it there; I even lift the carpet. I crawl on all fours, my mouth has gone dry, I wander around the room like a madman. Finally I lift the mat on my desk, and there it is.

I leave it lying there while I think of what to say if Helga comes in, and if she asks, perhaps casually, what I'm reading. I must have an answer ready, something simple and as matter-of-fact as possible, avoiding the slightest tremor in my voice, which would immediately make her suspicious.

While I sit there considering various ideas and trying out one white lie after another, I see myself from a distance and see a mumbling old man behind his writing desk, and his satisfied expression as he concocts a long chain of lies, testing each link, and every possible follow-up question and the lie to counteract that with, and hey presto! Now he's really pleased with himself.

So much for your pure, sparkling love, I think.

Then I open the envelope.

She's sitting in the kitchen. It's black outside the window and rain's drumming on the roof. Outside the fields are soggy and dreary. The door to the coach-house is banging impatiently at regular intervals even though there's no wind. Occasionally she imagines she can see figures crossing the yard.

'Forgive me if I sound confused, I'm not getting much sleep these days. Ever since that dreadful evening at Porla, our last evening (at least there), my husband and I have together sunk lower than even I would ever have thought possible. Sometimes I almost have to pinch my arm to be sure it isn't all just a bad dream. But of course I have no regrets nonetheless. Or perhaps one thing: I regret I so badly underestimated the forces that can be released inside someone faced with the threat of being abandoned.

On the other hand, how could I ever have thought it would be otherwise? I've already told you how little I've meant to him all these years. Imagine for yourself what it must be like to live alone for years in a house that's totally dark, silent and deserted. You're brave enough to pack your bags and go to the door to leave for ever. But when you open the door all the lights go on, and suddenly every room in the house has become an inferno of voices shrieking in each other's faces.

That's how confusing the change I've seen in him has been. He cooks up one foul intrigue after another. He runs around the district complaining to everyone he comes across. He repeats his bitter harangues again and again to any lawyer, priest or magistrate who makes the mistake of opening the door when he knocks. There's a special spark in his eye that I've learned to fear. It's most often to be seen in the morning, when he's had some new idea about how to hurt me as much as possible. Then he storms out of the house, and spends the day trying to gather support for his new idea. When he comes home he gives me a little lecture about which important people have said this, and which educated gentlemen have said that.

But to go back to what I was saying: because I underestimated his anger, his bitterness and his vindictiveness, I often lose control when faced with his pettiness, and instead of keeping cool I have an unfortunate tendency to try and protect myself by scratching his face in the same way as he scratches mine, so the wretched spiral takes yet another turn downwards.

Thinking of you, and our memories from Porla, is all that keeps me going. My bulwark against madness.

Sometimes I try to be pedantic with him, and ask as pleasantly as I can why he's so obstinately against divorce, if as he claims he has evidence I'm such a repulsive and untrustworthy person. Then he goes as red as a lobster and starts a tedious sermon on the subject of promises and principles. I ask him, if promises and principles are so important, why has he broken all the same ones himself? Then he shouts that I have no basis whatever for taking such a view.

Then I answer that I not only have a basis for such a view but I also have a witness, and that is the man I love.

This usually makes him furious. But yesterday for the first time he shrugged his shoulders and smiled scornfully and said: 'So you always say. But tell me, where does this witness of yours live? He doesn't seem particularly anxious to make himself known.'

I've thought backwards and forwards and I don't know if I'm standing on my head or my heels. Perhaps it's idiotic to ask you about something like this. But however unsure I may be about other things, there's no getting away from the fact that what we heard that evening was dreadful.

The trouble is I'm beginning to suspect he may not be above exploiting the grotesque aspects of the story to his own advantage, simply by throwing up his hands and saying: You can hear for yourselves how absurd and far-fetched this is.

And if he does that, no one will believe me.

Perhaps all it needs is for you to write him a few lines to make clear to him that you were with me that evening, and that you heard everything. I know him. I'm sure that would rock his boat.

The most important thing of all is to get him to understand that I'm not alone. That of itself would make a world of difference. At the moment he seems convinced I am alone, and that if he keeps going long enough I shall crumble sooner or later, and then he'll have me where he wants me. Alone in this kitchen with the rain drumming on the roof and my life ebbing away.

Not that I have any idea what he wants me for. I'd rather not think about that. I'd rather think about the man I love.

I can't find words to tell you how much it hurts me to ask this of you. As you know it was my firm intention not to drag you into this miserable drama. I just don't know what to do.

But what made me write this letter to you nonetheless was the realisation that I hope with all my heart that if you ever landed in a similar dilemma, or in any other sort of dilemma, and didn't know what to do and had no one to turn to, that you'd turn to me. I'd feel proud and honoured and wildly happy.

I'm not trying to blackmail you. I never want to use my love for the purpose of extracting something. I'm just expressing what I feel in my heart. Of course I have no idea how easy or difficult it may be for you to respond to my cry for help. But no matter what you feel about it, my love remains firm and steady. The chair will always be there for you.

A hundred tender kisses from Anna.'

I fold up the letter and look around the room, searching automatically for somewhere to hide it. But there's no point. The only person I should hide the letter from is myself.

My eyes rest on the chair where Georg was sitting a moment ago.

Now she's sitting there. I smile at her. She smiles back. She holds out her arms, summoning me with her fingertips as if to say: Come on, hurry up, or I'll go under.

And I'm not afraid of anything. I'm not afraid to go to her and I'm not afraid to stay where I am. I'm not afraid to say yes and I'm not afraid to say no.

For a short moment the dream burns brightly. Then it goes out, and I wake up in that reality where all is fear.

I've preached about love all my life. I've thought about it, analysed it from every possible angle and wrapped it in so many words that I lost sight of the actual substance of it long ago.

I could do it because the subject amused me and captivated me so much. It has given me so many opportunities for uplifting flights of thought; it has set my imagination to work. I've spoken endlessly about love, to avoid hearing how mute my own heart is.

I've been particularly ready to pronounce on the problems and wrong turnings of love, and I've described fear of love as the greatest scourge of humanity, and the reason has of course always been, I now realise, that by this means I've been able to lull myself into believing that I myself am above this fear.

How could I possibly myself be the victim of something I can describe so eloquently and with so much insight?

Unfortunately, my dear Gregorius, says a voice, you should have understood, that it's precisely for this reason that fear is lodged more securely in you than in anyone else.

Somewhere it is still possible to find calm. Despite the fact that everything's trembling and quivering such as my fingers when I tie my shoelaces. I hastily glance at the mirror, expecting to see a deathly pale figure with staring eyes. But I look the same as usual.

I go down the stairs. Smells are emerging from the kitchen, some dark loaves about to be baked. Through the half-open door I see Märit put a bundle down on the bench; and when she opens it several onions roll out and one falls on the floor; her lips move in exasperation, she bends down and doesn't come up again.

I go through the drawing room and stand by the window. Helga's sitting out in the garden. I remember she was already there this morning. Perhaps she's left a life-size doll, like a scare-crow, to mislead me, and hurried off to Stortorget through the front door, using her own key.

She's got her Japanese silk coat on. She once joked that it makes the ideal dressing gown because you can wear it all day and still look presentable. It's windy and there's rain in the air. She's sitting with her back to the house and her face to the wall.

It's silent in the drawing room. Only the wind's wailing in the chinks of the windows.

Here comes Byström carrying a pail. It looks heavy. He's

holding it a little away from his body. Perhaps it's full of water.

He walks past Helga with slow, bandy-legged steps, walking surprisingly close to her as though he doesn't see her. Helga remains motionless as he passes, as if she can't see him either.

I make to turn the door handle, but my hand falls limply back again.

I feel a tightening over my chest. And the thought comes that if I don't find someone to confide in I'll go under. I turn and go through the drawing room and hall and continue down the steps and on to the gravel. I stumble, I feel I'm sinking, it's like wading through a bog.

I must see Dr Glas. There isn't anyone else. Well, Halvar of course, but he'll still be at Dalarö. He did go there after all.

The thought's often come to me and I've thrust it aside. But I remember Dr Lidin, and his thoughtful expression when I told him about Dr Glas's various prescriptions.

It's true he said things that could be considered disparaging of his young colleague. But the diagnosis perplexed him, that was clear. He wasn't able to dismiss it.

I wait at the edge of the road for some carts to roll by. The matted and streaked horses have been trotting through the rain, coming in from Roslagen.

Here comes a large cart. Three miserable sacks in one corner and two boys holding them. First I think they must be brothers, but they're holding hands so their arms form a rope around the sacks, and when the cart passes I see their eyes meeting, and they break into toothless smiles. That's not the way brothers look at each other.

I hurry across the street and trudge on up the hill. Suddenly I see the connection clearly. There was something Dr Glas wanted to say to me, or to us, but he didn't want to say it straight out. I stumble through the hiding places of my memory, pulling out conversation after conversation, and I think of all the talks Helga's had with him that I know nothing about.

Between Helga and me there is something that has been moving more and more slowly, until it became still, and stopped. We've turned our backs on each other and lifted our eyes towards the world.

But Dr Glas has been sitting there all the time, somewhere in the middle. He's been the junction. He's had the overview.

How was it really with her mysterious illness? At least it didn't seem serious enough for her to want to consult anyone else in the hope of a cure. And what about my weak heart? Not too bad, if one of the country's most skilled physicians was able to listen to it without hearing anything alarming.

I've reached the top of the hill. Far away in the north the rays of the sun are breaking through a mass of purple clouds. The air's permeated by a metallic scent like brackish water. From the left comes a desolate voice, it's a coachman who can't get past, there's a cart in his way; some men on it are moving about slowly and hurling great armfuls of planks down to the ground, one ominous crash after another. They ignore the coachman completely. His voice gets shriller and more pitiful till suddenly he sounds like a distant seagull, a lamenting cry over a dark bay.

An elderly couple totter arm in arm into the road to get past the cart. They are wearing fine clothes, she a billowing white dress of almost floor length, he a long black coat and a tall hat that looks heavy and unsteady on his small head. They blink nervously and jump every time an armful of planks hits the ground. One of the workmen on the cart follows them with his eyes, nods after them to his workmate and grins.

I increase my pace, causing my trouser legs to rustle irritably as I cross the churchyard. I feel discomfort in my stomach, as though I've eaten something rotten, and there's a singing in my head.

There is a door that's always been there, flashing past the corner of my eye as I've hurried to and fro, always on the way to somewhere else. Now I'm standing before it; there is a gleaming frame
around it with a strong white light coming from inside, and now I
summon up all my strength, narrow my eyes and rush up to it.

I glance down the street before I knock, with my fist in the air,
it hangs like a frightened snake about to strike and I hesitate. It
looks like spring down there, like a day in March, just as bare and
dirty, as newly awoken, the street muddy and wet with melting
snow and ice.

I take a step back when the door opens. There is his housekeeper, she stands so far back in the hall that I can only make out her
long, pale, narrow face, while a dismal green brooch stares at me
from her neck-band like an eye.

'I'm afraid the doctor's out.'

I nod slowly and look down the street again. The housekeeper
repeats the same words, but in a more surly tone.

She closes the door. I go slowly down the steps.

I wonder why she was so brusque with me? I feel an impulse to
go back and demand an explanation. But there is so much one can't
know. Perhaps I interrupted her cooking and she was afraid the
food might burn.

I'm overcome by fatigue. I stick my hand inside my coat to make
sure Anna's letter's still there. For a moment she's walking beside
me; we fall into step and look at each other and I shake my head in
distress as if to say: I'm so sorry, my darling, I really did try to
overcome my paralysis, but you can see for yourself what happened.

As if everything stood or fell with Dr Glas.

I don't take the shortest way home. It's a long time since I last
did that. I persuade myself a walk would do me good. One can
persuade oneself of anything to avoid having to go straight home.

There's the waste ground. There's a small crowd standing in front of the heap of gravel and tiles and dirty pieces of glass. They look like students, about twenty of them. Shabby suits and white necks. An elderly man is standing in front of them pontificating. I can't make out his words but his tone is bombastic and pedantic, and he's articulating with crushing slowness. The students shift their weight impatiently from one leg to the other. A boy with red hair turns; our eyes meet and he stares suspiciously at me.

I turn away and walk faster, looking straight ahead with my hands behind my back. Perhaps by now they're all staring after me, wondering who I am and what I'm doing there. Perhaps their teacher has stopped speaking and is following their eyes, but I can't hear any more.

Who is that man? I want to know that too. I want to join them, to run clumsily up the hill towards them. Let's form a chorus. Let's shout the question together. After a count of three, let's hear it, let it resound to the skies: Who is that man?

And I gather them around me and they sit down in the damp grass with stiff, embarrassed movements, and I tell them about an ordinary day, sometime in March, muddy roads, dripping birches. There are the red buildings, you see, the dormitories, the lecture rooms and the office, and there's the slope where we used to sit in the evenings throwing pebbles at the forest and talking about all the great and serious matters that were beginning to engage us.

We were young theological students from every corner of the country. Some were quick and bold, with soulful eyes and healthy teeth; they enjoyed a certain shy respect because everyone knew they'd go far in life. Others had known each other before coming to the college, in some cases since childhood; their fathers had worked together as pastors or deans and their children had got to know each other under the kitchen table while the voices of the adults rumbled overhead, and they'd amused themselves whittling boats out of bark as they lay on their stomachs by the nearest stream.

I was finding it difficult to make friends. But then something happened; little by little people began to talk to me and I began to respond to them. It was wonderful not to be the one left out any longer and to be able to speak my mind without the response always being a crushing silence.

This was a morning of quick, nervous repartee. There was a man who was coming from Uppsala to give a talk; no one knew for sure what it was going to be about. But his lectures were highly thought of, and we'd been told that former students always talked about these particular lectures as a high point of their days there. It was rumoured that he was the archbishop's right hand, the man he turned to in difficulties. It was also rumoured that his visits were an annual good turn to the college as a favour to an old friend from his own student days.

He was going to talk to us in the largest hall, the one in the new building a little distance away. We walked there in a group, quiet and composed. I remember the sound of our footsteps, the mist over the fields, the pollarded ash trees that lined the way.

We went in and sat down, and he arrived, slightly late, a tall man with a luxuriant moustache and a severe expression behind glasses so strong that they made his eyes seem twice the normal size, like a mythical being behind the lectern.

He introduced himself, I think his name was Bigert, and then began with a story to relax the tension, and we felt that we liked him, had confidence in him, and were interested in him.

He said we must close our eyes and give the story our full attention, and on no account open our eyes or make a sound.

It was the story of a dog. Bigert's voice changed as he began his narration; it sounded soft, unhurried, tired.

The dog had the misfortune of being owned by a disorderly

drunkard who lived on the outskirts of the village. He'd made endless attempts to find work or a woman to be his wife, but failing again and again he became bitter and angry, and he drank to comfort himself.

He took all his bitterness out on his dog. There was always something about the dog that annoyed him. Either the animal was too lively and made irritating noises that made his headache worse, or it was depressingly gloomy and passive and lay in a corner giving him accusing looks, or so he thought.

The man hit and kicked the dog and devised sadistic punishments for it, he dragged its basket out into the backyard and forced it to sleep in the rain, he kept it on the verge of starvation and prised open its jaws when it came home to see if he could find traces of food it might have ferreted out from rubbish heaps or dustbins.

But the dog stayed with him, and always greeted its master with a hopeful glint in its little brown eyes. If there seemed the slightest hope it might for once avoid curses, kicks and blows, its little tail would begin to swing uncertainly from side to side, but all too soon its master would force it to bend its head in submission again, lowering its eyes and sticking its tail between its legs.

One morning the man didn't get out of bed, he had no more strength. The dog realised something wasn't right, put its forelegs on the bed and howled anxiously.

With the last of his strength the man managed to raise his hand and hit the dog on the nose. The animal crept under the table but continued to howl piteously. Gradually the sound attracted the attention of neighbours, who did their best to revive the alcoholic old man, but it was too late.

The man was laid in a coffin and lowered to his final rest in a corner of the churchyard. No one came to his funeral. But after the priest and grave diggers slunk away in the pouring rain the dog padded out from the shadows, still submissive from the blows it had received, and lay down on the newly dug grave, and howled to the sky...

I don't know when the first tears began to come. I do know with certainty that a sob shook me at the point where the dog hopefully wagged his tail. I found it best to hide my eyes behind my hand as the tears streamed down, and I breathed heavily through my mouth.

I could see the animal so clearly before me. It looked like a dog I used to pat when I was small, when I was allowed to come to the market. It was just the right size. Not a ridiculous little lapdog, but also not so large you might be afraid of it. It was mottled white, black and brown, and had a funny little beard around its mouth. It was so happy and energetic. When I squatted in front of it, it would leap up on my knee to lick my face and snort happily.

This was the dog life treated so badly. But it never gave up. It never tired of hoping for something better. Even when its tormentor was dead and it should have been overjoyed to be liberated, it lay on his grave as if weeping for sorrow over all the wasted chances of a life so hopelessly misspent.

Bigert had stopped talking. Then he cleared his throat and went on in his normal voice. I slowly took my hands away from my eyes, blinking at the light and trying to wipe away my tears discreetly.

When I looked around I had a shock. Everyone in the hall was staring at me. A mass of faces. One had even stood up on his bench to be able to see better. Some could hardly keep a straight face. Most looked openly astonished, as though something unheard of had happened, something almost incomprehensible, as if they had an exotic beast among them, a rhinoceros or crocodile.

No one said anything. Occasionally a bench creaked or a heavy boot scraped on the floor. Tiny sounds, but in the silence they cut through my head like knives.

Bigert cleared his throat again. He rapped on the desk and asked everyone to face the front.

He took a piece of chalk, tossing it from hand to hand, then went over to the blackboard and began to talk about the story in such a way that I gradually realised it had been intended as an example of everything turgid, false and melodramatic.

We were urged to recall all the circumstances and details that sank the story in this swamp of tastelessness.

Soon everyone had his hand up. A stream of suggestions were offered. Bigert got increasingly enthusiastic, moving backwards and forwards between the lectern and the blackboard. The detail of the hopefully wagging tail evoked particular mirth. At one point Bigert's eyes fell on me, and he said perhaps we shouldn't get overexcited, since there were obviously sensitive souls present.

Everyone laughed. I smiled too, and, I think, pulled a funny face.

Then he put down the chalk and started his lecture.

It was about the temptations of sentimentality, and that sentimentality was the path of the lazy priest, an obstacle between man and God.

I had nothing to hide behind, nothing to blame.

They had all sat in silence during his story, and I was sure none of them had been sneaking glances at his bench-mate to see what attitude they were expected to take. Entirely unprompted, they'd found the answers to Bigert's questions deep in their own souls, and all had come to the same conclusion. They'd had no difficulty telling true from false and genuine from artificial. All except me.

I hadn't just let myself be duped by continuing to walk when everyone else had come to a halt, but had rushed headlong into tastelessness, thinking the story the most gripping and moving one I'd ever heard.

Who is that man?

That's what he's like.

Years ago he wept over dogs. Now he's weeping over a woman, and he doesn't even know himself which one he's weeping over: whether she's the one turning away from him or the one holding out her arms to him.

The key to the church usually hangs on a hook in a cupboard; I move carefully through the dark hall and grope in the cupboard, but my fingers find nothing but dry wood, an empty hook.

I go out again and look at the church. The lights are off and it looks gloomy. The sound of my own footsteps on the gravel makes me shudder. Something is crushed at every step. And eyes on my back. I could turn around and look at one empty window after another, but it would be no use. The same instant I resume my walk the heavy gaze is there, from each window, eight black panes, like a she-spider in her net, stock-still, ready to pounce.

The churchyard's deserted, it seems autumn has arrived, it's strangely quiet in the streets. The lanterns outside the taverns are swinging backwards and forwards in the wind.

I go to the side door of the church; it's unlocked. I enter the silence, automatically wiping my shoes on the little mat.

I see Helga's head, light and beautiful, ahead of me. Yet somehow her head disfigures the empty church. I see a giant sword sweep over the rows of pews, I see her cut off like a weed and harmony restored.

She must have heard me come in but she's still sitting with her head bowed. I go forward and sit down beside her. She looks up a moment, her lips move, she gives a friendly nod then looks down again and closes her eyes.

I clasp my hands on my knees and look straight ahead, remembering how many times I've sat here in this desolate half-darkness, trying to collect myself for prayer.

The church has been my refuge when the vicarage has seemed stifling and cramped, when its walls have crept closer and its roof has sunk, and silence has descended like a lid.

All the times when I've tried to collect myself to pray, but instead sat looking around, looking up, breathing.

I've sat on God's knee like a child and let Him point out to me the kingdom He's given us and the greatness we carry within us. I've sat in rapture, mouth open, and let Him show me everything we have it in us to become. All this might, all this splendour and beauty. All this space, all this light; and my gaze has rested on the altar-piece and all it can tell me, and on the exquisite roundel of the cupola, and I have sat in God's warmth and understood what He has wanted to tell me: that all this, however magnificent it may seem, is still as *nothing* compared to the greatness we bear within us.

I feel a movement, it's Helga's hand on mine.

'It's beautiful here this evening,' she says.

'Yes.'

'I hope I'm not disturbing you in any way. I know you often come here in the evenings.' She laughs. 'Perhaps I thought it was the best way to get to sit beside you for a while. You've had so many things to keep you busy since you came home.'

I abstractedly pinch her fingers, the joints and knuckles. As one does with one's own hand.

There's something light-hearted in her voice, something soft and tentative. It fills me with both dread and bitterness. I don't know why. Her voice is like a shadow at my feet. There may be people who would bend down before the shadow, full of trust. But I'm not that sort of person. Before I've had a chance to think, I've kicked out.

'I'm surprised to hear that,' I say.

Her hand stiffens and pulls away from me. Not a violent movement. Just calm and decisive.

'Why do you say that?'

I shake my head. I can feel, with almost frightening clarity, how everything I wanted to say to her has dispersed and vanished. Before me I see a fortress, where recently all those inside were collected together and ready to do battle on the defences, excited and armed to the teeth. Now suddenly they have all dropped their weapons and rushed in to find shelter, closing the gates behind them. It happened so alarmingly quickly.

'Come on, answer me!'

She hasn't raised her voice but it still fills the whole church. Fills it till it bulges.

I raise my head and look straight at her.

'Sometimes,' I say, 'I get the impression you don't want to sit next to me at all.'

She stares back.

Her mouth has taken on that familiar expression. I've seen it so many times. It makes me feel like a disobedient little boy. A boy with a lively imagination. He uses it for all kinds of things. Sometimes he uses it to distract attention from something silly he's done. And Helga's face becomes heavy and grey with exhaustion, boredom, and even distaste, before this little boy, who seems incapable of ever learning to take responsibility for his actions.

'What really happened?' she says.

'What do you mean?'

'At Porla. You haven't seemed yourself. What happened?'

'Nothing.'

The silence, I can't describe it. There it is again. The irrevocable.

I open my mouth and a stream of words emerges, about drinking spa water, walks, concerts; my words are dry and scared, and I run alongside and point at them as if to say: Look, they're true, every one, just look how true they are, they couldn't be truer.

She looks away. She seems not to be listening. She strokes her chin reflectively with her index finger, and then interrupts me.

'In other words, there's nothing you think you should tell me about?'

'No...'

It's my voice. It sounds questioning, almost injured.

I feel an impulse to stroke her cheek and put on a humorous voice, and I already have a sentence ready, something in the style of: Well, of course I could tell you – that I love you.

But before I can lift my hand she gets up to leave. Her steps are soft and distinct on the thick carpet, like heartbeats.

The door slams and I'm alone in the dark.

I sit there a long time, and try to understand what's happened.

I sit in the pew waiting for God's warmth. I wait and wait. But it stays cold. Perhaps around me, perhaps inside me, I don't know any longer.

During all these years I've navigated so skilfully between truths that I've never needed to lie. But now it's happened. I've sat before God, and before this altar where we became man and wife, and lied to her.

I look around myself, but with new eyes. All these paintings and tapestries, all these sculptures and ornaments, all evidence and symbols of God's almighty power.

Now I know all about lying. I was there when it was conceived, when it grew and when it was born. It was conceived in fear, grew in fear and was born in fear. I could never have imagined that there

403

was anything I feared more than God's wrath. Clearly I was wrong.

And my mind remains cold. Almost exhilarated by thoughts of lying and fear. I'm gripped by a wish to set them down on paper. To write something enlightened and knowledgeable on the subject.

I get up and go. God's eye following me must be horrified.

I'd meant to spend the evening writing a letter to Anna. The letter she asked me for. But let that be, at least for this evening. She deserves something better.

*I*t's Mother's name-day. I ask Helga if she'd like to come, but she says she doesn't feel like it. Then she turns a page in the newspaper.

I sip my coffee and turn my face up to the sun. She would never have spoken so frankly before. But when you think about it, perhaps this is not such a bad thing. I can hardly blame her for not feeling like going to see Mother when I don't even feel like it myself.

Just think: the sun's finding its way through the branches and pouring its warmth over me, there's a scent of freshly cut grass, and the wonderful taste of coffee. Just think: this could be the beginning of something new and untried. Like her words just now. They hurt me a bit of course. But she was completely honest.

Still facing the sun, I rest a hand on her leg above the knee. I do something playful with the movement: I squeeze hard, move my hand about a little, enjoy the feel of her flesh quivering under my palm; like a butcher, I think. Helga says nothing; my hand is allowed to stay.

I'm sure she's broken off her relationship with him. Several days have passed, and she's only taken some short walks. She said she wanted to buy a hat, and after an hour she came home with a new hat. She spends her time mostly in the garden.

Perhaps she is grieving for him. The thought wakes an unexpected tenderness in me. What if we could grieve together? Perhaps that's to set my sights a little too high. But we have an autumn before us now, and a winter, and I look forward to it if not with confidence, at least with a certain curiosity.

Not even the moment when I sat before my wife, and before God, and lied in cold blood feels quite so ominous any longer.

Perhaps even Helga will come to see things in perspective when she's had a chance to think in peace and quiet. Perhaps it will lead to a certain amount of soul-searching.

Some sparrows come and hop about in front of the bench, pecking cake crumbs. One of the bolder ones leaps up on the table and looks at us with its gentle eyes. Helga says something about them spreading infection but she doesn't sound particularly worried. I dismiss her theory with the sort of affectionate sarcasm that is welcomed in all marriages as a sign of spring and as a promise that difficulties are over, at least for the present, and that warmer times are on the way.

For a moment it's autumn; not this autumn but an autumn in the future, and we are sitting wrapped in blankets with cups of something hot before us; we're more tired than we are now but it's a pleasant tiredness, and we are quieter than now, but it's a pleasant quietness, and we are thinking back to this summer when our marriage went through a bloody war and bled so profusely that we thought it would never stop bleeding.

When we think back to this summer we shudder. But then we smile.

In the midst of everything I come to think of Professor Wallgren. When he made his decision, with his revolver against his temple. There he sat. Perhaps cold and damp already from sitting on the ground. And the plaintive song of the jackdaws from some corner of the park, Observatorielunden. A lonely tram screeching in a cloud of dust. And he thought he knew for certain that nothing could ever change for the better.

I wish he could have sat with Helga and me on the bench in our garden. I'd pat his hand gently, and feel infinitely old and wise when I told him that he was wrong.

Things do get better, not necessarily because one straightens things out or chases one's demons away, but because sooner or later one is so exhausted that all one can do is leave things in peace.

Which of course might sound indifferent and resigned, particularly to such sophisticated ears as Professor Wallgren's. I might admit that he was right on that point. But you can't say that he found a better way out of the dilemma.

Perhaps I'd just like to say to him that there's a time for everything. There's a time for struggling, and a time for rest. If you endlessly seek to fight, that too can become an end in itself. Then eventually it'll come to be all you know, it will have made a home in you, and you will seek it out regardless of whether you have good reason to do so. And when you no longer have anyone to fight, you'll start fighting yourself.

I push away the cup and get up. I stand for a moment behind Helga, stroking her shoulders gently. I stand there for a long time, I don't understand what I'm waiting for. Oh yes, I do. I'm waiting for her to turn her head and look at me warmly, or put her hand on mine. When she doesn't, I pretend to fix my eyes on her newspaper.

Then I say goodbye and tell her I won't be long.

I go into the street and begin to walk southwards. I think about Mother. I think about her three name-days, and how evenly they're spread through the year. When I was little I used to say her three names silently to myself like a spell, abracadabra, and then I received all the powers and abilities she had. Now her three names are the last tired fingers with which she still clings to my mind. Soon she'll be too tired, soon the last wave of tide-water will lift her up and she'll float into oblivion.

At the square, Oxtorget, there's a bakery where they sell fancy cakes made with raspberries, cream and jelly. They have a special name I never manage to remember. All I can do is point. Mother likes them. At least she expressed great delight last time I brought them. On the other hand, she expresses great delight about almost everything.

I'm sitting in a droshky with the box of cakes on my knees and one hand on top of the box. We pass over Strömmen water and along Skeppsbron. The coachman keeps scratching the back of his head and neck. His hand moves lower and lower till it's between his shoulder-blades.

At Stadsgården a large passenger steamer is putting into port, hiding Skeppsholmen and half of Kastellholmen. The Union Jack's waving from its stern. Sailors are moving to and fro on its lower deck, disappearing into doors and emerging again. On the upper deck men in black are leaning on the rail and women in white stand half a pace behind them, sunlit parasols gleaming like haloes behind their heads. The coachman shouts something and points at the steamer, but he speaks some incomprehensible dialect and I pretend not to hear. The droshky stops at the bottom of the hill; I pay and get out. At the laundry the half-open skylight windows emit clouds of steam. Not far away two boys are sitting in the shade gutting herrings, their hands shiny with silver and blood, they throw the fish heads and entrails into a barrel a few metres away; they are good at hitting the barrel and enjoy their own skill. The barrel is leaking fish blood, a narrow rivulet soaking down into the gutter, a red streak between the paving-stones I'm stepping over.

There are flags waving outside the nursing home. I walk up the hill with the absurd thought that blood might have got onto the cakes; I make a move to untie the string around the carton to check.

Inside the nursing home it's cool and there's a smell of linen and marble. The nurses nod to me and smile in a special way; they always do, I haven't thought of it before, but it's a smile that makes me think of myself as a fine person, a good son, an example to everyone else.

I go upstairs. I am thinking about what I shall say to her, the first sentence, and suddenly I can't remember which of her names is in the calendar today. I try a process of elimination – what did I say last time I congratulated her? But it's impossible. On the other hand, she probably won't remember either.

She's lying in bed. She hasn't noticed me yet. She's lying turned to the window. The view's enchanting: all of Stockholm is out there, from the flag on Kastellet to Saltsjön's angry little waves.

But all she can see is the blue sky. Her hair is uncombed, and she's wearing yellow hospital linen. Two of her fingers are constantly flicking against one another on the coverlet as though trying to climb somewhere. She looks serious, but there's a hint of a nervous smile, as if she's just heard something menacing but is determined to keep up her spirits and persuade herself it's not so bad.

I knock on the doorpost and go in. Mother turns towards me and looks at me with a puzzled expression on her face, but I know she recognises me. She reaches towards me with her hands, fingers groping and scratching the air as if she's drowning. I take her hands and kiss her forehead, which is warm and remarkably taut, as if there's nothing but bone under the skin.

I pull up a chair and sit down by the bed.

'Congratulations on your name-day, darling Mamma.'

'Yes… How has… how has…'

Her mouth starts trembling and she begins to blink.

'Thank you, everything's fine with me.'

'Yes… And how… how have you…'

She begins to pluck and pull at the sheet. The more impatient she gets with not finding the right words, the more vigorous her plucking movements become.

I lay my hand over hers. I tell her about my stay at Porla. About all the walks I took, and how slim and active I've become. She listens and nods vigorously, eyes wide open. 'Obediently', I think. Her hand moves impatiently in mine, as if it would like to creep further in, as if it would like to be enclosed in all my fingers, or to enclose my fingers. Her hand is living a life of its own inside mine; I begin to think it must be insane with hunger, that it must have been hungry all its life and never had a chance to eat its fill.

This could frighten me. I know it has before. But I only feel sad. Soon I shall leave her with her hunger, and soon she will die.

Everything about her seems so small. Her head, nose, shoulders. Her arms are so thin. I look at her feet under the sheet; she takes up such a small space in the bed.

How long her days must seem. These white walls, the flowers in the vase, the blue sky outside the window, the clouds passing, then it gets dark, then it gets light again.

She gave birth to four sons, now there's only one left. Even if her thoughts were lucid, the whole of her life could seem like something she might have dreamed.

This thought has always filled me with unease. But as I sit holding her hand I suddenly think it's beautiful.

All our hard work and aspirations, all our dreams and hopes. All the things we list when we meet someone we don't know as we try to tell them who we are. My name's this or that, I live here or there, I work with this or that. And this is my family, and these are their names.

Little by little it all vanishes, rubbed out by soft waves.

Relatives die and work becomes too difficult. All that's left is a little flickering flame of life. Everything is back where it once began. So we meet God. Naked, stripped bare. Nothing to hold on to, nothing to hide behind.

The thought is dizzying. It tickles my chest, it hums in my head, it's like staring down from a great height. I'm ready to fall. But not yet.

I go on talking. I tell her I met a woman at Porla, and came to love her. I tell her the woman's name was Anna. I describe her as best I can: her clothes, her hair, the little scar on her upper lip. I even tell about her husband, the little superintendent.

It's a long time since I told my mother such intimate things. It seems strange and at the same time familiar. It's hard to find the right words.

A veil comes over Mother's eyes, and she seems to be listening more attentively than before. When I have said all I have to say she takes my hand between hers and strokes my wrist. She nods and opens her mouth, but all that comes out is:

'Yes... yes... So you've... so you've...'

Then I recognise the expression on her face. I've seen it so often before. She looks like this when she wants to tell me I deserve something. When she approves and wants to show me I have her full support.

But it's not a light-hearted expression. There is an undertone of pity. As though she feels sorry for me, and believes I've deserved all that's good and fine and beautiful, indeed, that I've really earned the right to be happy.

Even perhaps that I've earned it more than others.

I have to smile when I think of this. Mother smiles back. Her teeth look too large for her mouth. She reaches out her hand to me.

'Such beautiful... You have such beautiful...'

I lean down close to her. Her fingers touch my head with light,

411

jerky movements like a bird hopping about, and I understand she wants to say I have beautiful hair. She always says this, to Helga as well. Of course I haven't much hair left. But perhaps she thinks it's beautiful even so.

When I raise my head she caresses my cheek. I stiffen when I sense the smell of excrement on her fingers.

I stare at her hands. They look clean. Perhaps it's in her cuticles. I feel an urge to go out and call a nurse. To hiss at someone, to say something icy and threatening. Then I realise there's no point.

I murmur something about having to go home soon. I leave the room and go out to the corridor. There's a nurse sitting in the office, checking one list against another. She can barely hide her irritation at being interrupted in her work, and she pointedly makes sure her fingers keep the place in each respective column.

I say we'd like a pot of coffee with spoons and plates, I add that it's Mother's name-day and that she needs to wash her hands. My voice sounds thin and plaintive. The nurse is very young and her face is broad and hard. She says she'll do what she can.

Mother has turned towards the window again. The same frightened little smile. I have the unpleasant thought that if I were to greet her as if we hadn't met for six months, she'd brighten up and start scratching and groping for me again in exactly the same way as she did just now.

But perhaps this wouldn't be because of her illness, but because her faith in me is so great.

I keep my eyes on the floor. I sit down on the chair and start untying the carton. Something drips from one corner. I don't understand why I so obstinately think of blood.

I hold the cakes up so she can see them. She chuckles and gives me a mischievous look as though we're planning something that's forbidden. Something we should be keeping secret. Then we sit in silence, waiting for our coffee.

*I*t's a long walk home. But it will do me good.

The sun's hot over Skeppsbron. My footsteps spread through my whole body, like muffled drumbeats sounding all the way up to my head. During the walk I feel increasingly lonely, more so with every stranger I pass. All with their fathers and mothers, sick or healthy, their husbands or wives, faithful or unfaithful, all with an interior world that no one else has been able to enter.

I should have asked Helga to come with me. I should have insisted on it. Perhaps then I could have walked down Skeppsbron without feeling like a frozen star in the night sky. I don't understand it, this constant longing for someone with whom I wouldn't need to be a stranger. It seems never-ending.

At the Royal Palace it's the changing of the guard; an officer's glaring furiously at a troop of recruits standing with lips pressed together and trembling epaulettes.

I cross the bridge, passing the murmur from the shops and the sleepy rustle of wrapping paper, and assistants who have left their places and are standing blinking in the sunlight and turning in confusion now to one side, now to the other.

I keep uneasily in the middle. I feel thirsty after my walk. I slow down in front of a shop selling pilsner and lemonade, but the man behind the counter bores into me from a distance with his eyes as if reading my thoughts and nods to me as if we were old acquaintances. I hurry on.

I think of a boy I prepared for confirmation many years ago. He was small and dark-haired, and I remember he had curiously pointed teeth. He was ambitious and eager for knowledge in a way that set him apart from the others. He often stayed behind after lessons, asking how one became a priest, and offered to help me with small tasks. This boy – I can't remember his name – possessed in large measure every praiseworthy quality imaginable, yet there was something about him that made me a little wary of him. My voice became falsely cheerful when I talked to him, and I didn't find it easy to give him a friendly smile. I developed a nagging bad conscience about him.

One evening I was taking a walk along Strömmen. It was late and there weren't many people out. Suddenly I heard a well-known voice, light and eager, which seemed to be coming out of empty nothing. I went over to the rail and looked down. The boy was there below on the little landing stage, holding up a lantern, and in front of him a fisherman on all fours was trying to sort out something entangled in his net. The boy was overwhelming the fisherman with questions and the fisherman was giving him monosyllabic and impatient answers.

I called out to the boy to come up. I remember his pale face looking up at me, his bewilderment and shame. Eventually he came up and I started to take him home. He talked virtually nonstop, a strange mixture of things the fisherman had told him and his own thoughts, inspired by his confirmation classes.

Suddenly he stopped at a street corner and said goodbye. I stood there watching him walk down the badly-lit street. But something made me suspicious. He was walking so slowly, and constantly glancing back over his shoulder.

When he was almost out of sight he went in through a doorway.

I followed. Perhaps he was trying to deceive me and had deliberately gone into the wrong building. Then I heard drunken bawling from inside, surly voices and fearful cries from the boy. I turned and went home.

On Sunday we had our class as usual. I said nothing to the boy about what I'd heard. But I felt able to smile at him in a new way. I can't remember whether he smiled back.

I go around the corner at the Jacob church. At the water shop there is a man sitting reading a newspaper, and I stop suddenly when I see that it's Dr Glas.

The sight of his pale, worried face over the paper fills me with a feeling of triumph, but a certain unease too. I remember how I rushed to his surgery a few days ago and how it's already beginning to seem unreal. There were so many urgent topics I wanted to talk to him about, but at that time everything had gathered like a hard knot in my chest, and now when I try to remember it all, it's been dispersed and ground to powder, and stowed away in so many different compartments of my mind that it makes me feel faint and exhausted even to think of it.

But most of all, I'm afraid. A few days ago I would have been able to put all those questions to him without any fear of the answers he might give.

That moment is past.

I go up to him and greet him. He looks up from his paper, and gets up with what seems like a little sigh. When I take his hand and look into his watery, close-set eyes a wave of fury rises in me, for all the times I've sat before him with my voice shaking with anxiety and anguish.

'May I sit down?' I say. 'I thought I'd have a small glass of mineral water before dinner. Couldn't be bad for my heart, surely?'

I'm not sure whether he takes in the sharp undertone, and I don't quite hear his answer either.

I sit down. The doctor folds his paper carefully. He asks me a few questions about Porla, and I answer them, without giving any particular thought to the matter.

He seems to have overcome his confusion and waves to the waitress, looking at me with kindly interest. I sense myself softening slightly, and regret my initial sarcasm.

The girl comes and takes our orders. She's small and rosy, and smiles at us with her mouth half-open. I follow her with my eyes as she disappears.

When I turn to the doctor I discover that he is still looking at me, and I get the unpleasant feeling that he hasn't taken his eyes off me for an instant and can read my thoughts about the girl.

I grope for small talk. Porla, Ronneby, the landscape, the weather, and all the time I'm thinking of my suffocating paralysis, and how only a few days ago I rushed off to the doctor's home as if he must have the answer to all the questions that have tormented me for so long.

Now the doctor is sitting opposite me. But I say not a word. I simply daren't hear what he would answer. I'm very curious. The torment of uncertainty is even greater. But fear is the greatest factor of all. It always has been.

Fear could make me run off. In some ways, that would be my preference. It would prompt questions. I'd have to explain myself. Something would happen.

But I stay put. I behave normally. I'm my usual self.

Then I hear a voice. No louder than a whisper. This is what happens, it whispers. This is what happens when you stay in the shadows. When you become a stranger to the whole world.

The doctor bends his head and takes a shiny object from his waistcoat pocket. It looks like a small box. He takes something out of the box and puts it in his mouth. He washes it down with water.

I ask a question; he answers that it's a heart medication, and he tells me about it. There's something in his voice I don't think I've heard before. An intimacy.

When he holds out the box and offers me a pill, I thank him and take one, and it's not until I put it in my mouth that I'm struck by the irony of the situation. That I take a heart pill from him when I had really wanted to tell him that Dr Lidin had found nothing wrong with my heart.

But I suppose it's an automatic reflex. You meet someone you want to confide in, he offers you something and you accept it, in the hope that it's a small but significant step on the long road, from one human being to another.

I swallow the pill. The water tastes sweet and fresh.

I already feel better. Exactly as though I've just taken a small but significant step. Soon perhaps I will open my mouth to ask those questions.

$\mathcal{A}$fterword

On the first page of Hjalmar Söderberg's 1905 novel *Doctor Glas*, the doctor exclaims, 'But why, of all people, must I keep running into the Rev. Gregorius? I never see that man without remembering an anecdote I once heard told of Schopenhauer. One evening the austere philosopher was sitting, alone as usual, in a corner of his café, when the door opens and in comes a person of disagreeable mien. His features distorted with disgust and horror, Schopenhauer gives him one look, leaps up, and begins thumping him over the head with his stick. All this, merely on account of his appearance!'[1]

A few pages later:

'That people such as him can be allowed to exist in the world! Who doesn't remember the old question so often debated by any bunch of poor fellows at a café table: if you could kill a Chinese mandarin by pressing a button on a wall, or through a simple act of will, and then inherit his wealth — would you do it? It's a question I could never be bothered to answer, perhaps because I have never felt the bitterness and hardship of poverty. But I do think that if I could kill that priest by pressing a button on the wall I would do it.'

Towards the end of the novel, that opportunity appears.

Dr Glas and Pastor Gregorius bump into each other near the Jacob church. They sit down together at a café, and drink some water. The doctor pretends to take a tablet for his digestion, and offers one to the Pastor. The tablet, in fact, is cyanide. The doctor had prepared them himself a few years earlier, when he was contemplating suicide. The Pastor takes the tablet, and swallows it.

Doctor Glas is written in the first person, in the form of a diary kept by the doctor over the course of a hot and dusty summer. At the beginning of the book Helga Gregorius comes to the doctor's office, and tells him that she has conceived a strong dislike for her husband, and she asks him for a favour: she wants him to tell the Pastor that she, '... suffers from some illness, some gynaecological complaint, and that he must give up his conjugal rights, at least for some time'.

Dr Glas is in love with Helga, and does as she asks.

Tyko Gabriel Glas is thirty-three years old. He has never made love with a woman. He is a captivating character. He is well bred and well read, he believes in the future, and he has an icy streak in his personality. In a class of school children he would be the clever bully. He has a sharp eye for human weakness. But he would never shout out hurtful comments. He would whisper them in someone's ear, knowing that they would be passed on. The doctor would stay in the shadows, and take pleasure in his deeds from a distance.

Many Swedes read Söderberg's book at school. A young reader is easily amused by the doctor's acid remarks, and can identify with his fear of touch, and share his repulsion at the sight of the fat hypocrite, Gregorius.

Doctor Glas, for me, is the novel I return to when I periodically lose faith in literature.

It is as though this novel has always known something about me that I still had to discover for myself. I slowly made myself at home in it. I slowly liberated myself from the grip of Dr Glas himself.

And then the day came. I had reached the point in the story when Gregorius is in the doctor's surgery. The doctor does as Helga has asked him: he tells the Pastor that Helga is ill, and that they must live in abstinence for at least six months.

'I can't tell you how sorry I feel for her,' says the Pastor. 'We had so much hoped and wished that we might be granted a little child.'

Dr Glas doesn't care what the Pastor says. Why should he? Children mean nothing to him. At a certain point in the book he sees a woman he recognises, who several years earlier had begged him to perform an abortion for her, which he had refused. Now he sees her with a husband and child, and thinks, 'Well, my little lady, and what do you say now – wasn't I right? The scandal passed; but you still have your little boy and can delight in him... Yet I wonder whether that is really the child? No, it can't be. This lad is four, at most five, and it's at least seven or eight years since that old story. It was at the very beginning of my practice. What can have happened to the first child? Perhaps it came to grief in some way. Well, that's of no importance – they seem to have repaired the damage since.'

The possibility that a child may be unique and irreplaceable does not exist for the doctor.

But suddenly something moved in me: what if the Pastor was telling the truth? What if he actually does long to be a father before he dies. He is approaching his sixties. This is his second childless marriage. He is worried about his health. What if being childless is the bane of his life?

That thought was the starting point. That was when my

curiosity was awakened. I began to break away from Dr Glas's magic circle.

But *Gregorius* is more than just playing games with narrative perspective. I didn't draw his name from a hat at random as though I could equally well have written a novel about Marie in Ernest Hemingway's *To Have and Have Not*.

Pastor Gregorius is carved out by Hjalmar Söderberg with a definite aim in mind. He appears in a book that is, in his own words, both 'a thought-provoking tract and a fully-formed novel', and the question that Dr Glas seeks an answer to is whether there can ever be any justification for killing another human being. The portrait of Gregorius is so skilfully painted that even modern readers soon begin to feel their humanitarian instincts crack.

How do you prepare yourself to commit murder?

If you wish to avoid going under yourself, you have to ensure a certain distance from the victim. You must see to it that the victim appears different, a different kind of human being. Then you must make him a little less human than the rest of us.

To succeed, you must take one small step at a time.

The Nazis were good at this. When they occupied Holland during the Second World War they issued an edict forbidding Jews to sit on the trams – standing room only. A little later Jews were forbidden to stand on the trams as well. Then they were not allowed to travel by tram at all. In stages, the Dutch people became used to the idea that the Jews were different. The next stage was to show that they were a threat. And then they just had to carry on. Finally it must have seemed logical to the Dutch that their Jewish neighbours should be packed into lorries and taken away.

Dr Glas uses exactly the same methods. Pastor Gregorius is not like us. Everyone dislikes him. His wife finds him repulsive, and betrays him with somebody younger and slimmer. But the Pastor sails through the narrative, curiously unaffected by all the gossip behind his back. And Dr Glas gradually strips the Pastor of every trace of humanity, one piece at a time.

I imagined that my novel would be a movement in the opposite direction, and that piece by piece I would succeed in making him more human, making him one of us.

I often played with the thought that I was writing in order to save the Pastor's life. That Dr Glas was reading over my shoulder and that if I only succeeded in making Gregorius human enough he might abstain from offering him that tablet.

(Note: 'human'. Not the same thing as 'sympathetic'.)

But the doctor still offered him the tablet. I was sad for several weeks. I had created life, and the doctor had snuffed it out. But for every new reader the Pastor comes to life again. I don't know how it happens.

Bengt Ohlsson
Stockholm, February 2006

[1] Published in English by the Harvill Press 2002, translated by Paul Britten Austin.

For news about current and forthcoming titles
from Portobello Books and for a sense of purpose
visit the website **www.portobellobooks.com**

encouraging voices,
supporting writers,
challenging readers

Portobello
BOOKS